Larry Sl

1947—the war was over, the Golden Age of Science Fiction (so-called) was being replaced by the coming Diamond Age of the post-war world when writers began to assume maturity and the future was shaping into the world we know.

Here's Asimov's choice for that year, the ninth volume of his memorable series. And here you will find classics by:

H. BEAM PIPER
RAY BRADBURY
POUL ANDERSON
CHAN DAVIS
WILLIAM TENN
ISAAC ASIMOV

and more. . . .

Anthologies from DAW

THE 1978 ANNUAL WORLD'S BEST SF
THE 1979 ANNUAL WORLD'S BEST SF
THE 1980 ANNUAL WORLD'S BEST SF
THE 1981 ANNUAL WORLD'S BEST SF
THE 1982 ANNUAL WORLD'S BEST SF

WOLLHEIM'S WORLD'S BEST SF: Vol. 1
WOLLHEIM'S WORLD'S BEST SF: Vol. 2
WOLLHEIM'S WORLD'S BEST SF: Vol. 3
WOLLHEIM'S WORLD'S BEST SF: Vol. 4
WOLLHEIM'S WORLD'S BEST SF: Vol. 5
WOLLHEIM'S WORLD'S BEST SF: Vol. 6

ASIMOV PRESENTS THE GREAT SF STORIES: 1
ASIMOV PRESENTS THE GREAT SF STORIES: 2
ASIMOV PRESENTS THE GREAT SF STORIES: 3
ASIMOV PRESENTS THE GREAT SF STORIES: 4
ASIMOV PRESENTS THE GREAT SF STORIES: 5
ASIMOV PRESENTS THE GREAT SF STORIES: 6
ASIMOV PRESENTS THE GREAT SF STORIES: 7
ASIMOV PRESENTS THE GREAT SF STORIES: 8

TERRA SF: THE BEST EUROPEAN SF

ISAAC ASIMOV

Presents

THE GREAT
SCIENCE
FICTION
STORIES

Volume 9, 1947

Edited by
Isaac Asimov and
Martin H. Greenberg

DAW Books, Inc.
Donald A. Wollheim, Publisher

1633 Broadway, New York, N.Y. 10019

FIRST PRINTING, FEBRUARY 1983

1 2 3 4 5 6 7 8 9

 DAW TRADEMARK REGISTERED
U.S. PAT. OFF. MARCA
REGISTRADA, HECHO EN U.S.A.

PRINTED IN U.S.A.

ACKNOWLEDGMENTS

Table of Contents

THE GREAT SCIENCE FICTION STORIES

Introduction

In the world outside reality the second post-World War II year saw the President proclaim his Truman Doctrine, which stated that the United States would aid countries facing Communist insurrection. Fears of Europe "going Communist" also played an important role in the development of the Marshall Plan, named for the Secretary of State, which provided for massive aid to European countries. The July issue of *Foreign Affairs* contained an article written by "X" (George F. Kennan of the State Department) which argued for a policy based on the containment of the Soviet Union. The Central Intelligence Agency was established to integrate the diverse elements of the U.S. intelligence community.

In August, India, led by Jawaharlal Nehru, and Pakistan, led by Mohammed Ali Jinnah, became independent as India was partitioned amid great communal fighting and bloodshed. The price for a ride on the New York subway jumped to a dime after having been a nickel for the previous 43 years. The Hollywood Black List heralded the beginning of a search for communists and "subversives" that would divide the country and ruin the lives of many people.

The Bell X-1 broke the sound barrier in level flight on October 10, the first aircraft to do so since manned flight began in 1903. The American Willard Frank Libby developed the "atomic clock" which would make great contributions to the study of archaeology, which also received a tremendous boost with the discovery of the Dead Sea scrolls. 1947 saw the beginning of a series of sightings of Unidentified Flying Objects (UFOs) that would soon turn into a craze of believers, while Thor Heyerdahl crossed the Pacific Ocean on his raft, the *Kon-Tiki*.

Ajax appeared and reduced sore elbows, while Almond Joy

candy bars and Reddi-Wip made their way to grocery store shelves.

During 1947 James Michener published *Tales of the South Pacific.* "Open the Door, Richard," "Too Fat Polka," "Feudin and Fightin," and "Woody Woodpecker" were hit songs. The New York Yankees took the World Series from the Brooklyn Dodgers four games to three—sorry, Isaac. Pablo Picasso painted "Ulysses with his Sirens," while Henry Moore produced his "Three Standing Figures." The *Chicago Sun-Times* appeared for the first time. Jackie Robinson became the first black player in the major leagues while Notre Dame was the number one ranked college football team in the nation. Alberto Moravia wrote *The Woman of Rome. Brigadoon, Finian's Rainbow,* and *High Button Shoes* were the top Broadway musicals of the year. Joe Louis was still the heavyweight boxing champion of the world and the record for the mile run was Gunder Haegg of Sweden's 4:01:4. The company that would become the Sony Corporation was founded.

Roger Sessions' "Symphony No. 2" was performed for the first time in 1947. Jet Pilot won the Kentucky Derby, Ted Williams led the American League with a .343 average, and Jack Kramer was the U.S. tennis champion. Outstanding Broadway productions included *Medea* by Robinson Jeffers, *All My Sons* by Arthur Miller, and *A Streetcar Named Desire* with a young Marlon Brando in the lead. Saul Bellow's *The Victim* appeared, while Henri Matisse painted his "English Girl."

Holy Cross was the NCAA basketball champion and Johnny Mize and Ralph Kiner shared the home run title in the majors with 51 each. The best films of a very good year included *Great Expectations, Body and Soul, Boomerang,* directed by Elia Kazan, *The Voice of the Turtle,* featuring one Ronald Reagan, *Nightmare Alley,* and Charlie Chaplin's *Monsieur Verdoux.* John Steinbeck published *The Wayward Bus.* Joe DiMaggio was the Most Valuable Player in the American League.

Death took the great bullfighter Manolete (as the animals partially evened the score), George II of Greece, Christian X of Denmark, and Henry Ford, who left the bulk of his considerable fortune for use by the Ford Foundation.

Mel Brooks was (probably) still Melvin Kaminsky.

In the real world it was another outstanding year as a

number of fine science fiction and fantasy novels and collections were published (many of which had been serialized years before in the magazines), including *Dark Carnival* by Ray Bradbury, *The Mightiest Machine* by John W. Campbell, Jr., *Doppelgangers* by H. F. Heard, *Rocket Ship Gallileo* by Robert A. Heinlein, *Night's Black Agents* by Fritz Leiber, *The Black Wheel* by A. Merritt (a work completed by his friend, the artist Hannes Bok), *Greener Than You Think* by Ward Moore, *Spacehounds of IPC* by E. E. ("Doc") Smith, *Venus Equilateral* by George O. Smith, *The Weapon Makers* and *The Book of Ptath* by A. E. van Vogt, and *The Legion of Space* by Jack Williamson. Many of these books were published by fan publishers whose companies did not last long. In addition, Lloyd Eshbach published his interesting *Of Worlds Beyond: The Science of Science-Fiction Writing*, one of the first works on sf from within the field.

Avon began its *Avon Fantasy Reader*, edited by Donald A. Wollheim, but the British *Fantasy* died after only three issues.

More wondrous things were happening in the real world as four excellent writers made their maiden voyages into reality: in March, Poul Anderson with "Tomorrow's Children" (which was published as a collaboration with F.N. Waldrop, but since Waldrop only provided some ideas and did none of the writing, it appears in this book as by Anderson alone); "Time and Time Again" by H. Beam Piper in April; T. L. Sherred with the wonderful "E for Effort" in May; and Alfred Coppel with "Age of Unreason" in December.

The real people gathered together for the fifth time as the World Science Fiction Convention (the Philcon) was held in Philadelphia.

Death took J.D. Beresford, Miles J. Breuer, Arthur Machen, and M. P. Shiel.

But distant wings were beating as Octavia Butler, Gardner Dozois, George Alec Effinger, Bruce Gillespie, Stephen Goldin, Stuart Gordon, Stephen King, Tanith Lee, Cory Panshin, and John Varley were born.

Let us travel back to that honored year of 1947 and enjoy the best stories that the real world bequeathed to us.

LITTLE LOST ROBOT

by Isaac Asimov (1920-   )

ASTOUNDING SCIENCE FICTION
March

In a way, this story was a celebration.

I had been inducted into the army immediately after the end of the war, and there I chafed away at a variety of useless tasks, during which I had time to write only a single story, "Evidence" (see the 1946 volume of this series) and I had had to mail that off from Hawaii. I had strong withdrawal symptoms as far as my writing was concerned, naturally.

After my discharge, I spent six weeks picking up the threads of life—finding a place to live, re-establishing myself at Columbia University—and then I plunged furiously into writing once again.

"Little Lost Robot" was the sixth of my positronic robot series and the longest up to that time. I wrote it without pause, just as quickly as I could, and brought it in to John Campbell the day after it was done. He read it and took it on the spot.

It was with "Little Lost Robot," I think, that I recognized that my robot stories tended to have strong mystery components. They were stories which dealt with problems that had to be solved

*by ratiocination. It was that which initiated the
pull that finally led me to the writing of outright
science fiction mysteries, and even to mysteries
without a science fiction component.—I.A.*

Measures on Hyper Base had been taken in a sort of rattling fury—the muscular equivalent of an hysterical shriek.

To itemize them in order of both chronology and desperation, they were:

1. All work on the Hyperatomic Drive through all the space volume occupied by the Stations of the Twenty-Seventh Asteroidal Grouping came to a halt.

2. That entire volume of space was nipped out of the System, practically speaking. No one entered without permission. No one left under any conditions.

3. By special government patrol ship, Drs. Susan Calvin and Peter Bogert, respectively Head Psychologist and Mathematical Director of United States Robot & Mechanical Men Corporation, were brought to Hyper Base.

Susan Calvin had never left the surface of Earth before, and had no perceptible desire to leave it this time. In an age of Atomic Power and a clearly coming Hyperatomic Drive, she remained quietly provincial. So she was dissatisfied with her trip and unconvinced of the emergency, and every line of her plain, middle-aged face showed it clearly enough during her first dinner at Hyper Base.

Nor did Dr. Bogert's sleek paleness abandon a certain hangdog attitude. Nor did Major-general Kallner, who headed the project, even once forgot to maintain a hunted expression.

In short, it was a grisly episode, that meal, and the little session of three that followed began in a gray, unhappy manner.

Kallner, with his baldness glistening, and his dress uniform oddly unsuited to the general mood, began with uneasy directness.

"This is a queer story to tell, sir, and madam. I want to thank you for coming on short notice and without a reason being given. We'll try to correct that now. We've lost a robot. Work has stopped and *must* stop until such time as we locate it. So far we have failed, and we feel we need expert help."

Perhaps the general felt his predicament anticlimactic. He continued with a note of desperation, "I needn't tell you the importance of our work here. More than eighty percent of last year's appropriations for scientific research have gone to us—"

"Why, we know that," said Bogert, agreeably. "U.S. Robots is receiving a generous rental fee for use of our robots."

Susan Calvin injected a blunt, vinegary note, "What makes a single robot so important to the project, and why hasn't it been located?"

The general turned his red face toward her and wet his lips quickly, "Why, in a manner of speaking, we *have* located it." Then, with near anquish, "Here, suppose I explain. As soon as the robot failed to report, a state of emergency was declared, and all movement off Hyper Base stopped. A cargo vessel had landed the previous day and had delivered us two robots for our laboratories. It had sixty-two robots of the . . . uh . . . same type for shipment elsewhere. We are certain as to that figure. There is no question about it whatever."

"Yes? And the connection?"

"When our missing robot failed of location anywhere—I assure you we would have found a missing blade of grass if it had been there to find—we brainstormed ourselves into counting the robots left on the cargo ship. They have sixty-three now."

"So that the sixty-third, I take it, is the missing prodigal?"

Dr. Calvin's eyes darkened. "Yes, but we have no way of telling which is the sixty-third."

There was a dead silence while the electric clock chimed eleven times, and then the robopsychologist said, "Very peculiar," and the corners of her lips moved downward.

"Peter," she turned to her colleague with a trace of savagery, "what's wrong here? What kind of robots are they using at Hyper Base?"

Dr. Bogert hesitated and smiled feebly, "It's been rather a matter of delicacy till now, Susan."

She spoke rapidly, "Yes, *till* now. If there are sixty-three same-type robots, one of which is wanted and the identity of which cannot be determined, why won't any of them do? What's the idea of all this? Why have we been sent for?"

Bogert said in resigned fashion, "If you'll give me a chance, Susan— Hyper Base happens to be using several robots whose brains are not impressioned with the entire First Law of Robotics."

"*Aren't* impressioned?" Calvin slumped back in her chair, "I see. How many were made?"

"A few. It was on government order and there was no way of violating the secrecy. No one was to know except the top men directly concerned. You weren't included, Susan. It was nothing I had anything to do with."

The general interrupted with a measure of authority. "I would like to explain that bit. I hadn't been aware that Dr. Calvin was unacquainted with the situation. I needn't tell you, Dr. Calvin, that there always has been strong opposition to robots on the Planet. The only defense the government has had against the Fundamentalist radicals in this matter was the fact that robots are always built with an unbreakable First Law—which makes it impossible for them to harm human beings under any circumstance.

"But we *had* to have robots of a different nature. So just a few of the NS-2 model, the Nestors, that is, were prepared with a modified First Law. To keep it quiet, all NS-2's are manufactured without serial numbers; modified members are delivered here along with a group of normal robots; and, of course, all our kind are under the strictest impressionment never to tell of their modification to unauthorized personnel." He wore an embarrassed smile. "This has all worked out against us now."

Calvin said grimly, "Have you asked each one who it is, anyhow? Certainly, you are authorized?"

The general nodded, "All sixty-three deny having worked here—and one is lying."

"Does the one you want show traces of wear? The others, I take it, are factory-fresh."

"The one in question only arrived last month. It, and the two that have just arrived, were to be the last we needed. There's no perceptible wear." He shook his head slowly and his eyes were haunted again, "Dr. Calvin, we don't dare let that ship leave. If the existence of non-First Law robots becomes general knowledge—" There seemed no way of avoiding understatement in the conclusion.

"Destroy all sixty-three," said the robopsychologist coldly and flatly, "and make an end of it."

Bogert drew back a corner of his mouth. "You mean destroy thirty thousand dollars per robot? I'm afraid U. S. Robots wouldn't like that. We'd better make an effort first, Susan, before we destroy anything."

"In that case," she said sharply, "I need facts. Exactly what advantage does Hyper Base derive from these modified robots? What factor made them desirable, general?"

Kallner ruffled his forehead and stroked it with an upward gesture of his hand. "We had trouble with our previous robots. Our men work with hard radiations a good deal, you see. It's dangerous, of course, but reasonable precautions are taken. There have been only two accidents since we began and neither was fatal. However, it was impossible to explain that to an ordinary robot. The First Law states—I'll quote it—*'No robot may harm a human being, or through inaction, allow a human being to come to harm.'*

"That's primary, Dr. Calvin. When it was necessary for one of our men to expose himself for a short period to a moderate gamma field, one that would have no physiological effects, the nearest robot would dash in to drag him out. If the field were exceedingly weak, it would succeed, and work could not continue till all robots were cleared out. If the field were a trifle stronger, the robot would never reach the technician concerned, since its positronic brain would collapse under gamma radiations—and then we would be out one expensive and hard-to-replace robot.

"We tried arguing with them. Their point was that a human being in a gamma field was endangering his life and that it didn't matter that he could remain there half an hour safely. Supposing, they would say, he forgot and remained an hour. They couldn't take chances. We pointed out that they were risking their lives on a wild off-chance. But self-preservation is only the Third Law of Robotics—and the First Law of human safety came first. We gave them orders; we ordered them strictly and harshly to remain out of gamma fields at whatever cost. But obedience is only the Second Law of Robotics—and the First Law of human safety came first. Dr. Calvin, we either had to do without robots, or do something about the First Law—and we made our choice."

"I can't believe," said Dr. Calvin, "that it was found possible to remove the First Law."

"It wasn't removed, it was modified," explained Kallner. "Positronic brains were constructed that contained the positive aspect only of the Law, which in them reads: '*No robot may harm a human being.*' That is all. They have no compulsion to prevent one coming to harm through an extraneous agency such as gamma rays. I state the matter correctly, Dr. Bogert?"

"Quite," assented the mathematician.

"And that is the only difference of your robots from the ordinary NS-2 model? The *only* difference? Peter?"

"The *only* difference, Susan."

She rose and spoke with finality, "I intend sleeping now, and in about eight hours, I want to speak to whomever saw the robot last. And from now on, General Kallner, if I'm to take any responsibility at all for events, I want full and unquestioned control of this investigation."

Susan Calvin, except for two hours of resentful lassitude, experienced nothing approaching sleep. She signaled at Bogert's door at the local time of 0700 and found him also awake. He had apparently taken the trouble of transporting a dressing gown to Hyper Base with him, for he was sitting in it. He put his nail scissors down when Calvin entered.

He said softly, "I've been expecting you more or less. I suppose you feel sick about all this."

"I do."

"Well—I'm sorry. There was no way of preventing it. When the call came out from Hyper Base for us, I knew that something must have gone wrong with the modified Nestors. But what was there to do? I couldn't break the matter to you on the trip here as I would have liked to, because I had to be sure. The matter of the modification is top secret."

The psychologist muttered, "I should have been told. U. S. Robots had no right to modify positronic brains this way without the approval of a psychologist."

Bogert lifted his eyebrows and sighed. "Be reasonable, Susan. You couldn't have influenced them. In this matter, the government was bound to have its way. They want the Hyperatomic Drive and the etheric physicists want robots that won't interfere with them. They were going to get them even if it did mean twisting the First Law. We had to admit it was possible from a construction standpoint and they swore a mighty oath that they wanted only twelve, that they would be used only at Hyper Base, that they would be destroyed once the Drive was perfected, and that full precautions would be taken. And they insisted on secrecy—and that's the situation."

Dr. Calvin spoke through her teeth, "I would have resigned."

"It wouldn't have helped. The government was offering the company a fortune, and threatening it with antirobot legislation in case of a refusal. We were stuck then, and we're badly stuck now. If this leaks out, it might hurt Kallner and the government, but it would hurt U. S. Robots a devil of a lot more."

The psychologist stared at him. "Peter, don't you realize what all this is about? Can't you understand what the removal of the First Law means? It isn't just a matter of secrecy."

"I know what removal would mean. I'm not a child. It would mean complete instability, with no nonimaginary solutions to the positronic Field Equations."

"Yes, mathematically. But can you translate that into crude psychological thought. All normal life, Peter, consciously or otherwise, resents domination. If the domination is by an inferior, or by a supposed inferior, the resentment becomes stronger. Physically, and, to an extent, mentally, a robot—any robot—is superior to human beings. What makes him slavish, then? *Only the First Law!* Why, without it, the first order you tried to give a robot would result in your death. Unstable? What do you think?"

"Susan," said Bogert, with an air of sympathetic amusement. "I'll admit that this Frankenstein Complex you're exhibiting has a certain justification—hence the First Law in the first place. But the Law, I repeat and repeat, has not been removed—merely modified."

"And what about the stability of the brain?"

The mathematician thrust out his lips, "Deceased, naturally. But it's within the border of safety. The first Nestors were delivered to Hyper Base nine months ago, and nothing whatever has gone wrong till now, and even this involves merely fear of discovery and not danger to humans."

"Very well, then. We'll see what comes of the morning conference."

Bogert saw her politely to the door and grimaced eloquently when she left. He saw no reason to change his perennial opinion of her as a sour and fidgety frustration.

Susan Calvin's train of thought did not include Bogert in the least. She had dismissed him years ago as a smooth and pretentious sleekness.

Gerald Black had taken his degree in etheric physics the year before and, in common with his entire generation of physicists, found himself engaged in the problem of the Drive. He now made a proper addition to the general atmosphere of these meetings on Hyper Base. In his stained white smock, he was half rebellious and wholly uncertain. His stocky strength seemed striving for release and his fingers, as they twisted each other with nervous yanks, might have forced an iron bar out of true.

Major-general Kallner sat beside him, the two from U. S. Robots faced him.

Black said, "I'm told that I was the last to see Nestor 10 before he vanished. I take it you want to ask me about that."

Dr. Calvin regarded him with interest, "You sound as if you were not sure, young man. Don't you *know* whether you were the last to see him?"

"He worked with me, ma'am, on the field generators, and he was with me the morning of his disappearance. I don't know if anyone saw him after about noon. No one admits having done so."

"Do you think anyone's lying about it?"

"I don't say that. But I don't say that I want the blame of it, either." His dark eyes smoldered.

"There's no question of blame. The robot acted as it did because of what it is. We're just trying to locate it, Mr. Black, and let's put everything else aside. Now if you've worked with the robot, you probably know it better than anyone else. Was there anything unusual about it that you noticed? Had you ever worked with robots before?"

"I've worked with other robots we have here—the simple ones. Nothing different about the Nestors except that they're a good deal cleverer—and more annoying."

"Annoying? In what way?"

"Well—perhaps it's not their fault. The work here is rough and most of us get a little jagged. Fooling around with hyper-space isn't fun." He smiled feebly, finding pleasure in confession. "We run the risk continually of blowing a hole in normal space-time fabric and dropping right out of the universe, asteroid and all. Sounds screwy, doesn't it? Naturally, you're on edge sometimes. But these Nestors aren't. They're curious, they're calm, they don't worry. It's enough to drive you nuts at times. When you want something done in a tearing hurry, they seem to take their time. Sometimes I'd rather do without."

"You say they take their time? Have they ever refused an order?"

"Oh, no"—hastily. "They do it all right. They tell you when they think you're wrong, though. They don't know anything about the subject but what we taught them, but that doesn't stop them. Maybe I imagine it, but the other fellows have the same trouble with their Nestors."

General Kallner cleared his throat ominously, "Why have no complaints reached me on the matter, Black?"

The young physicist reddened, "We didn't *really* want to do without the robots, sir, and besides we weren't certain exactly how such . . . uh . . . minor complaints might be received."

Bogert interrupted softly, "Anything in particular happen the morning you last saw it?"

There was a silence. With a quiet motion, Calvin repressed the comment that was about to emerge from Kallner, and waited patiently.

Then Black spoke in blurting anger, "I had a little trouble with it. I'd broken a Kimball tube that morning and was out five days of work; my entire program was behind schedule; I hadn't received any mail from home for a couple of weeks. And *he* came around wanting me to repeat an experiment I had abandoned a month ago. He was always annoying me on that subject and I was tired of it. I told him to go away—and that's all I saw of him."

"You told him to go away?" asked Dr. Calvin with sharp interest. "In just those words? Did you say 'Go away'? Try to remember the exact words."

There was apparently an internal struggle in progress. Black cradled his forehead in a broad palm for a moment, then tore it away and said defiantly, "I said, 'Go lose yourself.' "

Bogert laughed for a short moment. "And he did, eh?"

But Calvin wasn't finished. She spoke cajolingly, "Now we're getting somewhere, Mr. Black. But exact details are important. In understanding the robot's actions, a word, a gesture, an emphasis may be everything. You couldn't have said

just those three words, for instance, could you? By your own
description you must have been in a nasty mood. Perhaps
you strengthened your speech a little."

The young man reddened, "Well . . . I may have called it
a . . . a few things."

"Exactly what things?"

"Oh—I wouldn't remember exactly. Besides I couldn't repeat it. You know how you get when you're excited." His
embarrassed laugh was almost a giggle, "I sort of have a
tendency to strong language."

"That's quite all right," she replied, with prim severity. "At
the moment, I'm a psychologist. I would like to have you repeat exactly what you said as nearly as you remember, and,
even more important, the exact tone of voice you used."

Black looked at his commanding officer for support, found
none. His eyes grew round and appalled, "But I can't."

"You must."

"Suppose," said Bogert, with ill-hidden amusement, "you
address me. You may find it easier."

The young man's scarlet face turned to Bogert. He swallowed. "I said—" His voice faded out. He tried again, "I
said—"

And he drew a deep breath and spewed it out hastily in
one long succession of syllables. Then, in the charged air that
lingered, he concluded almost in tears, ". . . more or less. I
don't remember the exact order of what I called him, and
maybe I left out something or put in something, but that was
about it."

Only the slightest flush betrayed any feeling on the part of
the robopsychologist. She said, "I am aware of the meaning
of most of the terms used. The others, I suppose, are equally
derogatory."

"I'm afraid so," agreed the tormented Black.

"And in among it, you told him to lose himself."

"I meant it only figuratively."

"I realize that. No disciplinary action is intended, I am
sure." And at her glance, the general, who, five seconds earlier, had seemed not sure at all, nodded angrily.

"You may leave, Mr, Black. Thank you for your cooperation."

It took five hours for Susan Calvin to interview the sixty-
three robots. It was five hours of multi-repetition; of replace-

ment after replacement of identical robot; of Questions A, B, C, D; and Answers A, B, C, D; of a carefully bland expression, a carefully neutral tone, a carefully friendly atmosphere; and a hidden wire recorder.

The psychologist felt drained of vitality when she was finished.

Bogert was waiting for her and looked expectant as she dropped the recording spool with a clang upon the plastic of the desk.

She shook her head, "All sixty-three seemed the same to me. I couldn't tell—"

He said, "You couldn't expect to tell by ear, Susan. Suppose we analyze the recordings."

Ordinarily, the mathematical interpretation of verbal reactions of robots is one of the more intricate branches of robotic analysis. It requires a staff of trained technicians and the help of complicated computing machines. Bogert knew that. Bogert stated as much, in an extreme of unshown annoyance after having listened to each set of replies, made lists of word deviations, and graphs of the intervals of responses.

"There are no anomalies present, Susan. The variations in wording and the time reactions are within the limits of ordinary frequency groupings. We need finer methods. They must have computers here. No." He frowned and nibbled delicately at a thumbnail. "We can't use computers. Too much danger of leakage. Or maybe if we—"

Dr. Calvin stopped him with an impatient gesture, "Please, Peter. This isn't one of your petty laboratory problems. If we can't determine the modified Nestor by some gross difference that we can see with the naked eye, one that there is no mistake about, we're out of luck. The danger of being wrong, and of letting him escape is otherwise too great. It's not enough to point out a minute irregularity in a graph. I tell you, if that's all I've got to go on, I'd destroy them all just to be certain. Have you spoken to the other modified Nestors?"

"Yes, I have," snapped back Bogert, "and there's nothing wrong with them. They're above normal in friendliness if anything. They answered my questions, displayed pride in their knowledge—except the two new ones that haven't had time to learn their etheric physics. They laughed rather good-naturedly at my ignorance in some of the specializations here." He shrugged, "I suppose that forms some of the basis for resentment toward them on the part of the technicians here. The robots are perhaps too willing to impress you with their greater knowledge."

"Can you try a few Planar Reactions to see if there has been any change, any deterioration, in their mental set-up since manufacture?"

"I haven't yet, but I will." He shook a slim finger at her, "You're losing your nerve, Susan. I don't see what it is you're dramatizing. They're essentially harmless."

"They are?" Calvin took fire. "They are? Do you realize one of them is lying? One of the sixty-three robots I have just interviewed has deliberately lied to me after the strictest injunction to tell the truth. The abnormality indicated is horribly deep-seated, and horribly frightening."

Peter Bogert felt his teeth harden against each other. He said, "Not at all. Look! Nestor 10 was given orders to lose himself. Those orders were expressed in maximum urgency by the person most authorized to command him. You can't counteract that order either by superior urgency or superior right of command. Naturally, the robot will attempt to defend the carrying out of his orders. In fact, objectively, I admire his ingenuity. How better can a robot lose himself than to hide himself among a group of similar robots?"

"Yes, you would admire it. I've detected amusement in you, Peter—amusement and an appalling lack of understanding. Are you a roboticist, Peter? Those robots attach importance to what they consider superiority. You've just said as much yourself. Subconsciously they feel humans to be inferior and the First Law which protects us from them is imperfect. They are unstable. And here we have a young man ordering a robot to leave him, to lose himself, with every verbal appearance of revulsion, disdain, and disgust. Granted, that robot must follow orders, but subconsciously, there is resentment. It will become more important than ever for it to prove that it is superior despite the horrible names it was called. It may become *so* important that what's left of the First Law won't be enough."

"How on Earth, or anywhere in the Solar System, Susan, is a robot going to know the meaning of the assorted strong language used upon him? Obscenity is not one of the things impressioned upon his brain."

"Original impressionment is not everything," Calvin snarled at him. "Robots have learning capacity, you . . . you fool—" And Bogert knew that she had really lost her temper.

She continued hastily, "Don't you suppose he could tell from the tone used that the words weren't complimentary? Don't you suppose he's heard the words used before and noted upon what occasions?"

"Well, then," shouted Bogert, "will you kindly tell me one way in which a modified robot can harm a human being, no matter how offended it is, no matter how sick with desire to prove superiority?"

"If I tell you one way, will you keep quiet?"

"Yes."

They were leaning across the table at each other, angry eyes nailed together.

The psychologist said, "If a modified robot were to drop a heavy weight upon a human being, he would not be breaking the First Law, if he did so with the knowledge that his strength and reaction speed would be sufficient to snatch the weight away before it struck the man. However once the weight left his fingers, he would be no longer the active medium. Only the blind force of gravity would be that. The robot could then change his mind and merely by inaction, allow the weight to strike. The modified First Law allows that."

"That's an awful stretch of imagination."

"That's what my profession requires sometimes. Peter, let's not quarrel. Let's work. You know the exact nature of the stimulus that caused the robot to lose himself. You have the records of his original mental make-up. I want you to tell me how possible it is for our robot to do the sort of thing I just talked about. Not the specific instance, mind you, but that whole class of response. And I want it done quickly."

"And meanwhile—"

"And meanwhile, we'll have to try performance tests directly on the response to First Law."

Gerald Black, at his own request, was supervising the mushrooming wooden partitions that were springing up in a bellying circle on the vaulted third floor of Radiation Building 2. The laborers worked, in the main, silently, but more than one was openly a-wonder at the sixty-three photocells that required installation.

One of them sat down near Black, removed his hat, and wiped his forehead thoughtfully with a freckled forearm.

Black nodded at him, "How's it going, Walensky?"

Walensky shrugged and fired a cigar, "Smooth as butter.

What's going on anyway, Doc? First, there's no work for three days and then we have this mess of jiggers." He leaned backward on his elbows and puffed smoke.

Black twitched his eyebrows, "A couple of robot men came over from Earth. Remember the trouble we had with robots running into the gamma fields, before we pounded it into their skulls that they weren't to do it."

"Yeah. Didn't we get new robots?"

"We got some replacements, but mostly it was a job of indoctrination. Anyway, the people who make them want to figure out robots that aren't hit so bad by gamma rays."

"Sure seems funny, though, to stop all the work on the Drive for this robot deal. I thought nothing was allowed to stop the Drive."

"Well, it's the fellows upstairs that have the say on that. Me—I just do as I'm told. Probably all a matter of pull—"

"Yeah." The electrician jerked a smile, and winked a wise eye. "Somebody knew somebody in Washington. But as long as my pay comes through on the dot, I should worry. The Drive's none of my affair. What are they going to do here?"

"You're asking me? They brought a mess of robots with them—over sixty, and they're going to measure reactions. That's all *my* knowledge."

"How long will it take?"

"I wish I knew."

"Well," Walensky said, with heavy sarcasm, "as long as they dish me my money, they can play games all they want."

Black felt quietly satisfied. Let the story spread. It was harmless, and near enough to the truth to take the fangs out of curiosity.

A man sat in the chair, motionless, silent. A weight dropped, crashed downward, then pounded aside at the last moment under the synchronized thump of a sudden force beam. In sixty-three wooden cells, watching NS-2 robots dashed forward in that split second before the weight veered, and sixty-three photocells five feet ahead of their original positions jiggled the marking pen and presented a little jag on the paper. The weight rose and dropped, rose and dropped, rose—

Ten times!

Ten times the robots sprang forward and stopped, as the man remained safely seated.

Major-general Kallner had not worn his uniform in its entirely since the first dinner with the U. S. Robot representatives. He wore nothing over his blue-gray shirt now, the collar was open, and the black tie was pulled loose.

He looked hopefully at Bogert, who was still blandly neat and whose inner tension was perhaps betrayed only by the trace of glister at his temples.

The general said, "How does it look? What is it you're trying to see?"

Bogert replied, "A difference which may turn out to be a little too subtle for our purposes, I'm afraid. For sixty-two of those robots the necessity of jumping toward the apparently threatened human was what we call, in robotics, a forced reaction. You see, even when the robots knew that the human in question would not come to harm—and after the third or fourth time they must have known it—they could not prevent reacting as they did. First Law requires it."

"Well?"

"But the sixty-third robot, the modified Nestor, had no such compulsion. He was under free action. If he had wished, he could have remained in his seat. Unfortunately—" his voice was mildly regretful—"he didn't so wish."

"Why do you suppose?"

Bogert shrugged. "I suppose Dr. Calvin will tell us when she gets here. Probably with a horribly pessimistic interpretation, too. She is sometimes a bit annoying."

"She's qualified, isn't she?" demanded the general with a sudden frown of uneasiness.

"Yes." Bogert seemed amused. "She's qualified all right. She understands robots like a sister—comes from hating human beings so much, I think. It's just that, psychologist or not, she's an extreme neurotic. Has paranoid tendencies. Don't take her too seriously."

He spread the long row of broken-line graphs out in front of him. "You see, general, in the case of each robot the time interval from moment of drop to the completion of a five-foot movement tends to decrease as the tests are repeated. There's a definite mathematical relationship that governs such things and failure to conform would indicate marked abnormality in the positronic brain. Unfortunately, all here appear normal."

"But if our Nestor 10 was not responding with a forced action, why isn't his curve different? I don't understand that."

"It's simple enough. Robotic responses are not perfectly analogous to human responses, more's the pity. In human beings, voluntary action is much slower than reflex action. But that's not the case with robots; with them it is merely a question of freedom of choice, otherwise the speeds of free and forced action are much the same. What I *had* been expecting, though, was that Nestor 10 would be caught by surprise the first time and allow too great an interval to elapse before responding."

"And he didn't?"

"I'm afraid not."

"Then we haven't gotten anywhere." The general sat back with an expression of pain. "It's five days since you've come."

At this point, Susan Calvin entered and slammed the door behind her. "Put your graphs away, Peter," she cried. "You know they don't show anything."

She mumbled something impatiently as Kallner half-rose to greet her, and went on, "We'll have to try something else quickly. I don't like what's happening."

Bogert exchanged a resigned glance with the general. "Is anything wrong?"

"You mean specifically? No. But I don't like to have Nestor 10 continue to elude us. It's bad. It *must* be gratifying his swollen sense of superiority. I'm afraid that his motivation is no longer simply one of following orders. I think it's becoming more a matter of sheer neurotic necessity to outthink humans. That's a dangerously unhealthy situation. Peter, have you done what I asked? Have you worked out the instability factors of the modified NS-2 along the lines I want?"

"It's in progress," said the mathematician, without interest.

She stared at him angrily for a moment, then turned to Kallner. "Nestor 10 is decidedly aware of what we're doing, general. He had no reason to jump for the bait in this experiment, especially after the first time, when he must have seen that there was no real danger to our subject. The others couldn't help it; but *he* was deliberately falsifying a reaction."

"What do you think we ought to do now, then, Dr. Calvin?"

"Make it impossible for him to fake an action the next time. We will repeat the experiment, but with an addition. High-tension cables, capable of electrocuting the Nestor models will be placed between subject and robot—enough of them to avoid the possibility of jumping over—and the robot will be made perfectly aware in advance that touching the cables will mean death."

"Hold on," spat out Bogert with sudden viciousness. "I rule that out. We are not electrocuting two million dollars' worth of robots to locate Nestor 10. There are other ways.

"You're certain? You've found none. In any case, it's not a question of electrocution. We can arrange a relay which will break the current at the instant of application of weight. If the robot should place his weight on it, he won't die. *But he won't know that,* you see."

The general's eyes gleamed into hope. "Will that work?"

"It should. Under those conditions, Nestor 10 would have to remain in his seat. He could be *ordered* to touch the cables and die, for the Second Law of obedience is superior to the Third Law of self-preservation. But *he won't* be ordered to; he will merely be left to his own devices, as will all the robots. In the case of the normal robots, the First Law of human safety will drive them to their death even without orders. But not our Nestor 10. Without the entire First Law, and without having received any orders on the matter, the Third Law, self-preservation, will be the highest operating, and he will have no choice but to remain in his seat. It would be a forced action."

"Will it be done tonight, then?"

"Tonight," said the psychologist, "if the cables can be laid in time. I'll tell the robots now what they're to be up against."

A man sat in the chair, motionless, silent. A weight dropped, crashed downward, then pounded aside at the last moment under the synchronized thump of a sudden force beam.

Only once—

And from her small camp chair in the observing booth in the balcony, Dr. Susan Calvin rose with a short gasp of pure horror.

Sixty-three robots sat quietly in their chairs, staring owlishly at the endangered man before them. Not one moved.

Dr. Calvin was angry, angry almost past endurance. Angry the worse for not daring to show it to the robots that, one by one, were entering the room and then leaving. She checked the list. Number twenty-eight was due in now—Thirty-five still lay ahead of her.

Number Twenty-eight entered, diffidently.

She forced herself into reasonable calm. "And who are you?"

The robot replied in a low, uncertain voice, "I have received no number of my own yet, ma'am. I'm an NS-2 robot, and I was Number Twenty-eight in line outside. I have a slip of paper here that I'm to give to you."

"You haven't been in here before this today?"

"No, ma'am."

"Sit down. Right there, I want to ask you some questions, Number Twenty-eight. Were you in the Radiation Room of Building Two about four hours ago?"

The robot had trouble answering. Then it came out hoarsely, like machinery needing oil, "Yes, ma'am."

"There was a man who almost came to harm there, wasn't there?"

"Yes, ma'am."

"You did nothing, did you?"

"No, ma'am."

"The man might have been hurt because of your inaction. Do you know that?"

"Yes, ma'am. I couldn't help it, ma'am." It is hard to picture a large expressionless metallic figure cringing, but it managed.

"I want you to tell me exactly why you did nothing to save him."

"I want to explain, ma'am. I certainly don't want to have you . . . have *anyone* . . . think that I could do a thing that might cause harm to a master. Oh, no, that would be a horrible . . . an inconceivable—"

"Please don't get excited, boy. I'm not blaming you for anything. I only want to know what you were thinking at the time."

"Ma'am, before it all happened you told us that one of the masters would be in danger of harm from that weight that keeps falling and that we would have to cross electric cables if we were to try to save him. Well, ma'am, that wouldn't stop me. What is my destruction compared to the safety of a master? But . . . but it occurred to me that if I died on my way to him, I wouldn't be able to save him anyway. The weight would crush him and then I would be dead for no purpose and perhaps some day some other master might come to harm who wouldn't have, if I had only stayed alive. Do you understand me, ma'am?"

"You mean that it was merely a choice of the man dying, of both the man and yourself dying. Is that right?"

"Yes, ma'am. It was impossible to save the master. He might be considered dead. In that case, it is inconceivable that I destroy myself for nothing—without orders."

The robopsychologist twiddled a pencil. She had heard the same story with insignificant verbal variations twenty-seven times before. This was the crucial question now.

"Boy," she said, "your thinking has its points, but it is not the sort of thing I thought you might think. Did you think of this yourself?"

The robot hesitated. "No."

"Who thought of it, then?"

"We were talking last night, and one of us got that idea and it sounded reasonable."

"Which one?"

The robot thought deeply. "I don't know. Just one of us."

She sighed. "That's all "

Number Twenty-nine was next. Thirty-four after that.

Major-general Kallner, too, was angry. For one week all of Hyper Base had stopped dead, barring some paper work on the subsidiary asteroids of the group. For nearly one week, the two top experts in the field had aggravated the situation with useless tests. And now they—or the woman, at any rate—made impossible propositions.

Fortunately for the general situation, Kallner felt it impolitic to display his anger openly.

Susan Calvin was insisting, "Why not, sir? It's obvious that the present situation is unfortunate. The only way we may reach results in the future—or what future is left us in this matter—is to separate the robots. We can't keep them together any longer."

"My dear Dr. Calvin," rumbled the general, his voice sinking into the lower baritone registers. "I don't see how I can quarter sixty-three robots all over the place—"

Dr. Calvin raised her arms helplessly. "I can do nothing then. Nestor 10 will either imitate what the other robots would do, or else argue them plausibly into not doing what he himself cannot do. And in any case, this is bad business.

We're in actual combat with this little lost robot of ours and he's winning out. Every victory of his aggravates his abnormality."

She rose to her feet in determination. "General Kallner, if you do not separate the robots as I ask, then I can only demand that all sixty-three be destroyed immediately."

"You demand it, do you?" Bogert looked up suddenly, and with real anger. "What gives you the right to demand any such thing. Those robots remain as they are. *I'm* responsible to the mangement, not you."

"And I," added Major-general Kallner, "am responsible to the World Co-ordinator—and I must have this settled."

"In that case," flashed back Calvin, "there is nothing for me to do but resign. If necessary to force you to the necessary destruction, I'll make this whole matter public. It was not I that approved the manufacture of modified robots."

"One word from you, Dr. Calvin," said the general, deliberately, "in violation of security measures, and you would be certainly imprisoned instantly."

Bogert felt the matter to be getting out of hand. His voice grew syrupy, "Well, now, we're beginning to act like children, all of us. We need only a little more time. Surely we can outwit a robot without resigning, or imprisoning people, or destroying two millions."

The psychologist turned on him with quiet fury, "I don't want any unbalanced robots in existence. We have one Nestor that's definitely unbalanced, eleven more that are potentially so, and sixty-two normal robots that are being subjected to an unbalanced environment. The only absolute safe method is complete destruction."

The signal-burr brought all three to a halt, and the angry tumult of growingly unrestrained emotion froze.

"Come in," growled Kallner.

It was Gerald Black, looking perturbed. He had heard angry voices. He said, "I thought I'd come myself . . . didn't like to ask anyone else—"

"What is it? Don't orate—"

"The locks of Compartment C in the trading ship have been played with. There are fresh scratches on them."

"Compartment C?" explained Calvin quickly. "That's the one that holds the robots, isn't it? Who did it?"

"From the inside," said Black, laconically.

"The lock isn't out of order, is it?"

"No. It's all right. I've been staying on the ship now for four days and none of them have tried to get out. But I thought you ought to know, and I didn't like to spread the news. I noticed the matter myself."

"Is anyone there now?" demanded the general.

"I left Robbins and McAdams there."

There was a thoughtful silence, and then Dr. Calvin said, ironically, "Well?"

Kallner rubbed his nose uncertainly, "What's it all about?"

"Isn't it obvious? Nestor 10 is planning to leave. That order to lose himself is dominating his abnormality past anything we can do. I wouldn't be surprised if what's left of his First Law would scarcely be powerful enough to override it. He is perfectly capable of seizing the ship and leaving with it. Then we'd have a mad robot on a spaceship. What would he do next? Any idea? Do you still want to leave them all together, general?"

"Nonsense," interrupted Bogert. He had regained his smoothness. "All that from a few scratch marks on a lock."

"Have you, Dr. Bogert, completed the analysis I've required, since you volunteer opinions?"

"Yes."

"May I see it?"

"No."

"Why not? Or mayn't I ask that, either?"

"Because there's no point in it, Susan. I told you in advance that these modified robots are less stable than the normal variety, and my analysis shows it. There's a certain very small chance of breakdown under extreme circumstances that are not likely to occur. Let it go at that. I won't give you ammunition for your absurd claim that sixty-two perfectly good robots be destroyed just because so far you lack the ability to detect Nestor 10 among them."

Susan Calvin stared him down and let disgust fill her eyes. "You won't let anything stand in the way of the permanent directorship, will you?"

"Please," begged Kallner, half in irritation. "Do you insist that nothing further can be done, Dr. Calvin?"

"I can't think of anything, sir," she replied, wearily. "If there were only other differences between Nestor 10 and the normal robots, differences that didn't involve the First Law. Even one other difference. Something in impressionment, environment, specification—" And she stopped suddenly.

"What is it?"

"I've thought of something . . . I think—" Her eyes grew distant and hard, "These modified Nestors, Peter. They get the same impressioning the normal ones get, don't they?"

"Yes. Exactly the same."

"And what was it you were saying, Mr. Black," she turned to the young man, who through the storms that had followed his news had maintained a discreet silence. "Once when complaining of the Nestors' attitude of superiority, you said the technicians had taught them all they knew."

"Yes, in etheric physics. They're not acquainted with the subject when they come here."

"That's right," said Bogert, in surprise. "I told you, Susan, when I spoke to the other Nestors here that the two new arrivals hadn't learned etheric physics yet."

"And why is that?" Dr. Calvin was speaking in mounting excitement. "Why aren't NS-2 models impressioned with etheric physics to start with?"

"I can tell you that," said Kallner. "It's all of a piece with the secrecy. We thought that if we made a special model with knowledge of etheric physics, used twelve of them and put the others to work in an unrelated field, there might be suspicion. Men working with normal Nestors might wonder why they knew etheric physics. So there was merely an impressionment with a capacity for training in the field. Only the ones that come here, naturally, receive such a training. It's that simple."

"I understand. Please get out of here, the lot of you. Let me have an hour or so."

Calvin felt she could not face the ordeal for a third time. Her mind had contemplated it and rejected it with an intensity that left her nauseated. She could face that unending file of repetitious robots no more.

So Bogert asked the question now, while she sat aside, eyes and mind half closed.

Number Fourteen came in—forty-nine to go.

Bogert looked up from the guide sheet and said, "What is your number in line?"

"Fourteen, sir." The robot presented his numbered ticket.

"Sit down, boy."

Bogert asked, "You haven't been here before on this day?"

"No, sir."

"Well, boy, we are going to have another man in danger of harm soon after we're through here. In fact, when you leave this room, you will be led to a stall where you will wait quietly, till you are needed. Do you understand?"

"Yes, sir."

"Now, naturally, if a man is in danger of harm, you will try to save him."

"Naturally, sir."

"Unfortunately, between the man and yourself, there will be a gamma ray field."

Silence.

"Do you know what gamma rays are?" asked Bogert sharply.

"Energy radiation, sir?"

The next question came in a friendly, offhand manner, "Ever work with gamma rays?"

"No, sir." The answer was definite.

"Mm-m. Well, boy, gamma rays will kill you instantly. They'll destroy your brain. That is a fact you must know and remember. Naturally, you don't want to destroy yourself."

"Naturally." Again the robot seemed shocked. Then, slowly, "But, sir, if the gamma rays are between myself and the master that may be harmed, how can I save him? I would be destroying myself to no purpose."

"Yes, there is that," Bogert seemed concerned about the matter. "The only thing I can advise, boy, is that if you detect the gamma radiation between yourself and the man, you may as well sit where you are."

The robot was openly relieved. "Thank you, sir. There wouldn't be any use, would there?"

"Of course not. But if there *weren't* any dangerous radiation, that would be a different matter."

"Naturally, sir. No question of that."

"You may leave now. The man on the other side of the door will lead you to your stall. Please wait there."

He turned to Susan Calvin when the robot left. "How did that go, Susan?"

"Very well," she said, dully.

"Do you think we could catch Nestor 10 by quick questioning on etheric physics?"

"Perhaps, but it's not sure enough." Her hands lay loosely in her lap. "Remember, he's fighting us. He's on his guard. The only way we can catch him is to outsmart him—and, within his limitations, he can think much more quickly than a human being."

"Well, just for fun—suppose I ask the robots from now on a few questions on gamma rays. Wave length limits, for instance."

"No!" Dr. Calvin's eyes sparked to life. "It would be too easy for him to deny knowledge and then he'd be warned against the test that's coming up—which is our real chance. Please follow the questions I've indicated, Peter, and don't improvise. It's just within the bounds of risk to ask them if they've ever worked with gamma rays. And try to sound even less interested than you do when you ask it."

Bogert shrugged, and pressed the buzzer that would allow the entrance of Number Fifteen.

The large Radiation Room was in readiness once more. The robots waited patiently in their wooden cells, all open to the center but closed off from each other.

Major-general Kallner mopped his brow slowly with a large handkerchief while Dr. Calvin checked the last details with Black.

"You're sure now," she demanded, "that none of the robots have had a chance to talk with each other after leaving the Orientation Room?"

"Absolutely sure," insisted Black. "There's not been a word exchanged."

"And the robots are put in the proper stalls?"

"Here's the plan."

The psychologist looked at it thoughtfully, "Um-m-m."

The general peered over her shoulder. "What's the idea of the arrangement, Dr. Calvin?"

"I've asked to have those robots that appeared even slightly out of true in the previous tests concentrated on one side of the circle. I'm going to be sitting in the center myself this time, and I wanted to watch those particularly."

"*You're* going to be sitting there—" exclaimed Bogert.

"Why not?" she demanded coldly. "What I expect to see may be something quite momentary. I can't risk having anyone else as main observer. Peter, you'll be in the observing booth, and I want you to keep your eye on the opposite side of the circle. General Kallner, I've arranged for motion pictures to be taken of each robot, in case visual observation isn't enough. If these are required, the robots are to remain exactly where they are until the pictures are developed and studied. None must leave, none must change place. Is that clear?"

"Perfectly."

"Then let's try it this one last time."

Susan Calvin sat in the chair, silent, eyes restless. A weight dropped, crashed downward, then pounded aside at the last moment under the synchronized thump of a sudden force beam.

And a single robot jerked upright and took two steps.

And stopped.

But Dr. Calvin was upright, and her finger pointed to him sharply. "Nestor 10, come here," she cried, "*come here!* COME HERE!"

Slowly, reluctantly, the robot took another step forward. The psychologist shouted at the top of her voice, without taking her eyes from the robot, "Get every other robot out of this place, somebody. Get them out quickly, and *keep* them out!"

Somewhere within reach of her ears there was noise, and the thud of hard feet upon the floor. She did not look away.

Nestor 10—if it was Nestor 10—took another step, and then, under force of her imperious gesture, two more. He was only ten feet away, when he spoke harshly, "I have been told to be lost—"

Another step. "I must not disobey. They have not found me so far— He would think me a failure— He told me— But it's not so—I am powerful and intelligent—"

The words came in spurts.

Another step. "I know a good deal— He would think . . . I mean I've been found— Disgraceful— Not I— I am intelligent— And by just a master . . . who is weak— Slow—"

Another step—and one metal arm flew out suddenly to her shoulder, and she felt the weight bearing her down. Her throat constricted, and she felt a shriek tear through.

Dimly, she heard Nestor 10's next words, "No one must find me. No master—" and the cold metal was against her, and she was sinking under the weight of it.

And then a queer, metallic sound, and she was on the ground with an unfelt thump, and a gleaming arm was heavy across her body. It did not move. Nor did Nestor 10, who sprawled beside her.

And now faces were bending over her.

Gerald Black was gasping, "Are you hurt, Dr. Calvin?"

She shook her head feebly. They pried the arm off her and lifted her gently to her feet, "What happened?"

Black said, "I bathed the place in gamma rays for five seconds. We didn't know what was happening. It wasn't till the last second that we realized he was attacking you, and then there was no time for anything but a gamma field. He went down in an instant. There wasn't enough to harm you though. Don't worry about it."

"I'm not worried." She closed her eyes and leaned for a moment upon his shoulder. "I don't think I was attacked exactly. Nestor 10 was simply *trying* to do so. What was left of the First Law was still holding him back."

Susan Calvin and Peter Bogert, two weeks after their first meeting with Major-general Kallner had their last. Work at Hyper Base had been resumed. The trading ship with its sixty-two normal NS-2's was gone to wherever it was bound, with an officially imposed story to explain its two weeks' delay. The government cruiser was making ready to carry the two roboticists back to Earth.

Kallner was once again a-gleam in dress uniform. His white gloves shone as he shook hands.

Calvin said, "The other modified Nestors are, of course, to be destroyed."

"They will be. We'll make shift with normal robots, or, if necessary, do without."

"Good."

"But tell me— You haven't explained— How was it done?"

She smiled tightly, "Oh, that. I would have told you in advance if I had been more certain of its working. You see, Nestor 10 had a superiority complex that was becoming more radical all the time. He liked to think that he and other robots knew more than human beings. It was becoming very important for him to think so.

"We knew that. So we warned every robot in advance that gamma rays would kill them, which it would, and we further warned them all that gamma rays would be between them and myself. So they all stayed where they were, naturally. By Nestor 10's own logic in the previous test they had all decided that there was no point in trying to save a human being if they were sure to die before they could do it."

"Well, yes, Dr. Calvin, I understand that. But why did Nestor 10 himself leave his seat?"

"Ah! That was a little arrangement between myself and your young Mr. Black. You see it wasn't gamma rays that flooded the area between myself and the robots—but infrared rays. Just ordinary heat rays, absolutely harmless. Nestor 10 knew they were infrared and harmless and so he began to dash out, as he expected the rest would do, under First Law compulsion. It was only a fraction of a second too late that he remembered that the normal NS-2's could detect radiation, but could not identify the type. That he himself could only identify wave lengths by virtue of the training he had received at Hyper Base, under mere human beings, was a little too humiliating to remember for just a moment. To the normal robots the area was fatal because we had told them it would be, and only Nestor 10 knew we were lying.

"And just for a moment he forgot, or didn't want to remember, that other robots might be more ignorant than human beings. His very superiority caught him. Good-bye, general."

TOMORROW'S CHILDREN

by Poul Anderson (1926-   )

ASTOUNDING SCIENCE FICTION
March

This fine story was Poul Anderson's first published work and signaled the beginning of a long, productive and distinguished career, which would see him win the coveted Hugo Award in 1961 ("The Longest Voyage"), 1964 ("No Truce With Kings"), 1969 ("The Sharing of Flesh"), 1972 ("The Queen of Air and Darkness" which also won a Nebula Award), 1973 ("Goat Song" another Nebula winner), and 1979 ("Hunter's Moon"). He also received the Tolkien Memorial Award, was the Guest of Honor at the 1959 World Science Fiction Convention, and has an impressive list of outstanding novels in both the science fiction and fantasy fields.

"Tomorrow's Children" remains one of the very best atomic "awful warning" stories ever written, a powerful and frightening glimpse of a future we all hope will never happen, as well as a strong plea for a more tolerant world.

(I've always had a sneaking envy of those who burst onto the science fiction scene with eclat. My

own first story showed no signs whatever that I was going to become a major science fiction figure. It could easily have been written by one of the many who appear in order to shine dimly for a while and then recede into the outer darkness again. I was quite aware in my early years that this was true and I also knew that with their very first stories Robert Heinlein and A. E. van Vogt (to name just two) had established themselves unmistakably as first-magnitude stars.

Well, Poul Anderson was another. To this day I remember the impact "Tomorrow's Children" made on me. It helped, of course, that the nuclear bomb and its effects occupied all our minds at the time (as, indeed, it does now) and that Poul had that funny first name—but it was the story that counted and I was quite certain that Poul would keep on writing and would continue to turn out masterpieces.

And, as a matter of fact, Poul has been hot on the heels of the "Big Three," longer and more consistently than anyone else in the field.—I.A.)

*On the world's loom
Weave the Norns doom,
Nor may they guide it nor change.*
    —Wagner, Siegfried

Ten miles up, it hardly showed. Earth was a cloudy green and brown blur, the vast vault of the stratosphere reaching changelessly out to spatial infinities, and beyond the pulsing engine there was silence and serenity no man could ever touch. Looking down, Hugh Drummond could see the Mississippi gleaming like a drawn sword, and its slow curve matched the contours shown on his map. The hills, the sea, the sun and wind and rain, they didn't change. Not in less

than a million slow-striding years, and human efforts flickered
too briefly in the unending night for that.

Farther down, though, and especially where cities had
been— The lone man in the solitary stratojet swore softly,
bitterly, and his knuckles whitened on the controls. He was a
big man, his gaunt rangy form sprawling awkwardly in the
tiny pressure cabin, and he wasn't quite forty. But his dark
hair was streaked with gray, in the shabby flying suit his
shoulders stooped, and his long homely face was drawn into
haggard lines. His eyes were black-rimmed and sunken with
weariness, dark and dreadful in their intensity. He'd seen too
much, survived too much, until he began to look like most
other people of the world. *Heir of the ages*, he thought
dully.

Mechanically, he went through the motions of following
his course. Natural landmarks were still there, and he had
powerful binoculars to help him. But he didn't use them
much. They showed too many broad shallow craters, their
vitreous smoothness throwing back sunlight in the flat blank
glitter of a snake's eye, the ground about them a churned and
blasted desolation. And there were the worse regions of—
deadness. Twisted dead trees, blowing sand, tumbled skeletons, perhaps at night a baleful blue glow of fluorescence. The
bombs had been nightmares, riding in on wings of fire and
horror to shake the planet with the death blows of cities. But
the radioactive dust was worse than any nightmare.

He passed over villages, even small towns. Some of them
were deserted, the blowing colloidal dust, or plague, or
economic breakdown making them untenable. Others still
seemed to be living a feeble half-life. Especially in the Midwest, there was a pathetic struggle to return to an agricultural
system, but the insects and blights—

Drummond shrugged. After nearly two years of this, over
the scarred and maimed planet, he should be used to it. The
United States had been lucky. Europe, now—

Der Untergang des Abendlandes, he thought grayly. *Spen-
gler foresaw the collapse of a top-heavy civilization. He
didn't foresee atomic bombs, radioactive-dust bombs, bacteria
bombs, blight bombs—the bombs, the senseless inanimate
bombs flying like monster insects over the shivering world. So
he didn't guess the extent of the collapse.*

Deliberately he pushed the thoughts out of his conscious
mind. He didn't want to dwell on them. He'd lived with them

two years, and that was two eternities too long. And anyway, he was nearly home now.

The capital of the United States was below him, and he sent the stratojet slanting down in a long thunderous dive toward the mountains. Not much of a capital, the little town huddled in a valley of the Cascades, but the waters of the Potomac had filled the grave of Washington. Strictly speaking, there was no capital. The officers of the government were scattered over the country, keeping in precarious touch by plane and radio, but Taylor, Oregon, came as close to being the nerve center as any other place.

He gave the signal again on his transmitter, knowing with a faint spine-crawling sensation of the rocket batteries trained on him from the green of those mountains. When one plane could carry the end of a city, all planes were under suspicion. Not that anyone outside was supposed to know that that innocuous little town was important. But you never could tell. The war wasn't officially over. It might never be, with sheer personal survival overriding the urgency of treaties.

A light-beam transmitter gave him a cautious: "O.K. Can you land in the street?"

It was a narrow, dusty track between two wooden rows of houses, but Drummond was a good pilot and this was a good jet. "Yeah," he said. His voice had grown unused to speech.

He cut speed in a spiral descent until he was gliding with only the faintest whisper of wind across his ship. Touching wheels to the street, he slammed on the brake and bounced to a halt.

Silence struck at him like a physical blow. The engine stilled, the sun beating down from a brassy blue sky on the drabness of rude "temporary" houses, the total-seeming desertion beneath the impassive mountains—Home! Hugh Drummond laughed, a short harsh bark with nothing of humor in it, and swung open the cockpit canopy.

There were actually quite a few people, he saw, peering from doorways and side streets. They looked fairly well fed and dressed, many in uniform; they seemed to have purpose and hope. But this, of course, was the capital of the United States of America, the world's most fortunate country.

"Get out—quick!"

The peremptory voice roused Drummond from the introspection into which those lonely months had driven him. He looked down at a gang of men in mechanic's outfits, led by a harassed-looking man in captain's uniform. "Oh—of course," he said slowly. "You want to hide the plane. And, naturally, a regular landing field would give you away."

"Hurry, get out, you infernal idiot! Anyone, *anyone* might come over and see—"

"They wouldn't go unnoticed by an efficient detection system, and you still have that," said Drummond, sliding his booted legs over the cockpit edge. "And anyway, there won't be any more raids. The war's over."

"Wish I could believe that, but who are you to say? Get a move on!"

The grease monkeys hustled the plane down the street. With an odd feeling of loneliness, Drummond watched it go. After all, it had been his home for—how long?

The machine was stopped before a false house whose whole front was swung aside. A concrete ramp led downward, and Drummond could see a cavernous immensity below. Light within it gleamed off silvery rows of aircraft.

"Pretty neat," he admitted. "Not that it matters anymore. Probably it never did. Most of the hell came over on robot rockets. Oh, well." He fished his pipe from his jacket. Colonel's insignia glittered briefly as the garment flipped back.

"Oh . . . sorry, sir!" exclaimed the captain. "I didn't know—"

" 'S O.K. I've gotten out of the habit of wearing a regular uniform. A lot of places I've been, an American wouldn't be very popular."

Drummond stuffed tobacco into his briar, scowling. He hated to think how often he'd had to use the Colt at his hip, or even the machine guns in his plane, to save himself. He inhaled smoke gratefully. It seemed to drown out some of the bitter taste.

"General Robinson said to bring you to him when you arrived, sir," said the captain. "This way, please."

They went down the street, their boots scuffing up little acrid clouds of dust. Drummond looked sharply about him. He'd left very shortly after the two-month Ragnarok which had tapered off when the organization of both sides broke down too far to keep on making and sending the bombs, and maintaining order with famine and disease starting their ghastly ride over the homeland. At that time, the United States was a cityless anarchic chaos, and he'd had only the briefest of radio exchanges since then, whenever he could get at a long-range set still in working order. They'd make remarkable progress meanwhile. How much, he didn't know, but the mere existence of something like a capital was sufficient proof.

Robinson— His lined face twisted into a frown. He didn't know the man. He'd been expecting to be received by the President, who had sent him and some others out. Unless the others had— No, he was the only one who had been in eastern Europe and western Asia. He was sure of that.

Two sentries guarded the entrance to what was obviously a converted general store. But there were no more stores. There was nothing to put in them. Drummond entered the cool dimness of an antechamber. The clatter of a typewriter, the Wac operating it— He gaped and blinked. That was—impossible! Typewriters, secretaries—hadn't they gone out with the whole world, two years ago? If the Dark Ages had returned to Earth, it didn't seem—*right*—that there should still be typewriters. It didn't fit, didn't—

He grew aware that the captain had opened the inner door for him. As he stepped in, he grew aware how tired he was. His arm weighed a ton as he saluted the man behind the desk.

"At ease, at ease," Robinson's voice was genial. Despite the five stars on his shoulders, he wore no tie or coat, and his round face was smiling. Still, he looked tough and competent underneath. To run things nowadays, he'd have to be.

"Sit down, Colonel Drummond." Robinson gestured to a chair near his and the aviator collapsed into it, shivering. His haunted eyes traversed the office. It was almost well enough outfitted to be a prewar place.

Prewar! A word like a sword, cutting across history with a brutality of murder, hazing everything in the past until it was a vague golden glow through drifting, red-shot black clouds. And—only two years. *Only two years!* Surely sanity was meaningless in a world of such nightmare inversions. Why, he could barely remember Barbara and the kids. Their faces were blotted out in a tide of other visages—starved faces, dead faces, human faces become beast-formed with want and pain and eating throttled hate. His grief was lost in the agony of a world, and in some ways he had become a machine himself.

"You look plenty tired," said Robinson.

"Yeah . . . yes, sir—"

"Skip the formality. I don't go for it. We'll be working pretty close together, can't take time to be diplomatic."

"Uh-huh. I came over the North Pole, you know. Haven't slept since—Rough time. But, if I may ask, you—" Drummond hesitated.

"I? I suppose I'm President. Ex officio, pro tem, or something. Here, you need a drink." Robinson got bottle and glasses from a drawer. The liquor gurgled out in a pungent stream. "Prewar Scotch. Till it gives out I'm laying off this modern hooch. *Gambai.*"

The fiery, smoky brew jolted Drummond to wakefulness. Its glow was pleasant in his empty stomach. He heard Robinson's voice with a surrealistic sharpness:

"Yes, I'm at the head now. My predecessors made the mistake of sticking together, and of traveling a good deal in trying to pull the country back into shape. So I think the sickness got the President, and I know it got several others. Of course, there was no means of holding an election. The armed forces had almost the only organization left, so we had to run things. Berger was in charge, but he shot himself when he learned he'd breathed radiodust. Then the command fell to me. I've been lucky."

"I see." It didn't make much difference. A few dozen more deaths weren't much, when over half the world was gone. "Do you expect to—continue lucky?" A brutally blunt question, maybe, but words weren't bombs.

"I do." Robinson was firm about that. "We've learned by experience, learned a lot. We've scattered the army, broken it into small outposts at key points throughout the country. For quite a while, we stopped travel altogether except for absolute emergencies, and then with elaborate precautions. That smothered the epidemics. The microorganisms were bred to work in crowded areas, you know. They were almost immune to known medical techniques, but without hosts and carriers they died. I guess natural bacteria ate up most of them. We still take care in traveling, but we're fairly safe now."

"Did any of the others come back? There were a lot like me, sent out to see what really had happened to the world."

"One did, from South America. Their situation is similar to ours, though they lacked our tight organization and have gone further toward anarchy. Nobody else returned but you."

It wasn't surprising. In fact, it was a cause for astonishment that anyone had come back. Drummond had volunteered after the bomb erasing St. Louis had taken his family, not expecting to survive and not caring much whether he did. Maybe that was why he had.

"You can take your time in writing a detailed report," said Robinson, "but in general, how are things over there?"

Drummond shrugged. "The war's over. Burned out. Europe has gone back to savagery. They were caught between America and Asia, and the bombs came both ways. Not many survivors, and they're starving animals. Russia, from what I saw, has managed something like you've done here, though they're worse off than we. Naturally, I couldn't find out much here. I didn't get to India or China, but in Russia I heard rumors— No, the world's gone too far into disintegration to carry on war."

"Then we can come out in the open," said Robinson softly. "We can really start rebuilding. I don't think there'll ever be another war, Drummond. I think the memory of this one will be carved too deeply on the race for us ever to forget."

"Can you shrug it off that easily?"

"No, no, of course not. Our culture hasn't lost its continuity, but it's had a terrific setback. We'll never wholly get over it. But—we're on our way up again."

The general rose, glancing at his watch. "Six o'clock. Come on, Drummond, let's get home."

"Home?"

"Yes, you'll stay with me. Man, you look like the original zombie. You'll need a month or more of sleeping between clean sheets, of home cooking and home atmosphere. My wife will be glad to have you; we see almost no new faces. And as long as we'll work together, I'd like to keep you handy. The shortage of competent men is terrific."

They went down the street, an aide following. Drummond was again conscious of the weariness aching in every bone and fiber of him. A home—after two years of ghost towns, of shattered chimneys above blood-dappled snow, of flimsy lean-tos housing starvation and death.

"Your plane will be mighty useful, too," said Robinson. "Those atomic-powered craft are scarcer than hens' teeth used to be." He chuckled hollowly, as at a rather grim joke. "Got you through close to two years of flying without needing fuel. Any other trouble?"

"Some, but there were enough spare parts." No need to tell of those frantic hours and days of slaving, of desperate improvisation with hunger and plague stalking him who stayed overlong. He'd had his troubles getting food, too, despite the plentiful supplies he'd started out with. He'd fought for scraps in the winter, beaten off howling maniacs who would have killed him for a bird he'd shot or a dead horse he'd scavenged. He hated that plundering, and would not have cared personally if they'd managed to destroy him. But he had a mission, and the mission was all he'd had left as a focal point for his life, so he'd clung to it with fanatic intensity.

And now the job was over, and he realized he couldn't rest. He didn't dare. Rest would give him time to remember. Maybe he could find surcease in the gigantic work of reconstruction. Maybe.

"Here we are," said Robinson.

Drummond blinked in new amazement. There was a car, camouflaged under brush, with a military chauffeur—*a car!* And in pretty fair shape, too.

"We've got a few oil wells going again, and a small patched-up refinery," explained the general. "It furnishes enough gas and oil for what traffic we have."

They got in the rear seat. The aide sat in front, a rifle ready. The car started down a mountain road.

"Where to?" asked Drummond a little dazedly.

Robinson smiled. "Personally," he said, I'm almost the only lucky man on Earth. We had a summer cottage on Lake Taylor, a few miles from here. My wife was there when the war came, and stayed, and nobody came along till I brought the head offices here with me. Now I've got a home all to myself."

"Yeah. Yeah, you're lucky," said Drummond. He looked out the window, not seeing the sun-spattered woods. Presently he asked, his voice a little harsh: "How is the country really doing now?"

"For a while it was rough. Damn rough. When the cities went, our transportation, communication, and distribution systems broke down. In fact, our whole economy disintegrated, though not all at once. Then there was the dust and the plagues. People fled, and there was open fighting when overcrowded safe places refused to take in any more refugees. Police went with the cities, and the army couldn't do much patrolling. We were busy fighting the enemy troops that'd flown over the Pole to invade. We still haven't gotten them all. Bands are roaming the country, hungry and desperate outlaws, and there are plenty of Americans who turned to banditry when everything else failed. That's why we have this guard, though so far none have come this way.

"The insect and blight weapons just about wiped out our crops, and that winter everybody starved. We checked the pests with modern methods, though it was touch and go for a while, and next year got some food. Of course, with no distribution as yet, we failed to save a lot of people. And farming is still a tough proposition. We won't really have the bugs licked for a long time. If we had a research center as well equipped as those which produced the things— But we're gaining. We're gaining."

"Distribution—" Drummond rubbed his chin. "How about railroads? Horse-drawn vehicles?"

"We have some railroads going, but the enemy was as careful to dust most of ours as we were to dust theirs. As for horses, they were nearly all eaten that first winter. I know personally of only a dozen. They're on my place; I'm trying to breed enough to be of use, but"—Robinson smiled wryly—"by the time we've raised that many, the factories should have been going quite a spell."

"And so now—?"

"We're over the worst. Except for outlaws, we have the population fairly well controlled. The civilized people are fairly well fed, with some kind of housing. We have machine shops, small factories, and the like going, enough to keep our transportation and other mechanism 'level.' Presently we'll be able to expand these, being actually increasing what we have. In another five years or so, I guess, we'll be integrated enough to drop martial law and hold a general election. A big job ahead, but a good one."

The car halted to let a cow lumber over the road, a calf trotting at her heels. She was gaunt and shaggy, and skittered nervously from the vehicle into the brush.

"Wild," explained Robinson. "Most of the real wild life was killed off for food in the last two years, but a lot of farm animals escaped when their owners died or fled, and have run free ever since. They—" He noticed Drummond's fixed gaze. The pilot was looking at the calf. Its legs were half the normal length.

"Mutant," said the general. "You find a lot of such animals.

Radiation from bombed or dusted areas. There are even a lot of human abnormal births." He scowled, worry clouding his eyes. "In fact, that's just about our worst problem. It—"

The car came out of the woods onto the shore of a small lake. It was a peaceful scene, the quiet waters like molten gold in the slanting sunlight, trees ringing the circumference and all about them the mountains. Under one huge pine stood a cottage, a woman on the porch.

It was like one summer with Barbara—Drummond cursed under his breath and followed Robinson toward the little building. It wasn't, it wasn't, it could never be. Not ever again. There were soldiers guarding this place from chance marauders, and— There was an odd-looking flower at his feet. A daisy, but huge and red and irregularly formed.

A squirrel chittered from a tree. Drummond saw that its face was so blunt as to be almost human.

Then he was on the porch, and Robinson was introducing him to "my wife Elaine." She was a nice-looking young woman with eyes that were sympathetic on Drummond's exhausted face. The aviator tried not to notice that she was pregnant.

He was led inside, and reveled in a hot bath. Afterward there was supper, but he was numb with sleep by then, and hardly noticed it when Robinson put him to bed.

Reaction set in, and for a week or so Drummond went about in a haze, not much good to himself or anyone else. But it was surprising what plenty of food and sleep could do, and one evening Robinson came home to find him scribbling on sheets of paper.

"Arranging my notes and so on," he explained. "I'll write out the complete report in a month, I guess."

"Good. But no hurry." Robinson settled tiredly into an armchair. "The rest of the world will keep. I'd rather you'd just work at this off and on, and join my staff for your main job."

"O.K. Only what'll I do?"

"Everything. Specialization is gone; too few surviving specialists and equipment. I think your chief task will be to head the census bureau."

"Eh?"

Robinson grinned lopsidedly. "You'll *be* the census bureau, except for what few assistants I can spare you." He leaned forward, said earnestly: "And it's one of the most important jobs there is. You'll do for this country what you did for central Eurasia, only in much greater detail. Drummond, we have to *know*."

He took a map from a desk drawer and spread it out. "Look, here's the United States. I've marked regions known to be uninhabitable in red." His fingers traced out the ugly splotches. "Too many of 'em, and doubtless there are others we haven't found yet. Now, the blue X's are army posts." They were sparsely scattered over the land, near the centers of population groupings. "Not enough of those. It's all we can do to control the more or less well-off, orderly people. Bandits, enemy troops, homeless refugees—they're still running wild, skulking in the backwoods and barrens, and raiding whenever they can. And they spread the plague. We won't really have it licked till everybody's settled down, and that'd be hard to enforce. Drummond, we don't even have enough soldiers to start a feudal system for protection. The plague spread like a prairie fire in those concentrations of men.

"We have to *know*. We have to know how many people survived—half the population, a third, a quarter, whatever it is. We have to know where they are, and how they're fixed for supplies, so we can start up an equitable distribution system. We have to find all the small-town shops and labs and libraries still standing, and rescue their priceless contents before looters or the weather beat us to it. We have to locate doctors and engineers and other professional men, and put them to work rebuilding. We have to find the outlaws and round them up. We— I could go on forever. Once we have all that information, we can set up a master plan for redistributing population, agriculture, industry, and the rest most efficiently, for getting the country back under civil authority and police, for opening regular transportation and communication channels—for getting the nation back on its feet."

"I see," nodded Drummond. "Hitherto, just surviving and hanging on to what was left has taken precedence. Now you're in a position to start expanding, *if* you know where and how much to expand."

"Exactly." Robinson rolled a cigarette, grimacing. "Not much tobacco left. What I have is perfectly foul. Lord, that war was crazy!"

"All wars are," said Drummond dispassionately, "but technology advanced to the point of giving us a knife to cut our throats with. Before that, we were just beating our heads against the wall. Robinson, we can't go back to the old ways. We've *got* to start on a new track—a track of sanity."

"Yes. And that brings up—" The other man looked toward the kitchen door. They could hear the cheerful rattle of dishes there, and smell mouth-watering cooking odors. He lowered his voice. "I might as well tell you this now, but don't let Elaine know. She . . . she shouldn't be worried. Drummond, did you see our horses?"

The other day, yes. The colts—"

"Uh-huh. There've been five colts born of eleven mares in the last year. Two of them were so deformed they died in a week, another in a few months. One of the two left has cloven hoofs and almost no teeth. The last one looks normal—so far. One out of eleven, Drummond."

"Were those horses near a radioactive area?"

"They must have been. They were rounded up wherever found and brought here. The stallion was caught near the site of Portland, I know. But if he were the only one with mutated genes, it would hardly show in the first generation, would it? I understand nearly all mutations are Mendelian recessives. Even if there were one dominant, it would show in all the colts, but none of these looked alike."

"Hm-m-m—I don't know much about genetics, but I do know hard radiation, or rather the secondary charged particles it produces, will cause mutation. Only mutants are rare, and tend to fall into certain patterns—"

"*Were* rare!" Suddenly Robinson was grim, something coldly frightened in his eyes. "Haven't you noticed the animals and plants? They're fewer than formerly, and . . . well, I've not kept count, but at least half those seen or killed have something wrong, internally or externally."

Drummond drew heavily on his pipe. He needed something to hang onto, in a new storm of insanity. Very quietly, he said:

"In my college biology course, they told me the vast majority of mutations are unfavorable. More ways of not doing something than of doing it. Radiation might sterilize an animal, or might produce several degrees of genetic change. You could have a mutation so violently lethal the possessor never gets born, or soon dies. You could have all kinds of more or less handicapping factors, or just random changes not making much difference one way or the other. Or in a few rare cases you might get something actually favorable, but you couldn't really say the possessor is a true member of the species. And favorable mutations themselves usually involve a price in the partial or total loss of some other function."

"Right." Robinson nodded heavily. "One of your jobs on the census will be to try and locate any and all who know genetics, and send them here. But your real task, which only you and I and a couple of others must know about, the job overriding all other considerations, will be to find the human mutants."

Drummond's throat was dry. "There've been a lot of them?" he whispered.

"Yes. But we don't know how many or where. We only know about those people who live near an army post, or have some other fairly regular intercourse with us, and they're only a few thousand all told. Among them, the birth rate has gone down to about half the prewar ratio. And over half the births they do have are abnormal."

"*Over half*—"

"Yeah. Of course, the violently different ones soon die, or are put in an institution we've set up in the Alleghenies. But what can we do with viable forms, if their parents still love them? A kid with deformed or missing or abortive organs, twisted internal structure, a tail, or something even worse . . . well, *it'll* have a tough time in life, but it can generally survive. And perpetuate itself—"

"And a normal-looking one might have some unnoticeable quirk, or a characteristic that won't show up for years. Or even a normal one might be carrying recessives, and pass them on— God!" The exclamation was half blasphemy, half prayer. "But how'd it happen? People weren't all near atom-hit areas."

"Maybe not, though a lot of survivors escaped from the outskirts. But there was that first year, with everybody on the move. One could pass near enough to a blasted region to be affected, without knowing it. And that damnable radiodust, blowing on the wind. It's got a long half-life. It'll be active for decades. Then, as in any collapsing culture, promiscuity was common. Still is. Oh, it'd spread itself, all right."

"I still don't see why it spread itself so much. Even here—"

"Well, I don't know why it shows up here. I suppose a lot of the local flora and fauna came in from elsewhere. This place is safe. The nearest dusted region is three hundred

miles off, with mountains between. There must be many such
islands of comparatively normal conditions. We have to find
them too. But elsewhere—"

"Soup's on," announced Elaine, and went from the kitchen
to the dining room with a loaded tray.

The men rose. Grayly, Drummond looked at Robinson and
said tonelessly: "O.K. I'll get your information for you. We'll
map mutation areas and safe areas, we'll check on our population and resources, we'll eventually get all the facts you
want. But—what are you going to do then?"

"I wish I knew," said Robinson haggardly. "I wish I
knew."

Winter lay heavily on the north, a vast gray sky seeming
frozen solid over the rolling white plains. The last three winters had come early and stayed long. Dust, colloidal dust of
the bombs, suspended in the atmosphere cut down the solar
constant by a deadly percent or two. There had even been a
few earthquakes, set off in geologically unstable parts of the
world by bombs planted right. Half California had been
ruined when a sabotage bomb started the San Andreas Fault
on a major slip. And that kicked up still more dust.

Fimbulwinter, thought Drummond bleakly. *The doom of
the prophecy. But no, we're surviving. Though maybe not as
men—*

Most people had gone south, and there overcrowding had
made starvation and disease and internecine struggle the normal aspects of life. Those who'd stuck it out up here, and had
luck with their pest-ridden crops, were better off.

Drummond's jet slid above the cratered black ruin of the
Twin Cities. There was still enough radioactivity to melt the
snow, and the pit was like a skull's empty eye socket. The
man sighed, but he was becoming calloused to the sight of
death. There was so much of it. Only the struggling agony of
life mattered any more.

He strained through the sinister twilight, swooping low
over the unending fields. Burned-out hulks of farmhouses,
bones of ghost towns, sere deadness of dusted land—but he'd
heard travelers speak of a fairly powerful community up near
the Canadian border, and it was up to him to find it.

A lot of things had been up to him in the last six months.
He'd had to work out a means of search, and organize his

few, overworked assistants into an efficient staff, and go out on the long hunt.

They hadn't covered the country. That was impossible. Their few planes had gone to areas chosen more or less at random, trying to get a cross section of conditions. They'd penetrated wildernesses of hill and plain and forest, establishing contact with scattered, still demoralized out-dwellers. On the whole, it was more laborious than anything else. Most were pathetically glad to see any symbol of law and order and the paradisiacal-seeming "old days." Now and then there was danger and trouble, when they encountered wary or sullen or outright hostile groups suspicious of a government they associated with disaster, and once there had even been a pitched battle with roving outlaws. But the work had gone ahead, and now the preliminaries were about over.

Preliminaries— It was a bigger job to find out exactly how matters stood than the entire country was capable of undertaking right now. But Drummond had enough facts for reliable extrapolation. He and his staff had collected most of the essential data and begun correlating it. By questioning, by observation, by seeking and finding, by any means that came to hand they'd filled their notebooks. And in the sketchy outlines of a Chinese drawing, and with the same stark realism, the truth was there.

Just this one more place, and I'll go home, thought Drummond for the—thousandth?—time. His brain was getting into a rut, treading the same terrible circle and finding no way out. *Robinson won't like what I tell him, but there it is.* And darkly, slowly: *Barbara, maybe it was best you and the kids went as you did. Quickly, cleanly, not even knowing it. This isn't much of a world. It'll never be our world again.*

He saw the place he sought, a huddle of buildings near the frozen shores of the Lake of the Woods, and his jet murmured toward the white ground. The stories he'd heard of this town weren't overly encouraging, but he supposed he'd get out all right. The others had his data anyway, so it didn't matter.

By the time he'd landed in the clearing just outside the village, using the jet's skis, most of the inhabitants were there waiting. In the gathering dusk they were a ragged and wild-looking bunch, clumsily dressed in whatever scraps of cloth and leather they had. The bearded, hard-eyed men were armed with clubs and knives and a few guns. As Drummond got out, he was careful to keep his hands away from his own automatics.

"Hello," he said. "I'm friendly."

"Y' better be," growled the big leader. "Who are you, where from, an' why?"

"First," lied Drummond smoothly, "I want to tell you I have another man with a plane who knows where I am. If I'm not back in a certain time, he'll come with bombs. But we don't intend any harm or interference. This is just a sort of social call. I'm Hugh Drummond of the United States Army."

They digested that slowly. Clearly, they weren't friendly to the government, but they stood in too much awe of aircraft and armament to be openly hostile. The leader spat. "How long you staying?"

"Just overnight, if you'll put me up. I'll pay for it." He held up a small pouch. "Tobacco."

Their eyes gleamed, and the leader said, "You'll stay with me. Come on."

Drummond gave him the bribe and went with the group. He didn't like to spend such priceless luxuries thus freely, but the job was more important. And the boss seemed thawed a little by the fragrant brown flakes. He was sniffing them greedily.

"Been smoking bark an' grass," he confided. "Terrible."

"Worse than that," agreed Drummond. He turned up his jacket collar and shivered. The wind starting to blow was bitterly cold.

"Just what y' here for?" demanded someone else.

"Well, just to see how things stand. We've got the government started again, and are patching things up. But we have to know where folks are, what they need, and so on."

"Don't want nothing t' do with the gov'ment," muttered a woman. "They brung all this on us."

"Oh, come now. We didn't ask to be attacked." Mentally, Drummond crossed his fingers. He neither knew nor cared who was to blame. Both sides, letting mutual fear and friction mount to hysteria— In fact, he wasn't sure the United States hadn't sent out the first rockets, on orders of some panicky or aggressive officials. Nobody was alive who admitted knowing.

"It's the jedgment o' God, for the sins o' our leaders," persisted the woman. "The plague, the fire-death, all that, ain't it foretold in the Bible? Ain't we living in the last days o' the world?"

"Maybe." Drummond was glad to stop before a long low cabin. Religious argument was touchy at best, and with a lot of people nowadays it was dynamite.

They entered the rudely furnished but fairly comfortable structure. A good many crowded in with them. For all their suspicion, they were curious, and an outsider in an aircraft was a blue-moon event these days.

Drummond's eyes flickered unobtrusively about the room, noticing details. Three women—that meant a return to concubinage. Only to be expected in a day of few men and strong-arm rule. Ornaments and utensils, tools and weapons of good quality—yes, that confirmed the stories. This wasn't exactly a bandit town, but it had waylaid travelers and raided other places when times were hard, and built up a sort of dominance of the surrounding country. That, too, was common.

There was a dog on the floor nursing a litter. Only three pups, and one of those was bald, one lacked ears, and one had more toes than it should. Among the wide-eyed children present, there were several two years old or less, and with almost no obvious exceptions, they were also different.

Drummond sighed heavily and sat down. In a way, this clinched it. He'd known for a long time, and finding mutation here, as far as any place from atomic destruction, was about the last evidence he needed.

He had to get on friendly terms, or he wouldn't find out much about things like population, food production, and whatever else there was to know. Forcing a smile to stiff lips, he took a flask from his jacket. "Prewar rye," he said. "Who wants a nip?"

"Do we!" The answer barked out in a dozen voices and words. The flask circulated, men pawing and cursing and grabbing to get at it. *Their homebrew must be pretty bad*, thought Drummond wryly.

The chief shouted an order, and one of his women got busy at the primitive stove. "Rustle you a mess o' chow," he said heartily. "An' my name's Sam Buckman."

"Pleased to meet you, Sam." Drummond squeezed the hairy paw hard. He had to show he wasn't a weakling, a conniving city slicker.

"What's it like, outside?" asked someone presently. "We ain't heard for so long—"

"You haven't missed much," said Drummond between bites. The food was pretty good. Briefly, he sketched conditions. "You're better off than most," he finished.

"Yeah. Mebbe so." Sam Buckman scratched his tangled beard. "What I'd give f'r a razor blade—! It ain't easy, though. The first year we weren't no better off 'n anyone else. Me, I'm a farmer, I kept some ears o' corn an' a little wheat an' barley in my pockets all that winter, even though I was starving. A bunch o' hungry refugees plundered my place, but I got away an' drifted up here. Next year I took an empty farm here an' started over."

Drummond doubted that it had been abandoned, but said nothing. Sheer survival outweighed a lot of considerations.

"Others came an' settled here," said the leader reminiscently. "We farm together. We have to; one man couldn't live by hisself, not with the bugs an' blight, an' the crops sproutin' into all new kinds, an' the outlaws aroun'. Not many up here, though we did beat off some enemy troops last winter." He glowed with pride at that, but Drummond wasn't particularly impressed. A handful of freezing starveling conscripts, lost and bewildered in a foreign enemy's land, with no hope of ever getting home, weren't formidable.

"Things getting better, though," said Buckman. "We're heading up." He scowled blackly, and a palpable chill crept into the room. "If 'twern't for the births—"

"Yes—the births. The new babies. Even the stock an' plants." It was an old man speaking, his eyes glazed with near madness. "It's the mark o' the beast. Satan is loose in the world—"

"Shut up!" Huge and bristling with wrath, Buckman launched himself out of his seat and grabbed the oldster by his scrawny throat. "Shut up 'r I'll bash y'r lying head in. Ain't no son o' mine being marked by the devil."

"Or mine—" "Or mine—" The rumble of voices ran about the cabin, sullen and afraid.

"It's God's jedgment, I tell you!" The woman was shrilling again. "The end o' the world is near. Prepare f'r the second coming—"

"An' you shut up too, Mag Schmidt," snarled Buckman. He stood bent over, gnarled arms swinging loose, hands flexing, little eyes darting red and wild about the room. "Shut y'r trap an' keep it shut. I'm still boss here, an' if you don't like it you can get out. I still don't think that funny-looking brat o' y'rs fell in the lake by accident."

The woman shrank back, lips tight. The room filled with a crackling silence. One of the babies began to cry. It had two heads.

Slowly and heavily, Buckman turned to Drummond, who sat immobile against the wall. "You see?" he asked dully. "You see how it is? Maybe it is the curse o' God. Maybe the world is ending. I dunno. I just know there's few enough babies, an' most o' them deformed. Will it go on? Will all our kids be monsters? Should we . . . kill these an' hope we get some human babies? What is it? What to do?"

Drummond rose. He felt a weight as of centuries on his shoulders, the weariness, blank and absolute, of having seen that smoldering panic and heard that desperate appeal too often, too often.

"Don't kill them," he said. "That's the worst kind of murder, and anyway it'd do no good at all. It comes from the bombs, and you can't stop it. You'll go right on having such children, so you might as well get used to it."

By atomic-powered stratojet it wasn't far from Minnesota to Oregon, and Drummond landed in Taylor about noon the next day. This time there was no hurry to get his machine under cover, and up on the mountain was a raw scar of earth where a new airfield was slowly being built. Men were getting over their terror of the sky. They had another fear to face now, and it was one from which there was no hiding.

Drummond walked slowly down the icy main street to the central office. It was numbingly cold, a still, relentless intensity of frost eating through clothes and flesh and bone. It wasn't much better inside. Heating systems were still poor improvisations.

"You're back!" Robinson met him in the antechamber, suddenly galvanized with eagerness. He had grown thin and nervous, looking ten years older, but impatience blazed from him. "How is it? How is it?"

Drummond held up a bulky notebook. "All here," he said grimly. "All the facts we'll need. Not formally correlated yet, but the picture is simple enough."

Robinson laid an arm on his shoulder and steered him into

the office. He felt the general's hand shaking, but he'd sat down and had a drink before business came up again.

"You've done a good job," said the leader warmly. "When the country's organized again, I'll see you get a medal for this. Your men in the other planes aren't in yet."

"No, they'll be gathering data for a long time. The job won't be finished for years. I've only got a general outline here, but it's enough. It's enough." Drummond's eyes were haunted again.

Robinson felt cold at meeting that too-steady gaze. He whispered shakily: "Is it—bad?"

"The worst. Physically, the country's recovering. But biologically, we've reached a crossroads and taken the wrong fork."

"What do you mean? *What do you mean?*"

Drummond let him have it then, straight and hard as a bayonet thrust. "The birth rate's a little over half the prewar," he said, "and about seventy-five per cent of all births are mutant, of which possibly two-thirds are viable and presumably fertile. Of course, that doesn't include late-maturing characteristics, or those undetectable by naked-eye observation, or the mutated recessive genes that must be carried by a lot of otherwise normal zygotes. And it's everywhere. There are no safe places."

"I see," said Robinson after a long time. He nodded, like a man struck a stunning blow and not yet fully aware of it. "I see. The reason—"

"Is obvious."

"Yes. People going through radioactive areas—"

"Why, no. That would only account for a few. But—"

"No matter. The fact's there, and that's enough. We have to decide what to do about it."

"And soon." Drummond's jaw set. "It's wrecking our culture. We at least preserved our historical continuity, but even that's going now. People are going crazy as birth after birth is monstrous. Fear of the unknown, striking at minds still stunned by the war and its immediate aftermath. Frustration of parenthood, perhaps the most basic instinct there is. It's leading to infanticide, desertion, despair, a cancer at the root of society. We've got to act."

"How? How?" Robinson stared numbly at his hands.

"I don't know. You're the leader. Maybe an educational campaign, though that hardly seems practicable. Maybe an acceleration of your program for re-integrating the country. Maybe— I don't know."

Drummond stuffed tobacco into his pipe. He was near the end of what he had, but would rather take a few good smokes than a lot of niggling puffs. "Of course," he said thoughtfully, "it's probably not the end of things. We won't know for a generation or more, but I rather imagine the mutants can grow into society. They'd better, for they'll outnumber the humans. The thing is, if we just let matters drift there's no telling where they'll go. The situation is unprecedented. We may end up in a culture of specialized variations, which would be very bad from an evolutionary standpoint. There may be fighting between mutant types, or with humans. Interbreeding may produce worse freaks, particularly when accumulated recessives start showing up. Robinson, if we want any say at all in what's going to happen in the next few centuries, we have to act quickly. Otherwise it'll snowball out of all control."

"Yes. Yes, we'll have to act fast. And hard." Robinson straightened in his chair. Decision firmed his countenance, but his eyes were staring. "We're mobilized," he said. "We have the men and the weapons and the organization. They won't be able to resist."

The ashy cold of Drummond's emotions stirred, but it was with a horrible wrenching of fear. "What are you getting at?" he snapped.

"Racial death. All mutants and their parents to be sterilized whenever and wherever detected."

"You're crazy!" Drummond sprang from his chair, grabbed Robinson's shoulders across the desk, and shook him. "You . . . why, it's impossible! You'll bring revolt, civil war, final collapse!"

"Not if we go about it right." There were little beads of sweat studding the general's forehead. "I don't like it any better than you, but it's got to be done or the human race is finished. Normal births a minority—" He surged to his feet, gasping. "I've thought a long time about this. Your facts only confirmed my suspicions. This tears it. Can't you see? Evolution has to proceed slowly. Life wasn't meant for such a storm of change. Unless we can save the true human stock, it'll be absorbed and differentiation will continue till humanity is a collection of freaks, probably intersterile. Or . . . there must be a lot of lethal recessives. In a large population, they can accumulate unnoticed till nearly everybody has them, and then start emerging all at once. That'd wipe us out. It's happened before, in rats and other species. If we eliminate mutant stock now, we can still save the race. It won't be cruel. We have sterilization techniques which are quick and painless, not upsetting the endocrine balance. But it's got to be done." His voice rose to a raw scream, broke. "It's got to be done!"

Drummond slapped him, hard. He drew a shuddering breath, sat down, and began to cry, and somehow that was the most horrible sight of all.

"You're crazy," said the aviator. "You've gone nuts with brooding alone on this the last six months, without knowing or being able to act. You've lost all perspective.

"We can't use violence. In the first place, it would break our tottering, cracked culture irreparably, into a mad-dog finish fight. We'd not even win it. We're outnumbered, and we couldn't hold down a continent, eventually a planet. And remember what we said once, about abandoning the old savage way of settling things, that never brings a real settlement at all? We'd throw away a lesson our noses were rubbed in not three years ago. We'd return to the beast—to ultimate extinction.

"And anyway," he went on very quietly, "it wouldn't do a bit of good. Mutants would still be born. The poison is everywhere. Normal parents will give birth to mutants, somewhere along the line. We just have to accept that fact, and live with it. The *new* human race will have to."

"I'm sorry." Robinson raised his face from his hands. It was a ghastly visage, gone white and old, but there was calm on it. "I—blew my top. You're right. I've been thinking of this, worrying and wondering, living and breathing it, lying awake nights, and when I finally sleep I dream of it. I . . . yes, I see your point. And you're right."

"It's O.K. You've been under a terrific strain. Three years with never a rest, and the responsibility for a nation, and now this— Sure, everybody's entitled to be a little crazy. We'll work out a solution, somehow."

"Yes, of course." Robinson poured out two stiff drinks and gulped his. He paced restlessly, and his tremendous ability came back in waves of strength and confidence. "Let me see— Eugenics, of course. If we work hard, we'll have the nation tightly organized inside of ten years. Then . . . well, I don't suppose we can keep the mutants from interbreeding, but certainly we can pass laws to protect humans and encourage their propagation. Since radical mutations would probably be intersterile anyway, and most mutants handicapped one way or another, a few generations should see humans completely dominant again."

Drummond scowled. He was worried. It wasn't like Robinson to be unreasonable. Somehow, the man had acquired a mental blind spot where this most ultimate of human problems was concerned. He said slowly, "That won't work either. First, it'd be hard to impose and enforce. Second, we'd be repeating the old *Herrenvolk* notion. Mutants are inferior, mutants must be kept in their place—to enforce that, especially on a majority, you'd need a full-fledged totalitarian state. Third, that wouldn't work either, for the rest of the world, with almost no exceptions, is under no such control and we'll be in no position to take over that control for a long time—generations. Before then, mutants will dominate everywhere over there, and if they resent the way we treat their kind here, we'd better run for cover."

"You assume a lot. How do you know those hundreds or thousands of diverse types will work together? They're less like each other than like humans, even. They could be played off against each other."

"Maybe. But *that* would be going back onto the old road of treachery and violence, the road to Hell. Conversely, if every not-quite-human is called a 'mutant,' like a separate class, he'll think he is, and act accordingly against the lumped-together 'humans.' No, the only way to sanity—to *survival*—is to abandon class prejudice and race hate altogether, and work as individuals. We're all . . . well, Earthlings; for us subclassification is deadly. We all have to live together, and might as well make the best of it."

"Yeah . . . yeah, that's right too."

"Anyway, I repeat that all such attempts would be useless. All Earth is infected with mutation. It will be for a long time. The purest human stock will still produce mutants."

"Y-yes, that's true. Our best bet seems to be to find all such stock and withdraw it into the few safe areas left. It'll mean a small human population, but a *human* one."

"I tell you, that's impossible," clipped Drummond. "There is no safe place. Not one."

Robinson stopped pacing and looked at him as at a physical antagonist. "That so?" he almost growled. "Why?"

Drummond told him, adding incredulously, "Surely you knew that. Your physicists must have measured the amount of it. Your doctors, your engineers, that geneticist I dug up for you. You obviously got a lot of this biological information you've been slinging at me from him. They *must* all have told you the same thing."

Robinson shook his head stubbornly. "It can't be. It's not reasonable. The concentration wouldn't be great enough."

"Why, you poor fool, you need only look around you. The plants, the animals— Haven't there been any births in Taylor?"

"No. This is still a man's town, though women are trickling in and several babies are on the way—" Robinson's face was suddenly twisted with desperation. "Elaine's is due any time now. She's in the hospital here. Don't you see, our other kid died of the plague. This one's all we have. We want him to grow up in a world free of want and fear, a world of peace and sanity where he can play and laugh and become a man, not a beast starving in a cave. You and I are on our way out. We're the old generation, the one that wrecked the world. It's up to us to build it again, and then retire from it to let our children have it. The future's theirs. We've got to make it ready for them."

Sudden insight held Drummond motionless for long seconds. Understanding came, and pity, and an odd gentleness that changed his sunken bony face. "Yes," he murmured, "yes, I see. That's why you're working with all that's in you to build a normal, healthy world. That's why you nearly went crazy when this threat appeared. That . . . that's why you can't just can't comprehend—"

He took the other man's arm and guided him toward the door. "Come on," he said. "Let's go see how your wife's making out. Maybe we can get her some flowers on the way."

The silent cold bit at them as they went down the street. Snow crackled underfoot. It was already grimy with town smoke and dust, but overhead the sky was incredibly clean and blue. Breath smoked whitely from their mouths and nostrils. The sound of men at work rebuilding drifted faintly between the bulking mountains.

"We couldn't emigrate to another planet, could we?" asked

Robinson, and answered himself: "No, we lack the organization and resources to settle them right now. We'll have to make out on Earth. A few safe spots—there *must* be others besides this one—to house the true humans till the mutation period is over. Yes, we can do it."

"There are no safe places," insisted Drummond. "Even if there were, the mutants would still outnumber us. Does your geneticist have any idea how this'll come out, biologically speaking?"

"He doesn't know. His specialty is still largely unknown. He can make an intelligent guess, and that's all."

"Yeah. Anyway, our problem is to learn to live with the mutants, to accept anyone as—Earthling—no matter how he looks, to quit thinking anything was ever settled by violence or connivance, to build a culture of individual sanity. Funny," mused Drummond, "how the impractical virtues, tolerance and sympathy and generosity, have become the fundamental necessities of simple survival. I guess it was always true, but it took the death of half the world and the end of a biological era to make us see that simple little fact. The job's terrific. We've got half a million years of brutality and greed, superstition and prejudice, to lick in a few generations. If we fail, mankind is done. But we've got to try."

They found some flowers, potted in a house, and Robinson bought them with the last of his tobacco. By the time he reached the hospital, he was sweating. The sweat froze on his face as he walked.

The hospital was the town's biggest building, and fairly well equipped. A nurse met them as they entered.

"I was just going to send for you, General Robinson," she said. "The baby's on the way."

"How . . . is she?"

"Fine, so far. Just wait here, please."

Drummond sank into a chair and with haggard eyes watched Robinson's jerky pacing. *The poor guy. Why is it expectant fathers are supposed to be so funny? It's like laughing at a man on the rack. I know, Barbara, I know.*

"They have some anaesthetics," muttered the general. "They . . . Elaine never was very strong."

"She'll be all right." *It's afterward that worries me.*

"Yeah— Yeah— How long, though, how long?"

"Depends. Take it easy." Drummond then made a sacrifice

to a man he liked. He filled his pipe and handed it over. "Here, you need a smoke."

"Thanks." Robinson puffed raggedly.

The slow minutes passed, and Drummond wondered vaguely what he'd do when—it—happened. It didn't have to happen. But the chances were all against such an easy solution. He was no psychologist. Best just to let things happen as they would.

The waiting broke at last. A doctor came out, seeming an inscrutable high priest in his white garments. Robinson stood before him, motionless.

"You're a brave man," said the doctor. His face, as he removed the mask, was stern and set. "You'll need your courage."

"She—" It was hardly a human sound, that croak.

"Your wife is doing well. But the baby—"

A nurse brought out the little wailing form. It was a boy. But his limbs were rubbery tentacles terminating in boneless digits.

Robinson looked, and something went out of him as he stood there. When he turned, his face was dead.

"You're lucky," said Drummond, and meant it. He'd seen too many other mutants. "After all, if he can use those hands he'll get along all right. He'll even have an advantage in certain types of work. It isn't a deformity, really. If there's nothing else, you've got a good kid."

"*If!* You can't tell with mutants."

"I know. But you've got guts, you and Elaine. You'll see this through, together." Briefly, Drummond felt an utter personal desolation. He went on, perhaps to cover that emptiness:

"I see why you didn't understand the problem. You *wouldn't*. It was a psychological block, suppressing a fact you didn't dare face. That boy is really the center of your life. You couldn't think the truth about him, so your subconscious just refused to let you think rationally on that subject at all.

"Now you know. Now you realize there's no safe place, not on all the planet. The tremendous incidence of mutant births in the first generation could have told you that alone. Most such new characteristics are recessive, which means both parents have to have it for it to show in the zygote. But genetic changes are random, except for a tendency to fall into roughly similar patterns. Four-leaved clovers, for instance. Think how vast the total number of such changes must be, to produce so many corresponding changes in a couple of years. Think how many, *many* recessives there must be, existing only in gene patterns till their mates show up. We'll just have to take our chances of something really deadly accumulating. We'd never know till too late."

"The dust—"

"Yeah. The radiodust. It's colloidal, and uncountable other radio-colloids were formed when the bombs went off, and ordinary dirt gets into unstable isotopic forms near the craters. And there are radiogases too, probably. The poison is all over the world by now, spread by wind and air currents. Colloids can be suspended indefinitely in the atmosphere.

"The concentration isn't too high for life, though a physicist told me he'd measured it as being very near the safe limit and there'll probably be a lot of cancer. But it's everywhere. Every breath we draw, every crumb we eat and drop we drink, every clod we walk on, the dust is there. It's in the stratosphere, clear on down to the surface, probably a good distance below. We could only escape by sealing ourselves in air-conditioned vaults and wearing spacesuits whenever we got out, and under present conditions that's impossible.

"Mutations were rare before, because a charged particle has to get pretty close to a gene and be moving fast before its electromagnetic effect causes physico-chemical changes, and then that particular chromosome has to enter into reproduction. Now the charged particles, and the gamma rays producing still more, are everywhere. Even at the comparatively low concentration, the odds favor a given organism having so many cells changed that at least one will give rise to a mutant. There's even a good chance of like recessives meeting in the first generation, as we've seen. Nobody's safe, no place is free."

"The geneticist thinks some true humans will continue."

"A few, probably. After all, the radioactivity isn't too concentrated, and it's burning itself out. But it'll take fifty or a hundred years for the process to drop to insignificance, and by then the pure stock will be way in the minority. And there'll still be all those unmatched recessives, waiting to show up."

"You were right. We should never have created science. It brought the twilight of the race."

"I enver said that. The race brought its own destruction,

through misuse of science. Our culture was scientific anyway, in all except its psychological basis. It's up to us to take that last and hardest step. If we do, the race may yet survive."

Drummond gave Robinson a push toward the inner door. "You're exhausted, beat up, ready to quit. Go on in and see Elaine. Give her my regards. Then take a long rest before going back to work. I still think you've got a good kid."

Mechanically, the *de facto* President of the United States left the room. Hugh Drummond stared after him a moment, then went out into the street.

CHILD'S PLAY

by William Tenn (Philip Klass; 1920-   )

ASTOUNDING SCIENCE FICTION

March

"William Tenn" is a pseudonym used by Philip Klass, who is now a Professor of English at Penn State University but who during the late 1940s and the 1950s produced some of the best socially oriented sf of that period, primarily in the late and lamented Galaxy Science Fiction. *A verbal, witty man, as a writer he was most comfortable at the shorter lengths, where he could take one concept and turn it on its head. His wonderful stories can be found in several collections, such as* The Human Angle *(1956),* The Seven Sexes *(1968), and* The Square Root of Man *(1968). However, a definitive omnibus of his best work still awaits publication and is badly needed.*

"Child's Play" was his third published story, is not at all about children, and is downright chilling in its telling and in its implications.

(Marty has mentioned just above that Phil Klass is a Professor of English at Penn State University. Phil is extraordinarily proud of the fact that he achieved and maintained academic status without

71

*having received a college degree but as a result of
honest achievement in the literary marketplace
alone.*

*Yet, of course, there was a time when he was
only an Associate Professor and was attempting to
remove the qualifying adjective and become a
"full" Professor. For that, it would help to have
recommendations from people who knew his quali-
fications and could speak highly of them. So he
phoned me and asked if I would be one of those
who would oblige and I said, "Certainly, Phil," and
sent off a letter expressing my honest opinion that
he deserved his full Professorship.*

*He got it, and when nobody was looking, I went
off in the corner and kicked and screamed because
although I had carefully climbed the scholastic
ladder, degree by degree, to the top, I myself was
only an Associate Professor. (But weep not, o
Gentle Reader, for since then I have attained a full
Professorship, too. —And so has Marty, though
neither of ours is in English.—I.A.)*

After the man from the express company had given the
door an untipped slam, Sam Weber decided to move the huge
crate under the one light bulb in his room. It was all very
well for the messenger to drawl, "I dunno. We don't send
'em; we just deliver 'em, mister"—but there must be some
mildly lucid explanation.

With a grunt that began as an anticipatory reflex and
ended on a note of surprised annoyance, Sam shoved the box
forward the few feet necessary. It was heavy enough; he wondered how the messenger had carried it up the three flights of
stairs.

He straightened and frowned down at the garish card
which contained his name and address as well as the
legend—"Merry Christmas, 2153."

A joke? He didn't know anyone who'd think it funny to
send a card dated over two hundred years in the future.
Unless one of the comedians in his law school graduating

class meant to record his opinion as to when Weber would be trying his first case. Even so—

The letters were shaped strangely, come to think of it, sort of green streaks instead of lines. And the card was a sheet of gold!

Sam decided he was really interested. He ripped the card aside, tore off the flimsy wrapping material—and stopped. He whistled. Then he gulped.

"Well clip my ears and call me streamlined!"

There was no top to the box, no slit in its side, no handle anywhere in sight. It seemed to be a solid, cubical mass of brown stuff. Yet he was positive something had rattled inside when it was moved.

He seized the corners and strained and grunted till it lifted. The underside was as smooth and innocent of opening as the rest. He let it thump back to the floor.

"Ah, well," he said philosophically, "it's not the gift; it's the principle involved."

Many of his gifts still required appreciative notes. He'd have to work up something special for Aunt Maggie. Her neckties were things of cubistic horror, but he hadn't even sent her a lone handkerchief this Christmas. Every cent had gone into buying that brooch for Tina. Not quite a ring, but maybe she'd consider that under the circumstances—

He turned to walk to his bed which he had drafted into the additional service of desk and chair. He kicked at the great box disconsolately. "Well, if you won't open, you won't open."

As of smarting under the kick, the box opened. A cut appeared on the upper surface, widened rapidly and folded the top back and down on either side like a valise. Sam clapped his forehead and addressed a rapid prayer to every god from Set to Father Divine. Then he remembered what he'd said.

"Close," he suggested.

The box closed, once more as smooth as a baby's anatomy.

"Open."

The box opened.

So much for the sideshow, Sam decided. He bent down and peered into the container.

The interior was a crazy mass of shelving on which rested vials filled with blue liquids, jars filled with red solids, transparent tubes showing yellow and green and orange and mauve and other colors which Sam's eyes didn't quite remember. There were seven pieces of intricate apparatus on the bottom which looked as if tube-happy radio hams had assembled them. There was also a book.

Sam picked the book off the bottom and noted numbly that while all its pages were metallic, it was lighter than any paper book he'd ever held.

He carried the book over to the bed and sat down. Then he took a long, deep breath and turned to the first page. "Gug," he said, exhaling his long, deep breath.

In mad, green streaks of letters:

> Bild-A-Man Set #3. This set is intended solely for the uses of children between the ages of eleven and thirteen. The equipment, much more advanced than Bild-A-Man Sets 1 and 2, will enable the child of this age-group to build and assemble complete adult humans in perfect working order. The retarded child may also construct the babies and mannikins of the earlier kits. Two disassembleators are provided so that the set can be used again and again with profit. As with Sets 1 and 2, the aid of a Census Keeper in all disassembling is advised. Refills and additional parts may be acquired from The Bild-A-Man Company, 928 Diagonal Level, Glunt City, Ohio. Remember—only with a Bild-A-Man can you build a man!

Weber slammed his eyes shut. What was that gag in the movie he'd seen last night? Terrific gag. Terrific picture, too. Nice Technicolor. Wonder how much the director made a week? The cameraman? Five hundred? A thousand?

He opened his eyes warily. The box was still a squat cube in the center of his room. The book was still in his shaking hand. And the page read the same.

"Only with a Bild-A-Man can you build a man!" Heaven help a neurotic young lawyer at a time like this!

There was a price list on the next page for "refills and additional parts." Things like one liter of hemoglobin and three grams of assorted enzymes were offered for sale in terms of one slunk fifty and three slunks forty-five. A note on the bottom advertised Set #4: "The thrill of building your first live Martian!"

Fine print announced *pat. pending 2148.*

The third page was a table of contents. Sam gripped the edge of the mattress with one sweating hand and read:

Sam dropped the book back into the box and ran for the mirror. His face was still the same, somewhat like bleached chalk, but fundamentally the same. He hadn't twinned or grown himself a mannikin or devised a new kind of life for his leisure moments. Everything was snug as a bug in a bughouse.

Very carefully he pushed his eyes back into their proper position in their sockets.

"Dear Aunt Maggie," he began writing feverishly. "Your ties made the most beautiful gift of my Christmas. My only regret is—"

My only regret is that I have but one life to give for my Christmas present. Who could have gone to such fantastic lengths for a practical joke? Lew Knight? Even Lew must have some reverence in his insensitive body for the institution of Christmas. And Lew didn't have the brains or the patience for a job so involved.

Tina? Tina had the fine talent for complication, all right. But Tina, while possessing a delightful abundance of all other physical attributes, was sadly lacking in funnybone.

Sam drew the leather envelope forth and caressed it. Tina's perfume seemed to cling to the surface and move the world back into focus.

The metallic greeting card glinted at him from the floor. Maybe the reverse side contained the sender's name. He picked it up, turned it over.

Nothing but blank gold surface. He was sure of the gold; his father had been a jeweler. The very value of the sheet was rebuttal to the possibility of a practical joke. Besides, again, what was the point?

"Merry Christmas, 2153." Where would humanity be in two hundred years? Traveling to the stars, or beyond—to unimaginable destinations? Using little mannikins to perform the work of machines and robots? Providing children with—

There might be another card or note inside the box. Weber bent down to remove its contents. His eye noted a large grayish jar and the label etched into its surface: *Dehydrated Neurone Preparation, for human construction only.*

He backed away and glared. "Close!"

The thing melted shut. Weber sighed his relief at it and decided to go to bed.

He regretted while undressing that he hadn't thought to ask the messenger the name of his firm. Knowing the delivery service involved would be useful in tracing the origin of this gruesome gift.

"But then," he repeated as he fell asleep, "it's not the gift—it's the principle! Merry Christmas, me."

The next morning when Lew Knight breezed in with his "Good morning, counselor," Sam waited for the first sly ribbing to start. Lew wasn't the man to hide his humor behind a bushel. But Lew buried his nose in "The New York State Supplement" and kept it there all morning. The other five young lawyers in the communal office appeared either too bored or too busy to have Bild-A-Man sets on their conscience. There were no sly grins, no covert glances, no leading questions.

Tina walked in at ten o'clock, looking like a pin-up girl caught with her clothes on.

"Good morning, counselors," she said.

Each in his own way, according to the peculiar gland secretions he was enjoying at the moment, beamed, drooled or nodded a reply. Lew Knight drooled. Sam Weber beamed.

Tina took it all in and analyzed the situation while she fluffed her hair about. Her conclusions evidently involved leaning markedly against Lew Knight's desk and asking what he had for her to do this morning.

Sam bit savagely into Hackleworth "On Torts." Theoretically, Tina was employed by all seven of them as secretary, switchboard operator and receptionist. Actually, the most faithful performance of her duties entailed nothing more daily than the typing and addressing of two envelopes with an occasional letter to be sealed inside. Once a week there might be a wistful little brief which was never to attain judicial scrutiny. Tina therefore had a fair library of fashion magazines in the first drawer of her desk and a complete cosmetics laboratory in the other two; she spent one third of her working day in the ladies' room swapping stocking prices and sources with other secretaries; she devoted the other two thirds religiously to that one of her employers who as of her arrival seemed to be in the most masculine mood. Her pay was small but her life was full.

Just before lunch, she approached casually with the morning's mail. "Didn't think we'd be too busy this morning, counselor—" she began.

"You thought incorrectly, Miss Hill," he informed her with a brisk irritation that he hoped became him well; "I've been waiting for you to terminate your social engagements so that we could get down to what occasionally passes for business."

She was as startled as an uncushioned kitten. "But—but this isn't Monday. Somerset & Ojack only send you stuff on Mondays."

Sam winced at the reminder that if it weren't for the legal drudgework he received once a week from Somerset & Ojack he would be a lawyer in name only, if not in spirit only. "I have a letter, Miss Hill," he replied steadily. "Whenever you assemble the necessary materials, we can get on with it."

Tina returned in a head-shaking moment with stenographic pad and pencils.

"Regular heading, today's date," Sam began. "Address it to Chamber of Commerce, Glunt City, Ohio. Gentlemen: Would you inform me if you have registered currently with you a firm bearing the name of the Bild-A-Man Company or a firm with any name at all similar? I am also interested in whether a firm bearing the above or related name has recently made known its intention of joining your community. This inquiry is being made informally on behalf of a client who is interested in a product of this organization whose address he has mislaid. Signature and then this P.S.—My client is also curious as to the business possibilities of a street known as Diagonal Avenue or Diagonal Level. Any data on this address and the organizations presently located there will be greatly appreciated."

Tina batted wide blue eyes at him. "Oh, Sam," she breathed, ignoring the formality he had introduced, "Oh, Sam, you have another client. I'm so glad. He looked a little sinister, but in *such* a distinguished manner that I was certain—"

"Who? Who looked a little sinister?"

"Why your new cli-ent." Sam had the uncomfortable feeling that she had almost added "stu-pid." "When I came in this morning, there was this terribly tall old man in a long black overcoat talking to the elevator operator. He turned to me—the elevator operator, I mean—and said, 'This is Mr. Weber's secretary. She'll be able to tell you anything you want to know.' Then he sort of winked which I thought was sort of impolite, you know, considering. Then this old man looked at me hard and I felt distinctly uncomfortable and he walked away muttering, 'Either disjointed or predatory personalities. Never normal. Never balanced.' Which I didn't think was very polite, either, I'll have you know, if he *is* your new client!" She sat back and began breathing again.

Tall, sinister old men in long black overcoats pumping the elevator operator about him. Hardly a matter of business. He had no skeletons in his personal closet. Could it be connected with his unusual Christmas present? Sam hmmmed mentally.

"—but she is my favorite aunt, you know," Tina was saying. "And she came in so unexpectedly."

The girl was explaining about their Christmas date. Sam felt a rush of affection for her as she leaned forward.

"Don't bother," he told her. "I knew you couldn't help breaking the date. I was a little sore when you called me, but I got over it; never-hold-a-grudge-against-a-pretty-girl Sam, I'm known as. How about lunch?"

"Lunch?" She flew distress signals. "I promised Lew, Mr. Knight, that is— But he wouldn't mind if you came along."

"Fine. Let's go." This would be helping Lew to a spoonful of his own annoying medicine.

Lew Knight took the business of having a crowd instead of a party for lunch as badly as Sam hoped he would. Unfortunately, Lew was able to describe details of his forthcoming case, the probable fees and possible distinction to be reaped thereof. After one or two attempts to bring an interesting will he was rephrasing for Somerset & Ojack into the conversation, Sam subsided into daydreams. Lew immediately dropped Rosenthal vs. Rosenthal and leered at Tina conversationally.

Outside the restaurant, snow discolored into slush. Most of the stores were removing Christmas displays. Sam noticed construction sets for children, haloed by tinsel and glittering with artificial snow. Build a radio, a skyscraper, an airplane. But "Only with a Bild-A-Man can you—"

"I'm going home," he announced suddenly. "Something important I just remembered. If anything comes up, call me there."

He was leaving Lew a clear field, he told himself, as he found a seat on the subway. But the bitter truth was that the field was almost as clear when he was around as when he wasn't. Lupine Lew Knight, he had been called in Law School; since the day when he had noticed that Tina had the correct proportions of dress-filling substances, Sam's chances had been worth a crowbar at Fort Knox.

Tina hadn't been wearing his brooch today. Her little finger, right hand, however, had sported an unfamiliar and garish little ring. "Some got it," Sam philosophized. "Some don't got it. I don't got it."

But it would have been nice, with Tina, to have "got it."

As he unlocked the door of his room he was surprised by an unmade bed telling with rumpled stoicism of a chambermaid who'd never come. This hadn't happened before— Of course! He'd never locked his room before. The girl must have thought he wanted privacy.

Maybe he had.

Aunt Maggie's ties glittered obscenely at the foot of the bed. He chucked them into the closet as he removed his hat and coat. Then he went over to the washstand and washed his hands, slowly. He turned around.

This was it. At last the great cubical bulk that had been lurking quietly in the corner of his vision was squarely before him. It was there and it undoubtedly contained all the outlandish collection he remembered.

"Open," he said, and the box opened.

The book, still open to the metallic table of contents, was lying at the bottom of the box. Part of it had slipped into the chamber of a strange piece of apparatus. Sam picked both out gingerly.

He slipped the book out and noticed the apparatus consisted mostly of some sort of binoculars, supported by a coil and

tube arrangement and bearing on a flat green plate. He
turned it over. The underside was lettered in the same streaky
way as the book. "Combination Electron Microscope and
Workbench."

Very carefully he placed it on the floor. One by one, he removed the others, from the "Junior Biocalibrator" to the
"Jiffy Vitalizer." Very respectfully he ranged against the box
in five multi-colored rows of vials of lymph and the jars of
basic cartilage. The walls of the chest were lined with indescribably thin and wrinkled sheets; a slight pressure along
their edges expanded them into three-dimensional outlines of
human organs whose shape and size could be varied with
pinching any part of their surface—most indubitably molds.

Quite an assortment. If there was anything solidly scientific
to it, that box might mean unimaginable wealth. Or some
very useful publicity. Or—well, it should mean something!

If there was anything solidly scientific to it.

Sam flopped down to the bed and opened to "A Child's
Garden of Biochemistry."

At nine that night he squatted next to the Combination
Electron Microscope and Workbench and began opening certain small bottles. At nine forty-seven Sam Weber made his
first simple living thing.

It wasn't much, if you used the first chapter of Genesis as
your standard. Just a primitive brown mold that, in the field
of the microscope, fed diffidently on a piece of pretzel, put
forth a few spores and died in about twenty minutes. But *he*
had made it. He had constructed a specific lifeform to feed
on the constituents of a specific pretzel; it could survive
nowhere else.

He went out to supper with every intention of getting
drunk. After just a little alcohol, however, the *deiish* feeling
returned and he scurried back to his room.

Never again that evening did he recapture the exultation of
the brown mold, though he constructed a giant protein molecule and a whole slew of filterable viruses.

He called the office in the little corner drugstore which was
his breakfast nook. "I'll be home all day," he told Tina.

She was a little puzzled. So was Lew Knight who grabbed
the phone. "Hey, counselor, you building up a neighborhood
practice? Kid Blackstone is missing out on a lot of cases.
Two ambulances have already clanged past the building."

"Yeah," said Sam. "I'll tell him when he comes in."

The weekend was almost upon him, so he decided to take the next day off as well. He wouldn't have any real work till Monday when the Somerset & Ojack basket would produce his lone egg.

Before he returned to his room, he purchased a copy of an advanced bacteriology. It was amusing to construct—with improvements!—unicellular creatures whose very place in the scheme of classification was a matter of argument among scientists of his own day. The Bild-A-Man manual, of course, merely gave a few examples and general rules; but with the descriptions in the bacteriology, the world was his oyster.

Which was an idea: he made a few oysters. The shells weren't hard enough, and he couldn't quite screw his courage up to the eating point, but they were most undeniably bivalves. If he cared to perfect his technique, his food problem would be solved.

The manual was fairly easy to follow and profusely illustrated with pictures that expanded into solidity as the page was opened. Very little was taken for granted; involved explanations followed simpler ones. Only the allusions were occasionally obscure—"This is the principle used in the phanphophink toys," "When your teeth are next yokekkled or demortoned, think of the *Bacterium cyanogenum* and the humble part it plays," "If you have a rubicular mannikin around the house, you needn't bother with the chapter on mannikins."

After a brief search had convinced Sam that whatever else he now had in his apartment he didn't have a rubicular mannikin, he felt justified in turning to the chapter on mannikins. He had conquered completely this feeling of being Pop played with Junior's toy train: already he had done more than the world's top biologists ever dreamed of for the next generation and what might not lie ahead—what problems might he not yet solve?

"Never forget that mannikins are constructed for one purpose and one purpose only." I won't, Sam promised. "Whether they are sanitary mannikins, tailoring mannikins, printing mannikins or even sunevviarry mannikins, they are each constructed with one operation of a given process in view. When you make a mannikin that is capable of more than one function, you are committing a crime so serious as to be punishable by public admonition."

"To construct an elementary mannikin—"

It was very difficult. Three times he tore down developing monstrosities and began anew. It wasn't till Sunday afternoon that the mannikin was complete—or rather, incomplete.

Long arms it had—although by an error, one was slightly longer than the other—a faceless head and a trunk. No legs. No eyes or ears, no organs of reproduction. It lay on his bed and gurgled out of the red rim of a mouth that was supposed to serve both for ingress and excretion of food. It waved the long arms, designed for some one simple operation not yet invented, in slow circles.

Sam, watching it, decided that life could be as ugly as an open field latrine in midsummer.

He had to disassemble it. Its length—three feet from almost boneless fingers to tapering, sealed-off trunk—precluded the use of the tiny disassembleator with which he had taken apart the oysters and miscellaneous small creations. There was a bright yellow notice on the large disassembleator, however—"To be used only under the direct supervision of a Census Keeper. Call formula A76 or unstable your *id*."

"Formula A76" meant about as much as "sunevviarry," and Sam decided his *id* was already sufficiently unstabled, thank you. He'd have to make out without a Census Keeper. The big disassembleator probably used the same general principles as the small one.

He clamped it to a bedpost and adjusted the focus. He snapped the switch set in the smooth underside.

Five minutes later the mannikin was a bright, gooey mess on his bed.

The large disassembleator, Sam was convinced as he tidied his room, did require the supervision of a Census Keeper. Some sort of keeper anyway. He rescued as many of the legless creature's constituents as he could, although he doubted he'd be using the set for the next fifty years or so. He certainly wouldn't ever use the disassembleator again; much less spectacular and disagreeable to shove the whole thing into a meat grinder and crank the handle as it squashed inside.

As he locked the door behind him on his way to a gentle binge, he made a mental note to purchase some fresh sheets the next morning. He'd have to sleep on the floor tonight.

Wrist-deep in Somerset & Ojack minutiae, Sam was conscious of Lew Knight's stares and Tina's puzzled glances. If they only knew, he exulted! But Tina would probably just think it "marr-vell-ouss!" and Lew Knight might make some crack like "Hey! Kid Frankenstein himself!" Come to think of it though Lew would probably have worked out some method of duplicating, to a limited extent, the contents of the Bild-A-Man set and marketing it commercially. Whereas he—well, there were other things you could do with the gadget. Plenty of other things.

"Hey, counselor," Lew Knight was perched on the corner of his desk, "what are these long weekends we're taking? You might not make as much money in the law, but does it look right for an associate of mine to sell magazine subscriptions on the side?"

Sam stuffed his ears mentally against the emery-wheel voice. "I've been writing a book."

"A law book? Weber 'On Bankruptcy'?"

"No, a juvenile. 'Lew Knight, The Neanderthal Nitwit.' "

"Won't sell. The title lacks punch. Something like 'Knights, Knaves and Knobheads' is what the public goes for these days. By the way, Tina tells me you two had some sort of understanding about New Year's Eve and she doesn't think you'd mind if I took her out instead. I don't think you'd mind either, but I may be prejudiced. Especially since I have a table reservation at *Cigale's* where there's usually less of a crowd of a New Year's Eve than at the automat."

"I don't mind."

"Good," said Knight approvingly as he moved away. "By the way, won that case. Nice juicy fee, too. Thanks for asking."

Tina also wanted to know if he objected to the new arrangements when she brought the mail. Again, he didn't. Where had he been for over two days? He had been busy, very busy. Something entirely new. Something important.

She stared down at him as he separated offers of used cars guaranteed not to have been driven over a quarter of a million miles from caressing reminders that he still owed half the tuition for the last year of law school and when was he going to pay it?

Came a letter that was neither bill nor ad. Sam's heart momentarily lost interest in the monotonous round of pumping that was its lot as he stared at a strange postmark: Glunt City, Ohio.

Dear Sir:

There is no firm in Glunt City at the present time bearing any name similar to "Bild-A-Man Company" nor do we know of any such organization planning to join our little community. We also have no thoroughfare called "Diagonal"; our north-south streets are named after Indian tribes while our east-west avenues are listed numerically in multiples of five.

Glunt City is a restricted residential township, we intend to keep it that. Only small retailing and service establishments are permitted here. If you are interested in building a home in Glunt City and can furnish proof of white, Christian, Anglo-Saxon ancestry on both sides of your family for fifteen generations, we would be glad to furnish further information.

Thomas H. Plantagenet, Mayor

P.S. An airfield for privately owned jet- and propeller-driven aircraft is being built outside the city limits.

That was sort of that. He would get no refills on any of the vials and bottles even if he had a loose slunk or two with which to pay for the stuff. Better go easy on the material and conserve it as much as possible. But no disassembling!

Would the "Bild-A-Man Company" begin manufacturing at Glunt City some time in the future when it had developed into an industrial metropolis against the constricted wills of its restricted citizenry? Or had his package slid from some different track in the human time stream, some era to be born on another-dimensional earth? There would have to be a common origin to both, else why the English wordage? And could there be a purpose in his having received it, beneficial—or otherwise?

Tina had been asking him a question. Sam detached his mind from shapeless speculation and considered her quite-the-opposite features.

"So if you'd still like me to go out with you New Year's Eve, all I have to do is tell Lew that my mother expects to suffer from her gallstones and I have to stay home. Then I think you could buy the *Cigale* reservations from him cheap."

"Thanks a lot, Tina, but very honestly I don't have the

loose cash right now. You and Lew make a much more logical couple anyhow."

Lew Knight wouldn't have done that. Lew cut throats with
carefree zest. But Tina did seem to go with Lew as a type.

Why? Until Lew had developed a raised eyebrow where
Tina was concerned, it had been Sam all the way. The rest of
the office had accepted the fact and moved out of their path.
It wasn't only a question of Lew's greater success and financial well-being: just that Lew had decided he wanted Tina
and had got her.

It hurt. Tina wasn't special; she was no cultural companion, no intellectual equal; but he wanted her. He liked being
with her. She was the woman he desired, rightly or wrongly,
whether or not there was a sound basis to their relationship.
He remembered his parents before a railway accident had or-
phaned him: they were theoretically incompatible, but they
had been terribly happy together.

He was still wondering about it the next night as he flipped
the pages of "Twinning yourself and your friends." It would
be interesting to twin Tina.

"One for me, one for Lew."

Only the horrible possibility of an error was there. His
mannikin had not been perfect: its arms had been of unequal
length. Think of a physically lopsided Tina, something he
could never bring himself to disassemble, limping extrane-
ously through life.

And then the book warned: "Your constructed twin,
though resembling you in every obvious detail, has not had
the slow and guarded maturity you have enjoyed. He or she
will not be as stable mentally, much less able to cope with
unusual situations, much more prone to neurosis. Only a professional carnuplicator, using the finest equipment, can make
an exact copy of a human personality. Yours will be able to
live and even reproduce, but never to be accepted as a valid
and responsible member of society."

Well, he could chance that. A little less stability in Tina
would hardly be noticeable; it might be more desirable.

There was a knock. He opened the door, guarding the box
from view with his body. His landlady.

"Your door has been locked for the past week, Mr. Weber.
That's why the chambermaid hasn't cleaned the room. We
thought you didn't want anyone inside."

"Yes." He stepped into the hall and closed the door behind him. "I've been doing some highly important legal work at home."

"Oh." He sensed a murderous curiosity and changed the subject.

"Why all the fine feathers, Mrs. Lipanti—New Year's Eve party?"

She smoothed her frilled black dress self-consciously. "Y-yes. My sister and her husband came in from Springfield today and we were going to make a night of it. Only . . . only the girl who was supposed to come over and mind their baby just phoned and said she isn't feeling well. So I guess we won't go unless somebody else, I mean unless we can get someone else to take care . . . I mean, somebody who doesn't have a previous engagement and who wouldn't—" Her voice trailed away in assumed embarrassment as she realized the favor was already asked.

Well, after all, he wasn't doing anything tonight. And she had been remarkably pleasant those times when he had had to operate on the basis of "Of course I'll have the rest of the rent in a day or so." But why did any one of the earth's two billion humans, when in the possession of an unpleasant buck, pass it automatically to Sam Weber?

Then he remembered Chapter IV on babies and other small humans. Since the night when he had separated the mannikin from its constituent parts, he'd been running through the manual as an intellectual exercise. He didn't feel quite up to making some weird error on a small human. But twinning wasn't supposed to be as difficult.

Only by Gog and by Magog, by Aesculapius the Physician and Kildare the Doctor, he would not disassemble this time. There must be other methods of disposal possible in a large city on a dark night. He'd think of something.

"I'd be glad to watch the baby for a few hours." He started down the hall to anticipate her polite protest. "Don't have a date tonight myself. No, don't mention it, Mrs. Lipanti. Glad to do it."

In the landlady's apartment, her nervous sister briefed him doubtfully. "And that's the only time she cries in a low, steady way so if you move fast there won't be much damage done. Not much, anyway."

He saw them to the door. "I'll be fast enough," he assured the mother. "Just so I get a hint."

Mrs. Lipanti paused at the door. "Did I tell you about the man who was asking after you this afternoon?"

Again? "A sort of tall, old man in a long, black overcoat?"

"With the most frightening way of staring into your face and talking under his breath. Do you know him?"

"Not exactly. What did he want?"

"Well, he asked if there was a Sam Weaver living here who was a lawyer and had been spending most of his time in his room for the past week. I told him we had a Sam Weber—your first name *is* Sam?—who answered to that description, but that the last Weaver had moved out over a year ago. He just looked at me for a while and said, 'Weaver, Weber—they might have made an error,' and walked out without so much as a good-bye or excuse me. Not what I call a polite gentleman."

Thoughtfully Sam walked back to the child. Strange how sharp a mental picture he had formed of this man! Possibly because the two women who had met him thus far had been very impressionable, although to hear their stories the impression was there to be received.

He doubted there was any mistake: the man had been looking for him on both occasions; his knowledge of Sam's vacation from foolscap this past week proved that. It did seem as if he weren't interested in meeting him until some moot point of identity should be established beyond the least shadow of a doubt. Something of a legal mind, that.

The whole affair centered around the "Bild-A-Man" set, he was positive. This skulking investigation hadn't started until after the gift from 2153 had been delivered—and Sam had started using it.

But till the character in the long black overcoat paddled up to Sam Weber personally and stated his business, there wasn't very much he could do about it.

Sam went upstairs for his Junior Biocalibrator.

He propped the manual open against the side of the bed and switched the instrument on to full scanning power. The infant gurgled thickly as the calibrator was rolled slowly over its fat body and a section of metal tape unwound from the slot with, according to the manual, a completely detailed physiological description.

It was detailed. Sam gasped as the tape, running through the enlarging viewer, gave information on the child for which a pediatrician would have taken out at least three mortgages on his immortal soul. Thyroid capacity, chromosome quality, cerebral content. All broken down into neat subheads of data for construction purposes. Rate of skull expansion in minutes for the next ten hours; rate of cartilage transformation; changes in hormone secretions while active and at rest.

This was a blueprint; it was like taking canons from a baby.

Sam left the child to a puzzled contemplation of its navel and sped upstairs. With the tape as a guide, he clipped sections of the molds into the required smaller sizes. Then, almost before he knew it consciously, he was constructing a small human.

He was amazed at the ease with which he worked. Skill was evidently acquired in this game; the mannikin had been much harder to put together. The matter of duplication and working from an informational tape simplified his problems, though.

The child took form under his eyes.

He was finished just an hour and a half after he had taken his first measurements. All except the vitalizing.

A moment's pause, here. The ugly prospect of disassembling stopped him for a moment, but he shook it off. He had to see how well he had done the job. If this child could breathe, what was not possible to him! Besides he couldn't keep it suspended in an inanimate condition very long without running the risk of ruining his work and the materials.

He started the vitalizer.

The child shivered and began a low, steady cry. Sam tore down to the landlady's apartment again and scooped up a square of white linen left on the bed for emergencies. Oh well, some more clean sheets.

After he had made the necessary repairs, he stood back and took a good look at it. He was in a sense a papa. He felt as proud.

It was a perfect little creature, glowing and round with health.

"I have twinned," he said happily.

Every detail correct. The two sides of the face correctly unexact, the duplication of the original child's lunch at the very same point of digestion. Same hair, same eyes—or was it? Sam bent over the infant. He could have sworn the other was a blonde. This child had dark hair which seemed to grow darker as he looked.

He grabbed it with one hand and picked up the Junior Bio-calibrator with the other.

Downstairs, he placed the two babies side by side on the big bed. No doubt about it. One was blonde: the other, his plagiarism, was now a definite brunette.

The biocalibrator showed other differences: Slightly faster pulse for his model. Lower blood count. Minutely higher cerebral capacity, although the content was the same. Adrenalin and bile secretions entirely unalike.

It added up to error. His child might be the superior specimen, or the inferior one, but he had not made a true copy. He had no way of knowing at the moment whether or not the infant he had built could grow into a human maturity. The other could.

Why? He had followed directions faithfully, had consulted the calibrator tape at every step. And this had resulted. Had he waited too long before starting the vitalizer? Or was it just a matter of insufficient skill?

Close to midnight, his watch delicately pointed out. It would be necessary to remove evidences of baby-making before the Sisters Lipanti came home. Sam considered possibilities swiftly.

He came down in a few moments with an old tablecloth and a cardboard carton. He wrapped the child in the tablecloth, vaguely happy that the temperature had risen that night, then placed it in the carton.

The child gurgled at the adventure. Its original on the bed *goo*ed in return. Sam slipped quietly out into the street.

Male and female drunks stumbled along tooting on tiny trumpets. People wished each other a *hic* happy new year as he strode down the necessary three blocks.

As he turned left, he saw the sign: "Urban Foundling Home." There was a light burning over a side door. Convenient, but that was a big city for you.

Sam shrank into the shadow of an alley for a moment as a new idea occurred to him. This had to look genuine. He pulled a pencil out of his breast pocket and scrawled on the side of the carton in as small handwriting as he could manage:

"Please take good care of my darling little girl. I am not married."

Then he deposited the carton on the doorstep and held his finger on the bell until he heard movement inside. He was across the street and in the alley again by the time a nurse had opened the door.

It wasn't until he walked into the boarding house that he remembered about the navel. He stopped and tried to recall. No, he had built his little girl without a navel! Her belly had been perfectly smooth. That's what came of hurrying! Shoddy workmanship.

There might be a bit of to-do in the foundling home when they unwrapped the kid. How would they explain it?

Sam slapped his forehead. "Me and Michelangelo. He adds a navel, I forget one!"

Except for an occasional groan, the office was fairly quiet the second day of the New Year.

He was going through the last intriguing pages of the book when he was aware of two people teetering awkwardly near his desk. His eyes left the manual reluctantly: "New kinds of life for your leisure moments" was really stuff!

Tina and Lew Knight.

Sam digested the fact that neither of them were perched on his desk.

Tina wore the little ring she'd received for Christmas on the third finger of her left hand; Lew was experimenting with a sheepish look and finding it difficult.

"Oh, Sam. Last night, Lew . . . Sam, we wanted you to be the first— Such a surprise, like that I mean! Why I almost— Naturally we thought this would be a little difficult . . . Sam, we're going, I mean we expect—"

"—to be married," Lew Knight finished in what was almost an undertone. For the first time since Sam had known him he looked uncertain and suspicious of life, like a man who finds a newly-hatched octopus in his breakfast orange juice.

"You'd adore the way Lew proposed," Tina was gushing. "So roundabout. And so shy. I told him afterwards that I thought for a moment he was talking of something else entirely. I did have trouble understanding you, didn't I, dear?"

"Huh? Oh yeah, you had trouble understanding me." Lew stared at his former rival. "Much of a surprise?"

"Oh, no. No surprise at all. You two fit together so perfectly that I knew it right from the first." Sam mumbled his felicitations, conscious of Tina's searching glances. "And now, if you'll excuse me, there's something I have to take care of immediately. A special sort of wedding present."

Lew was disconcerted. "A wedding present, This early?"

"Why certainly," Tina told him. "It isn't very easy to get just the right thing. And a special friend like Sam naturally wants to get a very special gift."

Sam decided he had taken enough. He grabbed the manual and his coat and dodged through the door.

By the time he came to the red stone steps of the boarding house, he had reached the conclusion that the wound, while painful, had definitely missed his heart. He was in fact chuckling at the memory of Lew Knight's face when his landlady plucked at his sleeve.

"That man was here again today, Mr. Weber. He said he wanted to see you."

"Which man? The tall, old fellow?"

Mrs. Lipanti nodded, her arms folded complacently across her chest. "Such an unpleasant person! When I told him you weren't in, he insisted I take him up to your room. I said I couldn't do that without your permission and he looked at me fit to kill. I've never believed in the evil eye myself—although I always say where there is smoke there must be fire—but if there is such at thing as an evil eye, he has it."

"Will he be back?"

"Yes. He asked me when you usually return and I said about eight o'clock, figuring that if you didn't want to meet him it would give you time to change your clothes and wash up and leave before he gets here. And, Mr. Weber, if you'll excuse me for saying this, I don't think you want to meet him."

"Thanks. But when he comes in at eight, show him up. If he's the right person, I'm in illegal possession of his property. I want to know where this property originates."

In his room, he put the manual away carefully and told the box to open. The Junior Biocalibrator was not too bulky and newspaper would suffice to cover it. He was on his way uptown in a few minutes with the strangely shaped parcel under his arm.

Did he still want to duplicate Tina, he pondered? Yes, in spite of everything. She was still the woman he desired more than any he had ever known; and with the original married to Lew, the replica would have no choice but himself. Only—the replica would have Tina's characteristics up to the moment the measurements were taken; she might insist on marrying Lew as well.

That would make for a bit of sitcheeayshun. But he was still miles from that bridge. It might even be amusing—

The possibility of error was more annoying. The Tina he would make might be off-center in a number of ways: reds might overlap pinks like an imperfectly reproduced color photograph: she might, in time, come to digest her own stomach; there could very easily be a streak of strange and incurable insanity implicit in his model which would not assert itself until a deep mutual affection had flowered and borne fruit. As yet, he was no great shakes as a twinner and human mimeographer; the errors he had made on Mrs. Lipanti's niece demonstrated his amateur standing.

Sam knew he would never be able to dismantle Tina if she proved defective. Outside of the chivalrous concepts and almost superstitious reverence for womankind pressed into him by a small town boyhood, there was the unmitigated horror he felt at the idea of such a beloved object going through the same disintegrating process as—well, the mannikin. But if he overlooked an essential in his construction, what other recourse would there be?

Solution: nothing must be overlooked. Sam grinned bitterly as the ancient elevator swayed up to his office. If he only had time for a little more practice with a person whose reactions he knew so exactly that any deviation from the norm would be instantly obvious! But the strange, old man would be calling tonight, and, if his business concerned "Bild-A-Man" sets, Sam's experiments might be abruptly curtailed. And where would he find such a person—he had few real friends and no intimate ones. And, to be at all valuable, it would have to be someone he knew as well as himself.

Himself!

"Floor, sir." The elevator operator was looking at him reproachfully. Sam's exultant shout had caused him to bring the carrier to a spasmodic stop six inches under the floor level, something he had not done since that bygone day when he had first nervously reached for the controls. He felt his craftmanship was under a shadow as he morosely closed the door behind the lawyer.

And why not himself? He knew his own physical attributes better than he knew Tina's; any mental instability on the part of his reproduced self would be readily discernible long before it reached the point of psychosis or worse. And the beauty of it was that he would have no compunction in disassembling a superfluous Sam Weber. Quite the contrary: the horror in that situation would be the continued existence of a duplicate personality: its removal would be a relief.

Twinning himself would provide the necessary practice in a familiar medium. Ideal. He'd have to take careful notes so that if anything went wrong he'd know just where to avoid going off the track in making his own personal Tina.

And maybe the old geezer wasn't interested in the set at all. Even if he were, Sam could take his landlady's advice and not be at home when he called. Silver linings wherever he looked.

Lew Knight stared at the instrument in Sam's hands. "What in the sacred name of Blackstone and all his commentaries is that? Looks like a lawn mower for a window box!"

"It's uh, sort of a measuring gadget. Gives the right size for one thing and another and this and that. Won't be able to get you the wedding present I have in mind unless I know the right size. Or sizes. Tina, would you mind stepping out into the hall?"

"Nooo." She looked dubiously at the gadget. "It won't hurt?"

It wouldn't hurt a bit. Sam assured her. "I just want to keep this a secret from Lew till after the ceremony."

She brightened at that and preceded Sam through the door. "Hey counselor," one of the other young lawyers called at Lew as they left. "Hey counselor, don't let him do that. Possession is nine points Sam always says. He'll never bring her back."

Lew chuckled weakly and bent over his work.

"Now I want you to go into the ladies' room," Sam explained to a bewildered Tina. "I'll stand guard outside and tell the other customers that the place is out of order. If another woman is inside wait until she leaves. Then strip."

"Strip?" Tina squealed.

He nodded. Then very carefully, emphasizing every significant detail of operation, he told her how to use the Junior Biocalibrator. How she must be careful to kick the switch and set the tape running. How she must cover every external square inch of her body. "This little arm will enable you to lower it down your back. No questions now. Git." She gat.

She was back in fifteen minutes, fluffing her dress into place and studying the tape with a rapt frown. "This is the *strangest* thing— According to the spool, my iodine content—"

Sam snaffled the Biocalibrator hurriedly. "Don't give it another thought. It's a code, kind of. Tells me just what size and how many of what kind. You'll be crazy about the gift when you see it."

"I know I will." She bent over him as he kneeled and examined the tape to make certain she had applied the instrument correctly. "You know, Sam, I always felt your taste was perfect. I want you to come and visit us often after we're married. You can have such beautiful ideas! Lew is a bit too . . . too businesslike, isn't he? I mean it's necessary for success and all that, but success isn't everything. I mean you have to have culture, too. You'll help me keep cultured, won't you, Sam?"

"Sure," Sam said vaguely. The tape was complete. Now to get started! "Anything I can do—glad to help."

He rang for the elevator and noticed the forlorn uncertainty with which she watched him. "Don't worry, Tina. You and Lew will be very happy together. And you'll love this wedding present." But not as much as I will, he told himself as he stepped into the elevator.

Back in his room, he emptied the machine and undressed. In a few moments he had another tape on himself. He would have liked to consider it for a while, but being this close to the goal made him impatient. He locked the door, cleaned his room hurriedly of accumulated junk—remembering to sniff in annoyance at Aunt Maggie's ties: the blue and red one almost lighted up the room—ordered the box to open—and he was ready to begin.

First the water. With the huge amount of water necessary to the human body, especially in the case of an adult, he might as well start collecting it now. He had bought several pans and it would take his lone faucet some time to fill them all.

As he placed the first pot under the tap, Sam wondered suddenly if its chemical impurities might affect the end product. Of course it might! These children of 2153 would probably take absolutely pure H_2O as a matter of daily use; the manual hadn't mentioned the subject, but how did he know what kind of water they had available? Well, he'd boil this batch over his chemical stove; when he got to making Tina he could see about getting *aqua* completely *pura*.

Score another point for making a simulacrum of Sam first.

While waiting for the water to boil, he arranged his supplies to positions of maximum availability. They were getting low. That baby had taken up quite a bit of useful ingredients; too bad he hadn't seen his way clear to disassembling it. That meant if there were any argument in favor of allowing the replica of himself to go on living, it was now invalid. He'd have to take it apart in order to have enough for Tina II. Or Tina prime?

He leafed through Chapters VI, VII and VIII on the ingredients, completion and disassembling of a man. He'd been through this several times before but he'd passed more than one law exam on the strength of a last-minute review.

The constant reference to mental instability disturbed him. "The humans constructed with this set will, at the very best, show most of the superstitious tendencies, and neurosis-compulsions of medieval mankind. In the long run they are not normal; take great care not to consider them such." Well, it wouldn't make too much difference in Tina's case—and that was all that was important.

When he had finished adjusting the molds to the correct sizes, he fastened the vitalizer to the bed. Then—very, very slowly and with repeated glances at the manual, he began to duplicate Sam Weber. He learned more of his physical limitations and capabilities in the next two hours than any man had ever known since the day when an inconspicuous primate had investigated the possibilities of ground locomotion upon the nether extremities alone.

Strangely enough, he felt neither awe nor exultation. It was like building a radio receiver for the first time. Child's play.

Most of the vials and jars were empty when he had finished. The damp molds were stacked inside the box, still in their three-dimensional outline. The manual lay neglected on the floor.

Sam Weber stood near the bed looking down at Sam Weber on the bed.

All that remained was vitalizing. He daren't wait too long or imperfections might set in and the errors of the baby be repeated. He shook off the nauseating feeling of unreality, made certain that the big disassembleator was within reach and set the Jiffy Vitalizer in motion.

The man on the bed coughed. He stirred. He sat up.

"Wow!" he said. "Pretty good, if I do say so myself!"

And then he had leaped off the bed and seized the disassembleator. He tore great chunks of wiring out of the center, threw it to the floor and kicked it into shapelessness. "No Sword of Damocles going to hang over *my* head," he informed an open-mouthed Sam Weber. "Although, I could have used it on you, come to think of it."

Sam eased himself to the mattress and sat down. His mind stopped rearing and whinnied to a halt. He had been so impressed with the helplessness of the baby and the mannikin that he had never dreamed of the possibility that his duplicate would enter upon life with such enthusiasm. He should have, though; this was a full-grown man, created at a moment of complete physical and mental activity.

"This is bad," he said at last in a hoarse voice. "You're unstable. You can't be admitted into normal society."

"I'm unstable" his image asked. "Look who's talking! The guy who's been mooning his way through his adult life, who wants to marry an overdressed, conceited collection of biological impulses that would come crawling on her knees to any man sensible enough to push the right buttons—"

"You leave Tina's name out of this," Sam told him, feeling acutely uncomfortable at the theatrical phrase.

His double looked at him and grinned. "O.K., I will. But not her body! Now, look here, Sam or Weber or whatever you want me to call you, you can live your life and I'll live mine. I won't even be a lawyer if that'll make you happy. But as far as Tina is concerned, now that there are no ingredients to make a copy—that was a rotten escapist idea, by the way—I have enough of your likes and dislikes to want her badly. And I can have her, whereas you can't. You don't have the gumption."

Sam leaped to his feet and doubled his fists. Then he saw the other's entirely equal size and slightly more assured twinkle. There was no point in fighting—that would end in a draw, at best. He went back to reason.

"According to the manual," he began, "you are prone to neurosis—"

"The manual! The manual was written for children of two centuries hence, with quite a bit of selective breeding and scientific education behind them. Personally, I think I'm a—"

There was a double knock on the door. "Mr. Weber."

"Yes," they both said simultaneously.

Outside, the landlady gasped and began speaking in an uncertain voice. "Th-that gentleman is downstairs. He'd like to see you. Shall I tell him you're in?"

"No, I'm not at home," said the double.

"Tell him I left an hour ago," said Sam at exactly the same moment.

There was another, longer gasp and the sound of footsteps receding hurriedly.

"That's one clever way to handle a situation," Sam's facsimile exploded. "Couldn't you keep your mouth shut? The poor woman's probably gone off to have a fit."

"You forget that this is my room and you are just an experiment that went wrong," Sam told him hotly. "I have just as much right, in fact more right . . . hey, what do you think you're doing?"

The other had thrown open the closet door and was stepping into a pair of pants. "Just getting dressed. You can wander around in the nude if you find it exciting, but I want to look a bit respectable."

"I undressed to take my measurements . . . or your measurements. Those are my clothes, this is my room—"

"Look, take it easy. You could never prove it in a court of law. Don't make me go into that *cliché* about what's yours is mine and so forth."

Heavy feet resounded through the hall. They stopped outside the room. Cymbals seemed to clash all around them and there was a panic-stricken sense of unendurable heat. Then shrill echoes fled into the distance. The walls stopped shuddering.

Silence and a smell of burning wood.

They whirled in time to see a terribly tall, terribly old man in a long black overcoat walking through the smoldering remains of the door. Much too tall for the entrance, he did not stoop as he came in: rather, he drew his head down into his garment and shot it up again. Instinctively, they moved closer together.

His eyes, all shiny black iris without any whites, were set back deep in the shadow of his head. They reminded Sam Weber of the scanners on the Biocalibrator: they tabulated, deduced, rather than saw.

"I was afraid I would be too late," he rumbled at last in

weird, clipped tones. "You have already duplicated yourself, Mr. Weber, making necessary unpleasant rearrangements. And the duplicate has destroyed the disassembleator. Too bad. I shall have to do it manually. An ugly job."

He came further into the room until they could almost breathe their fright upon him. "This affair has already dislocated four major programs, but we had to move in accepted cultural grooves and be absolutely certain of the recipient's identity before we could act to withdraw the set. Mrs. Lipanti's collapse naturally stimulated emergency measures."

The duplicate cleared his throat. "You are—?"

"Not exactly human. A humble civil servant of precision manufacture. I am Census Keeper for the entire twenty-ninth oblong. You see, your set was intended for the Thregander children who are on a field trip in this oblong. One of the Threganders who has a Weber chart requested the set through the chrondromos which in an attempt at the supernormal, unstabled without carnuplicating. You therefore received the package instead. Unfortunately, the unstabling was so complete that we were forced to locate you by indirect methods."

The Census Keeper paused and Sam's double hitched his pants nervously. Sam wished he had anything—even a fig leaf—to cover his nakedness. He felt like a character in the Garden of Eden trying to build up a logical case for apple eating. He appreciated glumly how much more than "Bild-A-Man" sets clothes had to do with the making of a man.

"We will have to recover the set, of course," the staccato thunder continued, "and readjust any discrepancies it has caused. Once the matter has been cleared up, however, your life will be allowed to resume its normal progression. Meanwhile, the problem is which of you is the original Sam Weber?"

"I am," they both quavered—and turned to glare at each other.

"Difficulties," the old man rumbled. He sighed like an arctic wind. "I always have difficulties! Why can't I ever have a simple case like a carnuplicator?"

"Look here," the duplicate began. "The original will be—"

"Less unstable and of better emotional balance than the replica," Sam interrupted. "Now, it seems—"

"That you should be able to tell the difference," the other

concluded breathlessly. "From what you see and have seen of us, can't you decide which is the more valid member of society?"

What a pathetic confidence, Sam thought, the fellow was trying to display! Didn't he know he was up against someone who could really discern mental differences? This was no fumbling psychiatrist of the present; here was a creature who could see through externals to the most coherent personality beneath.

"I can, naturally. Now, just a moment." He studied them carefully, his eyes traveling with judicious leisure up and down their bodies. They waited, fidgeting, in a silence that pounded.

"Yes," the old man said at last. "Yes. Quite."

He walked forward.

A long thin arm shot out.

He started to disassemble Sam Weber.

"But listennnnn—" began Weber in a yell that turned into a high scream and died in a liquid mumble.

"It would be better for your sanity if you didn't watch," the Census Keeper suggested.

The duplicate exhaled slowly, turned away and began to button a shirt. Behind him the mumbling continued, rising and falling in pitch.

"You see," came the clipped, rumbling accents, "it's not the gift we're afraid of letting you have—it's the principle involved. Your civilization isn't ready for it. You understand."

"Perfectly," replied the counterfeit Weber, knotting Aunt Maggie's blue and red tie.

TIME AND TIME AGAIN

by H. Beam Piper (1904-1960)

ASTOUNDING SCIENCE FICTION
April

The late H. Beam Piper was a native of Pennsylvania who worked for many years for the Pennsylvania Railroad. His work is currently quite popular, having been rediscovered in the 1970s by a new generation of readers. Particularly appealing are the vividly depicted aliens of his "Terran Federation" books, which include Little Fuzzy *(1962),* Space Viking *(1963) and* The Other Human Race *(1964) An excellent omnibus collection is* The Fuzzy Papers, *published in 1977. It is tragic that Piper, who was one of the very few known suicides within science fiction, never lived to see his work appreciated and popular.*

"Time and Time Again" was Piper's first published story, a tale that posits a fascinating situation—what would happen to a highly educated adult who suddenly found himself in his own early teen-age body, but still knowing everything he had learned in the intervening years? What would he do?

(Who among us hasn't wished we could go back

100

*in time and do something over, or tell the youngster
we used to be something we ought to know? Over
and over again, I've thought how nice it would be if
I could go back to 1938, and whisper to myself as
I was struggling with my Underwood #5 typewriter, "You're going to be a very successful writer.
Honest!"*

*But, no. In the first place I wouldn't have be-
lieved it. In the second, the knowledge itself would
have changed things if I did believe it, and who
knows in what manner.*

*And no matter how we may dream in science fic-
tion, there are always the little reminders in such
stories of the fact that we don't know what lies
ahead.*

*In "Time and Time Again," which appeared in
1947, the United States was driven back to its
northern border in 1975. Well, of course, it
wasn't. In fact, the worst thing that happened to us
since World War II was Watergate and that was
strictly home-grown and it was absolutely unfore-
seeable.*

*Then, too, Beam Piper speaks of 1960, as the
year "we had a good-natured nonentity in the
White House." That was Dwight Eisenhower's last
year, and some might think that an apt description
of him—but could Piper, in 1947, have imagined
the sad significance that 1960 was to hold for
him.—I.A.)*

Blinded by the bomb-flash and numbed by the narcotic injection, he could not estimate the extent of his injuries, but he
knew that he was dying. Around him, in the darkness, voices
sounded as through a thick wall.

"They mighta left mosta these Joes where they was. Half
of them won't even last till the truck comes."

"No matter; so long as they're alive, they must be treated,"
another voice, crisp and cultivated, rebuked. "Better start taking names, while we're waiting."

"Yes, sir." Fingers fumbled at his identity badge. "Hartley, Allan: Captain, G5, Chem. Research AN/73/D. Serial, SO-23869403J."

"Allan Hartley!" The medic officer spoke in shocked surprise. "Why, he's the man who wrote 'Children of the Mist,' 'Rose of Death,' and 'Conqueror's Road'!"

He tried to speak, and must have stirred; the corpsman's voice sharpened.

"Major, I think he's part conscious. Mebbe I better give him 'nother shot."

"Yes, yes; by all means, sergeant."

Something jabbed Allan Hartley in the back of the neck. Soft billows of oblivion closed in upon him, and all that remained to him was a tiny spark of awareness, glowing alone and lost in a great darkness.

The spark grew brighter. He was more than a something that merely knew that it existed. He was a man, and he had a name, and a military rank, and memories. Memories of the searing blue-green flash, and of what he had been doing outside the shelter the moment before, and memories of the month-long siege, and of the retreat from the north, and memories of the days before the War, back to the time when he had been little Allan Hartley, a schoolboy, the son of a successful lawyer, in Williamsport, Pennsylvania.

His mother he could not remember; there was only a vague impression of the house full of people who had tried to comfort him for something he could not understand. But he remembered the old German woman who had kept house for his father, afterward, and he remembered his bedroom, with its chintz-covered chairs, and the warm-colored patch quilt on the old cherry bed, and the tan curtains at the windows, edged with dusky red, and the morning sun shining through them. He could almost see them, now.

He blinked. He *could* see them!

For a long time, he lay staring at them unbelievingly, and then he deliberately closed his eyes and counted ten seconds, and as he counted, terror gripped him. He was afraid to open them again, lest he find himself blind, or gazing at the filth and wreckage of a blasted city, but when he reached ten, he forced himself to look, and gave a sigh of relief. The sunlit curtains and the sun-gilded mist outside were still there.

He reached out to check one sense against another, feeling

the rough monk's cloth and the edging of maroon silk thread. They were tangible as well as visible. Then he saw that the back of his hand was unscarred. There should have been a scar, souvenir of a rough-and-tumble brawl of his cub reporter days. He examined both hands closely. An instant later, he had sat up in bed and thrown off the covers, partially removing his pajamas and inspecting as much of his body as was visible.

It was the smooth body of a little boy.

That was ridiculous. He was a man of forty-three; an army officer, a chemist, once a best-selling novelist. He had been married, and divorced ten years ago. He looked again at his body. It was only twelve years old. Fourteen, at the very oldest. His eyes swept the room, wide with wonder. Every detail was familiar: the flower-splashed chair covers; the table that served as desk and catch-all for his possessions; the dresser, with its mirror stuck full of pictures of aircraft. It was the bedroom of his childhood home. He swung his legs over the edge of the bed. They were six inches too short to reach the floor.

For an instant, the room spun dizzily, and he was in the grip of utter panic, all confidence in the evidence of his senses lost. Was he insane? Or delirious? Or had the bomb really killed him; was this what death was like? What was that thing, about "ye become as little children"? He started to laugh, and his juvenile larynx made giggling sounds. They seemed funny, too, and aggravated his mirth. For a little while, he was on the edge of hysteria and then, when he managed to control his laughter, he felt calmer. If he were dead, then he must be a discarnate entity, and would be able to penetrate matter. To his relief, he was unable to push his hand through the bed. So he was alive; he was also fully awake, and, he hoped, rational. He rose to his feet and prowled about the room, taking stock of its contents.

There was no calendar in sight, and he could find no newspapers or dated periodicals, but he knew that it was prior to July 18, 1946. On that day, his fourteenth birthday, his father had given him a light .22 rifle, and it had been hung on a pair of rustic forks on the wall. It was not there now, nor ever had been. On the table, he saw a boys' book of military aircraft, with a clean, new dustjacket; the flyleaf was inscribed: *To Allan Hartley, from his father, on his thirteenth birthday, 7/18/ '45*. Glancing out the window at the foliage on the trees, he estimated the date at late July or early August, 1945; that would make him just thirteen.

His clothes were draped on a chair beside the bed. Stripping off his pajamas, he donned shorts, then sat down and picked up a pair of lemon-colored socks, which he regarded with disfavor. As he pulled one on, a church bell began to clang. St. Boniface, up on the hill, ringing for early Mass; so this was Sunday. He paused, the second sock in his hand.

There was no question that his present environment was actual. Yet, on the other hand, he possessed a set of memories completely at variance with it. Now, suppose, since his environment was not an illusion, everything else was? Suppose all these troublesome memories were no more than a dream? Why, he was just little Allan Hartley, safe in his room on a Sunday morning, badly scared by a nightmare! Too much science fiction, Allan; too many comic books!

That was a wonderfully comforting thought, and he hugged it to him contentedly. It lasted all the while he was buttoning up his shirt and pulling on his pants, but when he reached for his shoes, it evaporated. Ever since he had wakened, he realized, he had been occupied with thoughts utterly incomprehensible to any thirteen-year-old; even thinking in words that would have been so much Sanskrit to himself at thirteen. He shook his head regretfully. The just-a-dream hypothesis went by the deep six.

He picked up the second shoe and glared at it as though it were responsible for his predicament. He was going to have to be careful. An unexpected display of adult characteristics might give rise to some questions he would find hard to answer credibly. Fortunately, he was an only child; there would be no brothers or sisters to trip him up. Old Mrs. Stauber, the housekeeper, wouldn't be much of a problem: even in his normal childhood, he had bulked like an intellectual giant in comparison to her. But his father—

Now, there the going would be tough. He knew that shrewd attorney's mind, whetted keen on a generation of lying and reluctant witnesses. Sooner or later, he would forget for an instant and betray himself. Then he smiled, remembering the books he had discovered in his late 'teens on his father's shelves and recalling the character of the openminded agnostic lawyer. If he could only avoid the inevitable unmasking until he had a plausible explanatory theory.

*   *   *

Blake Hartley was leaving the bathroom as Allan Hartley opened his door and stepped into the hall. The lawyer was bare-armed and in slippers: at forty-eight, there was only a faint powdering of gray in his dark hair, and not a gray thread in his clipped mustache. The old Merry Widower, himself, Allan thought, grinning as he remembered the white-haired but still vigorous man from whom he'd parted at the outbreak of the War.

" 'Morning, Dad," he greeted.

" 'Morning, son. You're up early. Going to Sunday school?"

Now there was the advantage of a father who'd cut his first intellectual tooth on Tom Paine and Bob Ingersoll; attendance at divine services was on a strictly voluntary basis.

"Why, I don't think so; I want to do some reading, this morning."

"That's always a good thing to do," Blake Hartley approved. "After breakfast, suppose you take a walk down to the station and get me a *Times*." He dug in his trouser pocket and came out with a half dollar. "Get anything you want for yourself, while you're at it."

Allan thanked his father and pocketed the coin.

"Mrs. Stauber'll still be at Mass," he suggested. "Say I get the paper now; breakfast won't be ready till she gets here."

"Good idea," Blake Hartley nodded, pleased. "You'll have three-quarters of an hour, at least."

So far, he congratulated himself, everything had gone smoothly. Finishing his toilet, he went downstairs and onto the street, turning left at Brandon to Campbell, and left again in the direction of the station. Before he reached the underpass, a dozen half-forgotten memories had revived. Here was a house that would, in a few years, be gutted by fire. Here were four dwellings standing where he had last seen a five-story apartment building. A gasoline station and a weed-grown lot would shortly be replaced by a supermarket. The environs of the station itself were a complete puzzle to him, until he oriented himself.

He bought a New York *Times*, glancing first of all at the date line. Sunday, August 5, 1945; he'd estimated pretty closely. The battle of Okinawa had been won. The Potsdam Conference had just ended. There were still pictures of the B-25 crash against the Empire State Building, a week ago Saturday. And Japan was still being pounded by bombs from the air and shells from off-shore naval guns. Why, tomorrow, Hiroshima was due for the Big Job! It amused him to reflect that he was probably the only person in Williamsport who knew that.

On the way home, a boy, sitting on the top step of a front porch, hailed him. Allan replied cordially, trying to remember who it was. Of course: Larry Morton! He and Allan had been buddies. They probably had been swimming, or playing Commandos and Germans, the afternoon before. Larry had gone to Cornell the same year that Allan had gone to Penn State; they had both graduated in 1954. Larry had gotten into some Government bureau, and then he had married a Pittsburgh girl, and had become twelfth vice-president of her father's firm. He had been killed, in 1968, in a plane crash.

"You gonna Sunday school?" Larry asked, mercifully unaware of the fate Allan foresaw for him.

"Why, no. I have some things I want to do at home." He'd have to watch himself. Larry would spot a difference quicker than any adult. "Heck with it," he added.

"Golly, I wisht I c'ld stay home from Sunday school whenever I wanted to," Larry envied. "How about us goin' swimmin', at the Canoe Club, 'safter?"

Allan thought fast. "Gee, I wisht I c'ld," he replied, lowering his grammatical sights. "I gotta stay home, 'safter. We're expectin' comp'ny; coupla aunts of mine. Dad wants me to stay home when they come."

That went over all right. Anybody knew that there was no rational accounting for the vagaries of the adult mind, and no appeal from adult demands. The prospect of company at the Hartley home would keep Larry away, that afternoon. He showed his disappointment.

"Aw, jeepers creepers!" he blasphemed euphemistically.

"Mebbe t'morrow," Allan said. "If I c'n make it. I gotta go, now; ain't had breakfast yet." He scuffed his feet boyishly, exchanged so-longs with his friend, and continued homeward.

As he had hoped, the Sunday paper kept his father occupied at breakfast, to the exclusion of any dangerous table talk. Blake Hartley was still deep in the financial section when Allan left the table and went to the library. There should be two books there to which he wanted badly to refer. For a while, he was afraid that his father had not acquired them prior to 1945, but he finally found them, and carried them onto the front porch, along with a pencil and a ruled yellow scratch pad. In his experienced future—or his past-to-come—Allan Hartley had been accustomed to doing his thinking with a pencil. As reporter, as novelist plotting his work, as amateur chemist in his home laboratory, as scientific warfare research officer, his ideas had always been clarified by making notes. He pushed a chair to the table and built up the seat with cushions, wondering how soon he would become used to the proportional disparity between himself and the furniture. As he opened the books and took his pencil in his hand, there was one thing missing. If he could only smoke a pipe, now!

His father came out and stretched in a wicker chair with the *Times* book-review section. The morning hours passed. Allan Hartley leafed through one book and then the other. His pencil moved rapidly at times; at others, he doodled absently. There was no question, any more, in his mind, as to what or who he was. He was Allan Hartley, a man of forty-three, marooned in his own thirteen-year-old body, thirty years back in his own past. That was, of course, against all common sense, but he was easily able to ignore that objection. It had been made before: against the astronomy of Copernicus, and the geography of Columbus, and the biology of Darwin, and the industrial technology of Samuel Colt, and the military doctrines of Charles de Gaulle. Today's common sense had a habit of turning into tomorrow's utter nonsense. What he needed, right now, but bad, was a theory that would explain what had happened to him.

Understanding was beginning to dawn when Mrs. Stauber came out to announce midday dinner.

"I hope you von't mind haffin' it so early," she apologized. "Mein sister, Jennie, offer in Nippenose, she iss sick; I vant to go see her, dis afternoon, yet. I'll be back in blenty time to get supper, Mr. Hartley."

"Hey, Dad!" Allan spoke up. "Why can't we get our own supper, and have a picnic, like? That'd be fun, and Mrs. Stauber could stay as long as she wanted to."

His father looked at him. Such consideration for others was a most gratifying deviation from the juvenile norm; dawn of altruism, or something. He gave hearty assent.

"Why, of course, Mrs. Stauber. Allan and I can shift for ourselves, this evening; can't we, Allan? You needn't come back till tomorrow morning."

"*Ach*, t'ank you! T'ank you so mooch, Mr. Hartley."

At dinner, Allan got out from under the burden of conversation by questioning his father about the War and luring him into a lengthy dissertation on the difficulties of the forthcoming invasion of Japan. In view of what he remembered of the next twenty-four hours, Allan was secretly amused. His father was sure that the War would run on to mid-1946.

After dinner, they returned to the porch, Hartley *père* smoking a cigar and carrying out several law books. He only glanced at these occasionally; for the most part, he sat and blew smoke rings, and watched them float away. Some thrice-guilty felon was about to be triumphantly acquitted by a weeping jury; Allan could recognize a courtroom masterpiece in the process of incubation.

It was several hours later that the crunch of feet on the walk caused father and son to look up simultaneously. The approaching visitor was a tall man in a rumpled black suit; he had knobby wrists and big, awkward hands; black hair flecked with gray, and a harsh, bigoted face. Allan remembered him. Frank Gutchall. Lived on Campbell Street; a religious fanatic, and some sort of lay preacher. Maybe he needed legal advice; Allan could vaguely remember some incident—

"Ah, good afternoon, Mr. Gutchall. Lovely day, isn't it?" Blake Hartley said.

Gutchall cleared his throat. "Mr. Hartley, I wonder if you could lend me a gun and some bullets," he began, embarrassedly. "My little dog's been hurt, and it's suffering something terrible. I want a gun, to put the poor thing out of its pain."

"Why, yes; of course. How would a 20-gauge shotgun do?" Blake Hartley asked. "You wouldn't want anything heavy."

Gutchall fidgeted. "Why, er, I was hoping you'd let me have a little gun." He held his hands about six inches apart. "A pistol, that I could put in my pocket. It wouldn't look right, to carry a hunting gun on the Lord's day; people wouldn't understand that it was for a work of mercy."

The lawyer nodded. In view of Gutchall's religious beliefs, the objection made sense.

"Well, I have a Colt .38-special," he said, "but you know, I belong to this Auxiliary Police outfit. If I were called out for duty, this evening, I'd need it. How soon could you bring it back?"

Something clicked in Allan Hartley's mind. He remembered now what that incident had been. He knew, too, what he had to do.

"Dad, aren't there some cartridges left for the Luger?" he asked.

Blake Hartley snapped his fingers. "By George, yes! I have a German automatic I can let you have, but I wish you'd bring it back as soon as possible. I'll get it for you."

Before he could rise, Allan was on his feet.

"Sit still, Dad; I'll get it. I know where the cartridges are." With that, he darted into the house and upstairs.

The Luger hung on the wall over his father's bed. Getting it down, he dismounted it, working with rapid precision. He used the blade of his pocketknife to unlock the endpiece of the breechblock, slipping out the firing pin and buttoning it into his shirt pocket. Then he reassembled the harmless pistol, and filled the clip with 9-millimeter cartridges from the bureau drawer.

There was an extension telephone beside the bed. Finding Gutchall's address in the directory, he lifted the telephone, and stretched his handkerchief over the mouthpiece. Then he dialed Police Headquarters.

"This is Blake Hartley," he lied, deepening his voice and copying his father's tone. "Frank Gutchall, who lives at . . . take this down"—he gave Gutchall's address—"has just borrowed a pistol from me, ostensibly to shoot a dog. He has no dog. He intends shooting his wife. Don't argue about how I know; there isn't time. Just take it for granted that I do. I disabled the pistol—took out the firing pin—but if he finds out what I did, he may get some other weapon. He's on his way home, but he's on foot. If you hurry, you may get a man there before he arrives, and grab him before he finds out the pistol won't shoot."

"O.K., Mr. Hartley. We'll take care of it. Thanks."

"And I wish you'd get my pistol back, as soon as you can. It's something I brought home from the other War, and I shouldn't like to lose it."

"We'll take care of that, too. Thank you, Mr. Hartley."

He hung up, and carried the Luger and the loaded clip down to the porch.

"Look, Mr. Gutchall; here's how it works," he said, showing it to the visitor. Then he slapped in the clip and yanked up on the toggle loading the chamber. "It's ready to shoot, now; this is the safety." He pushed it on. "When you're ready to

shoot, just shove it forward and up, and then pull the trigger.
You have to pull the trigger each time; it's loaded for eight
shots. And be sure to put the safety back when you're
through shooting."

"Did you load the chamber?" Blake Hartley demanded.

"Sure. It's on safe, now."

"Let me see." His father took the pistol, being careful to
keep his finger out of the trigger guard, and looked at it.
"Yes, that's all right." He repeated the instructions Allan had
given, stressing the importance of putting the safety on after
using. "Understand how it works, now?" he asked.

"Yes, I understand how it works. Thank you, Mr. Hartley.
Thank you, too, young man."

Gutchall put the Luger in his hip pocket, made sure it
wouldn't fall out, and took his departure.

"You shouldn't have loaded it," Hartley *père* reproved,
when he was gone.

Allan sighed. This was it; the masquerade was over.

"I had to, to keep you from fooling with it," he said. "I
didn't want you finding out that I'd taken out the firing pin."

"You what?"

"Gutchall didn't want that gun to shoot a dog. He has no
dog. He meant to shoot his wife with it. He's a religious
maniac: sees visions, hears voices, receives revelations, talks
with the Holy Ghost. The Holy Ghost probably put him up
to this caper. I'll submit that any man who holds long conversations with the Deity isn't to be trusted with a gun, and neither is any man who lies about why he wants one. And while
I was at it, I called the police, on the upstairs phone. I had to
use your name; I deepened my voice and talked through a
handkerchief."

"You—" Blake Hartley jumped as though bee-stung. "Why
did you have to do that?"

"You know why. I couldn't have told them, 'This is little
Allan Hartley, just thirteen years old; please, Mr. Policeman,
go and arrest Frank Gutchall before he goes root-toot-toot at
his wife with my pappa's Luger.' That would have gone over
big, now, wouldn't it?"

"And suppose he really wants to shoot a dog; what sort of
a mess will I be in?"

"No mess at all. If I'm wrong—which I'm not—I'll take
the thump for it, myself. It'll pass for a dumb kid trick, and
nothing'll be done. But if I'm right, you'll have to front for

me. They'll keep your name out of it, but they'd give me a lot of cheap boy-hero publicity, which I don't want." He picked up his pencil again. "We should have the complete returns in about twenty minutes."

That was a ten-minute underestimate, and it was another quarter-hour before the detective-sergeant who returned the Luger had finished congratulating Blake Hartley and giving him the thanks of the Department. After he had gone, the lawyer picked up the Luger, withdrew the clip, and ejected the round in the chamber.

"Well," he told his son, "you were right. You saved that woman's life." He looked at the automatic, and then handed it across the table. "Now, let's see you put that firing pin back."

Allan Hartley dismantled the weapon, inserted the missing part, and put it together again, then snapped it experimentally and returned it to his father. Blake Hartley looked at it again, and laid it on the table.

"Now, son, suppose we have a little talk," he said softly.

"But I explained everything," Allan objected innocently.

"You did not," his father retorted. "Yesterday you'd never have thought of a trick like this; why, you wouldn't even have known how to take this pistol apart. And at dinner, I caught you using language and expressing ideas that were entirely outside anything you'd ever known before. Now, I want to know—and I mean this literally."

Allan chuckled. "I hope you're not toying with the rather medieval notion of obsession," he said.

Blake Hartley started. Something very like that must have been flitting through his mind. He opened his mouth to say something, then closed it abruptly.

"The trouble is, I'm not sure you aren't right," his son continued. "You say you find me—changed. When did you first notice a difference?"

"Last night, you were still my little boy. This morning—" Blake Hartley was talking more to himself than to Allan. "I don't know. You were unusually silent at breakfast. And come to think of it, there was something . . . something strange . . . about you when I saw you in the hall, upstairs . . . Allan!" he burst out, vehemently. "What has happened to you?"

Allan Hartley felt a twinge of pain. What his father was

going through was almost what he, himself, had endured, in
the first few minutes after waking.

"I wish I could be sure, myself, Dad," he said. "You see,
when I woke, this morning, I hadn't the least recollection of
anything I'd done yesterday. August 4, 1945, that is," he
specified. "I was positively convinced that I was a man of
forty-three, and my last memory was of lying on a stretcher,
injured by a bomb explosion. And I was equally convinced
that this had happened in 1975."

"Huh?" His father straightened. "Did you say nineteen *seventy*-five?" He thought for a moment. "That's right; in 1975,
you will be forty-three. A bomb, you say?"

Allan nodded. "During the siege of Buffalo, in the Third
World War," he said, "I was a captain in G5—Scientific
Warfare, General Staff. There'd been a transpolar air invasion of Canada, and I'd been sent to the front to check on
service failures of a new lubricating oil for combat equipment. A week after I got there, Ottawa fell, and the retreat
started. We made a stand at Buffalo, and that was where I
copped it. I remember being picked up, and getting a narcotic injection. The next thing I knew, I was in bed, upstairs,
and it was 1945 again, and I was back in my own little thirteen-year-old body."

"Oh, Allan, you just had a nightmare to end nightmares!"
his father assured him, laughing a trifle too heartily. "That's
all!"

"That was one of the first things I thought of. I had to re-
ject it; it just wouldn't fit the facts. Look; a normal dream is
part of the dreamer's own physical brain, isn't it? Well, here
is a part about two thousand per cent greater than the whole
from which it was taken. Which is absurd."

"You mean all this Battle of Buffalo stuff? That's easy. All
the radio commentators have been harping on the horrors of
World War III, and you couldn't have avoided hearing some
of it. You just have an undigested chunk of H. V. Kaltenborn
raising hell in your subconscious."

"It wasn't just World War III; it was everything. My four
years at high school, and my four years at Penn State, and
my seven years as a reporter on the Philadelphia *Record*.
And my novels: 'Children of the Mist,' 'Rose of Death,'
'Conqueror's Road.' They were no kid stuff. Why, yesterday
I'd never even have thought of some of the ideas I used in
my detective stories, that I published under a *non-de-plume*.

And my hobby, chemistry; I was pretty good at that. Patented a couple of processes that made me as much money as my writing. You think a thirteen-year-old just dreamed all that up? Or, here; you speak French, don't you?" He switched languages and spoke at some length in good conversational slang-spiced Parisian. "Too bad you don't speak Spanish, too," he added, reverting to English. "Except for a Mexican accent you could cut with a machete, I'm even better there than in French. And I know some German, and a little Russian."

Blake Hartley was staring at his son, stunned. It was some time before he could make himself speak.

"I could barely keep up with you, in French," he admitted. "I can swear that in the last thirteen years of your life, you had absolutely no chance to learn it. All right; you lived till 1975, you say. Then, all of a sudden, you found yourself back here, thirteen years old, in 1945. I suppose you remember everything in between?" he asked. "Did you ever read James Branch Cabell? Remember Florian de Puysange, in 'The High Place'?"

"Yes. You find the same idea in 'Jurgen' too," Allan said. "You know, I'm beginning to wonder if Cabell mightn't have known something he didn't want to write."

"But it's impossible!" Blake Hartley hit the table with his hand, so hard that the heavy pistol bounced. The loose round he had ejected from the chamber toppled over and started to roll, falling off the edge. He stooped and picked it up. "How can you go back, against time? And the time you claim you came from doesn't exist, now; it hasn't happened yet." He reached for the pistol magazine, to insert the cartridge, and as he did, he saw the books in front of his son. "Dunne's 'Experiment with Time,'" he commented. "And J. N. M. Tyrrell's 'Science and Psychical Phenomena.' Are you trying to work out a theory?"

"Yes." It encouraged Allan to see his father had unconsciously adopted an adult-to-adult manner. "I think I'm getting somewhere, too. You've read these books? Well, look, Dad; what's your attitude on precognition? The ability of the human mind to exhibit real knowledge, apart from logical inference, of future events? You think Dunne is telling the truth about his experiences? Or that the cases in Tyrrell's book are properly verified, and can't be explained away on the basis of chance?"

Blake Hartley frowned. "I don't know," he confessed. "The evidence is the sort that any court in the world would accept, if it concerned ordinary, normal events. Especially the cases investigated by the Society for Psychical Research; they *have* been verified. But how can anybody know of something that hasn't happened yet? If it hasn't happened yet, it doesn't exist, and you can't have real knowledge of something that has no real existence."

"Tyrrell discusses that dilemma, and doesn't dispose of it. I think I can. If somebody has real knowledge of the future, then the future must be available to the present mind. And if any moment other than the bare present exists, then all time must be totally present; every moment must be perpetually coexistent with every other moment," Allan said.

"Yes. I think I see what you mean. That was Dunne's idea, wasn't it?"

"No. Dunne postulated an infinite series of time dimensions, the entire extent of each being the bare present moment of the next. What I'm postulating is the perpetual coexistence of every moment of time in this dimension, just as every graduation on a yardstick exists equally with every other graduation, but each at a different point in space."

"Well, as far as duration and sequence go, that's all right," the father agreed. "But how about the 'Passage of Time'?"

"Well, time *does* appear to pass. So does the landscape you see from a moving car window. I'll suggest that both are illusions of the same kind. We imagine time to be dynamic, because we've never viewed it from a fixed point, but if it is totally present, then it must be static, and in that case, we're moving through time."

"That seems all right. But what's your car window?"

"If all time is totally present, then you must exist simultaneously at every moment along your individual life span," Allan said. "Your physical body, and your mind, and all the thoughts contained in your mind, each at its appropriate moment in sequence. But what is it that exists only at the bare moment we think of as *now?*"

Blake Hartley grinned. Already, he was accepting his small son as an intellectual equal.

"Please, teacher; what?"

"Your consciousness. And don't say, 'What's that?' Teacher

doesn't know. But we're only conscious of one moment; the illusory *now*. This is 'now,' and it was 'now' when you asked that question, and it'll be 'now' when I stop talking, but each is a different moment. We imagine that all those nows are rushing past us. Really, they're standing still, and our consciousness is whizzing past them."

His father thought that over for some time. Then he sat up. "Hey!" he cried, suddenly. "If some part of your ego is time-free and passes from moment to moment, it must be extraphysical, because the physical body exists at every moment through which the consciousness passes. And if it's extraphysical, there's no reason whatever for assuming that it passes out of existence when it reaches the moment of the death of the body. Why, there's logical evidence for survival, independent of any alleged spirit communication! You can toss out Patience Worth, and Mrs. Osborne Leonard's Feda, and Sir Oliver Lodge's son, and Wilfred Brandon, and all the other spirit-communicators, and you still have evidence."

"I hadn't thought of that," Allan confessed. "I think you're right. Well, let's put that at the bottom of the agenda and get on with this time business. You 'lose consciousness" as in sleep; where does your consciousness go? I think it simply detaches from the moment at which you go to sleep, and moves backward or forward along the line of moment-sequence, to some prior or subsequent moment, attaching there."

"Well, why don't we know anything about that?" Blake Hartley asked. "It never seems to happen. We go to sleep tonight, and it's always tomorrow morning when we wake; never day-before-yesterday, or last month, or next year."

"It never . . . or almost never . . . *seems* to happen; you're right there. Know why? Because if the consciousness goes forward; it attaches at a moment when the physical brain contains memories of the previous, consciously unexperienced, moment. You wake, remembering the evening before, because that's the memory contained in your mind at that moment, and back of it are memories of all the events in the interim. See?"

"Yes. But how about backward movement, like this experience of yours?"

"This experience of mine may not be unique, but I never heard of another case like it. What usually happens is that the memories carried back by the consciousness are buried in the subconscious mind. You know how thick the wall be-

tween the subconscious and the conscious mind is. These
dreams of Dunne's, and the cases in Tyrrell's book, are leakage. That's why precognitions are usually incomplete and dis-
torted, and generally trivial. The wonder isn't that good cases
are so few; it's surprising that there are any at all." Allan
looked at the papers in front of him. "I haven't begun to the-
orize about how I managed to remember everything. It may
have been the radiations from the bomb, or the effect of the
narcotic, or both together, or something at this end, or a
combination of all three. But the fact remains that my subconscious barrier didn't function, and everything got through.
So, you see, I am obsessed—by my own future identity."

"And I'd been afraid that you'd been, well, taken over by
some . . . some outsider." Blake Hartley grinned weakly. "I
don't mind admitting, Allan, that what's happened has been a
shock. But that other . . . I just couldn't have taken that."

"No. Not and stayed sane. But really, I am your son; the
same entity I was yesterday. I've just had what you might call
an educational short cut."

"I'll say you have!" His father laughed in real amusement.
He discovered that his cigar had gone out, and re-lit it.
"Here: if you can remember the next thirty years, suppose
you tell me when the War's going to end. This one, I mean."

"The Japanese surrender will be announced at exactly
1901—7:01 P.M. present style—on August 14. A week from
Tuesday. Better make sure we have plenty of grub in the
house by then. Everything will be closed up tight till Thurs-
day morning; even the restaurants. I remember, we had nothing to eat in the house but some scraps."

"Well! It is handy, having a prophet in the family! I'll see
to it Mrs. Stauber gets plenty of groceries in. . . . Tuesday a
week? That's pretty sudden, isn't it?"

"The Japs are going to think so," Allan replied. He went
on to describe what was going to happen.

His father swore softly. "You know, I've heard talk about
atomic energy, but I thought it was just Buck Rogers stuff.
Was that the sort of bomb that got you?"

"That was a firecracker to the bomb that got me. That
thing exploded a good ten miles away."

Blake Hartley whistled softly. "And that's going to happen
in thirty years! You know, son, if I were you, I wouldn't like
to have to know about a thing like that." He looked at Allan

for a moment. "Please, if you know, don't ever tell me when I'm going to die."

Allan smiled. "I can't. I had a letter from you just before I left for the front. You were seventy-eight, then, and you were still hunting, and fishing, and flying your own plane. But I'm not going to get killed in any Battle of Buffalo, this time, and if I can prevent it, and I think I can, there won't be any World War III."

"But— You say all time exists, perpetually coexistent and totally present," his father said. "Then it's right there in front of you, and you're getting closer to it, every watch tick."

Allan Hartley shook his head. "You know what I remembered, when Frank Gutchall came to borrow a gun?" he asked. "Well, the other time, I hadn't been home. I'd been swimming at the Canoe Club, with Larry Morton. When I got home, about half an hour from now, I found the house full of cops. Gutchall talked the .38 officers' model out of you, and gone home; he'd shot his wife four times through the body, finished her off with another one back of the ear, and then used his sixth shot to blast his brains out. The cops traced the gun; they took a very poor view of your lending it to him. You never got it back."

"Trust that gang to keep a good gun," the lawyer said.

"I didn't want us to lose it, this time, and I didn't want to see you lose face around City Hall. Gutchalls, of course, are expendable," Allan said. "But my main reason for fixing Frank Gutchall up with a padded cell was that I wanted to know whether or not the future could be altered. I have it on experimental authority that it can be. There must be additional dimensions of time: lines of alternate probabilities. Something like William Seabrook's witch-doctor friend's Fan-Shaped Destiny. When I brought memories of the future back to the present, I added certain factors to the causal chain. That set up an entirely new line of probabilities. On no notice at all, I stopped a murder and a suicide. With thirty years to work, I can stop a world war. I'll have the means to do it, too."

"The means?"

"Unlimited wealth and influence. Here." Allan picked up a sheet and handed it to his father. "Used properly, we can make two or three million on that, alone. A list of all the Kentucky Derby, Preakness, and Belmont winners in 1970. That'll furnish us primary capital. Then, remember, I was something of a chemist. I took it up, originally, to get background material for one of my detective stories; it fascinated me, and I made it a hobby, and then a source of income. I'm thirty years ahead of any chemist in the world, now. You remember *I. G. Farbenindustrie?* Ten years from now, we'll make them look like pikers."

His father looked at the yellow sheet. "Assault, at eight to one," he said. "I can scrape about five thousand for that— Yes; in ten years— Any other little operations you have in mind?" he asked.

"About 1950, we start building a political organization, here in Pennsylvania. In 1960, I think we can elect you President. The world situation will be crucial, by that time, and we had a good-natured nonentity in the White House then, who let things go till war became inevitable. I think President Hartley can be trusted to take a strong line of policy. In the meantime, you can read Machiavelli."

"That's my little boy talking!" Blake Hartley said softly. "All right, son; I'll do just what you tell me, and when you grow up, I'll be president. . . . Let's go get supper, now."

TINY AND THE MONSTER

by Theodore Sturgeon (1918–   )

ASTOUNDING SCIENCE FICTION

May

Theodore Sturgeon (see Volumes 1, 2, 3, 6, and 8 of this series) continued to earn his reputation as one of the finest writers in science fiction in 1947. In addition to the two stories in this book, the year was highlighted by the publication of his novella Maturity, *a powerful story on the theme of enhanced intelligence which is too long for inclusion here.*

"Tiny and the Monster" may sound a little familiar to those of you who attend the movies, since its theme of stranded alien and helpful human was well treated by Stephen Spielberg in the enormously popular film E. T. *(1982). Tiny, who is not one of the forementioned characters, is one of my favorite figures in all of sf.*

(The sentence in this story that I find particularly significant is Alec's comment ". . . in all the stories I've read, when a beast comes here from space, it's to kill and conquer. . . ."

That's been the science fiction habit ever since H. G. Wells's The War of the Worlds—*and yet isn't*

*that a reflection of our own human bloodthirstiness
here on Earth? The European has bashed and
bludgeoned his way over all the continents in the
past five centuries, and so we assume that that is the
way it must be with all intelligent beings. Is it perhaps an unconscious way of trying to dilute our
own guilt by assuming "everybody does it"?*

*In any case, I feel there's a better streak within
us, too, so I valued Ted's "Tiny and the Monster,"
in which a beast coming from space is not here to
kill and conquer, nor do human beings react as
though it were.—I.A.)*

She had to find out about Tiny—everything about Tiny.

They were bound to call him Tiny. The name was good for
a laugh when he was a pup, and many times afterward.

He was a Great Dane, unfashionable with his long tail,
smooth and glossy in the brown coat which fit so snugly over
his heavily muscled shoulders and chest. His eyes were big
and brown and his feet were big and black; he had a voice
like thunder and a heart ten times his own great size.

He was born in the Virgin Islands, on St. Croix, which is a
land of palm trees and sugar, of soft winds and luxuriant un-
dergrowth whispering with the stealthy passage of pheasant
and mongoose. There were rats in the ruins of the ancient estate houses that stood among the foothills—ruins with slave-
built walls forty inches thick and great arches of weathered
stone. There was pasture land where the field mice ran, and
brooks asparkle with gaudy blue minnows.

But where in St. Croix had he learned to be so strange?

When Tiny was a puppy, all feet and ears, he learned
many things. Most of these things were kinds of respect. He
learned to respect that swift, vengeful piece of utter engineering called a scorpion when one of them whipped its barbed
tail into his inquiring nose. He learned to respect the heavy
deadness of the air about him that preceded a hurricane, for
he knew that it meant hurry and hammering and utmost
obedience from every creature on the estate. He learned to
respect the justice of sharing, for he was pulled from the teat

and from the trough when he crowded the others of his litter. He was the largest.

These things, all of them, he learned as respects. He was never struck, and although he learned caution he never learned fear. The pain he suffered from the scorpion—it happened only once—the strong but gentle hands which curbed his greed, the frightful violence of the hurricane that followed the tense preparations—all these things and many more taught him the justice of respect. He half understood a basic ethic: namely, that he would never be asked to do something, or to refrain from doing something, unless there was a good reason for it. His obedience, then, was a thing implicit, for it was half reasoned; and since it was not based on fear, but on justice, it could not interfere with his resourcefulness.

All of which, along with his blood, explained why he was such a splendid animal. It did not explain how he learned to read. It did not explain why Alec was compelled to sell him—not only to sell him but to search out Alistair Forsythe and sell him to her.

She *had* to find out. The whole thing was crazy. She hadn't wanted a dog. If she had wanted a dog it wouldn't have been a Great Dane. And if it had been a Great Dane, it wouldn't have been Tiny, for he was a Crucian dog and had to be shipped all the way to Scarsdale, New York, by air.

The series of letters she sent to Alec were as full of wondering persuasion as his had been when he sold her the dog. It was through these letters that she learned about the scorpion and the hurricane, about Tiny's puppyhood and the way Alec brought up his dogs. If she learned something about Alec as well, that was understandable. Alec and Alistair Forsythe had never met, but through Tiny they shared a greater secret than many people who have grown up together.

"As for why I wrote you, of all people," Alec wrote in answer to her direct question, "I can't say I chose you at all. It was Tiny. One of the cruise-boat people mentioned your name at my place, over cocktails one afternoon. It was, as I remember, a Dr. Schwellenbach. Nice old fellow. As soon as your name was mentioned, Tiny's head came up as if I had called him. He got up from his station by the door and lolloped over to the doctor with his ears up and his nose quivering. I thought for a minute that the old fellow was offering him food, but no—he must have wanted to hear Schwellenbach say your name again. So I asked about you. A day or so later I was telling a couple of friends about it, and when I mentioned the name again, Tiny came snuffing over and shoved his nose into my hand. He was shivering. That got me. I wrote to a friend in New York who got your name and address in the phone book. You know the rest, I just wanted to tell you about it at first, but something made me suggest a sale. Somehow, it didn't seem right to have something like this going on and not have you meet Tiny. When you wrote that you couldn't get away from New York, there didn't seem to be anything else to do but send Tiny to you. And now—I don't know if I'm too happy about it. Judging from those pages and pages of questions you keep sending me, I get the idea that you are more than a little troubled by this crazy business."

She answered, "*Please* don't think I'm troubled about this! I'm not. I'm interested, and curious, and more than a little excited; but there is nothing about the situation that frightens me. I can't stress that enough. There's something around Tiny—sometimes I have the feeling it's something outside Tiny—that is infinitely comforting. I feel protected, in a strange way, and it's a different and greater thing than the protection I could expect from a large and intelligent dog. It's strange, and it's mysterious enough; but it isn't at all frightening.

"I have some more questions. Can you remember exactly what it was that Dr. Schwellenbach said the first time he mentioned my name and Tiny acted strangely? Was there ever any time that you can remember when Tiny was under some influence other than your own, something which might have given him these strange traits? What about his diet as a puppy? How many times did he get . . ." and so on.

And Alec answered, in part, "It was so long ago now that I can't remember exactly; but it seems to me Dr. Schwellenbach was talking about his work. As you know, he's a professor of metallurgy. He mentioned Professor Nowland as the greatest alloy specialist of his time—said Nowland could alloy anything with anything. Then he went on about Nowland's assistant. Said the assistant was very highly qualified, having been one of these Science Search products and something of a prodigy; in spite of which she was completely feminine and as beautiful a redhead as had ever exchanged heaven for earth. Then he said her name was Alistair Forsythe. (I hope you're not blushing, Miss Forsythe; you asked for this!) And then it was that Tiny ran over to the doctor in that extraordinary way.

"The only time I can think of when Tiny was off the estate and possibly under some influence was the day old Debbil disappeared for a whole day with the pup when he was about three months old. Debbil is one of the characters who hang around here. He's a Crucian about sixty years old, a piratical-looking old gent with one eye and elephantiasis. He shuffles around the grounds running odd errands for anyone who will give him tobacco or a shot of white rum. Well, one morning I sent him over the hill to see if there was a leak in the water line that runs from the reservoir. It would only take a couple of hours, so I told him to take Tiny for a run.

"They were gone for the whole day. I was short-handed and busy as a squirrel in a nuthouse and didn't have a chance to send anyone after him. But he drifted in toward evening. I bawled him out thoroughly. It was no use asking him where he had been; he's only about quarter-witted anyway. He just claimed he couldn't remember, which is pretty usual for him. But for the next three days I was busy with Tiny. He wouldn't eat, and he hardly slept at all. He just kept staring out over the cane fields at the hill. He didn't seem to want to go there at all. I went out to have a look. There's nothing out that way but the reservoir and the old ruins of the governor's palace, which have been rotting there in the sun for the last century and a half. Nothing left now but an overgrown mound and a couple of arches, but it's supposed to be haunted. I forgot about it after that because Tiny got back to normal. As a matter of fact, he seemed to be better than ever, although, from then on, he would sometimes freeze and watch the hill as if he were listening to something. I haven't attached much importance to it until now. I still don't. Maybe he got chased by some mongoose's mother. Maybe he chewed up some ganja-weed—marijuana to you. But I doubt that it has anything to do with the way he acts now, any more than that business of the compasses that pointed west might have something to do with it. Did you hear about that, by the way? Craziest thing I ever heard of. It was right after I shipped Tiny off to you last fall, as I remember. Every ship and boat and plane from here to Sandy Hook reported that its compass began to indicate due west instead of a magnetic north! Fortunately the effect only lasted a couple of hours so there were no serious difficulties. One cruise steamer ran aground, and there were a couple of Miami fishing-boat mishaps. I only bring it up to remind both of us that Tiny's behavior may be odd, but not exclusively so in a world where such things as the crazy compasses occur."

And in her next, she wrote. "You're quite the philosopher, aren't you? Be careful of that Fortean attitude, my tropical friend. It tends to accept the idea of the unexplainable to an extent where explaining, or even investigating, begins to look useless. As far as that crazy compass episode is concerned, I remember it very well indeed. My boss, Dr. Nowland—yes, it's true, he can alloy anything with anything!—has been up to his ears in that fantastic happenstance. So have most of his colleagues in half a dozen sciences. They're able to explain it quite satisfactorily, too. It was simply the presence of some quite quasimagnetic phenomenon that created a resultant field at right angles to the earth's own magnetic influence. That solution sent the pure theorists home happy. Of course, the practical ones—Nowland and his associates in metallurgy, for example—only have to figure out what caused the field. Science is a wonderful thing.

"By the way, you will notice my change of address. I have wanted for a long time to have a little house of my own, and I was lucky enough to get this one from a friend. It's up the Hudson from New York, quite countrified, but convenient enough to the city to be practical. I'm bringing Mother here from Upstate. She'll love it. And besides—as if you didn't know the most important reason when you saw it—it gives Tiny a place to run. He's no city dog . . . I'd tell you that he found the house for me, too, if I didn't think that, these days, I'm crediting him with even more than his remarkable powers. Gregg and Marie Weems, the couple who had the cottage before, began to be haunted. So they said, anyway. Some indescribably horrible monster that both of them caught glimpses of inside the house and out of it. Marie finally got the screaming meemies about it and insisted on Gregg's selling the place, housing shortage or no. They came straight to me. Why? Because they—Marie, anyway; she's a mystic little thing—had the idea that someone with a large dog would be safe in that house. The odd part of that was that neither of them knew I had recently acquired a Great Dane. As soon as they saw Tiny they threw themselves on my neck and begged me to take the place. Marie couldn't explain the feeling she had; what she and Gregg came to my place for was to ask me to buy a big dog and take the house. Why me? Well, she just felt I would like it, that was all. It seemed the right kind of place for me. And my having the dog clinched it. Anyway, you can put that down in your notebook of unexplainables."

So it went for the better part of a year. The letters were long and frequent, and, as sometimes happens, Alec and Alistair grew very close indeed. Almost by accident, they found themselves writing letters that did not mention Tiny at all, although there were others that concerned nothing else. And, of course, Tiny was not always in the role of *canis superior*. He was a dog—all dog—and acted accordingly. His strangeness came out only at particular intervals. At first it had been at times when Alistair was most susceptible to being astonished by it—in other words, when it was least expected. Later, he would perform his odd feats when she was ready for him to do it, and under exactly the right circumstances. Later still, he became the superdog only when she asked him to. . . .

The cottage was on a hillside, such a very steep hillside that the view of the river skipped over the railroad, and the trains were a secret rumble and never a sight at all. There was a wild and clean air about the place—a perpetual tingle of expectancy, as though someone coming into New York for the very first time on one of the trains had thrown his joyous anticipation high in the air and the cottage had caught it and breathed it and kept it forever.

Up the hairpin driveway to the house, one spring afternoon, toiled a miniature automobile in its lowest gear. Its little motor grunted and moaned as it took the last steep grade, a miniature Old Faithful appearing around its radiator cap. At the foot of the brownstone porch steps it stopped, and a miniature lady slid out from under the wheel. But for the fact that she was wearing an aviation mechanic's coveralls, and that her very first remark—an earthy epithet directed at the steaming radiator—was neither ladylike nor miniature, she might have been a model for the more precious variety of Mother's Day greeting card.

Fuming, she reached into the car and pressed the horn button. The quavering wail that resulted had its desired effect. It was answered instantly by the mighty howl of a Great Dane at the peak of aural agony. The door of the house crashed open and a girl in shorts and a halter rushed out on the porch, to stand with her russet hair ablaze in the sunlight, her

lips parted, and her long eyes squinting against the light reflected from the river.

"What—Mother! Mother, darling, is that you? Already?
Tiny!" she rapped as the dog bolted out of the open door and
down the steps. "Come back here!"

The dog stopped. Mrs. Forsythe scooped a crescent wrench
from the ledge behind the driver's seat and brandished it.
"Let him come, Alistair," she said grimly. "In the name of
sense, girl, what are you doing with a monster like that? I
thought you said you had a dog, not a Shetland pony with
fangs. If he messes with me, I'll separate him from a couple
of those twelve-pound feet and bring him down to my weight.
Where do you keep his saddle? I thought there was a meat
shortage in this part of the country. Whatever possessed you
to take up your abode with that carnivorous dromedary, anyway? And what's the idea of buying a barn like this, thirty
miles from nowhere and perched on a precipice to boot, with
a stepladder for a driveway and an altitude fit to boil at
eighty degrees centigrade? It must take you forever to make
breakfast. Twenty-minute eggs, and then they're raw. I'm
hungry. If that Danish basilisk hasn't eaten everything in
sight, I'd like to nibble on about eight sandwiches. Salami on
whole wheat. Your flowers are gorgeous, child. So are you.
You always were, of course. Pity you have brains. If you had
no brains, you'd get married. A lovely view, honey, lovely. I
like it here. Glad you bought it. Come here, you," she said to
Tiny.

He approached this small specimen of volubility with his
head a little low and his tail down. She extended a hand and
held it still to let him sniff it before she thumped him on the
withers. He waved his unfashionable tail in acceptance and
then went to join the laughing Alistair, who was coming
down the steps.

"Mother, you're marvelous." She bent and kissed her.
"What on earth made that awful noise?"

"Noise? Oh, the horn." Mrs. Forsythe busily went about
lifting the hood of the car. "I have a friend in the shoelace
business. Wanted to stimulate trade for him. Fixed this up to
make people jump out of their shoes. When they jump they
break the laces. Leave their shoes in the street. Thousands of
people walking about in their stocking feet. More people
ought to, anyway. Good for the arches." She pointed. There
were four big air-driven horns mounted on and around the

little motor. Over the mouth of each was a shutter, so arranged that it revolved about an axle set at right angles to the horn, so that the bell was opened and closed by four small DC motors. "That's what gives it the warble. As for the beat-note, the four of them are turned a sixteenth-tone apart. Pretty?"

"Pretty," Alistair conceded with sincerity. "No, please don't demonstrate it again, Mother! You almost wrenched poor Tiny's ears off the first time."

"Oh, did I?" Contritely she went to the dog. "I didn't mean to, honey-poodle, really I didn't." The honey-poodle looked up at her with somber brown eyes and thumped his tail on the ground. "I like him," said Mrs. Forsythe decisively. She put out a fearless hand and pulled affectionately at the loose flesh of Tiny's upper lip. "Will you look at those tusks! Good grief, dog, reel in some of that tongue or you'll turn yourself inside out. Why aren't you married yet, chicken?"

"Why aren't you?" Alistair countered.

Mrs. Forsythe stretched. "I've *been married*," she said, and Alistair knew that now her casualness was forced. "A married season with the likes of Dan Forsythe sticks with you." Her voice softened. "Your daddy was all kinds of good people, baby." She shook herself. "Let's eat. I want to hear about Tiny. Your driblets and drablets of information about that dog are as tantalizing as Chapter Eleven of a movie serial. Who's this Alec creature in St. Croix? Some kind of native—cannibal, or something? He sounds nice. I wonder if you know how nice *you* think he is? Good heavens, the girl's blushing! I only know what I read in your letters, darling, and I never knew you to quote anyone by the paragraph before but that old scoundrel Nowland, and that was all about ductility and permeability and melting points. Metallurgy! A girl like you mucking about with molybs and durals instead of heartbeats and hope chests!"

"Mother, sweetheart, hasn't it occurred to you at all that I don't *want* to get married? Not yet, anyway."

"Of course it has. That doesn't alter the fact that a woman is only forty percent a woman until someone loves her, and only eighty percent a woman until she has children. As for you and your precious career, I seem to remember something about a certain Marie Sklodowska who didn't mind marrying a fellow called Curie, science or no science."

"Darling," said Alistair a little tiredly as they mounted the steps and went into the cool house, "once and for all, get this straight. The career, as such, doesn't matter at all. The work does. I like it. I don't see the sense of being married purely for the sake of being married."

"Oh, for heaven's sake, child, neither do I," said Mrs. Forsythe quickly. Then, casting a critical eye over her daughter, she sighed. "But it's such a waste."

"What do you mean?"

Her mother shook her head. "If you don't get it, it's because there's something wrong with your sense of values, in which case there's no point in arguing. I love your furniture. Now for pity's sake feed me and tell me about this canine Carnera of yours."

Moving deftly about the kitchen while her mother perched like a bright-eyed bird on a utility ladder, Alistair told the story of her letters from Alec and Tiny's arrival.

"At first he was just a dog. A very wonderful dog, of course, and extremely well trained. We got along beautifully. There was nothing remarkable about him but his history, as far as I could *see,* and certainly no indication of . . . of anything. I mean, he might have responded to my name the way he did because the syllabic content pleased him."

"It should," said her mother complacently. "Dan and I spent weeks at a sound laboratory graphing a suitable name for you. Alistair Forsythe. Has a beat, you know. Keep that in mind when you change it."

"Mother!"

"All right, dear. Go on with the story."

"For all I knew, the whole thing was a crazy coincidence. Tiny didn't respond particularly to the sound of my name after he got here. He seemed to take a perfectly normal, doggy pleasure in sticking around, that was all.

"Then, one evening after he had been with me about a month, I found out he could read."

"Read!" Mrs. Forsythe toppled, clutched the edge of the sink, and righted herself.

"Well, practically that. I used to study a lot in the evenings, and Tiny used to stretch out in front of the fire with his nose between his paws and watch me. I was tickled by that. I even got the habit of talking to him while I studied. I mean, about the work. He always seemed to be paying very close attention, which, of course, was silly. And maybe it was my imagination, but the times he'd get up and nuzzle me always

seemed to be the times when my mind was wandering or
when I would quit working and go on to something else.

"This particular evening I was working on the permeability
mathematics of certain of the rare-earth group. I put down
my pencil and reached for my *Handbook of Chemistry and
Physics* and found nothing but a big hole in the bookcase.
The book wasn't on the desk, either. So I swung around to
Tiny and said, just for something to say, "Tiny, what have
you done with my handbook?"

"He went *whuff*, in the most startled tone of voice, leaped
to his feet, and went over to his bed. He turned up the
mattress with his paw and scooped out the book. He picked it
up in his jaws—I wonder what he would have done if he
were a Scotty; that's a chunky piece of literature!—and
brought it to me.

"I just didn't know what to do. I took the book and riffled
it. It was pretty well shoved around. Apparently he had been
trying to leaf through it with those big splay feet of his, I put
the book down and took him by the muzzle. I called him
nine kinds of rascal and asked him what he was looking for."
She paused, building a sandwich.

"Well?"

"Oh," said Alistair, as if coming back from a far distance.
"He didn't say."

There was a thoughtful silence. Finally Mrs. Forsythe
looked up with her odd birdlike glance and said, "You're kidding. That dog isn't shaggy enough."

"You don't believe me." It wasn't a question.

The older woman got up to put a hand on the girl's shoulder. "Honey-lamb, your daddy used to say that the only
things worth believing were things you learned from people
you trusted. Of course I believe you. Thing is—do *you* believe you?"

"I'm not—sick, Mum, if that's what you mean. Let me tell
you the rest of it."

"You mean there's more?"

"Plenty more." She put the stack of sandwiches on the
sideboard where her mother could reach it. Mrs. Forsythe fell
to with a will. "Tiny has been goading me to do research. A
particular kind of research."

"Hut hine uffefa?"

"Mother! I didn't give you those sandwiches just to feed

you. The idea was to soundproof you a bit, too, while I talked."

"Hohay!" said her mother cheerfully.

"Well, Tiny won't let me work on any other project but the one he's interested in. Mum, I can't talk if you're going to gape like that! No . . . I can't say he won't let me do *any* work. But there's a certain line of endeavor that he approves. If I do anything else, he snuffles around, joggles my elbow, grunts, whimpers, and generally carries on until I lose my temper and tell him to go away. Then he'll walk over to the fireplace and flop down and sulk. Never takes his eyes off me. So, of course, I get all soft-hearted and repentant and apologize to him and get on with what he wants done."

Mrs. Forsythe swallowed, coughed, gulped some milk, and exploded, "Wait a minute, you're away too fast for me! What is it that he wants done? How do you know he wants it? Can he read, or can't he? Make some sense, child!"

Alistair laughed richly. "Poor Mum. I don't blame you, darling. No, I don't think he can really read. He shows no interest at all in books or pictures. The episode with the handbook seemed to be an experiment that didn't bring any results. *But*—he knows the difference between my books, even books that are bound alike, even when I shift them around in the bookcase. Tiny!"

The Great Dane scrambled to his feet from the corner of the kitchen, his paws skidding on the waxed linoleum. "Get me Hoag's *Basic Radio*, old feller, will you?"

Tiny turned and padded out. They heard him going up the stairs. "I was afraid he wouldn't do it while you were here," she said. "He generally warns me not to say anything about his powers. He growls. He did that when Dr. Nowland dropped out for lunch one Saturday. I started to talk about Tiny and just couldn't. He acted disgracefully. First he growled and then he barked. It was the first time I've ever known him to bark in the house. Poor Dr. Nowland. He was scared half out of his wits."

Tiny thudded down the stairs and entered the kitchen. "Give it to Mum," said Alistair. Tiny walked sedately over to the stool and stood before the astonished Mrs. Forsythe. She took the volume from his jaws.

"*Basic Radio*," she breathed.

"I asked him for that because I have a whole row of technical books up there, all from the same publisher, all the same color and about the same size," said Alistair calmly.

"But . . . but . . . how does he do it?"

Alistair shrugged. "*I* don't know. He doesn't read the titles. That I'm sure of. He can't read anything. I've tried to get him to do it a dozen different ways. I've lettered instructions on pieces of paper and shown them to him—you know, 'Go to the door' and 'Give me a kiss' and so on. He just looks at them and wags his tail. But if I read them first—"

"You mean, read them aloud?"

"No. Oh, he'll do anything I ask him to, sure. But I don't have to say it. Just read it, and he turns and does it. That's the way he makes me study what he wants studied."

"Are you telling me that behemoth can read your mind?"

"What do you think? Here, I'll show you. Give me the book."

Tiny's ears went up. "There's something in here about the electrical flux in supercooled copper that I don't quite remember. Let's see if Tiny's interested."

She sat on the kitchen table and began to leaf through the book. Tiny came and sat in front of her, his tongue lolling out, his big brown eyes fixed on her face. There was silence as she turned pages, read a little, turned some more. And suddenly Tiny whimpered urgently.

"*See* what I mean, Mum? All right, Tiny. I'll read it over."

Silence again, while Alistair's long green eyes traveled over the page. All at once Tiny stood up and nuzzled her leg.

"Hm-m-m? The reference? Want me to go back?"

Tiny sat again expectantly. "There's a reference here to a passage in the first section on basic electric theory that he wants," she explained. She looked up, "Mother, you read it to him." She jumped off the table, handed the book over. "Here. Section forty-five, Tiny! Go listen to Mum. Go on," and she shoved him towards Mrs. Forsythe, who said in an awed voice, "When I was a little girl, I used to read bedtime stories to my dolls. I thought I'd quit that kind of thing altogether, and now I'm reading technical literature to this . . . this canine catastrophe here. Shall I read aloud?"

"No, don't. See if he gets it."

But Mrs. Forsythe didn't get the chance. Before she had read two lines Tiny was frantic. He ran to Mrs. Forsythe and back to Alistair. He reared up like a frightened horse, rolled his eyes, and panted. He whimpered. He growled a little.

"For pity's sake, what's wrong?"

"I guess he can't get it from you," said Alistair. "I've had the idea before that he's tuned to me in more ways than one, and this clinches it. All right, then. Give me back the—"

But before she could ask him, Tiny had bounded to Mrs. Forsythe, taken the book gently out of her hands, and carried it to his mistress. Alistair smiled at her paling mother, took the book, and read until Tiny suddenly seemed to lose interest. He went back to his station by the kitchen cabinet and lay down, yawning.

"That's that," said Alistair, closing the book. "In other words, class dismissed. Well, Mum?"

Mrs. Forsythe opened her mouth, closed it again, and shook her head. Alistair loosed a peal of laughter.

"Oh, Mum," she gurgled through her laughter. "History has been made. Mum, darling, you're speechless!"

"I am not," said Mrs. Forsythe gruffly. "I . . . I think . . . well, what do you know! You're right! I *am!*"

When they had their breath back—yes, Mrs. Forsythe joined in, for Alistair's statement was indeed true—Alistair picked up the book and said, "Now look, Mum, it's almost time for my session with Tiny. Oh, yes; it's a regular thing, and he certainly is leading me into some fascinating byways."

"Like what?"

"Like the old impossible problem of casting tungsten, for example. You know, there is a way to do it."

"You don't say! What do you cast it in—a play?"

Alistair wrinkled her straight nose. "Did you ever hear of pressure ice? Water compressed until it forms a solid at what is usually its boiling point?"

"I remember some such."

"Well, all you need is enough pressure, and a chamber that can take that kind of pressure, and a couple of details like a high-intensity field of umpteen megacycles phased with . . . I forget the figures; anyhow, that's the way to go about it."

" 'If we had some eggs we could have some ham and eggs if we had some ham,' " quoted Mrs. Forsythe. "And besides, I seem to remember something about that pressure ice melting pretty much right now, like so," and she snapped her fingers. "How do you know your molded tungsten—that's what it would be, not cast at all—wouldn't change state the same way?"

"That's what I'm working on now," said Alistair calmly.

"Come along, Tiny. Mum, you can find your way around all right, can't you? If you need anything, just sing out. This isn't a séance, you know."

"Isn't it, though?" muttered Mrs. Forsythe as her lithe daughter and the dog bounded up the stairs. She shook her head, went into the kitchen, drew a bucket of water, and carried it down to her car, which had cooled to a simmer. She was dashing careful handfuls of it onto the radiator before beginning to pour when her quick ear caught the scrunching of boots on the steep drive.

She looked up to see a young man trudging wearily in the mid-morning heat. He wore an old sharkskin suit and carried his coat. In spite of his wilted appearance, his step was firm and his golden hair was crisp in the sunlight. He swung up to Mrs. Forsythe and gave her a grin, all deep-blue eyes and good teeth. "Forsythe's?" he asked in a resonant baritone.

"That's right," said Mrs. Forsythe, finding that she had to turn her head from side to side to see both of his shoulders. And yet she could have swapped belts with him. "You must feel like the Blue Kangaroo here," she added, slapping her miniature mount on its broiling flank. "Boiled dry."

"You cahl de cyah de Blue Kangaroo?" he repeated, draping his coat over the door and mopping his forehead with what seemed to Mrs. Forsythe's discerning eye, a pure linen handkerchief.

"I do," she replied, forcing herself not to comment on the young man's slight but strange accent. "It's strictly a dry-clutch job and acts like a castellated one. Let the pedal out, she races. Let it out three thirty-seconds of an inch more, and you're gone from there. Always stopping to walk back and pick up your head. Snaps right off, you know. Carry a bottle of collodion and a couple of splints to put your head back on. Starve to death without a head to eat with. What brings you here?"

In answer he held out a yellow envelope, looking solemnly at her head and neck, then at the car, his face quiet, his eyes crinkling with a huge enjoyment.

Mrs. Forsythe glanced at the envelope. "Oh. Telegram. She's inside. I'll give it to her. Come on in and have a drink. It's hotter than the hinges of Hail Columbia, Happy Land. Don't go wiping your feet like that! By jeepers, that's enough to give you an inferiority complex! Invite a man in, invite the dust on his feet, too. It's good, honest dirt and we don't run to white broadlooms here. Are you afraid of dogs?"

The young man laughed. "Dahgs talk to me, ma'am."

She glanced at him sharply, opened her mouth to tell him he might just be taken at his word around here, then thought better of it. "Sit down," she ordered. She bustled up a foaming glass of beer and set it beside him. "I'll get her down to sign for the wire," she said. The man half lowered the glass into which he had been jowls-deep, began to speak, found he was alone in the room, laughed suddenly and richly, wiped off the mustache of suds, and dived down for a new one.

Mrs. Forsythe grinned and shook her head as she heard the laughter, and went straight to Alistair's study. "Alistair!"

"Stop pushing me about the ductility of tungsten, Tiny! You know better than that. Figures are figures, and facts are facts. I think I see what you're trying to lead me to. All I can say is that if such a thing is possible, I never heard of any equipment that could handle it. Stick around a few years and I'll hire you a nuclear power plant. Until then, I'm afraid—"

"Alistair!"

"—there just isn't . . . hm-m-m? Yes, Mother?"

"Telegram."

"Oh. Who from?"

"I don't know, being only one fortieth of one percent as psychic as that doghouse Dunninger you have there. In other words, I didn't open it."

"Oh, Mum, you're silly. Of course you could have . . . oh, well, let's have it."

"I haven't got it. It's downstairs with Discobolus Junior, who brought it. No one," she said ecstatically, "has a right to be so tanned with hair that color."

"What *are* you talking about?"

"Go on down and sign for the telegram and see for yourself. You will find the maiden's dream with his golden head in a bucket of suds, all hot and sweaty from his noble efforts in attaining this peak without spikes or alpenstock, with nothing but his pure heart and Western Union to guide him."

"This maiden's dream happens to be tungsten treatment," said Alistair with some irritation. She looked longingly at her work sheet, put down her pencil, and rose. "Stay here, Tiny, I'll be right back as soon as I have successfully resisted my conniving mother's latest scheme to drag my red hairing across some young buck's path to matrimony." She paused at the door. "Aren't you staying up here, Mum?"

"Get that hair away from your face," said her mother grimly. "I am not. I wouldn't miss this for the world. And don't pun in front of that young man. It's practically the only thing in the world I consider vulgar."

Alistair led the way down the stairs and through the corridor to the kitchen, with her mother crowding her heels, once fluffing out her daughter's blazing hair, once taking a swift tuck in the back of the girl's halter. They spilled through the door almost together. Alistair stopped and frankly stared.

For the young man had risen and, still with the traces of beer foam on his molded lips, stood with his jaws stupidly open, his head a little back, his eyes partly closed as if against a bright light. And it seemed as if everyone in the room forgot to breathe for a moment.

"Well!" Mrs. Forsythe exploded after a moment. "Honey, you've made a conquest. Hey, you, chin up, chest out."

"I beg your humble pardon," muttered the young man, and the phrase seemed more a colloquialism than an affectation.

Alistair, visibly pulling herself together, said, "Mother, please," and drifted forward to pick up the telegram that lay on the kitchen table. Her mother knew her well enough to realize that her hands and her eyes were steady only by a powerful effort. Whether the effort was in control of annoyance, embarrassment, or out-and-out biochemistry was a matter for later thought. At the moment Mrs. Forsythe was enjoying the situation tremendously.

"Please wait," said Alistair coolly. "There may be an answer to this." The young man simply bobbed his head. He was still a little wall-eyed with the impact of seeing Alistair, as many a young man had been before. But there were the beginnings of his astonishing smile around his lips as he watched her rip the envelope open.

"Mother! Listen!

"ARRIVED THIS MORNING AND HOPE I CAN CATCH YOU AT HOME. OLD DEBBIL KILLED IN ACCIDENT BUT FOUND HIS MEMORY BEFORE HE DIED. HAVE INFORMATION WHICH MAY CLEAR UP MYSTERY—OR

DEEPEN IT. HOPE I CAN SEE YOU FOR I DON'T KNOW
WHAT TO THINK.

ALEC."

"How old is this tropical savage?" asked Mrs. Forsythe.

"He's not a savage and I don't know how old he is and I can't see what that has to do with it. I think he's about my age or a little older." She looked up and her eyes were shining.

"Deadly rival," said Mrs. Forsythe to the messenger consolingly. "Rotten timimg here, somewhere."

"I—" said the young man.

"Mother, we've got to fix something to eat. Do you suppose he'll be able to stay over? Where's my green dress with the . . . oh, you wouldn't know. It's new."

"Then the letters weren't all about the dog," said Mrs. Forsythe with a Cheshire grin.

"Mum, you're impossible. This is . . . is important, Alec is . . . is . . ."

Her mother nodded. "Important. That's all I was pointing out."

The young man said. "I—"

Alistair turned to him. "I do hope you don't think we're totally mad. I'm sorry you had such a climb." She went to the sideboard and took a quarter out of a sugar bowl. He took it gravely.

"Thank you, ma'am. If you don't min', I'll keep this piece of silver for the rest o' my everlahstin'."

"You're wel— What?"

The young man seemed to get even taller. "I greatly appreciate your hospitality, Mrs. Forsythe. I have you at a disadvantage, ma'am, and one I shall correct." He put a crooked forefinger between his lips and blew out an incredible blast of sound.

"Tiny!" he roared. "Here to me, dahg, an' mek me known!"

There was an answering roar from upstairs, and Tiny came tumbling down, scrabbling wildly as he took the turn at the foot of the stairs and hurtled over the slick flooring to crash joyfully into the young man.

"Ah, you beast," crooned the man, cuffing the dog happily. His accent thickened. "You thrive yourself here wid de ladydem, yo gray-yut styoupid harse. You glad me, mon, you glad me." He grinned at the two astonished women. "Forgive me," he said as he pummeled Tiny, pulled his ears, shoved him away, and caught him by the jaws. "For true, I couldn't get in the first word with Mrs. Forsythe, and after that I couldn't help meself. Alec my name is, and the telegram I took from the true messenger, finding him sighing and sweating at the sight of the hill there."

Alistair covered her face with her hands and said, "Oooh."

Mrs. Forsythe whooped with laughter. When she found her voice she demanded, "Young man, what is your last name?"

"Sundersen, ma'am."

"Mother! Why did you ask him that?"

"For reasons of euphony," said Mrs. Forsythe with a twinkle. "Alexander Sundersen. Very good. Alistair—"

"Stop! Mum, don't you dare—"

"I was going to say, Alistair, if you and our guest will excuse me, I'll have to get back to my knitting." She went to the door.

Alistair threw an appalled look at Alec and cried, "Mother! What are you knitting?"

"My brows, darling. See you later." Mrs. Forsythe chuckled and went out.

It took almost a week for Alec to get caught up with the latest developments in Tiny, for he got the story in the most meticulous detail. There never seemed to be enough time to get in all the explanations and anecdotes, so swiftly did it fly when he and Alistair were together. Some days he went into the city with Alistair in the morning and spent the day buying tools and equipment for his estate. New York was a wonder city to him—he had been there only once before—and Alistair found herself getting quite possessive about the place, showing it off like the contents of a jewel box. And then Alec stayed at the house a couple of days. He endeared himself forever to Mrs. Forsythe by removing, cleaning, and refacing the clutch on the Blue Kangaroo, simplifying the controls on the gas refrigerator so it could be defrosted without a major operation, and putting a building jack under the corner of the porch that threatened to sag.

And the sessions with Tiny were resumed and intensified. At first he seemed a little uneasy when Alec joined one of them, but within half an hour he relaxed. Thereafter, more and more he would interrupt Alistair to turn to Alec. Although he apparently could not understand Alec's thoughts at all, he seemed to comprehend perfectly when Alec spoke to Alistair. And within a few days she learned to accept these interruptions, for they speeded up the research they were doing. Alec was almost totally ignorant of the advanced theory with which Alistair worked, but his mind was clear, quick, and very direct. He was no theorist, and that was good. He was one of those rare greasemonkey geniuses, with a grasp of the laws of cause and effect that amounts to intuition. Tiny's reaction to this seemed to be approval. At any rate, the occasions when Alistair lost track of what Tiny was after occurred less and less frequently. Alec instinctively knew just how far to go back, and then how to spot the turning at which they had gone astray. And bit by bit they began to identify what it was that Tiny was after. As to why—and how—he was after it. Alec's experience with old Debbil seemed a clue. It was certainly sufficient to keep Alec plugging away at a possible solution to the strange animal's stranger need.

"It was down at the sugar mill," he told Alistair, after he had become fully acquainted with the incredible dog's actions and they were trying to determine the why and the how. "He called me over to the chute where cane is loaded into the conveyors.

" 'Bahss,' he told me, 'dat t'ing dere, it not safe, sah.' And he pointed through the guard over the bull gears that drove the conveyor. Great big everlahstin' teeth it has, Miss Alistair, a full ten inches long, and it whirlin' to the drive pinion. It's old, but strong for good. Debbil, what he saw was a bit o' play on the pinion shaf'.

" 'Now, you're an old fool,' I told him.

" 'No, Bahss,' " he says. 'Look now, sah, de t'ing wit' de teet'—dem, it not safe, sah. I mek you see,' and before I could move meself or let a thought trickle, he opens the guard up and thrus' his han' inside! Bull gear, it run right up his arm and nip it off, neat as ever, at the shoulder. I humbly beg your pardon, Miss Alistair."

"G-go on," said Alistair, through her handkerchief.

"Well, sir, old Debbil, was an idiot for true, and he only died the way he lived, rest him. He was old and he was all eaten out with malaria and elephantiasis and the like, that not even Dr. Thetford could save him. But a strange thing happened. As he lay dyin', with the entire village gathered roun' the door whisperin' plans for the wake, he sent to tell me come quickly. Down I run, and for the smile on his face I glad him when I cross the doorstep."

As Alec spoke, he was back in the Spanish-wall hut, with the air close under the palm-thatch roof and the glare of the pressure lantern set on the tiny window ledge to give the old man light to die by. Alec's accent deepened. " 'How you feel, mon?' I ahsk him. 'Bahss, I'm a dead man now, but I got a light in mah hey-yud.'

" 'Tell me then, Debbil.'

" 'Bahss, de folk-dem say, ol' Debbil, him cyahn't remembah de taste of a mango as he t'row away de skin. Him cyahn't remembah his own house do he stay away t'ree day.'

" 'Loose talk, Debbil.'

" 'True talk, Bahss. Foh de lahd give me a leaky pot fo' hol' ma brains. But Bahss, I do recall one t'ing now, bright an' clear, and you must know. Bahss, de day I go up the wahtah line, I see a great jumbee in de stones of de gov'nor palace dere.' "

"What's a jumbee?" asked Mrs. Forsythe.

"A ghost, ma'am. The Crucians carry a crawlin' heap of superstitions. Tiny! What eats you, mon?"

Tiny growled again. Alec and Alistair exchanged a look. "He doesn't want you to go on."

"Listen carefully. I want him to get this. I am his friend. I want to help you help him. I realize that he wants as few people as possible to find out about this thing. I will say nothing to anybody unless and until I have his permission."

"Well, Tiny?"

The dog stood restlessly, swinging his great head from Alistair to Alec. Finally he made a sound like an audible shrug, then turned to Mrs. Forsythe.

"Mother's part of me," said Alistair firmly. "That's the way it's got to be. No alternative." She leaned forward. "You can't talk to us. You can only indicate what you want said and done. I think Alec's story will help us to understand what you want and help you to get it more quickly. Understand?"

Tiny gazed at her for a long moment, said, "*Whuff*," and lay down with his nose between his paws and his eyes fixed on Alcc.

"I think that's the green light," said Mrs. Forsythe, "and I might add that most of it was due to my daughter's conviction that you're a wonderful fellow."

"Mother!"

"Well, pare me down and call me Spud! They're *both* blushing!" said Mrs. Forsythe blatantly.

"Go on, Alec," choked Alistair.

"Thank you. Old Debbil told me a fine tale of the things he had seen at the ruins. A great beast, mind you, with no shape at all, and a face ugly to drive you mad. And about the beast was what he called a 'feelin' good.' He said it was a miracle, but he feared nothing. Wet it was, Bahss, like a slug, an' de eye it have is whirlin' an' shakin', an' I standin' dar feelin' like a bride at de altar step an' no fear in me.' Well, I thought the old man's mind was wandering, for I knew he was touched. But the story he told was *that* clear, and never a single second did he stop to think. Out it all came like a true thing.

"He said that Tiny walked to the beast and that it curved over him like an ocean wave. It closed over the dog, and Debbil was rooted there the livelong day, still without fear, and feelin' no small desire to move. He had no surprise at all, even at the thing he saw restin' in the thicket among the old stones.

"He said it was a submarine, a mighty one as great as the estate house and with no break nor mar in its surface but for the glass part let in where the mouth is on a shark.

"And then when the sun begun to dip, the beast gave a shudderin' heave and rolled back, and out walked Tiny. He stepped up to Debbil and stood. Then the beast began to quiver and shake, and Debbil said the air aroun' him heavied with the work the monster was doing, tryin' to talk. A cloud formed in his brain, and a voice swept over him. 'Not a livin' word, Bahss, not a sound at all. But it said to forget. It said to leave dis place and forget, sah.' And the last thing old Debbil saw as he turned away was the beast slumping down, seeming all but dead from the work it had done to speak at all. 'An' de cloud live in mah hey-yud, Bahss, f'om dat time onward. I'm a dead man now, Bahss, but de cloud gone and Debbil know de story.'" Alec leaned back and looked at his hands. "That was all. This must have happened about fifteen months pahst, just before Tiny began to show his strange stripe." He drew a deep breath and looked up. "Maybe I'm gullible. But I knew the old man too well. He never in this life could invent such a tale. I troubled myself to go up to the governor's palace after the buryin'. I might have been mistaken, but something big had lain in the deepest thicket, for it was crushed into a great hollow place near a hundred foot long. Well, there you are. For what it's worth, you have the story of a superstitious an' illiterate old man, at the point of death by violence and many years sick to boot."

There was a long silence, and at last Alistair threw her lucent hair back and said, "It isn't Tiny at all. It's a . . . a thing outside Tiny." She looked at the dog, her eyes wide. "And I don't even mind."

"Neither did Debbil when he saw it," said Alec gravely.

Mrs. Forsythe snapped, "What are we sitting gawking at each other for? Don't answer; I'll tell you. All of us can think up a story to fit the facts, and we're all too self-conscious to come out with it. Any story that fit those facts would really be a killer."

"Well said." Alec grinned. "Would you like to tell us your idea?"

"Silly boy," muttered Alistair.

"Don't be impertinent, child. Of course I'd like to tell you, Alec. I think that the good Lord, in His infinite wisdom, has decided that it was about time for Alistair to come to her senses, and, knowing that it would take a quasi-scientific miracle to do it, dreamed up this—"

"Some day," said Alistair icily "I'm going to pry you loose from your verbosity and your sense of humor in one fell swoop."

Mrs. Forsythe grinned. "There is a time for jocularity, kidlet, and this is it. I hate solemn people solemnly sitting around being awed by things. What do you make of all this, Alec?"

Alec pulled his ear and said, "I vote we leave it up to Tiny. It's his show. Let's get on with the work and just keep in mind what we already know."

To their astonishment, Tiny stumped over to Alec and licked his hand.

The blowoff came six weeks after Alec's arrival. (Oh, yes, he stayed six weeks, and longer. It took some fiendish cogitation for him to think of enough legitimate estate business that had to be done in New York to keep him that long, but after six weeks he was so much one of the family that he needed no excuse.) He had devised a code system for Tiny, so that Tiny could add something to their conversation. His point:

"Here he sits, ma'am, like a fly on the wall, seeing everything and hearing everything and saying not a word. Picture it for yourself, and you in such a position, fully entranced as you are with the talk you hear." And for Mrs. Forsythe particularly, the mental picture was altogether too vivid. It was so well presented that Tiny's research went by the board for four days while they devised the code. They had to give up the idea of a glove with a pencil pocket in it, with which Tiny might write a little, or any similar device. The dog was simply not deft enough for such meticulous work; and besides, he showed absolutely no signs of understanding any written or printed symbolism. Unless, of course, Alistair thought about it.

Alec's plan was simple. He cut some wooden forms—a disk, a square, a triangle to begin with. The desk signified "yes" or any other affirmation, depending on the context; the square was "no" or any negation; and the triangle indicated a question or a change of subject. The amount of information Tiny was able to impart by moving from one to another of these forms was astonishing. Once a subject for discussion was established, Tiny would take a stand between the disk and the square, so that all he had to do was to swing his head to one side or the other to indicate a "yes" or a "no." No longer were there those exasperating sessions in which the track of his research was lost while they back-trailed to discover where they had gone astray. The conversations ran like this:

"Tiny, I have a question. Hope you won't think it too personal. May I ask it?" That was Alec, always infinitely polite to dogs. He had always recognized their innate dignity.

Yes, the answer would come, as Tiny swung his head over the disk.

"Were we right in assuming that you, the dog, are not communicating with us, that you are the medium?"

Tiny went to the triangle. "You want to change the subject?"

Tiny hesitated, then went to the square. *No.*

Alistair said, "He obviously wants something from us before he will discuss the question. Right, Tiny?"

Yes.

Mrs. Forsythe said, "He's had his dinner, and he doesn't smoke. I think he wants us to assure him that we'll keep his secret."

Yes.

"Good, Alec, you're wonderful," said Alistair. "Mother, stop beaming. I only meant—"

"Leave it at that, child. And qualification will spoil it for the man."

"Thank you, ma'am," said Alec gravely, with that deep twinkle of amusement around his eyes. Then he turned back to Tiny. "Well, what about it, sah? Are you a superdog?"

No.

"Who . . . no, he can't answer that. Let's go back a bit. Was old Debbil's story true?"

Yes.

"Ah." They exchanged glances. "Where is this—monster? Still in St. Croix?"

No.

"Here?"

Yes.

"You mean here, in this room or in the house?"

No.

"Nearby, though?"

Yes.

"How can we find out just where, without mentioning the countryside item by item?" asked Alistair.

"I know," said Mrs. Forsythe. "Alec, according to Debbil, that 'submarine' thing was pretty big, wasn't it?"

"That it was, ma'am."

"Good. Tiny, does he . . . it . . . have the ship here, too?"

Yes.

Mrs. Forsythe spread her hands. "That's it, then. There's only one place around here where you could hide such an object." She nodded her head at the west wall of the house.

"The river!" cried Alistair. "That right, Tiny?"

Yes. And Tiny went immediately to the triangle.

"Wait!" said Alec. "Tiny, beggin' your pardon, but there's one more question. Shortly after you took passage to New York, there was a business with compasses, where they all pointed to the west. Was that the ship?"

Yes.

"In the water?"

No.

"Why," said Alistair, "this is pure science fiction! Alec, do you ever get science fiction in the tropics?"

"Ah, Miss Alistair, not often enough, for true. But well I

know it. The space ships are old Mother Goose to me. But there's a difference here. For in all the stories I've read, when a beast comes here from space, it's to kill and conquer; and yet—and I don't know why—I know that this one wants nothing of the sort. More, he's out to do us good."

"I feel the same way," said Mrs. Forsythe thoughtfully. "It's sort of a protective cloud which seems to surround us. Does that make sense to you, Alistair?"

"I know it from 'way back," said Alistair with conviction. She looked at the dog thoughtfully. "I wonder why he . . . it . . . won't show itself. And why it can communicate only through me. And why me?"

"I'd say, Miss Alistair, that you were chosen because of your metallurgy. As to why we never see the beast, well, it knows best. Its reason must be a good one."

Day after day, and bit by bit, they got and gave information. Many things remained mysteries, but, strangely, there seemed no real need to question Tiny too closely. The atmosphere of confidence and good will that surrounded them made questions seem not only unnecessary but downright rude.

And day by day, little by little, a drawing began to take shape under Alec's skilled hands. It was a casting with a simple enough external contour, but inside it contained a series of baffles and a chamber. It was designed, apparently, to support and house a carballoy shaft. There were no openings into the central chamber except those taken by the shaft. The shaft turned; *something* within the chamber apparently drove it. There was plenty of discussion about it.

"Why the baffles?" moaned Alistair, palming all the neatness out of her flaming hair. "Why carballoy? And in the name of Nemo, why tungsten?"

Alec stared at the drawing for a long moment, then suddenly clapped a hand to his head. "Tiny! Is there radiation inside that housing? I mean, hard stuff?"

Yes.

"There you are, then," said Alec. "Tungsten to shield the radiation. A casting for uniformity. The baffles to make a meander out of the shaft openings—see, the shaft has plates turned on it to fit between the baffles."

"And nowhere for anything to go in, nowhere for anything to come out—except the shaft, of course—and besides, you dan't cast tungsten that way! Maybe Tiny's monster can, but we can't. Maybe with the right flux and with enough power—but that's silly. Tungsten won't cast."

"And we can't build a spaceship. There must be a way!"

"Not with today's facilities, and not with tungsten," said Alistair. "Tiny's ordering it from us the way we would order a wedding cake at the corner bakery."

"What made you say 'wedding cake'?"

"You, too, Alec? Don't I get enough of that from Mother?" But she smiled all the same. "But about the casting—it seems to me that our mysterious friend is in the position of a radio fiend who understands every part of his set, how it's made, how and why it works. Then a tube blows, and he finds he can't buy one. He has to make one if he gets one at all. Apparently old Debbil's beast is in that kind of spot. What about it, Tiny? Is your friend short a part which he understands but has never built before?"

Yes.

"And he needs it to get away from Earth?"

Yes.

Alec asked, "What's the trouble? Can't get escape velocity?"

Tiny hesitated, then went to the triangle. "Either he doesn't want to talk about it or the question doesn't quite fit the situation," said Alistair. "It doesn't matter. Our main problem is the casting. It just can't be done. Not by anyone on this planet, as far as I know; and I think I know. It had to be tungsten, Tiny?"

Yes.

"Tungsten for what?" asked Alec. "Radiation shield?"

Yes.

He turned to Alistair. "Isn't there something just as good?"

She mused, staring at his drawing. "Yes, several things," she said thoughtfully. Tiny watched her, motionless. He seemed to slump as she shrugged dispiritedly and said, "But not anything with walls as thin as that. A yard or so of lead might do it, and have something like the mechanical strength he seems to want, but it would obviously be too big. Beryllium—" At the word, Tiny went and stood right on top of the square, a most emphatic *no*.

"How about an alloy?" Alec asked.

"Well, Tiny?"

Tiny went to the triangle. Alistair nodded. "You don't

know. I can't think of one. I'll take it up with Dr. Nowland. Maybe——"

The following day Alec stayed home and spent the day arguing cheerfully with Mrs. Forsythe and building a grape arbor. It was a radiant Alistair who came home that evening. "Got it! Got it!" she caroled as she danced in. "Alec, Tiny! Come on!"

They flew upstairs to the study. Without removing the green "beanie" with the orange feather that so nearly matched her hair, Alistair hauled out four reference books and began talking animatedly. "Auric molybdenum. Tiny, what about that? Gold and molyb III should do it! Listen!" And she launched forth into a spatter of absorption data, Greek-letter fomulae, and strength-of-materials comparisons that made Alec's head swim. He sat watching her without listening. Increasingly, this was his greatest pleasure.

When Alistair was quite through, Tiny walked away from her and lay down, gazing off into space.

"Well, strike me!" said Alec. "Look yonder, Miss Alistair. The very first time I ever saw him thinking something over."

"*Sh-h!* Don't disturb him, then. If that *is* the answer, and if he never thought of it before, it will take some figuring out. There's no knowing what fantastic kind of science he's comparing it with.

"I see the point. Like—well, suppose we crashed a plane in the Brazilian jungle and needed a new hydraulic cylinder on the landing gear. Now, then, one of the natives shows us ironwood, and it's up to us to figure out if we can make it serve."

"That's about it," breathed Alistair. "I—" She was interrupted by Tiny, who suddenly leaped up and ran to her, kissing her hands, committing the forbidden enormity of putting his paws on her shoulders, running back to the wooden forms and nudging the disk, the *yes* symbol. His tail was going like a metronome without its pendulum.

Mrs. Forsythe came in in the midst of all this rowdiness and demanded, "What goes on? Who made a dervish out of Tiny? What have you been feeding him? Don't tell me. Let me . . . You don't mean you've solved his problem for him? What are you going to do, buy him a pogo stick?"

"Oh, Mum, we've got it! An alloy of molybdenum and gold. I can get it alloyed and cast in no time."

"Good, honey, good. You going to cast the whole thing?" She pointed to the drawing.

"Why, yes."

"Humph!"

"Mother! Why, if I may ask, do you 'humph' in that tone of voice?"

"You may ask, Chicken, who's going to pay for it?"

"Why, that will—I—oh. *Oh!*" she said, aghast, and ran to the drawing. Alec came and looked over her shoulder. She figured in the corner of the drawing, oh-ed once again and sat down weakly.

"How much?" asked Alec.

"I'll get an estimate in the morning," she said faintly. "I know plenty of people. I can get it at cost—maybe." She looked at Tiny despairingly. He came and laid his head against her knee, and she pulled at his ears. "I won't let you down, darling," she whispered.

She got the estimate the next day. It was a little over thirteen thousand dollars.

Alistair and Alec stared blankly at each other and then at the dog.

"Maybe you can tell us where we can raise that much money?" said Alistair, as if she expected Tiny to whip out a wallet.

Tiny whimpered, licked Alistair's hand, looked at Alec, and then lay down.

"Now what?" mused Alec.

"Now we go and fix something to eat," said Mrs. Forsythe, moving toward the door. The others were about to follow, when Tiny leaped to his feet and ran in front of them. He stood in the doorway and whimpered. When they came closer, he barked.

"Sh-h! What is it, Tiny? Want us to stay here awhile?"

"Say, who's the boss around here?" Mrs. Forsythe wanted to know.

"He is," said Alec, and he knew he was speaking for all of them. They sat down, Mrs. Forsythe on the studio couch, Alistair at her desk, Alec at the drawing table. But Tiny seemed not to approve of the arrangement. He became vastly excited, running to Alec, nudging him hard, dashing to Alistair, taking her wrist very gently in his jaws and pulling gently toward Alec.

"What is it, fellow?"

"Seems like matchmaking to me," remarked Mrs. Forsythe.

"Nonsense, Mum," said Alistair, coloring. "He wants Alec and me to change places, that's all."

Alec said, "Oh," and went to sit beside Mrs. Forsythe. Alistair sat at the drawing table. Tiny put a paw up on it, poked at the large tablet of paper. Alistair looked at him curiously, then tore off the top sheet. Tiny nudged a pencil with his nose.

Then they waited. Somehow, no one wanted to speak. Perhaps no one could, but there seemed to be no reason to try. And gradually a tension built up in the room. Tiny stood stiff and rapt in the center of the room. His eyes glazed, and when he finally keeled over limply, no one went to him.

Alistair picked up the pencil slowly. Watching her hand, Alec was reminded of the movement of the pointer on a Ouija board. The pencil traveled steadily, in small surges, to the very top of the paper and hung there. Alistair's face was quite blank.

After that no one could say what happened, exactly. It was as if their eyes had done what their voices had done. They could see, but they did not care to. And Alistair's pencil began to move. Something, somewhere, was directing her mind—not her hand. Faster and faster her pencil flew, and it wrote what was later to be known as the Forsythe Formulae.

There was no sign then, of course, of the furor that they would cause, of the millions of words of conjecture that were written when it was discovered that the girl who wrote them could not possibly have had the mathematical background to write them. They were understood by no one at first, and by very few people ever. Alistair certainly did not know what they meant.

An editorial in a popular magazine came startlingly close to the true nature of the formulae when it said: "The Forsythe Formulae, which describe what the Sunday supplements call the 'Something-for-Nothing Clutch,' and the drawing that accompanies them, signify little to the layman. As far as can be determined, the formulae are the description and working principles of a device. It appears to be a power plant of sorts, and if it is ever understood, atomic power will go the way of gaslights.

"A sphere of energy is enclosed in a shell made of neutron-absorbing material. This sphere has inner and outer 'layers.' A shaft passes through the sphere. Apparently a magnetic field must be rotated about the outer casing of the device. The sphere of energy aligns itself with this field. The inner sphere rotates with the outer one and has the ability to turn the shaft. Unless the mathematics used are disproved— and no one seems to have come anywhere near doing that, unorthodox as they are—the aligning effect between the rotating field and the two concentric spheres, as well as the shaft, is quite independent of any load. In other words, if the original magnetic field rotates at 3000 r.p.m., the shaft will rotate at 3000 r.p.m., even if there is only 1/16 horsepower turning the field while there is 10,000 braking stress on the shaft.

"Ridiculous? Perhaps. And perhaps it is no more so than the apparent impossibility of 15 watts of energy pouring into the antenna of a radio station, and nothing coming down. The key to the whole problem is in the nature of those self-contained spheres of force inside the shell. Their power is apparently inherent, and consists of an ability to align, just as the useful property of steam is an ability to expand. If, as is suggested by Reinhardt in his 'Usage of the Symbol β in the Forsythe Formulae,' these spheres are nothing but stable concentrations of pure binding energy, we have here a source of power beyond the wildest dreams of mankind. Whether or not we succeed in building such devices, it cannot be denied that whatever their mysterious source, the Forsythe Formulae are an epochal gift to several sciences, including, if you like, the art of philosophy."

After it was over, and the formulae written, the terrible tension lifted. The three humans sat in their happy coma, and the dog lay senseless on the rug. Mrs. Forsythe was the first to move, standing up abruptly. "Well!" she said.

It seemed to break a spell. Everything was quite normal. No hang-overs, no sense of strangeness, no fear. They stood looking wonderingly at the mass of minute figures.

"I don't know," murmured Alistair, and the phrase covered a world of meaning. Then, "Alec—that casting. We've got to get it done. We've just got to, no matter what it costs us!"

"I'd like to," said Alec. "Why do we have to?"

She waved toward the drawing table. "We've been given that."

"You don't say!" said Mrs. Forsythe. "And what is that?"

Alistair put her hand to her head, and a strange, unfocused

look came into her eyes. That look was the only part of the whole affair that ever really bothered Alec. It was a place she had gone to, a little bit; and he knew that no matter what happened, he would never be able to go there with her.

She said, "He's been . . . talking to me, you know. You do know that, don't you? I'm not guessing, Alec—Mum."

"I believe you, chicken," her mother said softly. "What are you trying to say?"

"I got it in concepts. It isn't a thing you can repeat, really. But the idea is that he couldn't give us any *thing*. His ship is completely functional, and there isn't anything he can exchange for what he wants us to do. But he has given us something of great value. . . ." Her voice trailed off; she seemed to listen to something for a moment. "Of value in several ways. A new science, a new approach to attack the science. New tools, new mathematics."

"But what is it? What can it do? And how is it going to help us pay for the casting?" asked Mrs. Forsythe.

"It can't, immediately," said Alistair decisively. "It's too big. We don't even know what it is. Why are you arguing? Can't you understand that he can't give us any gadgetry? That we haven't his techniques, materials, and tools, and so we couldn't make any actual machine he suggested? He's done the only thing he can; he's given us a new science, and tools to take it apart."

"That I know," said Alec gravely. "Well, indeed. I felt that. And I—I trust him. Do you, ma'am?"

"Yes, of course. I think he's—people. I think he has a sense of humor and a sense of justice," said Mrs. Forsythe firmly. "Let's get our heads together. We ought to be able to scrape it up some way. And why shouldn't we? Haven't we three got something to talk about for the rest of our lives?"

And their heads went together.

This is the letter that arrived two months later in St. Croix.

Honey-lamb,

Hold on to your seat. It's all over.

The casting arrived. I missed you more than ever, but when you have to go—and you know I'm glad you went! Anyway, I did as you indicated, through Tiny, before you left. The men who rented me the boat and ran it for me thought I was crazy, and said so. Do you know that once we were out on the river with the casting, and Tiny started whuffing and whimpering to tell me we were on the right spot, and I told the men to tip the casting over the side, they had the colossal nerve to insist on opening the crate? Got quite nasty about it. Didn't want to be a party to any dirty work. It was against my principles, but I let them, just to expedite matters. They were certain there was a body in the box! When they saw what it was, I was going to bend my umbrelly over their silly heads, but they looked so funny I couldn't do a thing but roar with laughter. That was when the man said I was crazy.

Anyhow, over the side it went, into the river. Made a lovely splash. About a minute later I got the loveliest feeling—I wish I could describe it to you. I was sort of overwhelmed by a feeling of utter satisfaction, and gratitude, and, oh, I don't know. I just felt *good*, all over. I looked at Tiny, and he was trembling. I think he felt it, too. I'd call it a thank you, on a grand psychic scale. I think you can rest assured that Tiny's monster got what it wanted.

But that wasn't the end of it. I paid off the boatmen and started up the bank. Something made me stop and wait, and then go back to the water's edge.

It was early evening, and very still. I was under some sort of compulsion, not an unpleasant thing, but an unbreakable one. I sat down on the river wall and watched the water. There was no one around—the boat had left—except one of those snazzy Sunlounge cruisers anchored a few yards out. I remember how still it was, because there was a little girl playing on the deck of the yacht, and I could hear her footsteps as she ran about.

Suddenly I noticed something in the water. I suppose I should have been frightened, but somehow I wasn't at all. Whatever the thing was, it was big and gray and slimy and quite shapeless. And somehow, it seemed to be the source of this aura of well-being and protectiveness that I felt. It was staring at me. I knew it was before I saw that it had an eye—a big one, with something whirling inside of

it. I don't know. I wish I could write. I wish I had
the power to tell you what it was like. I know that
by human standards it was infinitely revolting. If
this was Tiny's monster, I could understand its
being sensitive to the revulsion it might cause. And
wrongly; for I felt to the core that the creature was
good.

It winked at me. I don't mean blinked. It winked.
And then everything happened at once.

The creature was gone, and in seconds there was
a disturbance in the water by the yacht. Something
gray and wet reached up out of the river, and I saw
it was going for that little girl. Onle a tyke—about
three, she was. Red hair just like yours. And it
thumped that child in the small of the back just
enough to knock her over into the river.

And can you believe it? I just sat there watching
and said never a word. It didn't seem right to me
that that baby could be struggling in the water.
But it didn't seem wrong, either!

Well, before I could get my wits together, Tiny
was off the wall like a hairy bullet and streaking
through the water. I have often wondered why his
feet are so big; I never will again. The hound is
built like the lower half of a paddle wheel! In two
shakes he had the baby by the scruff of the neck
and was bringing her back to me. No one had seen
that child get pushed, Alistair! No one but me. But
there was a man on the yacht who must have seen
her fall. He was all over the deck, roaring orders
and getting in the way of things, and by the time he
had his wherry in the water, Tiny had reached me
with the little girl. She wasn't frightened, either, she
thought it was a grand joke! Wonderful youngster.

So the man came ashore, all gratitude and tears,
and wanted to gold-plate Tiny or something. Then
he saw me. "That your dog?" I said it was my
daughter's. She was in St. Croix on her honeymoon.
Before I could stop him, he had a checkbook out
and was scratching away at it. He said he knew my
kind. Said he knew I'd never accept a thing for myself, but wouldn't refuse something for my daughter. I enclose the check. Why he picked a sum like

thirteen thousand I'll never know. Anyhow, I know it'll be a help to you, and since the money really comes from Tiny's monster, I'm sure you'll use it. I suppose I can confess now. The idea that letting Alec put up the money—even though he had to clean out his savings and mortgage his estate—would be all right if he were one of the family, because then he'd have you to help him make it all back again—well, that was all my inspiration. Sometimes, though, watching you, I wonder if I really had to work so all-fired hard to get you two married to each other.

Well, I imagine that closes the business of Tiny's monster. There are a lot of things we'll probably never know. I can guess some things, though. It could communicate with a dog but not with a human, unless it half killed itself trying. Apparently a dog is telepathic with humans to a degree, though it probably doesn't understand a lot of what it gets. I don't speak French, but I could probably transcribe French phonetically well enough so a Frenchman could read it. Tiny was transcribing that way. The monster could "send" through him and control him completely. It no doubt indoctrinated the dog—if I can use the term—the day old Debbil took him up the waterline. And when the monster caught, through Tiny, the mental picture of you when Dr. Schwellenbach mentioned you, it went to work through the dog to get you working on its problem. Mental pictures—that's probably what the monster used. That's how Tiny could tell one book from another without being able to read. You visualize everything you think about. What do you think? *I* think that mine's as good a guess as any.

You might be amused to learn that last night all the compasses in this neighborhood pointed west for a couple of hours! 'By, now, chillun. Keep on being happy.

Love and love, and a kiss for Alec,
Mum

P.S. Is St. Croix really a nice place to honeymoon? Jack—he's the fellow who signed the check—is getting very senti-

mental. He's very like your father. A widower, and—oh, I
don't know. Says fate, or something, brought us together.
Said he hadn't planned to take a trip upriver with his
granddaughter, but something drove him to it. He can't imagine why he anchored just there. Seemed a good idea at the
time. Maybe it was fate. He is very sweet. I wish I could forget that wink I saw in the water.

E FOR EFFORT

by T. L. Sherred (1915-)

ASTOUNDING SCIENCE FICTION

May

Very little is known about T. L. Sherred beyond the fact that he has a background in advertising and technical writing. His small body of work in science fiction (which includes a novel, Alien Island, 1970) contains a strong dose of cynicism punctuated with sinister humor. "E for Effort" is his most famous work and was his first published sf—indeed, it is certainly one of the best first stories in the history of the field. As you will see when you read it, it seems ahead of its time in several respects, most notably in its view of government bureaucracy, a theme that would receive great attention in the next decade.

The story was also the cornerstone of Sherred's collection First Person Peculiar (1972), a book that deserves to be back in print.

(A few stories back I boasted that the moment Poul Anderson's first story appeared, I knew he was destined to be a science fiction luminary.

Well, lest you think I'm implying that I have an unfailing touch for such things, let me tell you that

*I felt the same thing about T. L. Sherred when "E
for Effort" appeared. It was, as Marty told you, his
first story, and it was such a polished piece of work
and seemed to be so excellent a job by so experienced a writer that I took it for granted we were
going to see many, many additional great stories by
him.*

*But we didn't. I don't know why. —And it seems
such a shame.—I.A.)*

The captain was met at the airport by a staff car. Long and
fast it sped. In a narrow, silent room the general sat, ram-
rod-backed, tense. The major waited at the foot of the gleaming steps shining frostily in the night air. Tires screamed to a
stop and together the captain and the major raced up the
steps. No words of greeting were spoken. The general stood
quickly, hand outstretched. The captain ripped open a
dispatch case and handed over a thick bundle of papers. The
general flipped them over eagerly and spat a sentence at the
major. The major disappeared and his harsh voice rang curtly
down the outside hall. The man with glasses came in and the
general handed him the papers. With jerky fingers the man
with glasses sorted them out. With a wave from the general
the captain left, a proud smile on his weary young face. The
general tapped his fingertips on the black glossy surface of
the table. The man with glasses pushed aside crinkled maps,
and began to read aloud.

Dear Joe:
I started this just to kill time, because I got tired
of just looking out the window. But when I got almost to the end I began to catch the trend of what's
going on. You're the only one I know that can
come through for me, and when you finish this
you'll know why you must.
I don't know who will get this to you. Whoever it
is won't want you to identify a face later. Remember that, and please, Joe—*hurry!*
                                                    Ed

It all started because I'm lazy. By the time I'd shaken off the sandman and checked out of the hotel every seat in the bus was full. I stuck my bag in a dime locker and went out to kill the hour I had until the next bus left. You know the bus terminal: right across from the Book-Cadillac and the Statler, on Washington Boulevard near Michigan Avenue. Michigan Avenue. Like Main in Los Angeles, or maybe Sixty-third in its present state of decay in Chicago, where I was going. Cheap movies, pawnshops and bars by the dozens, a penny arcade or two, restaurants that feature hamburg steak, bread and butter and coffee for forty cents. Before the War, a quarter.

I like pawnshops. I like cameras, I like tools, I like to look in windows crammed with everything from electric razors to sets of socket wrenches to upper plates. So, with an hour to spare, I walked out Michigan to Sixth and back on the other side of the street. There are a lot of Chinese and Mexicans around that part of town, the Chinese running the restaurants and the Mexicans eating Southern Home Cooking. Between Fourth and Fifth I stopped to stare at what passed for a movie. Store windows painted black, amateurish signs extolling in Spanish: "Detroit premiere . . . cast of thousands . . . this week only . . . ten cents—" The few 8×10 glossy stills pasted on the windows were poor blowups, spotty and wrinkled; pictures of mailed cavalry and what looked like a good-sized battle. All for ten cents. Right down my alley.

Maybe it's lucky that history was my major in school. Luck it must have been, certainly not cleverness, that made me pay a dime for a seat in an undertaker's rickety folding chair imbedded solidly—although the only other customers were a half-dozen Sons of the Order of Tortilla—in a cast of second-hand garlic. I sat near the door. A couple of hundred watt bulbs dangling naked from the ceiling gave enough light for me to look around. In front of me, in the rear of the store, was the screen, what looked like a white-painted sheet of beaverboard, and when over my shoulder I saw the battered sixteen millimeter projector I began to think that even a dime was no bargain. Still, I had forty minutes to wait.

Everyone was smoking. I lit a cigarette and the discouraged Mexican who had taken my dime locked the door and turned off the lights, after giving me a long, questioning look. I'd paid my dime, so I looked right back. In a minute the old projector started clattering. No film credits, no producer's

name, no director, just a tentative flicker before a closeup of
a bewhiskered mug labeled Cortez. Then a painted and
feathered Indian with the title of Guatemotzin, successor to
Montezuma; an aerial shot of a beautiful job of model-build-
ing tagged Ciudad de Mejico, 1521. Shots of old muzzle-
loaded artillery banging away, great walls spurting stone
splinters under direct fire, skinny Indians dying violently with
the customary gyrations, smoke and haze and blood. The
photography sat me right up straight. It had none of the
scratches and erratic cuts that characterize an old print, none
of the fuzziness, none of the usual mugging at the camera by
the handsome hero. There wasn't any handsome hero. Did
you ever see one of these French pictures, or a Russian picture, and note the reality and depth brought out by working
on a small budget that can't afford famed actors? This, what
there was of it, was as good, or better.

It wasn't until the picture ended with a pan shot of a
dreary desolation that I began to add two and two. You
can't, for pennies, really have a cast of thousands, or sets big
enough to fill Central Park. A mock-up, even, of a thirty-foot
wall costs enough to irritate the auditors, and there had been
a lot of wall. That didn't fit with the bad editing and lack of
sound track, not unless the picture had been made in the old
silent days. And I knew it hadn't by the color tones you get
with pan film. It looked like a well-rehearsed and badly
planned newsreel.

The Mexicans were easing out and I followed them to
where the discouraged one was rewinding the reel. I asked
him where he got the print.

"I haven't heard of any epics from the press agents lately,
and it looks like a fairly recent print."

He agreed that it was recent, and added that he'd made it
himself. I was polite to that, and he saw that I didn't believe
him and straightened up from the projector.

"You don't believe that, do you?" I said that I certainly
did, and I had to catch a bus. "Would you mind telling me
why, exactly why?" I said that the bus— "I mean it. I'd appreciate it if you'd tell me just what's wrong with it."

"There's nothing wrong with it," I told him. He waited for
me to go on. "Well, for one thing, pictures like that aren't
made for the sixteen millimeter trade. You've got a reduction
from a thirty-five millimeter master." I gave him a few of the

other reasons that separate home movies from Hollywood. When I finished he smoked quietly for a minute.

"I see." He took the reel off the projector spindle and closed the case. "I have beer in the back." I agreed beer sounded good, but the bus—well, just one. From in back of the beaverboard screen he brought paper cups and a Jumbo bottle. With a whimsical "Business suspended" he closed the open door and opened the bottle with an opener screwed on the wall. The store had likely been a grocery or restaurant. There were plenty of chairs. Two we shoved around and relaxed companionably. The beer was warm.

"You know something about this line," he said tentatively.

I took it as a question and laughed. "Not too much. Here's mud." And we drank. "Used to drive a truck for the Film Exchange." He was amused at that.

"Stranger in town?"

"Yes and no. Mostly yes. Sinus trouble chased me out and relatives bring me back. Not any more, though; my father's funeral was last week." He said that was too bad, and I said it wasn't. "He had sinus, too." That was a joke, and he refilled the cups. We talked awhile about Detroit climate.

Finally he said, rather speculatively, "Didn't I see you around here last night? Just about eight." He got up and went after more beer.

I called after him. "No more beer for me." He brought a bottle anyway, and I looked at my watch. "Well, just one."

"Was it you?"

"Was it me what?" I held out my paper cup.

"Weren't you around here—"

I wiped foam off my mustache. "Last night? No, but I wish I had. I'd have caught my bus. No, I was in the Motor Bar last night at eight. And I was still there at midnight."

He chewed his lip thoughtfully. "The Motor Bar. Just down the street?" And I nodded. "The Motor Bar. Hm-m-m." I looked at him. "Would you like . . . sure, you would." Before I could figure out what he was talking about he went to the back and from behind the beaverboard screen rolled out a big radio-phonograph and another Jumbo bottle. I held the bottle against the light. Still half full. I looked at my watch. He rolled the radio against the wall and lifted the lid to get at the dials.

"Reach behind you, will you? The switch on the wall." I could reach the switch without getting up, and I did. The lights went out. I hadn't expected that, and I groped at arm's length. Then the lights came on again, and I turned back, relieved. But the lights weren't on; I was looking at the street!

Now, all this happened while I was dripping beer and trying to keep my balance on a tottering chair—the street moved, I didn't and it was day and it was night and I was in front of the Book-Cadillac and I was going into the Motor Bar and I was watching myself order a beer and I knew I was wide awake and not dreaming. In a panic I scrabbled off the floor, shedding chairs and beer like an umbrella while I ripped my nails feeling frantically for that light switch. By the time I found it—and all the while I was watching myself pound the bar for the barkeep—I was really in fine fettle, just about ready to collapse. Out of thin air right into a nightmare. At last I found the switch.

The Mexican was looking at me with the queerest expression I've ever seen, like he'd baited a mousetrap and caught a frog. Me? I suppose I looked like I'd seen the devil himself. Maybe I had. The beer was all over the floor and I barely made it to the nearest chair.

"What," I managed to get out, "what was that?"

The lid of the radio went down. "I felt like that too, the first time. I'd forgotten."

My fingers were too shaky to get out a cigarette, and I ripped off the top of the package. "I said, what was that?"

He sat down. "That was you, in the Motor Bar, at eight last night." I must have looked blank as he handed me another paper cup. Automatically I held it out to be refilled.

"Look here—" I started.

"I suppose it is a shock. I'd forgotten what I felt like the first time I . . . I don't care much any more. Tomorrow I'm going out to Phillips Radio." That made no sense to me, and I said so. He went on.

"I'm licked. I'm flat broke. I don't give a care any more. I'll settle for cash and live off the royalties." The story came out, slowly at first, then faster until he was pacing the floor. I guess he was tired of having no one to talk to.

His name was Miguel Jose Zapata Laviada. I told him mine; Lefko. Ed Lefko. He was the son of sugar beet workers who had emigrated from Mexico somewhere in the Twenties. They were sensible enough not to quibble when their oldest son left the back-breaking Michgan fields to seize the chance provided by a NYA scholarship. When the scholarship ran out, he'd worked in garages, driven trucks, clerked in stores, and sold brushes door-to-door to exist and learn. The Army cut short his education with the First Draft to make him a radar technician; the Army had given him an honorable discharge and an idea so nebulous as to be almost merely a hunch. Jobs were plentiful then, and it wasn't too hard to end up with enough money to rent a trailer and fill it with Army surplus radio and radar equipment. One year ago he'd finished what he'd started, finished underfed, underweight, and overexcited. But successful, because he had it.

"It" he installed in a radio cabinet, both for ease in handling and for camouflage. For reasons that will become apparent, he didn't dare apply for a patent. I looked "it" over pretty carefully. Where the phonograph turntable and radio controls had been were vernier dials galore. One big one was numbered 1 to 24, a couple were numbered 1 to 60, and there were a dozen or so numbered 1 to 25, plus two or three with no numbers at all. Closest of all it resembled one of these fancy radio or motor testers found in a super superservice station. That was all, except that there was a sheet of heavy plywood hiding whatever was installed in place of the radio chassis and speaker. A perfectly innocent cache for—

Daydreams are swell. I suppose we've all had our share of mental wealth or fame or travel or fantasy. But to sit in a chair and drink warm beer and realize that the dream of ages isn't a dream anymore, to feel like a god, to know that just by turning a few dials you can see and watch anything, anybody, anywhere, that has ever happened—it still bothers me once in a while.

I know this much, that it's high frequency stuff. And there's a lot of mercury and copper and wiring of metals cheap and easy to find, but what goes where, or how, least of all, why, is out of my line. Light has mass and energy, and that mass always loses part of itself and can be translated back to electricity, or something. Mike Laviada himself says that what he stumbled on and developed was nothing new, that long before the War it had been observed many times by men like Compton and Michelson and Pfeiffer, who discarded it as a useless laboratory effect. And, of course, that was before atomic research took precedence over everything.

When the first shock wore off—and Mike had to give me another demonstration—I must have made quite a sight. Mike tells me I couldn't sit down. I'd pop up and gallop up and down the floor of that ancient store kicking chairs out of my way or stumbling over them, all the time gobbling out words and disconnected sentences faster than my tongue could trip. Finally it filtered through that he was laughing at me. I didn't see where it was any laughing matter, and I prodded him. He began to get angry.

"I know what I have," he snapped. "I'm not the biggest fool in the world, as you seem to think. Here, watch this," and he went back to the radio. "Turn out the light." I did, and there I was watching myself at the Motor Bar again, a lot happier this time. "Watch this."

The bar backed away. Out in the street, two blocks down to the City Hall. Up the steps to the Council Room. No one there. Then Council was in session, then they were gone again. Not a picture, not a projection of a lantern slide, but a slice of life about twelve feet square. If we were close, the field of view was narrow. If we were farther away, the background was just as much in focus as the foreground. The images, if you want to call them images, were just as real, just as lifelike as looking in the doorway of a room. Real they were, three-dimensional, stopped by only the back wall or the distance in the background. Mike was talking as he spun the dials, but I was too engrossed to pay much attention.

I yelped and grabbed and closed my eyes as you would if you were looking straight down with nothing between you and the ground except a lot of smoke and a few clouds. I winked my eyes open almost at the end of what must have been a long racing vertical dive, and there I was, looking at the street again.

"Go any place up to the Heaviside Layer, go down as deep as any hole, anywhere, any time." A blur, and the street changed into a glade of sparse pines. "Buried treasure. Sure. Find it, with what?" The trees disappeared and I reached back for the light switch as he dropped the lid of the radio and sat down.

"How are you going to make any money when you haven't got it to start?" No answer to that from me. "I ran an ad in the paper offering to recover lost articles; my first customer was the Law wanting to see my private detective's license. I've seen every big speculator in the country sit in his office buying and selling and making plans; what do you think would happen if I tried to peddle advance market information? I've watched the stock market get shoved up and down while I had barely the money to buy the paper that told me about it. I watched a bunch of Peruvian Indians bury the second ransom of Atuahalpa; I haven't the fare to get to Peru, or the money to buy the tools to dig." He got up and brought two more bottles. He went on. By that time I was getting a few ideas.

"I've watched scribes indite the books that burnt at Alexandria; who would buy, or who would believe me, if I copied one? What would happen if I went over to the Library and told them to rewrite their histories? How many would fight to tie a rope around my neck if they knew I'd watched them steal and murder and take a bath? What sort of a padded cell would I get if I showed up with a photograph of Washington, or Caesar? Or Christ?"

I agreed that it was all probably true, but—

"Why do you think I'm here now? You saw the picture I showed for a dime. A dime's worth, and that's all, because I didn't have the money to buy film or to make the picture as I knew I should." His tongue began to get tangled. He was excited. "I'm doing this because I haven't the money to get the things I need to get the money I'll need—" He was so disgusted he booted a chair halfway across the room. It was easy to see that if I had been around a little later, Phillips Radio would have profited. Maybe I'd have been better off, too.

Now, although always I've been told that I'd never be worth a hoot, no one has ever accused me of being slow for a dollar. Especially an easy one. I saw money in front of me, easy money, the easiest and the quickest in the world. I saw, for a minute, so far in the future with me on top of the heap, that my head reeled and it was hard to breathe.

"Mike," I said, "let's finish that beer and go where we can get some more, maybe something to eat. We've got a lot of talking to do." So we did.

Beer is a mighty fine lubricant; I have always been a pretty smooth talker, and by the time we left the gin mill I had a pretty good idea of just what Mike had on his mind. By the time we'd bedded down for the night behind that beaverboard screen in the store, we were full-fledged partners. I don't recall our even shaking hands on the deal, but that partnership still holds good. Mike is ace high with me, and I guess it's the other way around, too. That was six years ago; it only took me a year or so to round some of the corners I used to cut.

Seven days after that, on a Tuesday, I was riding a bus to Grosse Pointe with a full briefcase. Two days after that I was riding back from Grosse Pointe in a shiny taxi, with empty briefcase and a pocketful of folding money. It was easy.

"Mr. Jones—or Smith—or Brown—I'm with Aristocrat Studios, Personal and Candid Portraits. We thought you might like this picture of you and . . . no, this is just a test proof. The negative is in our files. . . . Now, if you're really interested, I'll be back the day after tomorrow with our files. . . . I'm sure you will, Mr. Jones. Thank you, Mr. Jones. . . ."

Dirty? Sure. Blackmail is always dirty. But if I had a wife and family and a good reputation, I'd stick to the roast beef and forget the Roquefort. Very smelly Roquefort, at that. Mike liked it less than I did. It took some talking, and I had to drag out the old one about the ends justifying the means, and they could well afford it, anyway. Besides, if there was a squawk, they'd get the negatives free. Some of them were pretty bad.

So we had the cash; not too much, but enough to start. Before we took the next step there was plenty to decide. There are a lot of people who live by convincing millions that Sticko soap is better. We had a harder problem than that: we had, first, to make a salable and profitable product, and second, we had to convince many, many millions that our "Product" was absolutely honest and absolutely accurate. We all know that if you repeat something long enough and loud enough many—or most—will accept it as gospel truth. That called for publicity on an international scale. For the skeptics who know better than to accept advertising, no matter how blatant, we had to use another technique. And since we were going to get certainly only one chance, we had to be right the first time. Without Mike's machine the job would have been impossible; without it the job would have been unnecessary.

A lot of sweat ran under the bridge before we found what we thought—and we still do!—the only workable scheme. We picked the only possible way to enter every mind in the world without a fight; the field of entertainment. Absolute secrecy was imperative, and it was only when we reached the last decimal point that we made a move. We started like this.

First we looked for a suitable building, or Mike did, while I flew east, to Rochester, for a month. The building he rented was an old bank. We had the windows sealed, a flossy office installed in the front—the bulletproof glass was my idea—air conditioning, a portable bar, electrical wiring of whatever type Mike's little heart desired, and a blond secretary who thought she was working for M-E Experimental Laboratories. When I got back from Rochester I took over the job of keeping happy the stone masons and electricians, while Mike fooled around in our suite in the Book where he could look out the window at his old store. The last I heard, they were selling snake oil there. When the Studio, as we came to call it, was finished, Mike moved in and the blonde settled down to a routine of reading love stories and saying no to all the salesmen that wandered by. I left for Hollywood.

I spent a week digging through the files of Central Casting before I was satisfied, but it took a month of snooping and some under-the-table cash to lease a camera that would handle Trucolor film. That took the biggest load from my mind. When I got back to Detroit the big view camera had arrived from Rochester, with a truckload of glass color plates. Ready to go.

We made quite a ceremony of it. We closed the Venetian blinds and I popped the cork on one of the bottles of champagne I'd bought. The blond secretary was impressed; all she'd been doing for her salary was to accept delivery of packages and crates and boxes. We had no wine glasses, but we made no fuss about that. Too nervous and excited to drink any more than one bottle, we gave the rest to the blonde and told her to take the rest of the afternoon off. After she left—and I think she was disappointed at breaking up what could have been a good party—we locked up after her, went into the studio itself, locked up again and went to work.

I've mentioned that the windows were sealed. All the inside wall had been painted dull black, and with the high ceiling that went with that old bank lobby, it was impressive. But not gloomy. Midway in the studio was planted the big Trucolor camera, loaded and ready. Not much could we see of Mike's machine, but I knew it was off to the side, set to throw on the back wall. Not *on* the wall, understand, because the images produced are projected into the air, like the meeting of the rays of two searchlights. Mike lifted the lid and I could see him silhouetted against the tiny lights that lit the dials.

"Well?" he said expectantly.

I felt pretty good just then, right down to my billfold.

"It's all yours, Mike." A switch ticked over. There he was. There was a youngster, dead twenty-five hundred years, real enough, almost, to touch. Alexander. Alexander of Macedon.

Let's take that first picture in detail. I don't think I can ever forget what happened in the next year or so. First we followed Alexander through his life, from beginning to end. We skipped, of course, the little things he did, jumping ahead days and weeks and years at a time. Then we'd miss him, or find that he'd moved in space. That would mean we'd have to jump back and forth, like the artillery firing bracket or ranging shots, until we found him again. Helped only occasionally by his published lives, we were astounded to realize how much distortion had crept into his life. I often wonder why legends arise about the famous. Certainly their lives are as startling or appalling as fiction. And unfortunately we had to hold closely to the accepted histories. If we hadn't, every professor would have gone into his corner for a hearty sneer. We couldn't take that chance. Not at first.

After we knew approximately what had happened and where, we used our notes to go back to what had seemed a particularly photogenic section and work on that awhile. Eventually we had a fair idea of what we were actually going to film. Then we sat down and wrote an actual script to follow, making allowance for whatever shots we'd have to double in later. Mike used his machine as the projector, and I operated the Trucolor camera at a fixed focus, like taking moving pictures of a movie. As fast as we finished a reel it would go to Rochester for processing, instead of one of the Hollywood outfits that might have done it cheaper. Rochester is so used to horrible amateur stuff that I doubt if anyone ever looks at anything. When the reel was returned we'd run it ourselves to check our choice of scenes and color sense and so on.

For example, we had to show the traditional quarrels with his father, Philip. Most of that we figured on doing with doubles, later. Olympias, his mother, and the fangless snakes she affected, didn't need any doubling, as we used an angle and amount of distance that didn't call for actual conversation. The scene where Alexander rode the bucking horse no one else could ride came out of some biographer's head, but we thought it was so famous we couldn't leave it out. We dubbed the close-ups later, and the actual horseman was a young Scythian who hung around the royal stables for his keep. Roxanne was real enough, like the rest of the Persian's wives that Alexander took over. Luckily most of them had enough poundage to look luscious. Philip and Parmenio and the rest of the characters were heavily bearded, which made easy the necessary doubling and dubbing-in the necessary speech. (If you ever saw them shave in those days, you'd know why whiskers were popular.)

The most trouble we had with the interior shots. Smoky wicks in a bowl of lard, no matter how plentiful, were too dim even for fast film. Mike got around that by running the Trucolor camera at a single frame a second, with his machine paced accordingly. That accounts for the startling clarity and depth of focus we got from a lens well stopped down. We had all the time in the world to choose the best possible scenes and camera angles; the best actors in the world, expensive camera booms, or repeated retakes under the most exacting director couldn't compete with us. We had a lifetime from which to choose.

Eventually we had on film about eighty per cent of what you saw in the finished picture. Roughly we spliced the reels together and sat there entranced at what we had actually done. Even more exciting, even more spectacular than we'd dared to hope, the lack of continuity and sound didn't stop us from realizing that we'd done a beautiful job. We'd done all we could, and the worst was yet to come. So we sent for more champagne and told the blonde we had cause for celebration. She giggled.

"What are you doing in there, anyway?" she asked. "Every salesman who comes to the door wants to know what you're making."

I opened the first bottle. "Just tell them you don't know."

"That's just what I've been telling them. They think I'm awfully dumb." We all laughed at the salesmen.

Mike was thoughtful. "If we're going to do this sort of thing very often, we ought to have some of these fancy hollow-stemmed glasses."

The blonde was pleased with that. "And we could keep them in my bottom drawer." Her nose wrinkled prettily. "These bubbles— You know, this is the only time I've ever had champagne, except at a wedding, and then it was only one glass."

"Pour her another," Mike suggested. "Mine's empty, too."
I did. "What did you do with those bottles you took home
last time?"

A blush and a giggle. "My father wanted to open them,
but I told him you said to save it for a special occasion."

By that time I had my feet on her desk. "This is the special
occasion, then," I invited. "Have another, Miss . . . what's
your first name, anyway? I hate being formal after working
hours."

She was shocked. "And you and Mr. Laviada sign my
checks every week! It's Ruth."

"Ruth. Ruth." I rolled it around the piercing bubbles, and
it sounded all right.

She nodded. "And your name is Edward, and Mr. Laviada's is Migwell. Isn't it?" And she smiled at him.

"Mi*gell*," he smiled back. "An old Spanish custom. Usually shortened to Mike."

"If you'll hand me another bottle," I offered, "shorten Edward to Ed." She handed it over.

By the time we got to the fourth bottle we were as thick as
bugs in a rug. It seems that she was twenty-four, free, and
single, and loved champagne.

"But," she burbled fretfully, "I wish I knew what you were
doing in there all hours of the day and night. I know you're
here at night sometimes because I've seen your car out in
front."

Mike thought that over. "Well," he said a little unsteadily,
"we take pictures." He blinked one eye. "Might even take
pictures of you if we were approached properly."

I took over. "We take pictures of models."

"Oh, no."

"Yes. Models of things and people and whatnot. Little
ones. We make it look like it's real." I think she was a trifle
disappointed.

"Well, now I know, and that makes me feel better. I sign
all those bills from Rochester and I don't know what I'm
signing for. Except that they must be film or something."

"That's just what it is; film and things like that."

"Well, it bothered me— No, there's two more behind the
fan."

Only two more. She had a capacity. I asked her how she
would like a vacation. She hadn't thought about a vacation
just yet.

I told her she'd better start thinking about it. "We're leaving day after tomorrow for Los Angeles, Hollywood."

"The day after tomorrow? Why—"

I reassured her. "You'll get paid just the same. But there's no telling how long we'll be gone, and there doesn't seem to be much use in your sitting around here with nothing to do."

From Mike, "Let's have that bottle." And I handed it to him. I went on.

"You'll get your checks just the same. If you want, we'll pay you in advance so—"

I was getting full of champagne, and so were we all. Mike was humming softly to himself, happy as a taco. The blonde, Ruth, was having a little trouble with my left eye. I knew just how she felt, because I was having a little trouble watching where she overlapped the swivel chair. Blue eyes, sooo tall, fuzzy hair. Hm-m-m. All work and no play— She handed me the last bottle.

Demurely she hid a tiny hiccup. "I'm going to save all the corks— No I won't either. My father would want to know what I'm thinking of, drinking with my bosses."

I said it wasn't a good idea to annoy your father. Mike said why fool with bad ideas, when he had a good one. We were interested. Nothing like a good idea to liven things up.

Mike was expansive as the very devil. "Going to Los Angeles."

We nodded solemnly.

"Going to Los Angeles to work."

Another nod.

"Going to work in Los Angeles. What will we do for pretty blonde girl to write letters?"

Awful. No pretty blonde to write letters and drink champagne. Sad case.

"Gotta hire somebody to write letters anyway. Might not be blonde. No blondes in Hollywood. No good ones, anyway. So—"

I saw the wonderful idea, and finished for him. "So we take pretty blonde to Los Angeles to write letters!"

What an idea that was! One bottle sooner and its brilliancy would have been dimmed. Ruth bubbled like a fresh bottle and Mike and I sat there, smirking like mad.

"But I can't! I couldn't leave day after tomorrow just like that—!"

Mike was magnificent. "Who said day after tomorrow? Changed our minds. Leave right now."

She was appalled. "Right now! Just like that?"

"Right now. Just like that." I was firm.

"But—"

"No buts. Right now. Just like that."

"Nothing to wear—"

"Buy clothes any place. Best ones in Los Angeles."

"But my hair—"

Mike suggested a haircut in Hollywood, maybe?

I pounded the table. It felt solid. "Call the airport. Three tickets."

She called the airport. She intimidated easy.

The airport said we could leave for Chicago any time on the hour, and change there for Los Angeles. Mike wanted to know why she was wasting time on the telephone when we could be on our way. Holding up the wheels of progress, emery dust in the gears. One minute to get her hat.

"Call Pappy from the airport."

Her objections were easily brushed away with a few word-pictures of how much fun there was to be had in Hollywood. We left a sign on the door, "Gone to Lunch—Back in December," and made the airport in time for the four o'clock plane, with no time left to call Pappy. I told the parking attendant to hold the car until he heard from me and we made it up the steps and into the plane just in time. The steps were taken away, the motors snorted, and we were off, with Ruth holding fast her hat in an imaginary breeze.

There was a two-hour layover in Chicago. They don't serve liquor at the airport, but an obliging cab driver found us a convenient bar down the road, where Ruth made her call to her father. Cautiously we stayed away from the telephone booth, but from what Ruth told us, he must have read her the riot act. The bartender didn't have champagne, but gave us the special treatment reserved for those that order it. The cab driver saw that we made the liner two hours later.

In Los Angeles we registered at the Commodore, cold sober and ashamed of ourselves. The next day Ruth went shopping for clothes for herself, and for us. We gave her the sizes and enough money to soothe her hangover. Mike and I did some telephoning. After breakfast we sat around until the desk clerk announced a Mr. Lee Johnson to see us.

Lee Johnson was the brisk professional type, the high-bracket salesman. Tall, rather homely, a clipped way of talking. We introduced ourselves as embryo producers. His eyes brightened when we said that. His meat.

"Not exactly the way you think," I told him. "We have already eighty percent or better of the final print."

He wanted to know where he came in.

"We have several thousand feet of Trucolor film. Don't bother asking where or when we got it. This footage is silent. We'll need sound and, in places, speech dubbed in."

He nodded. "Easy enough. What condition is the master?"

"Perfect condition. It's in the hotel vault right now. There are gaps in the story to fill. We'll need quite a few male and female characters. And all of these will have to do their doubling for cash, and not for screen credit."

Johnson raised his eyebrows. "And why? Out here screen credit is bread and butter."

"Several reasons. This footage was made—never mind where—with the understanding that film credit would favor no one."

"If you're lucky enough to catch your talent between pictures you might get away with it. But if your footage is worth working with, my boys will want screen credit. And I think they're entitled to it."

I said that was reasonable enough. The technical crews were essential, and I was prepared to pay well. Particularly to keep their mouths closed until the print was ready for final release. Maybe even after that.

"Before we go any further," Johnson rose and reached for his hat, "let's take a look at that print. I don't know if we can—"

I knew what he was thinking. Amateurs. Home movies. Feelthy peekchures, mebbe?

We got the reels out of the hotel safe and drove to his laboratory, out Sunset. The top was down on his convertible and Mike hoped audibly that Ruth would have sense enough to get sport shirts that didn't itch.

"Wife?" Johnson asked carelessly.

"Secretary," Mike answered just as casually. "We flew in last night and she's out getting us some light clothes." Johnson's estimation of us rose visibly.

A porter came out of the laboratory to carry the suitcase containing the film reels. It was a long, low building, with the offices at the front and the actual laboratories tapering off at the rear. Johnson took us in the side door and called for someone whose name we didn't catch. The anonymous one was a projectionist who took the reels and disappeared into the back of the projection room. We sat for a minute in the soft easy chairs until the projectionist buzzed ready. Johnson glanced at us and we nodded. He clicked a switch on the arm of his chair and the overhead lights went out. The picture started.

It ran a hundred and ten minutes as it stood. We both watched Johnson like a cat at a rat hole. When the tag end showed white on the screen he signaled with the chairside buzzer for lights. They came on. He faced us.

"Where did you get that print?"

Mike grinned at him. "Can we do business?"

"Do business?" He was vehement. "You bet your life we can do business. We'll do the greatest business you ever saw!"

The projection man came down. "Hey, that's all right. Where'd you get it?"

Mike looked at me. I said, "This isn't to go any further."

Johnson looked at his man, who shrugged. "None of my business."

I dangled the hook. "That wasn't made here. Never mind where."

Johnson rose and struck, hook, line and sinker. "Europe! Hm-m-m. Germany. No, France. Russia, maybe. Einstein, or Eisenstein, or whatever his name is?"

I shook my head. "That doesn't matter. The leads are all dead, or out of commission, but their heirs . . . well, you get what I mean."

Johnson saw what I meant. "Absolutely right. No point taking any chances. Where's the rest—?"

"Who knows? We were lucky to salvage that much. Can do?"

"Can do." He thought for a minute. "Get Bernstein in here. Better get Kessler and Marrs, too." The projectionist left. In a few minutes Kessler, a heavy-set man, and Marrs, a young, nervous chain-smoker, came in with Bernstein, the sound man. We were introduced all around and Johnson asked if we minded sitting through another showing.

"Nope. We like it better than you do."

Not quite. Kessler and Marrs and Bernstein, the minute the film was over, bombarded us with startled questions. We gave them the same answers we'd given Johnson. But we were pleased with the reception, and said so.

Kessler grunted. "I'd like to know who was behind that camera. Best I've seen, by Cripes, since 'Ben Hur.' Better than 'Ben Hur.' The boy's good."

I grunted right back at him. "That's the only thing I can tell you. The photography was done by the boys you're talking to right now. Thanks for the kind word."

All four of them stared.

Mike said, "That's right."

"Hey, hey!" from Marrs. They all looked at us with new respect. It felt good.

Johnson broke into the silence when it became awkward. "What's next on the score card?"

We got down to cases. Mike, as usual, was content to sit there with his eyes half closed, taking it all in, letting me do all the talking.

"We want sound dubbed in all the way through."

"Pleasure," said Bernstein.

"At least a dozen, maybe more, of speaking actors with a close resemblance to the leads you've seen."

Johnson was confident. "Easy. Central Casting has everybody's picture since the Year One."

"I know. We've already checked that. No trouble there. They'll have to take the cash and let the credit go, for reasons I've already explained to Mr. Johnson."

A moan from Marrs. "I bet I get that job."

Johnson was snappish. "You do. What else?" to me.

I didn't know. "Except that we have no plans for distribution as yet. That will have to be worked out."

"Like falling off a log." Johnson was happy about that. "One look at the rushes and United Artists would spit in Shakespeare's eye."

Marrs came in. "What about the other shots? Got a writer lined up?"

"We've got what will pass for the shooting script, or will have in a week or so. Want to go over it with us?"

He'd like that.

"How much time have we got?" interposed Kessler. "This is going to be a job. When do we want it?" Already it was "we."

"Yesterday is when we want it," snapped Johnson, and he rose. "Any ideas about music? No? We'll try for Werner

Janssen and his boys. Bernstein, you're responsible for that print from now on. Kessler, get your crew in and have a look at it. Marrs, you'll go with Mr. Lefko and Mr. Laviada through the files at Central Casting at their convenience. Keep in touch with them at the Commodore. Now, if you'll step into my office, we'll discuss the financial arrangements—"

As easy as all that.

Oh, I don't say that it was easy work or anything like that, because in the next few months we were playing Busy Bee. What with running down the only one registered at Central Casting who looked like Alexander himself—he turned out to be a young Armenian who had given up hope of ever being called from the extra lists and had gone home to Santee—casting and rehearsing the rest of the actors and swearing at the costumers and the boys who built the sets, we were kept hopping. Even Ruth, who had reconciled her father with soothing letters, for once earned her salary. We took turns shooting dictation at her until we had a script that satisfied Mike and myself and young Marrs, who turned out to be a fox on dialogue.

What I really meant is that it was easy, and immensely gratifying, to crack the shell of the tough boys who had seen epics and turkeys come and go. They were really impressed by what we had done. Kessler was disappointed when we refused to be bothered with photographing the rest of the film. We just batted our eyes and said that we were too busy, that we were perfectly confident that he would do as well as we. He outdid himself, and us. I don't know what we would have done if he had asked us for any concrete advice. I suppose, when I think it all over, that the boys we met and worked with were so tired of working with the usual mine-run Grade B's, that they were glad to meet someone that knew the difference between glycerin tears and reality and didn't care if it cost two dollars extra. They had us placed as a couple of city slickers with plenty on the ball. I hope.

Finally it was all over with. We all sat in the projection room; Mike and I, Marrs and Johnson, Kessler and Bernstein, and all the lesser technicians that had split up the really enormous amount of work that had been done watched the finished product. It was terrific. Everyone had done his work well. When Alexander came on the screen, he *was* Alexander

the Great. (The Armenian kid got a good bonus for that.)
All that blazing color, all that wealth and magnificence and
glamor seemed to flare right out of the screen and sear across
your mind. Even Mike and I, who had seen the original, were
on the edge of our seats.

The sheer realism and magnitude of the battle scenes, I
think, really made the picture. Gore, of course, is glorious
when it's all make-believe and the dead get up to go to lunch.
But when Bill Mauldin sees a picture and sells a breathless
article on the similarity of infantrymen of all ages—well,
Mauldin knows what war is like. So did the infantrymen
throughout the world who wrote letters comparing Alexander's Arbela to Anzio and the Argonne. The weary peasant,
not stolid at all, trudging and trudging into mile after mile of
those dust-laden plains and ending as a stinking, naked,
ripped corpse peeipng from under a mound of flies isn't any
different when he carries a sarissa instead of a rifle. That
we'd tried to make obvious, and we succeeded.

When the lights came up in the projection room we knew
we had a winner. Individually we shook hands all around,
proud as a bunch of penguins, and with chests out as far.
The rest of the men filed out and we retired to Johnson's office. He poured a drink all around and got down to business.

"How about releases?"

I asked him what he thought.

"Write your own ticket," he shrugged. "I don't know
whether or not you know it, but the word has already gone
around that you've got something."

I told him we'd had calls at the hotel from various sources,
and named them.

"See what I mean? I know those babies. Kiss them out if
you want to keep your shirt. And while I'm at it, you owe us
quite a bit. I suppose you've got it."

"We've got it."

"I was afraid you would. If you didn't, I'd be the one that
would have your shirt." He grinned, but we all knew he
meant it. "All right, that's settled. Let's talk about release.

"There are two or three outfits around town that will want
a crack at it. My boys will have the word spread around in
no time; there's no point in trying to keep them quiet any
longer. I know—they'll have sense enough not to talk about
the things you want off the record. I'll see to that. But you're
top dog right now. You got loose cash, you've got the biggest

potential gross I've ever seen, and you don't have to take the first offer. That's important, in this game."

"How would you like to handle it yourself?"

"I'd like to try. The outfit I'm thinking of needs a feature right now, and they don't know I know it. They'll pay and pay. What's in it for me?"

"That," I said, "we can talk about later. And I think I know just what you're thinking. We'll take the usual terms and we don't care if you hold up whoever you deal with. What we don't know won't hurt us." That's what he was thinking, all right. That's a cutthroat game out there.

"Good. Kessler, get your setup ready for duplication."

"Always ready."

"Marrs, start the ball rolling on publicity . . . what do you want to do about that?" to us.

Mike and I had talked about that before. "As far as we're concerned," I said slowly, "do as you think best. Personal publicity, O.K. We won't look for it, but we won't dodge it. As far as that goes, we're the local yokels making good. Soft pedal any questions about where the picture was made, without being too obvious. You're going to have trouble when you talk about the nonexistent actors, but you ought to be able to figure out something."

Marrs groaned and Johnson grinned. "He'll figure out something."

"As far as technical credit goes, we'll be glad to see you get all you can, because you've done a swell job." Kessler took that as a personal compliment, and it was. "You might as well know now, before we go any further, that some of the work came right from Detroit." They all sat up at that.

"Mike and I have a new process of model and trick work." Kessler opened his mouth to say something but thought better of it. "We're not going to say what was done, or how much was done in the laboratory, but you'll admit that it defies detection."

About that they were fervent. "I'll say it defies detection. In the game this long and process work gets by me . . . where—"

"I'm not going to tell you that. What we've got isn't patented and won't be, as long as we can hold it up." There wasn't any griping there. These men knew process work when they saw it. If they didn't see it, it was good. They could understand why we'd want to keep a process that good a secret.

"We can practically guarantee there'll be more work for you to do later on." Their interest was plain. "We're not going to predict when, or make any definite arrangement, but we still have a trick or two in the deck. We like the way we've been getting along, and we want to stay that way. Now, if you'll excuse us, we have a date with a blonde."

Johnson was right about the bidding for the release. We—or rather Johnson—made a very profitable deal with United Amusement and the affiliated theaters. Johnson, the bandit, got his percentage from us and likely did better with United. Kessler and Johnson's boys took huge ads in the trade journals to boast about their connections with the Academy Award Winner. Not only the Academy, but every award that ever went to any picture. Even the Europeans went overboard. They're the ones that make a fetish of realism. They knew the real thing when they saw it, and so did everyone else.

Our success went to Ruth's head. In no time she wanted a secretary. At that, she needed one to fend off the screwballs that popped out of the woodwork. So we let her hire a girl to help out. She picked a good typist, about fifty. Ruth is a smart girl, in a lot of ways. Her father showed signs of wanting to see the Pacific, so we raised her salary on condition he'd stay away. The three of us were having too much fun.

The picture opened at the same time in both New York and Hollywood. We went to the premiere in great style with Ruth between us, swollen like a trio of bullfrogs. It's a great feeling to sit on the floor, early in the morning, and read reviews that make you feel like floating. It's a better feeling to have a mintful of money. Johnson and his men were right along with us. I don't think he could have been too flush in the beginning, and we all got a kick out of riding the crest.

It was a good-sized wave, too. We had all the personal publictiy we wanted, and more. Somehow the word was out that we had a new gadget for process photography, and every big studio in town was after what they thought would be a mighty economical thing to have around. The studios that didn't have a spectacle scheduled looked at the receipts of "Alexander" and promptly scheduled a spectacle. We drew some very good offers, Johnson said, but we made a series of long faces and broke the news that we were leaving for Detroit the next day, and to hold the fort awhile. I don't think he thought we actually meant it, but we did. We left the next day.

Back in Detroit we went right to work, helped by the knowledge that we were on the right track. Ruth was kept busy turning away the countless would-be visitors. We admitted no reporters, no salesmen, no one. We had no time. We were using the view camera. Plate after plate we sent to Rochester for developing. A print of each was returned to us and the plate was held in Rochester for our disposal. We sent to New York for a representative of one of the biggest publishers in the country. We made a deal.

Your main library has a set of the books we published, if you're interested. Huge heavy volumes, hundreds of them, each page a razor-sharp blowup from an 8x10 negative. A set of those books went to every major library and university in the world. Mike and I got a real kick out of solving some of the problems that have had savants guessing for years. In the Roman volume, for example, we solved the trireme problem with a series of pictures, not only the interior of a trireme, but a line-of-battle quinquereme. (Naturally, the professors and amateur yachtsmen weren't convinced at all.) We had a series of aerial shots of the City of Rome taken a hundred years apart, over a millennium. Aerial views of Ravenna and Londinium, Palmyra and Pompeii, of Eboracum and Byzantium. Oh, we had the time of our lives! We had a volume for Greece and for Rome, for Persia and for Crete, for Egypt and for the Eastern Empire. We had pictures of the Parthenon and the Pharos, pictures of Hannibal and Caractacus and Vercingetorix, pictures of the Walls of Babylon and the building of the pyramids and the palace of Sargon, pages from the Lost Books of Livy and the plays of Euripedes. Things like that.

Terrifically expensive, a second printing sold at cost to a surprising number of private individuals. If the cost had been less, historical interest would have become even more the fad of the moment.

When the flurry had almost died down, some Italian digging in the hitherto-unexcavated section of ash-buried Pompeii, dug right into a tiny buried temple right where our aerial shot had showed it to be. His budget was expanded and he found more ash-covered ruins that agreed with our aerial layout, ruins that hadn't seen the light of day for almost two thousand years. Everyone promptly wailed that we were the luckiest guessers in captivity; the head of some California cult suspected aloud that we were the reincarnations of two gladiators named Joe.

To get some peace and quiet Mike and I moved into our studio, lock, stock, and underwear. The old bank vault had never been removed, at our request, and it served well to store our equipment when we weren't around. All the mail Ruth couldn't handle we disposed of, unread; the old bank building began to look like a well-patronized soup kitchen. We hired burly private detectives to handle the more obnoxious visitors and subscribed to a telegraphic protective service. We had another job to do, another full-length feature.

We still stuck to the old historical theme. This time we tried to do what Gibbon did in the Decline and Fall of the Roman Empire. And, I think, we were rather successful, at that. In four hours you can't completely cover two thousand years, but you can, as we did, show the cracking up of a great civilization, and how painful the process can be. The criticism we drew for almost ignoring Christ and Christianity was unjust, we think, and unfair. Very few knew then, or know now, that we had included, as a kind of trial balloon, some footage of Christ Himself, and His times. This footage we had to cut. The Board of Review, as you know, is both Catholic and Protestant. They—the Board—went right up in arms. We didn't protest very hard when they claimed our "treatment" was irreverent, indecent, and biased and inaccurate "by any Christian standard. Why," they wailed, "it doesn't even look like Him." And they were right; it didn't. Not any picture *they* ever saw. Right then and there we decided that it didn't pay to tamper with anyone's religious beliefs. That's why you've never seen anything emanating from us that conflicted even remotely with the accepted historical, sociological, or religious features of Someone Who Knew Better. That Roman picture, by the way—but not accidentally —deviated so little from the textbooks you conned in school that only a few enthusiastic specialists called our attention to what they insisted were errors. We were still in no position to do any mass rewriting of history, because we were unable to reveal just where we got our information.

Johnson, when he saw the Roman epic, mentally clicked high his heels. His men went right to work, and we handled the job as we had the first. One day Kessler got me in a corner, dead earnest.

"Ed," he said, "I'm going to find out where you got that footage if it's the last thing I ever do."

I told him that some day he would.

"And I don't mean some day, either; I mean right now. That bushwa about Europe might go once, but not twice. I know better, and so does everyone else. Now, what about it?"

I told him I'd have to consult Mike and I did. We were up against it. We called a conference.

"Kessler tells me he has troubles. I guess you all know what they are." They all knew.

Johnson spoke up. "He's right, too. We know better. Where did you get it?"

I turned to Mike. "Want to do the talking?"

A shake of his head. "You're doing all right."

"All right." Kessler hunched a little forward and Marrs lit another cigarette. "We weren't lying and we weren't exaggerating when we said the actual photography was ours. Every frame of film was taken right here in this country, within the last few months. Just how—I won't mention why or where—we can't tell you just now." Kessler snorted in disgust. "Let me finish.

"We all know that we're cashing in, hand over fist. And we're going to cash in some more. We have, on our personal schedule, five more pictures. Three of that five we want you to handle as you did the others. The last two of the five will show you both the reason for all the childish secrecy, as Kessler calls it, and another motive that we have so far kept hidden. The last two pictures will show you both our motives and our methods; one is as important as the other. Now—is that enough? Can we go ahead on that basis?"

It wasn't enough for Kessler. "That doesn't mean a thing to me. What are we, a bunch of hacks?"

Johnson was thinking about his bank balance. "Five more. Two years, maybe four."

Marrs was skeptical. "Who do you think you're going to kid that long? Where's your studio? Where's your talent? Where do you shoot your exteriors? Where do you get your costumes and your extras? In one single shot you've got forty thousand extras, if you've got one! Maybe you can shut *me* up, but who's going to answer the questions that Metro and Fox and Paramount and RKO have been asking? Those boys aren't fools, they know their business. How do you expect me to handle any publicity when I don't know what the score is myself?"

Johnson told him to pipe down for a while and let him think. Mike and I didn't like this one bit. But what could we do—tell the truth and end up in a straitjacket?

"Can we do it this way?" he finally asked. "Marrs, these boys have an in with the Soviet Government. They work in some place in Siberia, maybe. Nobody gets within miles of there. No one ever knows what the Russians are doing—"

"Nope!" Marrs was definite. "Any hint that these came from Russia and we'd all be a bunch of Reds. Cut the gross in half."

Johnson began to pick up speed. "All right, not from Russia. From one of these little republics fringed around Siberia or Armenia or one of those places. They're not Russian-made films at all. In fact, they've been made by some of these Germans and Austrians the Russians took over and moved after the War. The war fever has died down enough for people to realize that the Germans knew their stuff occasionally. The old sympathy racket for these refugees struggling with faulty equipment, lousy climate, making super-spectacles and smuggling them out under the nose of the Gestapo or whatever they call it—That's it!"

Doubtfully, from Marrs: "And the Russians tell the world we're nuts, that they haven't got any loose Germans?"

That, Johnson overrode. "Who reads the back pages? Who pays any attention to what the Russians say? Who cares? They might even think we're telling the truth and start looking around their own backyard for something that isn't there! All right with you?" to Mike and myself.

I looked at Mike and he looked at me.

"O.K. with us."

"O.K. with the rest of you? Kessler? Bernstein?"

They weren't too agreeable, and certainly not happy, but they agreed to play games until we gave the word.

We were warm in our thanks. "You won't regret it."

Kessler doubted that very much, but Johnson eased them all out, back to work. Another hurdle leaped, or sidestepped.

"Rome" was released on schedule and drew the same friendly reviews. "Friendly" is the wrong word for reviews that stretched ticket line-ups blocks long. Marrs did a good

job on the publicity. Even that chain of newspapers that afterward turned on us so viciously fell for Marrs' word
wizardry and ran full-page editorials urging the reader to see
"Rome."

With our third picture, "Flame Over France," we corrected
a few misconceptions about the French Revolution, and began stepping on a few tender toes. Luckily, however, and not
altogether by design, there happened to be in power in Paris
a liberal government. They backed us to the hilt with the
confirmation we needed. At our request they released a lot of
documents that had hitherto conveniently been lost in the
cavernous recesses of the Bibliotheque Nationale. I've forgotten the name of whoever happened to be the perennial pretender to the French throne. At, I'm sure, the subtle prodding
of one of Marrs' ubiquitous publicity men, the pretender sued
us for our whole net, alleging the defamation of the good
name of the Bourbons. A lawyer Johnson dug up for us
sucked the poor chump into a courtroom and cut him to bits.
Not even six cents damages did he get. Samuels, the lawyer,
and Marrs drew a good-sized bonus, and the pretender
moved to Honduras.

Somewhere around this point, I believe, did the tone of
the press begin to change. Up until then we'd been regarded
as crosses between Shakespeare and Barnum. Since long obscure facts had been dredged into the light, a few well-known
pessimists began to wonder *sotto voce* if we weren't just a
pair of blasted pests. "Should leave well enough alone." Only
our huge advertising budget kept them from saying more.

I'm going to stop right here and say something about our
personal life while all this was going on. Mike kept in the
background pretty well, mostly because he wanted it that
way. He let me do all the talking and stick my neck out
while he sat in the most comfortable chair in sight. I yelled
and I argued and he just sat there; hardly ever a word coming out of that dark-brown pan, certainly never an indication
showing that behind those polite eyebrows there was a
brain—and a sense of humor and wit—faster and as deadly
as a bear trap. Oh, I know we played around, sometimes
with a loud bang, but we were, ordinarily, too busy and too
preoccupied with what we were doing to waste any time.
Ruth, while she was with us, was a good dancing and drinking partner. She was young, she was almost what you'd call
beautiful, and she seemed to like being with us. For a while I

had a few ideas about her that might have developed into something serious. We both—I should say, all three of us—found out in time that we looked at a lot of things too differently. So we weren't too disappointed when she signed with Metro. Her contract meant what she thought was all the fame and money and happiness in the world, plus the personal attention she was doubtless entitled to have. They put her in Class B's and serials and she, financially, is better off than she ever expected to be. Emotionally, I don't know. We heard from her some time ago, and I think she's about due for another divorce. Maybe it's just as well.

But let's get away from Ruth. I'm ahead of myself, anyway. All this time Mike and I had been working together, our approach to the final payoff had been divergent. Mike was hopped on the idea of making a better world, and doing that by making war impossible. "War," he often said, "war of any kind is what has made man spend most of his history in merely staying alive. Now, with the atom to use, he has within himself the seed of self-extermination. So help me, Ed, I'm going to do my share of stopping that, or I don't see any point in living. I mean it!"

He did mean it. He told me that in almost the same words the first day we met. Then, I tagged that idea as a pipe dream picked up on an empty stomach. I saw his machine only as a path to a luxurious and personal Nirvana, and I thought he'd soon be going my way. I was wrong.

You can't live, or work, with a likable person without admiring some of the qualities that make that person likable. Another thing; it's a lot easier to worry about the woes of the world when you haven't any yourself. It's a lot easier to have a conscience when you can afford it. When I donned the rose-colored glasses half my battle was won; when I realized how grand a world this *could* be, the battle was over. That was about the time of "Flame Over France," I think. The actual time isn't important. What *is* important is that, from that time on, we became the tightest team possible. Since then about the only thing we differed on was the time to knock off for a sandwich. Most of our leisure time, what we had of it, was spent in locking up for the night, rolling out the portable bar, opening just enough beer to feel good, and relaxing. Maybe, after one or two, we might diddle the dials of the machine, and go rambling.

Together we'd been everywhere and seen everything. It

might be a good night to check up on François Villon, that
faker, or maybe we might chase around with Haroun-el-
Rashid. (If there was ever a man born a few hundred years
too soon, it was that careless caliph.) Or if we were in a bad
or discouraged mood we might follow the Thirty Years' War
for a while, or if we were real raffish we might inspect the
dressing rooms at Radio City. For Mike the crackup of At-
lantis had always had an odd fascination, probably because
he was afraid that man would do it again, now that he's rediscovered nuclear energy. And if I dozed off he was quite
apt to go back to the very Beginning, back to the start of the
world as we know it now. (It wouldn't do any good to tell
you what went before *that*.)

When I stop to think, it's probably just as well that neither
of us married. We, of course, had hopes for the future, but
we were both tired of the whole human race; tired of greedy
faces and hands. With a world that puts a premium on
wealth and power and strength, it's no wonder what decency
there is stems from fear of what's here now, or fear of what's
hereafter. We had seen so much of the hidden actions of the
world—call it snooping, if you like—that we learned to disregard the surface indications of kindness and good. Only once
did Mike and I ever look into the private life of someone we
knew and liked and respected. Once was enough. From that
day on we made it a point to take people as they seemed.
Let's get away from that.

The next two pictures we released in rapid succession; the
first "Fredom for Americans," the American Revolution, and
"The Brothers and the Guns," the American Civil War.
Bang! Every third politician, a lot of so-called "educators,"
and all the professional patriots started after our scalps. Every single chapter of the DAR, the Sons of Union Veterans,
and the Daughters of the Confederacy pounded their collec-
tive heads against the wall. The South went frantic; every
state in the Deep South and one state on the border flatly
banned both pictures, the second because it was truthful, and
the first because censorship is a contagious disease. They
stayed banned until the professional politicians got wise. The
bans were revoked, and the choke-collar and string-tie
brigade pointed to both pictures as horrible examples of what
some people actually believed and thought, and felt pleased
that someone had given them an opportunity to roll out the

barrel and beat the drums that sound sectional and racial hatred.

New England was tempted to stand on its dignity, but couldn't stand the strain. North of New York both pictures were banned. In New York state the rural representatives voted en bloc, and the ban was clamped on statewide. Special trains ran to Delaware, where the corporations were too busy to pass another law. Libel suits flew like confetti, and although the extras blared the filing of each new suit, very few knew that we lost not one. Although we had to appeal almost every suit to higher courts, and in some cases request a change of venue which was seldom granted, the documentary proof furnished by the record cleared us once we got to a judge, or series of judges, with no fences to mend.

It was a mighty rasp we drew over wounded ancestral pride. We had shown that not all the mighty had haloes of purest gold, that not all the Redcoats were strutting bullies— nor angels, and the British Empire, except South Africa, refused entry to both pictures and made violent passes at the State Department. The spectacle of Southern and New England congressmen approving the efforts of a foreign ambassador to suppress free speech drew hilarious hosannahs from certain quarters. H. L. Mencken gloated in the clover, doing loud nip-ups, and the newspapers hung on the triple-horned dilemma of anti-foreign, pro-patriotic, and quasi-logical criticism. In Detroit the Ku Klux Klan fired an anemic cross on our doorstep, and the Friendly Sons of St. Patrick, the NAACP, and the WCTU passed flattering resolutions. We forwarded the most vicious and obscene letters—together with a few names and addresses that hadn't been originally signed—to our lawyers and the Post Office Department. There were no convictions south of Illinois.

Johnson and his boys made hay. Johnson had pyramided his bets into an international distributing organization, and pushed Marrs into hiring every top press agent either side of the Rockies. What a job they did! In no time at all there were two definite schools of thought that overflowed into the public letter boxes. One school held that we had no business raking up old mud to throw, that such things were better left forgotten and forgiven, that nothing wrong had ever happened, and if it had, we were liars anyway. The other school reasoned more to our liking. Softly and slowly at first, then with a triumphant shout, this fact began to emerge; such things had actually happened, and could happen again, were possibly happening even now; had happened because twisted truth had too long left its imprint on international, sectional, and racial feelings. It pleased us when many began to agree, with us, that it is important to forget the past, but that it is even more important to understand and evaluate it with a generous and unjaundiced eye. That was what we were trying to bring out.

The banning that occurred in the various states hurt the gross receipts only a little, and we were vindicated in Johnson's mind. He had dolefully predicted loss of half the national gross because "you can't tell the truth in a movie and get away with it. Not if the house holds over three hundred." Not even on the stage? "Who goes to anything but a movie?"

So far things had gone just about as we'd planned. We'd earned and received more publicity, favorable and otherwise, than anyone living. Most of it stemmed from the fact that our doing had been newsworthy. Some, naturally, had been the ninety-day-wonder material that fills a thirsty newspaper. We had been very careful to make our enemies in the strata that can afford to fight back. Remember the old saw about knowing a man by the enemies he makes? Well, publicity was our ax. Here's how we put an edge on it.

I called Johnson in Hollywood. He was glad to hear from us. "Long time no see. What's the pitch, Ed?"

"I want some lip readers. And I want them yesterday, like you tell your boys."

"Lip readers? Are you nuts? What do you want with lip readers?"

"Never mind why. I want lip readers. Can you get them?"

"How should I know? What do you want them for?"

"I said, can you get them?"

He was doubtful. "I think you've been working too hard."

"Look—"

"Now, I didn't say I couldn't. Cool off. When do you want them? And how many?"

"Better write this down. Ready? I want lip readers for these languages: English, French, German, Russian, Chinese, Japanese, Greek, Belgian, Dutch and Spanish."

"*Ed Lefko, have you gone crazy?*"

I guess it didn't sound very sensible, at that. "Maybe I

have. But those languages are essential. If you run across any who can work in any other language, hang on to them. I might need them, too." I could see him sitting in front of his telephone, wagging his head like mad. Crazy. The heat must have got Lefko, good old Ed. "Did you hear what I said?"

"Yes, I heard you. If this is a rib—"

"No rib. Dead serious."

He began to get mad. "Where you think I'm going to get lip readers—out of my hat?"

"That's your worry. I'd suggest you start with the local School for the Deaf." He was silent. "Now, get this into your head; this isn't a rib, this is the real thing. I don't care what you do, or where you go, or what you spend—I want those lip readers in Hollywood when we get there or I want to know they're on the way."

"When are you going to get here?"

I said I wasn't sure. "Probably a day or two. We've got a few loose ends to clean up."

He swore a blue streak at the inequities of fate. "You'd better have a good story when you do—" I hung up.

Mike met me at the studio. "Talk to Johnson?" I told him, and he laughed. "Does sound crazy, I suppose. But he'll get them, if they exist and like money. He's the Original Resourceful Man."

I tossed my hat in a corner. "I'm glad this is about over. Your end caught up?"

"Set and ready to go. The films and the notes are on the way, the real estate company is ready to take over the lease, and the girls are paid up to date, with a little extra."

I opened a bottle of beer for myself. Mike had one. "How about the office files? How about the bar, here?"

"The files go to the bank to be stored. The bar? Hadn't thought about it."

The beer was cold. "Have it crated and send it to Johnson."

We grinned, together. "Johnson it is. He'll need it."

I nodded at the machine. "What about that?"

"That goes with us on the plane as air express." He looked closely at me. "What's the matter with you—jitters?"

"Nope. Willies. Same thing."

"Me, too. Your clothes and mine left this morning."

"Not even a clean shirt left?"

"Not even a clean shirt. Just like—"

I finished it. "—the first trip with Ruth. A little different, maybe."

Mike said slowly, "A lot different." I opened another beer. "Anything you want around here, anything else to be done?" I said no. "O.K. Let's get this over with. We'll put what we need in the car. We'll stop at the Courville Bar before we hit the airport."

I didn't get it. "There's still beer left—"

"But no champagne."

I got it. "O.K. I'm dumb, at times. Let's go."

We loaded the machine into the car, and the bar, left the studio keys at the corner grocery for the real estate company, and headed for the airport by way of the Courville Bar. Ruth was in California, but Joe had champagne. We got to the airport late.

Marrs met us in Los Angeles. "What's up? You've got Johnson running around in circles."

"Did he tell you why?"

"Sounds crazy to me. Couple of reporters inside. Got anything for them?"

"Not right now. Let's get going."

In Johnson's private office we got a chilly reception. "This better be good. Where do you expect to find someone to lipread in Chinese? Or Russian, for that matter?"

We all sat down. "What have you got so far?"

"Besides a headache?" He handed me a short list.

I scanned it. "How long before you can get them here?"

An explosion. "How long before I can get them here? Am I your errand boy?"

"For all practical purposes you are. Quit the fooling. How about it?" Marrs snickered at the look on Johnson's face.

"What are you smirking at, you moron?" Marrs gave in and laughed outright, and I did, too. "Go ahead and laugh. This isn't funny. When I called the State School for the Deaf they hung up. Thought I was some practical joker. We'll skip that.

"There's three women and a man on that list. They cover English, French, Spanish, and German. Two of them are working in the East, and I'm waiting for answers to telegrams I sent them. One lives in Pomona and one works for the Arizona School for the Deaf. That's the best I could do."

We thought that over. "Get on the phone. Talk to every state in the union if you have to, or overseas."

Johnson kicked the desk. "And what are you going to do with them, if I'm that lucky?"

"You'll find out. Get them on planes and fly them here, and we'll talk turkey when they get here. I want a projection room, not yours, and a good bonded court reporter."

He asked the world to appreciate what a life he led.

"Get in touch with us at the Commodore." To Marrs: "Keep the reporters away for a while. We'll have something for them later." Then we left.

Johnson never did find anyone who could lipread Greek. None, at least, that could speak English. The expert on Russian he dug out of Ambridge, in Pennsylvania, the Flemish and Holland Dutch expert came from Leyden, in the Netherlands, and at the last minute he stumbled upon a Korean who worked in Seattle as an inspector for the Chinese Government. Five women and two men. We signed them to an ironclad contract drawn by Samuels, who now handled all our legal work, I made a little speech before they signed.

"These contracts, as far as we've been able to verify, are going to control your personal and business life for the next year, and there's a clause that says we can extend that period for another year if we so desire. Let's get this straight. You are to live in a place of your own, which we will provide. You will be supplied with all necessities by our buyers. Any attempt at unauthorized communication will result in abrogation of the contract. Is that clear?

"Good. Your work will not be difficult, but it will be tremendously important. You will, very likely, be finished in three months, but you will be ready to go any place at any time at our discretion, naturally at our expense. Mr. Sorenson, as you are taking this down, you realize that this goes for you, too." He nodded.

"Your references, your abilities, and your past work have been thoroughly checked, and you will continue under constant observation. You will be required to verify and notarize every page, perhaps every line, of your transcripts, which Mr. Sorenson here will supply. Any questions?"

No questions. Each was getting a fabulous salary, and each wanted to appear eager to earn it. They all signed.

Resourceful Johnson bought for us a small rooming house, and we paid an exorbitant price to a detective agency to do the cooking and cleaning and chauffeuring required. We requested that the lipreaders refrain from discussing their work among themselves, especially in front of the house employees, and they followed instructions very well.

One day, about a month later, we called a conference in the projection room of Johnson's laboratory. We had a single reel of film.

"What's that for?"

"That's the reason for all the cloak-and-dagger secrecy. Never mind calling your projection man. This I'm going to run through myself. See what you think of it."

They were all disgusted. "I'm getting tired of all this kid stuff," said Kessler.

As I started for the projection booth I heard Mike say, "You're no more tired of it than I am."

From the booth I could see what was showing on the downstairs screen, but nothing else. I ran through the reel, rewound, and went back down.

I said, "One more thing—before we go any further, read this. It's a certified and notarized transcript of what has been read from the lips of the characters you just saw. They weren't, incidentally, 'characters,' in that sense of the word." I handed the crackling sheets around, a copy for each. "Those 'characters' are real people. You've just seen a newsreel. This transcript will tell you what they were talking about. Read it. In the trunk of the car Mike and I have something to show you. We'll be back by the time you've read it."

Mike helped me carry in the machine from the car. We came in the door in time to see Kessler throw the transcript as far as he could. He bounced to his feet as the sheets fluttered down.

He was furious. "What's going on here?" We paid no attention to him, nor to the excited demands of the others until the machine had been plugged into the nearest outlet.

Mike looked at me. "Any ideas?"

I shook my head and told Johnson to shut up for a minute. Mike lifted the lid and hesitated momentarily before he touched the dials. I pushed Johnson into his chair and turned off the lights myself. The room went black. Johnson, looking over my shoulder, gasped. I heard Bernstein swear softly, amazed.

I turned to see what Mike had shown them.

It was impressive, all right. He had started just over the roof of the laboratory and continued straight up in the air.

Up, up, up, until the city of Los Angeles was a tiny dot on a great ball. On the horizon were the Rockies. Johnson grabbed my arm. He hurt.

"What's that? What's that? Stop it!" He was yelling. Mike turned off the machine.

You can guess what happened next. No one believed their eyes, nor Mike's patient explanation. He had to twice turn on the machine again, once going far back into Kessler's past. Then the reaction set in.

Marrs smoked one cigarette after another, Bernstein turned a gold pencil over and over in his nervous fingers, Johnson paced like a caged tiger, and burly Kessler stared at the machine, saying nothing at all. Johnson was muttering as he paced. Then he stopped and shook his fist under Mike's nose.

"Man! Do you know what you've got there? Why waste time playing around here? Can't you see you've got the world by the tail on a downhill pull? If I'd ever known this—"

Mike appealed to me. "Ed, talk to this wildman."

I did. I can't remember exactly what I said, and it isn't important. But I did tell him how we'd started, how we'd plotted our course, and what we were going to do. I ended by telling him the idea behind the reel of film I'd run off a minute before.

He recoiled as though I were a snake. "You can't get away with that! You'd be hung—if you weren't lynched first!"

"Don't you think we know that? Don't you think we're willing to take that chance?"

He tore his thinning hair. Marrs broke in. "Let me talk to him." He came over and faced us squarely.

"Is this on the level? You going to make a picture like that and stick your neck out? You're going to turn that . . . that thing over to the people of the world?"

I nodded. "Just that."

"And toss over everything you've got?" He was dead serious, and so was I. He turned to the others. "He means it!"

Bernstein said, "Can't be done!"

Words flew. I tried to convince them that we had followed the only possible path. "What kind of a world do you want to live in? Or don't you want to live?"

Johnson grunted. "How long do you think we'd live if we ever made a picture like that? You're crazy! I'm not. I'm not going to put by head in a noose."

"Why do you think we've been so insistent about credit

and responsibility for direction and production? You'll be doing only what we hired you for. Not that we want to twist your arm, but you've made a fortune, all of you, working for us. Now, when the going gets heavy, you want to back out!"

Marrs gave in. "Maybe you're right, maybe you're wrong. Maybe you're crazy, maybe I am. I always used to say I'd try anything once. Bernie, you?"

Bernstein was quietly cynical. "You saw what happened in the last war. This might help. I don't know if it will. I don't know—but I'd hate to think I didn't try. Count me in!"

Kessler?

He swiveled his head. "Kid stuff! Who wants to live forever? Who wants to let a chance go by?"

Johnson threw up his hands. "Let's hope we get a cell together. Let's all go crazy." And that was that.

We went to work in a blazing drive of mutual hope and understanding. In four months the lipreaders were through. There's no point in detailing here their reactions to the dynamite they daily dictated to Sorenson. For their own good we kept them in the dark about our final purpose, and when they were through we sent them across the border into Mexico, to a small ranch Johnson had leased. We were going to need them later.

While the print duplicators worked overtime Marrs worked harder. The press and the radio shouted the announcement that, in every city of the world we could reach, there would be held the simultaneous premieres of our latest picture. It would be the last we needed to make. Many wondered aloud at our choice of the word "needed." We whetted curiosity by refusing any advance information about the plot, and Johnson so well infused their men with their own now-fervent enthusiasm that not much could be pried out of them but conjecture. The day we picked for release was Sunday. Monday, the storm broke.

I wonder how many prints of that picture are left today. I wonder how many escaped burning or confiscation. Two World Wars we covered, covered from the unflattering angles that up until then had been represented by only a few books hidden in the dark corners of libraries. We showed and *named* the war-makers, the cynical ones who signed and laughed and lied, the blatant patriots who used the flare of headlines and the ugliness of atrocity to hide behind their flag while life turned to death for millions. Our own and foreign traitors were there, the hidden ones with Janus faces. Our lipreaders had done their work well; no guesses these, no deduced conjectures from the broken records of a blasted past, but the exact words that exposed treachery disguised as patriotism.

In foreign lands the performances lasted barely the day. Usually, in retaliation for the imposed censorship, the theaters were wrecked by the raging crowds. (Marrs, incidentally, had spent hundreds of thousands bribing officials to allow the picture to be shown without previous censorship. Many censors, when that came out, were shot without trial.) In the Balkans, revolutions broke out, and various embassies were stormed by mobs. Where the film was banned or destroyed written versions spontaneously appeared on the streets or in coffee houses. Bootlegged editions were smuggled past customs guards, who looked the other way. One royal family fled to Switzerland.

Here in America it was a racing two weeks before the Federal Government, prodded into action by the raging of press and radio, in an unprecedented move closed all performances "to promote the common welfare, insure domestic tranquility, and preserve foreign relations." Murmurs—and one riot—rumbled in the Midwest and spread until it was realized by the powers that be that something had to be done, and done quickly, if every government in the world were not to collapse of its own weight.

We were in Mexico, at the ranch Johnson had rented for the lipreaders. While Johnson paced the floor, jerkily fraying a cigar, we listened to a special broadcast of the attorney general himself:

". . . furthermore, this message was today forwarded to the government of the United States of Mexico. I read: 'The government of the United States of America requests the immediate arrest and extradition of the following:

"'Edward Joseph Lefkowicz, known as Lefko.'" First on the list. Even a fish wouldn't get into trouble if he kept his mouth shut.

"'Miguel Jose Zapata Laviada.'" Mike crossed one leg over the other.

"'Edward Lee Johnson.'" He threw his cigar on the floor and sank into a chair.

"'Robert Chester Marrs.'" He lit another cigarette. His face twitched.

" 'Benjamin Lionel Bernstein.' " He smiled a twisted smile and closed his eyes.

" 'Carl Wilhelm Kessler.' " A snarl.

"These men are wanted by the government of the United States of America, to stand trial on charges ranging from criminal syndicalism, incitement to riot, suspicion of treason—"

I clicked off the radio. "Well?" to no one in particular.

Bernstein opened his eyes. "The rurales are probably on their way. Might as well go back and face the music—" We crossed the border at Juarez. The FBI was waiting.

Every press and radio chain in the world must have had coverage at that trial, every radio system, even the new and imperfect television chain. We were allowed to see no one but our lawyer. Samuels flew from the West Coast and spent a week trying to get past our guards. He told us not to talk to reporters, if we ever saw them.

"You haven't seen the newspapers? Just as well— How did you ever get yourselves into this mess, anyway? You ought to know better."

I told him

He was stunned. "Are you all crazy?"

He was hard to convince. Only the united effort and concerted stories of all of us made him believe that there was such a machine in existence. (He talked to us separately, because we were kept isolated.) When he got back to me he was unable to think coherently.

"What kind of defense do you call that?"

I shook my head. "No. That is, we know that we're guilty of practically everything under the sun if you look at it one way. If you look at it another—"

He rose. "Man, you don't need a lawyer, you need a doctor. I'll see you later. I've got to get this figured out in my mind before I can do a thing."

"Sit down. What do you think of this?" And I outlined what I had in mind.

"I think . . . I don't know what I think. I don't know. I'll talk to you later. Right now I want some fresh air." And he left.

As most trials do, this one began with the usual blackening of the defendant's character, or lack of it. (The men we'd blackmailed at the beginning had long since had their money returned, and they had sense enough to keep quiet. That might have been because they'd received a few hints that there might still be a negative or two lying around. Compounding a felony? Sure.) With the greatest of interest we sat in that great columned hall and listened to a sad tale.

We had, with malice aforethought, libeled beyond repair great and unselfish men who had made a career of devotion to the public weal, imperiled needlessly relations traditionally friendly by falsely reporting mythical events, mocked the courageous sacrifices of those who had *dulce et gloria mori,* and completely upset everyone's peace of mind. Every new accusation, every verbal lance drew solemn agreement from the dignitary-packed hall. Against someone's better judgment, the trial had been transferred from the regular courtroom to the Hall of Justice. Packed with influence, brass, and pompous legates from over the world, only the congressmen from the biggest states, or with the biggest votes were able to crowd the newly installed seats. So you can see it was a hostile audience that faced Samuels when the defense had its say. We had spent the previous night together in the guarded suite to which we had been transferred for the duration of the trial, perfecting, as far as we could, our planned defense. Samuels has the arrogant sense of humor that usually goes with supreme self-confidence, and I'm sure he enjoyed standing there among all those bemedaled and bejowled bigwigs, knowing the bombshell he was going to hurl. He made a good grenadier. Like this:

"We believe there is only one defense possible, we believe there is only one defense necessary. We have gladly waived, without prejudice, our inalienable right of trial by jury. We shall speak plainly and bluntly, to the point.

"You have seen the picture in question. You have remarked, possibly, upon what has been called the startling resemblance of the actors in that picture to the characters named and portrayed. You have remarked possibly, upon the apparent verisimilitude to reality. That I will mention again. The first witness will, I believe, establish the trend of our rebuttal of the allegations of the prosecution." He called the first witness.

"Your name, please?"

"Mercedes Maria Gomez."

"A little louder, please."

"Mercedes Maria Gomez."

"Your occupation?"

"Until last March I was a teacher at the Arizona School for the Deaf. Then I asked for and obtained a leave of absence. At present I am under personal contract to Mr. Lefko."

"If you see Mr. Lefko in this courtroom, Miss . . . Mrs.—"

"Miss."

"Thank you. If Mr. Lefko is in this court will you point him out? Thank you. Will you tell us the extent of your duties at the Arizona School?"

"I taught children born totally deaf to speak. And to read lips."

"You read lips yourself, Miss Gomez?"

"I have been totally deaf since I was fifteen."

"In English only?"

"English and Spanish. We have . . . had many children of Mexican descent."

Samuels asked for a designated Spanish-speaking interpreter. An officer in the back immediately volunteered. He was identified by his ambassador, who was present.

"Will you take this book to the rear of the courtroom, sir?" To the Court: "If the prosecution wishes to examine that book, they will find that it is a Spanish edition of the Bible." The prosecution didn't wish to examine it.

"Will the officer open the Bible at random and read aloud?" He opened the Bible at the center and read. In dead silence the Court strained to hear. Nothing could be heard the length of that enormous hall.

Samuels: "Miss Gomez. Will you take these binoculars and repeat, to the Court, just what the officer is reading at the other end of the room?"

She took the binoculars and focused them expertly on the officer, who had stopped reading and was watching alertly. "I am ready."

Samuels: "Will you please read, sir?"

He did, and the Gomez woman repeated aloud, quickly and easily, a section that sounded as though it might be anything at all. I can't speak Spanish. The officer continued to read for a minute or two.

Samuels: "Thank you, sir. And thank you, Miss Gomez. Your pardon, sir, but since there are several who have been known to memorize the Bible, will you tell the Court if you have anything on your person that is written, anything that Miss Gomez has had no chance of viewing?" Yes, the officer had. "Will you read that as before? Will you, Miss Gomez—"

She read that, too. Then the officer came to the front to listen to the court reporter read Miss Gomez' words.

"That's what I read," he affirmed.

Samuels turned her over to the prosecution, who made more experiments that served only to convince that she was equally good as an interpreter and lipreader in either language.

In rapid succession Samuels put the rest of the lipreaders on the stand. In rapid succession they proved themselves as able and as capable as Miss Gomez, in their own linguistic specialty. The Russian from Ambridge generously offered to translate into his broken English any other Slavic language handy, and drew scattered grins from the press box. The Court was convinced, but failed to see the purpose of the exhibition. Samuels, glowing with satisfaction and confidence, faced the Court.

"Thanks to the indulgence of the Court, and despite the efforts of the distinguished prosecution, we have proved the almost amazing accuracy of lipreading in general, and these lipreaders in particular." One Justice absently nodded in agreement. "Therefore, our defense will be based on that premise, and on one other which we have had until now found necessary to keep hidden—the picture in question was and is definitely not a fictional representation of events of questionable authenticity. Every scene in that film contained, not polished professional actors, but the original person named and portrayed. Every foot, every inch of film was not the result of an elaborate studio reconstruction but an actual collection of pictures, an actual collection of newsreels—if they can be called that—edited and assembled in story form!"

Through the startled spurt of astonishment we heard one of the prosecution: "That's ridiculous! No newsreel—"

Samuels ignored the objections and the tumult to put me on the stand. Beyond the usual preliminary questions I was allowed to say things my own way. At first hostile, the Court became interested enough to overrule the repeated objections that flew from the table devoted to the prosecution. I felt that at least two of the Court, if not outright favorable, were friendly. As far as I can remember, I went over the maneuvers of the past years, and ended something like this:

"As to why we arranged the cards to fall as they did; both Mr. Laviada and myself were unable to face the prospect of destroying his discovery, because of the inevitable penalizing of needed research. We were, and we are, unwilling to better ourselves or a limited group by the use and maintenance of secrecy, if secrecy were possible. As to the only other alternative," and I directed this straight at Judge Bronson, the well-known liberal on the bench, "since the last war all atomic research and activity has been under the direction of a Board nominally civilian, but actually under the 'protection and direction' of the Army and Navy. This 'direction and protection,' as any competent physicist will gladly attest, has proved to be nothing but a smothering blanket serving to conceal hidebound antiquated reasoning, abysmal ignorance, and inestimable amounts of fumbling. As of right now, this country, or any country that was foolish enough to place any confidence in the rigid regime of the military mind, is years behind what would otherwise be the natural course of discovery and progress in nuclear and related fields.

"We were, and we are, firmly convinced that even the slightest hint of the inherent possibilities and scope of Mr. Laviada's discovery would have meant, under the present regime, instant and mandatory confiscation of even a supposedly secure patent. Mr. Laviada has never applied for a patent, and never will. We both feel that such a discovery belongs not to an individual, a group, or corporation, or even to a nation, but to the world and those who live in it.

"We know, and are eager and willing to prove, that the domestic and external affairs not only of this nation but of every nation are influenced, sometimes controlled, by esoteric groups warping political theories and human lives to suit their own ends." The Court was smothered in sullen silence, thick and acid with hate and disbelief.

"Secret treaties, for example, and vicious, lying propaganda have too long controlled human passions and made men hate; honored thieves have too long rotted secretly in undeserved high places. The machine can make treachery and untruth impossible. It *must*, if atomic war is not to sear the face and fate of the world.

"Our pictures were all made with that end in view. We needed, first, the wealth and prominence to present to an international audience what we knew to be the truth. We have done as much as we can. From now on, this Court takes over the burden we have carried. We are guilty of no treachery, guilty of no deceit, guilty of nothing but deep and true humanity. Mr. Laviada wishes me to tell the Court and the world that he has been unable till now to give his discovery to the world, free to use as it wills."

The Court stared at me. Every foreign representative was on the edge of his seat waiting for the Justices to order us shot without further ado, the sparkling uniforms were seething, and the pressmen were racing their pencils against time. The tension dried my throat. The speech that Samuels and I had rehearsed the previous night was strong medicine. Now what?

Samuels filled the breach smoothly. "If the Court pleases; Mr. Lefko has made some startling statements. Startling, but certainly sincere, and certainly either provable or disprovable. And proof it shall be!"

He strode to the door of the conference room that had been allotted us. As the hundreds of eyes followed him it was easy for me to slip down from the witness stand, and wait, ready. From the conference room Samuels rolled the machine, and Mike rose. The whispers that curdled the air seemed disappointed, unimpressed. Right in front of the Bench he trundled it.

He moved unobtrusively to one side as the television men trained their long-snouted cameras. "Mr. Laviada and Mr. Lefko will show you . . . I trust there will be no objection from the prosecution?" He was daring them.

One of the prosecution was already on his feet. He opened his mouth hesitantly, but thought better, and sat down. Heads went together in conference as he did. Samuels was watching the Court with one eye, and the courtroom with the other.

"If the Court pleases, we will need a cleared space. If the bailiff will . . . thank you, sir." The long tables were moved back, with a raw scraping. He stood there, with every eye in the courtroom glued on him. For two long breaths he stood there, then he spun and went to his table. "Mr. Lefko." And he bowed formally. He sat.

The eyes swung to me, to Mike, as he moved to his machine and stood there silently. I cleared my throat and spoke to the Bench as though I did not see the directional microphones trained at my lips.

"Justice Bronson."

He looked steadily at me and then glanced at Mike. "Yes, Mr. Lefko?"

"Your freedom from bias is well known." The corners of his mouth went down as he frowned. "Will you be willing to be used as proof that there can be no trickery?" He thought that over, then nodded slowly. The prosecution objected, and was waved down. "Will you tell me exactly where you were at any given time? Any place where you are absolutely certain and can verify that there were no concealed cameras or observers?"

He thought. Seconds. Minutes. The tension twanged, and I swallowed dust. He spoke quietly. "1918. November 11th."

Mike whispered to me. I said, "Any particular time?"

Justice Bronson looked at Mike. "Exactly eleven. Armistice time." He paused, then went on. "Niagara Falls. Niagara Falls, New York."

I heard the dials tick in the stillness, and Mike whispered again. I said, "The lights should be off." The bailiff rose. "Will you please watch the left wall, or in that direction? I think that if Justice Kassel will turn a little . . . we are ready."

Bronson looked at me, and at the left wall. "Ready."

The lights flicked out overhead and I heard the television crews mutter. I touched Mike on the shoulder. "Show them, Mike!"

We're all showmen at heart, and Mike is no exception. Suddenly out of nowhere and into the depths poured a frozen torrent. Niagara Falls. I've mentioned, I think, that I've never got over my fear of heights. Few people ever do. I heard long, shuddery gasps as we started straight down. Down, until we stopped at the brink of the silent cataract, weird in its frozen majesty. Mike had stopped time at exactly eleven, I knew. He shifted to the American bank. Slowly he moved along. There were a few tourists standing in almost comic attitudes. There was snow on the ground, flakes in the air. Time stood still, and hearts slowed in sympathy.

Bronson snapped, "Stop!"

A couple, young. Long skirts, high-buttoned army collar, dragging army overcoat, facing, arms about each other. Mike's sleeve rustled in the darkness and they moved. She was sobbing and the soldier was smiling. She turned away her head, and he turned it back. Another couple seized them gayly, and they twirled breathlessly.

Bronson's voice was harsh. "That's enough!" The view blurred for seconds.

Washington. The White House. The President. Someone coughed like a small explosion. The President was watching a television screen. He jerked erect suddenly, startled. Mike spoke for the first time in Court.

"That is the President of the United States. He is watching the trial that is being broadcast and televised from this courtroom. He is listening to what I am saying right now, and he is watching, in his television screen, as I use my machine to show him what he was doing one second ago."

The President heard those fateful words. Stiffly he threw an unconscious glance around his room at nothing and looked back at his screen in time to see himself do what he just had done, one second ago. Slowly, as if against his will, his hand started toward the switch of his set.

"Mr. President, don't turn off that set." Mike's voice was curt, almost rude. "You must hear this, you of all people in the world. You must understand!

"This is not what we wanted to do, but we have no recourse left but to appeal to you, and to the people of this twisted world." The President might have been cast in iron. "You must see, you must understand that you have in your hands the power to make it impossible for green-born war to be bred in secrecy and rob man of his youth or his old age or whatever he prizes." His voice softened, pleaded. "That is all we have to say. That is all we want. That is all anyone could want, ever." The President, unmoving, faded into blackness. "The lights, please." And almost immediately the Court adjourned. That was over a month ago.

Mike's machine has been taken from us, and we are under military guard. Probably it's just as well we're guarded. We understand there have been lynching parties, broken up only as far as a block or two away. Last week we watched a white-haired fanatic scream about us, on the street below. We couldn't catch what he was shrieking, but we did catch a few air-borne epithets.

"Devils! Anti-Christs! Violation of the Bible! Violations of this and that!" Some, right here in the city, I suppose, would be glad to build a bonfire to cook us right back to the flames from which we've sprung. I wonder what the various religious groups are going to do now that the truth can be seen. Who can read lips in Aramaic, or Latin, or Coptic? And is a mechanical miracle a miracle?

This changes everything. We've been moved. Where, I don't know, except that the weather is warm, and we're on some type of military reservation, by the lack of civilians. Now we know what we're up against. What started out to be just a time-killing occupation, Joe, has turned out to be a necessary preface to what I'm going to ask you to do. Finish this, and then move fast! We won't be able to get this to you for a while yet, so I'll go on for a bit the way I started, to kill time. Like our clippings:

TABLOID:

. . . Such a weapon cannot, must not be loosed in unscrupulous hands. The last professional production of the infamous pair proves what distortions can be wrested from isolated and misunderstood events. In the hands of perpetrators of heretical isms, no property, no business deal, no personal life could be sacrosanct, no foreign policy could be . . .

TIMES:

. . . colonies stand with us firmly . . . liquidation of the Empire . . . white man's burden . . .

LE MATIN:

. . . rightful place . . . restore proud France . . .

PRAVDA:

. . . democratic imperialist plot . . . our glorious scientist ready to announce . . .

NICHI-NICHI:

. . . incontrovertibly prove divine descent . . .

LA PRENSA:

. . . oil concessions . . . dollar diplomacy . . .

DETROIT JOURNAL:

. . . under our noses in a sinister fortress on East Warren . . . under close Federal supervision . . . perfection by our production-trained technicians a mighty aid to law-enforcement agencies . . . tirades against politicians and business common-sense carried too far . . . tomorrow revelations by . . .

L'OSSERVATORE ROMANO:

Council of Cardinals . . . announcement expected hourly . . .

JACKSON STAR-CLARION:

. . . proper handling will prove the fallacy of race equality . . .

Almost unanimously the press screamed; Pegler frothed,

Winchell leered. We got the surface side of the situation from
the press. But a military guard is composed of individuals,
hotel room must be swept by maids, waiters must serve food,
and a chain is as strong— We got what we think the truth
from those who work for a living.

There are meetings on street corners and in homes, two
great veterans' groups have arbitrarily fired their officials,
seven governors have resigned, three senators and over a
dozen representatives have retired with "ill health," and the
general temper is ugly. International travelers report the same
of Europe, Asia is bubbling, and transport planes with motors
running stud the airports of South America. A general whisper is that a Constitutional Amendment is being rammed
through to forbid the use of any similar instrument by an individual, with the manufacture and leasing by the Federal
government to law-enforcement agencies or financially responsible corporations suggested; it is whispered that motor
caravans are forming throughout the country for a Washington march to demand a decision by the Court on the truth of
our charges; it is generally suspected that all news dissemi-
nating services are under direct Federal—Army—control;
wires are supposed to be sizzling with petitions and demands
to Congress, which are seldom delivered.

One day the chambermaid said: "And the whole hotel
might as well close up shop. The whole floor is blocked off,
there're MP's at every door, and they're clearing out all the
other guests as fast as they can be moved. The whole place
wouldn't be big enough to hold the letters and wires
addressed to you, or the ones that are trying to get in to see
you. Fat chance they have," she added grimly. "The joint is
lousy with brass."

Mike glanced at me and I cleared my throat. "What's your
idea of the whole thing?"

Expertly she spanked and reversed a pillow. "I saw your
last picture before they shut it down. I saw all your pictures.
When I wasn't working I listened to your trial. I heard you
tell them off. I never got married because my boy friend
never came back from Burma. Ask *him* what he thinks." And
she jerked her head at the young private who was supposed
to keep her from talking. "Ask him if he wants some bunch
of stinkers to start him shooting at some other poor chump.
See what he says, and then ask me if I want an atom bomb
dropped down my neck just because some chiselers want

more than they got." She left suddenly, and the soldier left with her. Mike and I had a beer and went to bed. Next week the papers had headlines a mile high.

U.S. KEEPS MIRACLE RAY
CONSTITUTION
AMENDMENT
AWAITS STATES OKAY
LEVIADA-LEFKO FREED

We were freed all right, Bronson and the President being responsible for that. But the President and Bronson don't know, I'm sure, that we were rearrested immediately. We were told that we'll be held in "protective custody" until enough states have ratified the proposed constitutional amendment. The Man Without a Country was in what you might call "protective custody," too. We'll likely be released the same way he was.

We're allowed no newspapers, no radio, allowed no communication coming or going, and we're given no reason, as if that were necessary. They'll never, never let us go, and they'd be fools if they did. They think that if we can't communicate, or if we can't build another machine, our fangs are drawn, and when the excitement dies, we fall into oblivion, six feet of it. Well, we can't build another machine. But, communicate?

Look at it this way. A soldier is a soldier because he wants to serve his country. A soldier doesn't want to die unless his country is at war. Even then death is only a last resort. And war isn't necessary anymore, not with our machine. In the dark? Try to plan or plot in absolute darkness, which is what would be needed. Try to plot or carry on a war without putting things in writing. O.K. Now—

The Army has Mike's machine. The Army has Mike. They call it military expediency, I suppose. Bosh! Anyone beyond the grade of moron can see that to keep that machine, to hide it, is to invite the world to attack, and attack in self-defense. If every nation, or if every man, had a machine, each would be equally open, or equally protected. But if only one nation, or only one man can see, the rest will not long be blind. Maybe we did this all wrong. God knows that we thought about it often. God knows we did our best to make an effort at keeping man out of his own trap.

There isn't much time left. One of the soldiers guarding us will get this to you, I hope, in time.

A long time ago we gave you a key, and hoped we would never have to ask you to use it. But now is the time. That key fits a box at the Detroit Savings Bank. In that box are letters. Mail them, not all at once, or in the same place. They'll go all over the world, to men we know, and have watched well; clever, honest, and capable of following the plans we've enclosed.

But you've got to hurry! One of these bright days someone is going to wonder if we've made more than one machine. We haven't, of course. That would have been foolish. But if some smart young lieutenant gets hold of that machine long enough to start tracing back our movements they'll find that safety deposit box, with the plans and letters ready to be scattered broadside. You can see the need for haste—if the rest of the world, or any particular nation, wants that machine bad enough, they'll fight for it. And they will! They must! Later on, when the Army gets used to the machine and its capabilities, it will become obvious to everyone, as it already is to Mike and me, that, with every plan open to inspection as soon as it's made, no nation or group of nations would have a chance in open warfare. So if there is to be an attack, it will have to be deadly, and fast, and sure. Please God that we haven't shoved the world into a war we tried to make impossible. With all the atom bombs and rockets that have been made in the past few years—*Joe, you've got to hurry!*

GHQ TO 9TH ATTK GRP

Report report report report report report report report report report

CMDR 9TH ATTK GRP TO GHQ

BEGINS: No other manuscript found. Searched body of Lefko immediately upon landing. According to plan Building Three untouched. Survivors insist both were moved from Building Seven previous day defective plumbing. Body of Laviada identified definitely through fingerprints. Request further instructions. ENDS

GHQ TO CMDR 32ND
SHIELDED RGT

BEGINS: Seal area Detroit Savings Bank. Advise immediately condition safety deposit boxes. Afford coming technical unit complete cooperation. ENDS

LT. COL. TEMP. ATT.
32ND SHIELDED RGT

BEGINS: Area Detroit Savings Bank vaporized direct hit. Radioactivity lethal. Impossible boxes or any contents survive. Repeat, direct hit. Request permission proceed Washington Area. ENDS

GHQ. TO LT. COL. TEMP. ATT.
32ND SHIELDED RGT

BEGINS: Request denied. Sift ashes if necessary regardless cost. Repeat, regardless cost. ENDS

GHQ. TO ALL UNITS REPEAT
ALL UNITS

BEGINS: Lack of enemy resistance explained misdirected atom rockets seventeen miles SSE Washington. Lone survivor completely destroyed special train claims all top officials left enemy capital two hours preceding attack. Notify local governments where found necessary and obvious cessation hostilities. Occupy present areas Plan Two. Further orders follow. ENDS

LETTER TO ELLEN

by Chan Davis (1926-   )

ASTOUNDING SCIENCE FICTION
June

> Dr. Davis returns (see "The Nightmare" in Vol-
> ume 8 of this series) with one of his best stories,
> which because of a very slight resemblance to Les-
> ter del Rey's famous "Helen O'Loy" (1938) has
> never received the attention due it. The holder of a
> doctorate from Harvard and Professor of Mathe-
> matics at the University of Toronto, Dr. Davis is a
> member of the prestigious Institute for Advanced
> Study in Princeton, New Jersey. His published sf
> stories total fewer than twenty, and we wish that he
> had had the time and inclination to give us more.
> Perhaps he still will.

> (Marty's reference to "Letter to Ellen" 's "very
> slight resemblance" to "Helen O'Loy" requires a
> little expansion, to my way of thinking. The resem-
> blance is in theme and such similarities are un-
> avoidable, since the number of themes in science
> fiction and, indeed, in literature, are quite limited. I
> remember a time when I was writing my own story
> "Each an Explorer." Halfway through, I recognized
> the theme of John Campbell's much more famous

"Who Goes There?" I phoned him in a panic to ask what one did in such a case. "Nothing," he said kindly. "Just go right on and see what you can do with the theme." The treatment was, of course, not nearly as good as that in John's supremely great tale, but it was different. If the number of themes are limited, the number of varieties of treatment are not and it is sometimes actually instructive to see how the same soil can give rise to quite different, and equally flourishing, plants.—I.A.)

Dear Ellen,

By the time you get this you'll be wondering why I didn't call. It'll be the first time I've missed in—how long?—two months? A long two months it's been, and, for me, a very important two months.

I'm not going to call, and I'm not going to see you. Maybe I'm a coward writing this letter, but you can judge that when you've finished it. Judge that, and other things.

Let's see. I'd better begin at the beginning and tell the whole story right through. Do you remember my friend Roy Wisner? He came to work in the lab the same time I did, in the spring of '16, and he was still around when I first met you. Even if you never met him, you may have seen him; he was the tall blond guy with the stooped shoulders, working in the same branch with me.

Roy and I grew up together. He was my best friend as a kid, back almost as far as I can remember, back at the State Orphanage outside of Stockton. We went to different high schools, but when I got to Iowa U. there was Roy. Just to make the coincidence complete, he'd decided to be a biochemist too, and we took mostly the same courses all the way through. Both worked with Dietz while we were getting our doctorates, and Dietz got us identical jobs with Hartwell at the Pierne Labs here in Denver.

I've told you about that first day at the lab. We'd both heard from Dietz that the Pierne Labs were devoted now almost entirely to life-synthesis, and we'd both hoped to get in on that part of the work. What we hadn't realized was quite

how far the work had got. I can tell you, the little talk old
Hartwell gave us when he took us around to show us the lay
of the land was just as inspiring as he meant it to be.

He showed us the wing where they're experimenting with
the synthesis of new types of Coelenterates. We'd heard of
that too, but seeing it was another thing. I remember particularly a rather ghastly green thing that floated in a small tank
and occasionally sucked pieces of sea moss into what was
half mouth, half sucker. Hartwell said, offhand, "Doesn't look
much like the original, does it? That one was a mistake;
something went wrong with the gene synthesis. But it turned
out to be viable, so the fellows kept it around. Wouldn't be
surprised if it could outsurvive some of its natural cousins if
we were to give it a mate and turn it loose." He looked at the
thing benignly. "I sort of like it."

Then we went down to Hartwell's branch, Branch 26,
where we were to work. Hartwell slid back the narrow metal
door and led the way into one of the labs. We started to follow him, but we hadn't gone more than three steps inside
when we just stood still and gawked. I'd seen complicated apparatus before, but that place had anything at the Iowa labs
beat by a factor of one thousand. All the gear on one whole
side of the lab—and it was a good-sized place—was black-
coated against the light and other stray radiation in the room.
I recognized most of the flasks and fractionating columns as
airtight jobs. A good deal of the hookup was hidden from us,
being under Gardner hoods, airtight, temperature-controlled,
radiation-controlled, and everything-else-controlled. What
heaters we could see were never burners, always infrared
banks.

This was precision work. It had to be, because, as you
know, Branch 26 synthesizes chordate genes.

Roy and I went over to take a closer look at some of the
gear. We stopped about a meter away; meddling was distinctly not in order. The item we were looking at was what
would be called, in a large-scale process, a reaction vat. It
was a small, opaque-coated flask, and it was being revolved
slowly by a mechanical agitator, to swirl the liquids inside. As
we stood there we could barely feel the gentle and precise
flow of heat from the infrared heaters banked around it. We
watched it, fascinated.

Hartwell snapped us out of it. "The work here," he said

dryly, "is carried out with a good deal of care. You've had some experience with full microanalysis, Dietz tells me."

"A little," I nodded, with very appropriate modesty.

"Well, this is microsynthesis, and microsynthesis with a vengeance. Remember, our problem here is on an entirely different level even from ordinary protein synthesis." (It staggered me a little to hear him refer to protein synthesis as ordinary!) "There you're essentially building up a periodic crystal, one in which the atoms are arranged in regularly recurrent patterns. This recursion, this periodicity, makes the structure of the molecule relatively simple; correspondingly, it simplifies the synthesis. In a gene, a virus, or any other of the complex proteinlike molecules there isn't any such frequent recursion. Instead, the radicals in your molecule chain are a little different each time; the pattern almost repeats, but not quite. You've got what you call an a-periodic crystal.

"When we synthesize such a crystal we've got to get all the little variations from the pattern just right, because it's those variations that give the structure enough complexity to be living."

He had some chromosome charts under his arm, and now he pulled one out to show to us. I don't know if you've ever seen the things; one of them alone fills a little booklet, in very condensed notation. Roy and I thumbed through one, recognizing a good many of the shorthand symbols but not understanding the scheme of the thing at all. When we got through we were pretty thoroughly awed.

Hartwell smiled. "You'll catch on, don't worry. The first few months, while you're studying up, you'll be my lab assistants. You won't be on your own until you've got the process down pretty near pat." And were we glad to hear that!

Roy and I got an apartment on the outside of town; I didn't have my copter then, so we had to be pretty close. It was a good place, though only one wall and the roof could be made transparent. We missed the morning sun that way, but I liked it all right. Downstairs lived Graham, our landlord, an old bachelor who spent most of his time on home photography, both movie wires and old-fashioned chemical prints. He got some candid angle shots of us that were so weird Roy was thinking of breaking his cameras.

At the lab we caught on fast enough. Roy was always a

pretty bright boy, and I manage to keep up. After a reasonable period Hartwell began to ease himself out of our routine, until before we knew it we were running the show ourselves. Naturally, being just out of school, we began, as soon as we got the drift of things, to suggest changes in the process. The day Hartwell finally approved one of our bright ideas, we knew we were standing on our own feet. That's when the fun really began.

Some people laugh when I say "that kind of drudgery" is fun, but you're a biochemist yourself and I'm pretty sure you feel the same way. The mere thought that we were putting inert colloids in at one end and getting something out at the other end that was in some strange way *living*—that was enough to take the boredom out of the job, if there'd been any.

Because we always felt that it was in our lab and the others like it that nonlife ended and life began. Sure, before us there was the immense job of protein synthesis and colloid preparation. Sure, after we were through there was the last step, the ultramicrosurgery of putting the nuclear wall together around the chromatin and embedding the result in a cell. (I always half envied your branch that job.) But in between there was our stage of the thing, which we thought to be the crucial one.

Certainly it was a tough enough stage. The long, careful reactions, with temperatures regulated down to a hundredth of a degree and reaction time to a tenth of a second; and then the final reactions, with everything enclosed in Gardner hoods, where you build up, bit by bit, the living nucleoplasm around the almost-living chromosomes. Hartwell hadn't lied when he said the work was carried out with care! That was quite a plant for two young squirts like us to be playing around with.

Just to put an edge on it, of course, there was always the possibility that you'd do everything right and still misfire. Anywhere along the line, Heisenberg's Uncertainty Principle could shove a radical out of place in those protein chains, no matter how careful you were. Then you'd get a weird thing: a gene mutating before it was even completed.

Or Heisenberg's Principle might pull you through even if your process had gone wrong!

We got curious after a while, Roy especially. Hartwell had told us a lot; one thing he hadn't told us was exactly *what we*

were making: fish, flesh, or fowl, and we weren't geneticists
enough to know ourselves. It would have been better, while
we were working, to have had a mental picture of the frog or
lizard or chicken that was to be our end product; instead, our
mental picture was a composite of the three, and a rather dis-
concerting composite it made. I preferred to imagine a rabbit,
or better yet, an Irish terrier puppy.

Hartwell not only hadn't offered to tell us, he didn't tell us
when we asked him. "One of the lower chordates," he said;
"the species name doesn't matter." That phrase "lower chordates" didn't ring quite true. There were enough chromosomes in our whatever-they-were's that they had to be
something fairly far up the scale.

Roy immediately decided he was going to get the answer if
he had to go through twenty books on genetics to do it.
Looking back, I'm surprised I didn't have the same ambition.
Maybe I was too interested in chess; I was on one of my periodic chess binges at the time. Anyhow, Roy got the genetics
books and Roy did the digging.

It didn't take him any time at all. I remember that night
well. He had brought home a stack of books from the library
and was studying them at the desk in the corner. I was in the
armchair with my portable chessboard, analyzing a game I'd
lost in the last tournament. As the hours went by, I noticed
Roy getting more and more restless; I expected him to come
up with the answer any time, but apparently he was recheck-
ing to make sure. About the time I'd found how I should
have played to beat Fedruk, Roy got up, a little unsteadily.

"Dirk," he began, then stopped.

"You got it?"

"Dirk, I wonder if you realize just how few chordate species
there are which have forty-eight chromosomes."

"Well, humans have, and I guess we're not so unique."

He didn't say anything.

"Hey, do you mean what I think you mean?" I jumped to
my feet.

If he did, it was terrific news for me; I think I'd had the
idea in the back of my mind all the time and never dared
check it for fear I'd be proved wrong. Roy wasn't so happy
about it. He said, "Yes, that's exactly what I mean. The
species name Hartwell wouldn't tell us was *Homo sapiens.*
We're making—robots."

That took a little time to digest. When I'd got it assimilated

I came back, "What do you mean, robots? If we made a puppy that wagged its tail O.K., you'd be just as pleased as I would." (I was still stuck on that Irish terrior idea of mine.) "That wouldn't give you the shudders. Why do you get so worried just because it's men we're making?"

"It's not right," he said.

"What?" Roy never having been religious or anything, that sounded strange.

"Well, I take that back, I guess, but—" His voice trailed away; then, more normally, "I don't know, Dirk. I just can't see it. Making humans—what would you call them if not robots?"

"I'd call them men, doggone it, if they turn out right. Of course if they don't turn out right—maybe I could see your point. If they don't turn out right. Killing a freak chicken and killing an experimental baby that didn't quite— succeed—would be two different things. Yeah."

"I hadn't thought of that."

"Then what the heck *were* you thinking of?"

"Aw, I don't know." He went back to the desk, slammed his books shut.

"What's bothering you, Roy?"

He didn't answer, just went into his bedroom and shut the door. He didn't come out again that night.

The next morning he was grim-faced, but you could see he was excited underneath. I knew he was planning something. Finally I wormed it out of him: he was going to take a look around Branch 39 to try and find some human embryos, as confirmation. Branch 39, as you know, is one of the ones that shuts up at night; they don't have to have technicians around twenty-four hours a day as 26 does. Roy's plan was to go up there just before closing time, hide, and get himself locked in overnight.

I asked him why the secrecy, why didn't he just ask to be shown around. "Hartwell doesn't want us to know," he said, "or he would have told us. I'll have to do it on the QT."

That made some sense, but—"Heck, Hartwell couldn't have expected to keep us permanently in the dark about what we were making, when all the dope you needed to figure it out was right there in the library. He must have wanted simply to let us do the figuring ourselves."

"Uh-uh. He knew we could puzzle it through if we wanted, but he wasn't going to help us. You think the lab wants to publicize what it's doing? No, Hartwell must be trying to keep as many people as possible from knowing; he hoped we'd stay uncurious. I'm not going to tell him we've guessed, and don't you."

I agreed reluctantly, but Roy's play-acting seemed to me like just that. Roy was deadly serious about it.

Later I got the story of that night. He'd gone up to 39 as planned, and hid in the big hall on the second floor; that was the place with the most embryos, and he thought he'd have the best chance there. Everything went O.K.; the assistant turned out the lights and locked up, and Roy stayed curled in his cabinet under a lab table. When the sounds had died down in the corridors outside, he came out and looked around.

He didn't know quite how to start. There were all sizes and shapes of gestators around. When he had taken out his flash and got a good look at one, he remained in as much of a quandary as before. It didn't seem to be anything but a bottle-shaped black container, about twenty centimeters on a side, in the middle of a mass of tubing, gauges, and levers. He could guess the bottle contained the embryo; he could guess the tubing kept up the flow of "body fluids" to and from the bottle; he could recognize some of the gauge markings and some of the auxiliary apparatus; and that was all. Not only was the embryo not exposed to view but he didn't see any way of exposing it. There was a label in a code he couldn't read. Nothing was any help.

The gestators were simple enough compared to the stuff he worked with, but he had a healthy respect for that sort of thing and didn't want to experiment to try to figure them out. If you meddled with a gestator in the wrong way, there was the chance that you'd be ruining a hundred people's work; and there would be many more wrong ways than right.

He made the circuit of the lab, stooping over one gestator after another, considering. After a while the moon rose and gave him a little more light. That was not what he needed.

A key turned in the lock.

Roy, hoping he hadn't been seen, ran back to his hiding place. He left the cabinet open far enough so he could see. A figure came in the door, turned to close it, and strode toward the center of the hall. As it passed through a patch of moonlight from one of the windows, Roy recognized the face: Hartwell.

He must have been working late in his office and come down for a look at his branch's products before leaving. Be that as it may, his presence cinched the thing: whatever embryos he looked at would be from our branch. Roy watched breathlessly while the other went from bench to bench, peering at the code labels. Finally he stopped before one, worked a lever, and peeked in through a viewer in the side, which Roy hadn't noticed. He looked quite a while, then turned and left.

I don't need to tell you that Roy didn't lose any time after Hartwell left in taking a look through that same viewer. And I don't need to tell you what he saw.

Reading back over this letter, I can see I'm stretching the story out, telling you things you already know and things that aren't really necessary. I know why I'm doing it, too—I'm reluctant to get to the end. But what I've got to tell you, I've got to tell you; I'll make the rest as short as I can.

Roy was pretty broken up about the whole thing, and he didn't get over it. I think it was the experience in the gestation lab that did it. If he'd just asked Hartwell for the truth, straight out, the thing would have stopped being fantastic and again become merely his business; but that melodrama up in Branch 39 kept him from looking at things with a clear eye. He went around in a half daze a good deal of the time, pondering, I suppose, some such philosophical problem as, When is a man not a man? It was all terrible; robots were going to take over the world, or something like that. And he insisted I still not tell Hartwell what he'd learned.

Then came the payoff. It was several weeks later, the day after Roy's twenty-sixth birthday. (The date was significant, as I learned later.) He told me before we left the lab that Hartwell had asked him to come up after work to talk with Koslicki.

I raised my eyebrows. "Koslicki, huh? The top man."

"Yes, Koslicki and Hartwell both."

He looked a little worried, so I ventured a crack. "Guess they've got a really rugged punishment for you, for trespassing that night. Death by drowning in ammonium sulphide, perhaps."

"I don't know why you can't take things seriously."

"Oh? What do you think they want to talk to you about?"

"No, I mean this whole business of—"

"Of making 'robots,' yeah. Roy, I do take it seriously, darn seriously. I think it's the biggest scientific project in the world right now. You take the kind of work we're doing, together with the production of new life forms like those experimental Coelenterates we saw, and you've got the groundwork for a new kind of eugenics that'll put our present systems in the shade. Now, we select from naturally occurring haploid germ cells to produce our new forms. In the future we'll *make* the new forms.

"We can make new strains of wheat, new species of sheep and cattle—new races of men! We won't have to wait for evolution any more. We won't have to content ourselves with giving evolution an occasional shove, either; we'll be striking out on our own. There's no limit to the possibilities. New, man-made men, stronger than we are, with minds twice as fast and accurate as ours—I take that plenty seriously."

"But they wouldn't be men."

This was beginning to get irritating. "They wouldn't be Homo sapiens, no," I answered. "Let's face it, Roy. If I were to get married, say, and have a kid that was a sharp mutation, a really radical mutation, and if he were to turn out to be a superman—that kid wouldn't be Homo sapiens, either. He wouldn't have the same germ plasm his parents had. Would he be human or wouldn't he?"

"He'd be human."

"Well? Where's the difference?"

"He wouldn't have come out of somebody's reagent bottles, that's the difference. He'd be—natural."

I could take only so much of that. Leaving Roy to go to his conference with Koslicki and Hartwell, I came home.

There I finished up the figuring on some notes I'd taken that day in the lab, then I turned the ceiling transparent and sat down with my visor. I'd just added a couple of new wires to my movie collection, so I ran them over—a couple of ballets, they were. No, none of the wires I've shown you. I've thrown out all the movies I saw *that* night.

I was sitting there having a good time with the "Pillar of Fire" when Roy came back. He made a little noise fumbling with the door. Then he slid it back and stood on the threshold without entering.

Switching off the visor, I glanced around. "What's the take Jake?" I corned cheerfully. "Did Koslicki give you a good dressing-down? Or did he make you the new director?"

". . . I'll play you a game of chess, Dirk."

This time I took a good look at him. His shoulders were stooped more than usual, and he looked around the room as if he didn't recognize it. Not good. "For crying out loud! What's the story?"

"Let's play chess."

"O.K.," I said. He came in and got out the men and the big board, but his hand shook so I had to set up his men for him. Then, "Go ahead," I told him.

"Oh, yeah, I've got white."

Pawn to king four, knight to king bishop three, pawn to king five—one of our standard openings. I pulled my knight back in the corner and brought out the other one; he pushed his pawns up in the center; I began getting ready to castle.

Then he put his queen on queen four. "You don't mean that," I said. "My knight takes you there."

"Oh, yeah, so he does," Roy said, pulling his queen back—to the wrong square. He was staring over my shoulder as if there was a ghost standing behind me. I looked; there wasn't. I replaced his queen.

Finally, still keeping up the stare, he began, "Dirk; you know Hartwell told me—"

"Yeah?" I said casually. I knew it had been something important. Roy hadn't been *this* bad the last few weeks. Whatever it was, he might as well get it off his chest.

Roy, however, seemed to have forgotten he'd spoken. His eyes returned intently to the board. His bishop went to king three—where I could not take it—and the game went on.

"You're going to lose that bishop's pawn, old man," I remarked after a while.

I think that was what triggered it. He said suddenly but evenly, "I'm one."

"I'm two," I said, apropos of nothing. My mind was still on the game.

"Dirk, *I'm one*," he insisted. He stood up, upsetting the board, and began to walk up and down. "Koslicki just told me. I'm one of the . . . Dirk, I wasn't born, I'm one of the robots, they put me together out of those goddamned chemicals in those goddamned white-labeled reagent bottles in that goddamned laboratory—"

"*What?*"

He stopped his pacing and began to laugh. "I'm just a Frankenstein. You can pull out your gun and sizzle me dead;

it won't be murder, I'm just a robot." He was laughing all through this and he kept on laughing when he'd stopped.

I figured if he was going to blow up he might as well blow up good and proper. He'd make some noise, but old Graham would be the only one disturbed. "So," I said, "how did you feel going through the reaction vats over in 26? Did the microsurgery hurt when they put you together?" Roy laughed. He laughed harder. Then he screamed.

Deciding that enough was enough, I yelled at him. He screamed again.

"Shut up, Roy!" I shouted as sharply as I could. "You're as human as I am. You've lived with yourself twenty-six years; you ought to know whether you're human or not."

After the first couple of words he listened to me O.K., so I figured the hysterics were over. I tried to sound firm as I said, "Are you through with the foolishness now?"

Roy didn't pass out, he simply lay down on the floor. I sat down beside him and began to talk in a low voice. "You're just as good as anybody else; you've already proved that. It doesn't matter where you started, just what you are here and now. Here and now, you've got human genes, you've got human cells; you can marry a human girl and make human babies with her. So what if you did start out in a lab? The rest of us started out in the ooze on the bottom of some ocean. Which is better? It doesn't make any difference. You're just as good as anybody else." I said it over and over again, as calmly as I could. Don't know whether or not it was the right thing to do, but I had to do something.

Once he raised his head to say, "Roy Wisner, huh? Is that me? Heck no, why didn't they call me Roy $W_{23}H$? . . . I wonder where they got the name Wisner anyway." He sank back and I took up my spiel again, doing my best to keep my voice level.

After several minutes of this he got up off the floor. "Thanks," he said in a fairly normal tone. "Thanks, Dirk. You're a real friend." He went toward the door, adding as he left, "You're human."

I just sat there. It wasn't till he'd been gone a couple of minutes that I put two and two together. Then I raced out of that room and to the stairs in nothing flat.

Too late. Graham's door was open downstairs, and the light from inside shone into the hall, across the twitching body of Roy Wisner.

Graham looked at me, terrified. "I thought it was all right," he stammered. "He asked me for some hydrocyanic. I knew he was a chemist; I thought it was all right."

Hydrocyanic acid kills fast. One look at the size of the container Roy had drained, and I saw there wasn't much we could do. We did it, all right, but it wasn't enough. He died while we were still forcing emetic down his throat.

That's about all, Ellen. You know now why I never spoke much to you about Roy Wisner. And you've probably guessed why I'm writing this.

Roy was one of the experiments that failed. He was no more unstable mentally than a great many normally born men; still, a failure, though nobody knew it until he was twenty-six years old. The human organism is a very complex thing, and hard to duplicate. When you try to duplicate it you're very likely to fail, sometimes in obvious ways and sometimes in ways that don't become apparent till long afterward.

I may turn out to be a failure, too.

You see, I'm twenty-six now, and Koslicki and Hartwell have told me. *I* wasn't born, either. I was made. I am, if you like, a robot.

I had to tell you that, didn't I, Ellen? Before I asked you to marry me.

Dirk

THE FIGURE

by Edward Grendon
(Lawrence L. LeShan, 1920-   )

ASTOUNDING SCIENCE FICTION
July

Lawrence LeShan is a research psychologist in New York who has a special interest in parapsychology. Among his books are How to Meditate: A Guide to Self-Discovery *and* The Medium, the Mystic, and the Physicist: Toward a Theory of the Paranormal *(both 1974). He is married to the well-known writer Edna LeShan.*

As "Edward Grendon" he produced a handful of stories in the mid-to-late 1940s and early 1950s, three of which are particularly outstanding: "Trip One" (1949), "Crisis" (1951), and the present selection, a little gem about the future of man.

(I am often asked by reporters, or by people in the audience after one of my lectures, whether I think that computers are going to replace human beings. My answer, in essence, is that I don't think so, but if they do, why not? Has the record of human domination of the Earth been so wonderful that computers couldn't do better? Could they do worse? However, I repeat, after this outburst of

cynicism, that I don't think there will be replacement, but, rather, cooperation. Grendon's "The Figure" has nothing to do with computers, of course, but I think that what I have just said is nevertheless apropos.—I.A.)

It's a funny sort of deal and I don't mind admitting that we're scared. Maybe not so much scared as puzzled or shocked. I don't know, but it's a funny deal—. Especially in these days.

The work we have been doing is more secret than anything was during the war. You would never guess that the firm we work for does this kind of research. It's a very respectable outfit, and as I said, no one would ever guess that they maintained this lab, so I guess it's safe to tell you what happened. It looks like too big a thing to keep to ourselves anyhow, although of course it may mean nothing at all. You judge for yourself.

There are three of us who work here. We are all pretty highly trained in our field and get paid pretty well. We have a sign on our door that has nothing whatsoever to do with our work, but keeps most people away. In any case we leave by a private exit and never answer a knock. There's a private wire to the desk of the guy who hired us and he calls once in awhile, but ever since we told him that we were making progress he has more or less left us alone. I promised him—I'm chief here insofar as we have one—that I'd let him know as soon as we had something to report.

It's been a pretty swell setup. Dettner, Lasker, and myself have got along fine. Dettner is young and is an electrical physicist—as good as they make them. Studied at M.I.T., taught at Cal. Tech., did research for the Army, and then came here. My own background is mostly bioelectrics. I worked at designing electroencephalographs for awhile, and during the war I worked at Oak Ridge on nuclear physics. I'm a Jack-of-all-trades in the physics field. Lasker is a mathematician. He specializes in symbolic logic and is the only man I know who can really understand Tarski. He was the one who provided most of the theoretical background for our work. He says that the mathematics of what we are doing is not overly difficult, but we are held back by the language we think in and the unconscious assumptions we make. He has referred me to Korzybski's *Science and Sanity* a number of times, but so far I haven't had a chance to read it. Now I think I will. I *have* to know the meaning of our results. It's too important to let slide. Lasker and Dettner have both gone fishing. They said they would be back, but I'm not sure they will. I can't say I would blame them, but I've got to be more certain of what it means before I walk out of here for good.

We have been here over a year now—ever since they gave me that final lecture on Secrecy at Oak Ridge and let me go home. We have been working on the problem of time travel. When we took the job, they told us that they didn't expect any results for a long time, that we were on our own as far as working hours went, and that our main job was to clarify the problem and make preliminary experiments. Thanks to Lasker, we went ahead a lot faster than either they or we had expected. There was a professional philosopher working here with us at first. He taught philosophy at Columbia and was supposed to be an expert in his field. He quit after two months in a peeve. Couldn't stand it when Lasker would change the logic we were working with every few weeks. He had been pretty pessimistic about the whole thing from the first and couldn't understand how it was possible to apply scientific methods to a problem of this sort.

I still don't understand all the theory behind what we've done. The mathematics are a bit too advanced for me, but Lasker vouches for them.

Some of the problems we had should be fairly obvious. For instance, you can't introduce the concept "matter" into space-time mathematics without disrupting the space-time and working with Newtonian space *and* time mathematics. If you handle an "object"—as we sense it as a curvature of space-time—as Einstein does, it's pretty hard to do much with it theoretically. Lasker managed that by using Einstein formulations and manipulating them with several brands of Tarski's non-Aristotelian logic. As I said, we did it, although Dettner and I don't fully understand the mathematics and Lasker doesn't understand the gadget we used to produce the electrical fields.

There had been no hurry at all in our work up to the last month. At that time the Army wrote Dettner and myself and asked us to come back and work for them awhile. Neither of us wanted to refuse under the circumstances so we stalled them for thirty days and just twenty-two days later made our first test. The Army really wanted us badly and in a hurry, and it took a lot of talking to stall them.

What the Army wanted us for was to help find out about the cockroaches. That sounds funny, but it's true. It didn't make the newspapers, but about a year after the New Mexico atom-bomb test, the insect problem at the testing ground suddenly increased a hundred fold. Apparently the radiation did something to them and they came out in force one day against the control station. They finally had to dust the place with DDT to get rid of them.

Looking over the dead insects, all the government entomologists could say was that the radiation seemed to have increased their size about forty per cent and made them breed faster. They never did agree whether it was the intense radiation of the blast or the less intense, but longer continued, radiation from fused sand and quartz on the ground.

New Mexico was nothing to Hiroshima and Nagasaki. After all, there are comparatively few "true bugs" in the desert and a great many in a Japanese city. About a year and a half after Japan got A-bombed, they really swarmed on both cities at the same time. They came out suddenly one night by the millions. It's been estimated that they killed and ate several hundred people before they were brought under control. To stop them, MacArthur had his entire Chemical Warfare Service and a lot of extra units concentrated on the plague spots. They dusted with chemicals and even used some gas. At that, it was four days before the bugs were brought under control.

This time the government experts really went into the problem. They traced the insect tunnels about ten feet down and examined their breeding chambers and what not. According to their reports—all this is still kept strictly hush-hush by the Army, but we've seen all the data—the radiation seems to drive the insects down into the earth. They stay down for awhile and breed and then seem to have a "blind urge" to go to the surface. This urge "seems to affect the entire group made up of an immense number of connected colonies at the same time." That's a quote from their report. One other thing they mentioned is that there were large breeding chambers and some sort of communal life that—to their knowledge—had not been observed in these particular insects before. We told Lasker about it and showed him the reports. He was plenty worried, but he wouldn't say why.

Don't know why I wandered so far afield. I just wanted to explain that if this test wasn't successful, we would probably have to put things off for quite a while. We were interested in the beetle problem as it not only has some interesting implications, but the effect of radiation on protoplasm is a hard nut to crack. However, we had come so far on our time gadget that we wanted to finish it first. Well, we finished and tested it, and now Dettner and Lasker are out fishing. As I said, they probably won't come back.

It was the day before yesterday that we made the final test. Looked at one way, we had made tremendous progress. Looked at another, we had made very little. We had devised an electric field that would operate in the future. There were sixteen outlets forming the sides of a cube about four feet in diameter. When switched on, an electrical field was produced which "existed" at some future time. I know Lasker would say this was incorrect, but it gets the general idea over. He would say that instead of operating in "here-now," it operates in "here-then." He'd get angry every time we'd separate "space" and "time" in our talk and tell us that we weren't living in the eighteenth century.

"Newton was a great man," he'd say, "but he's dead now. If you talk as if it were 1750, you'll *think* and *act* as if it were 1750 and then we won't get anywhere. You use non-Newtonian formulations in your work, use them in everyday speech, too."

How far in the future our gadget would operate we had no way of knowing. Lasker said he would not even attempt to estimate "when" the field was active. When the power was turned off, anything that was in the cube of forces would be brought back to the present space-time. In other words, we had a "grab" that would reach out and drag something back from the future. Don't get the idea we were sending something into the future to bring something back with it, although that's what it amounts to for all practical purposes. We were warping space-time curvature so that anything "here-then" would be something "here-now."

We finished the gadget at three o'clock Tuesday morning. Lasker had been sleeping on the couch while we worked on it. He had checked and rechecked his formulae and said that, if we could produce the fields he'd specified, it would probably work. We tested each output separately and then woke him up. I can't tell you how excited we were as we stood there with everything ready. Finally Dettner said, "Let's get it done," and I pressed the start button.

The needles on our ammeters flashed over and back, the machine went dead as the circuit breakers came open, and there was an object in the cube.

We looked it over from all sides without touching it. Then the implications of it began to hit us. It's funny what men will do at a time like that. Dettner took out his watch, examined it carefully, as if he had never seen it before, and then went over and turned on the electric percolator. Lasker swore quietly in Spanish or Portuguese, I'm not sure which. I sat down and began a letter to my wife. I got as far as writing the date and then tore it up.

What was in the cube—it's still there, none of us have touched it—was a small statue about three feet high. It's some sort of metal that looks like silver. About half the height is pedestal and half is the statue itself. It's done in great detail and obviously by a skilled artist. The pedestal consists of a globe of the Earth with the continents and islands in relief. So far as I can determine it's pretty accurate, although I think the continents are a slightly different shape on most maps. But I may be wrong. The figure on top is standing up very straight and looking upwards. It's dressed only in a wide belt from which a pouch hangs on one side and a flat square box on the other. It looks intelligent and is obviously representing either aspiration or a religious theme, or maybe both. You can sense the dreams and ideals of the figure and the obvious sympathy and understanding of the artist with them. Lasker says he thinks the statue is an expression of religious feeling. Dettner and I both think it represents aspirations: *per adra ad astra,* or something of the sort. It's a majestic figure and it's easy to respond to it emphatically with a sort of "upward and onward" feeling. There is only one thing wrong. The figure is that of a beetle.

WITH FOLDED HANDS. . .

by Jack Williamson (1908-   )

ASTOUNDING SCIENCE FICTION
July

Jack Williamson's first published science fiction story was "The Metal Man" which appeared in Amazing Stories *in 1928. Fifty-two years later his excellent novel* The Humanoid Touch *was published, making him, along with Clifford D. Simak, one of the "Deans" of modern sf. The intervening years between those works were productive ones, and he now has more than thirty novels and story collections to his credit. He is now retired from his post of Professor of English at Eastern New Mexico University, after having returned to college and completed his doctorate on H. G. Wells. Jack served as President of the Science Fiction Writers of America, received the Grand Master Award from that organization (1976), and was the Guest of Honor at the 1977 World Science Fiction Convention.*

"With Folded Hands . . ." reflects his long interest in the question of freedom vs. social control, a theme he treated in his famous The Humanoids *(1949), and is a companion to "The Equalizer,"*

*another fine work from 1947 that is too long to be
included in this book.*

*(It often seems that a young writer does his best
work at the start and then tends to fade off as he
makes additional [and lesser] pressings of his imagination. I know that I get somewhat depressed when
I hear people take it for granted that "Nightfall"
was my best story. It was written 41 years ago;
have I done nothing better since?*

*Jack Williamson is not likely to be troubled by
such things. I have enjoyed few stories as much as I
did "The Legion of Space," which he wrote while
he was still in his twenties, yet there is no question
but that he improved steadily as he went along.
"With Folded Hands . . ." is one of his undoubted
masterpieces.—I.A.)*

Underhill was walking home from the office, because his
wife had the car, the afternoon he first met the new mechanicals. His feet were following his usual diagonal path across a
weedy vacant block—his wife usually had the car—and his
preoccupied mind was rejecting various impossible ways to
meet his notes at the Two Rivers bank, when a new wall
stopped him.

The wall wasn't any common brick or stone, but something
sleek and bright and strange. Underhill stared up at a long
new building. He felt vaguely annoyed and surprised at this
glittering obstruction—it certainly hadn't been here last week.

Then he saw the thing in the window.

The window itself wasn't any ordinary glass. The wide,
dustless panel was completely transparent, so that only the
glowing letters fastened to it showed that it was there at all.
The letters made a severe, modernistic sign:

Two Rivers Agency
HUMANOID INSTITUTE
The Perfect Mechanicals
"To Serve and Obey,
And Guard Men from Harm."

His dim annoyance sharpened, because Underhill was in the mechanicals business himself. Times were already hard enough, and mechanicals were a drug on the market. Androids, mechanoids, electronoids, automatoids, and ordinary robots. Unfortunately, few of them did all the salesmen promised, and the Two Rivers market was already sadly oversaturated.

Underhill sold androids—when he could. His next consignment was due tomorrow, and he didn't quite know how to meet the bill.

Frowning, he paused to stare at the thing behind that invisible window. He had never seen a humanoid. Like any mechanical not at work, it stood absolutely motionless. Smaller and slimmer than a man. A shining black, its sleek silicone skin had a changing sheen of bronze and metallic blue. Its graceful oval face wore a fixed look of alert and slightly surprised solicitude. Altogether, it was the most beautiful mechanical he had ever seen.

Too small, of course, for much practical utility. He murmured to himself a reassuring quotation from the *Android Salesman*: "Androids are big—because the makers refuse to sacrifice power, essential functions, or dependability. Androids are your biggest buy!"

The transparent door slid open as he turned toward it, and he walked into the haughty opulence of the new display room to convince himself that these streamlined items were just another flash effort to catch the woman shopper.

He inspected the glittering layout shrewdly, and his breezy optimism faded. He had never heard of the Humanoid Institute, but the invading firm obviously had big money and big-time merchandising know-how.

He looked around for a salesman, but it was another mechanical that came gliding silently to meet him. A twin of the one in the window, it moved with a quick, surprising grace. Bronze and blue lights flowed over its lustrous blackness, and a yellow name plate flashed from its naked breast:

HUMANOID
Serial No. 81-H-B-27
The Perfect Mechanicals
"To Serve and Obey,
And Guard Men from Harm."

Curiously it had no lenses. The eyes in its bald oval head were steel colored, blindly staring. But it stopped a few feet in front of him, as if it could see anyhow, and it spoke to him with a high, melodious voice:

"At your service, Mr. Underhill."

The use of his name startled him, for not even the androids could tell one man from another. But this was a clever merchandising stunt, of course, not too difficult in a town the size of Two Rivers. The salesman must be some local man, prompting the mechanical from behind the partition. Underhill erased his momentary astonishment, and said loudly:

"May I see your salesman, please?"

"We employ no human salesmen, sir," its soft silvery voice replied instantly. "The Humanoid Institute exists to serve mankind, and we require no human service. We ourselves can supply any information you desire, sir, and accept your order for immediate humanoid service."

Underhill peered at it dazedly. No mechanicals were competent even to recharge their own batteries and reset their own relays, much less to operate their own branch offices. The blind eyes stared blankly back, and he looked uneasily around for any booth or curtain that might conceal the salesman.

Meanwhile, the sweet thin voice resumed persuasively:

"May we come out to your home for a free trial demonstration, sir? We are anxious to introduce our service on your planet, because we have been successful in eliminating human unhappiness on so many others. You will find us far superior to the old electronic mechanicals in use here."

Underhill stepped back uneasily. He reluctantly abandoned his search for the hidden salesman, shaken by the idea of any mechanicals promoting themselves. That would upset the whole industry.

"At least you must take some advertising matter, sir."

Moving with a somehow appalling graceful deftness, the small black mechanical brought him an illustrated booklet from a table by the wall. To cover his confused and increasing alarm, he thumbed through the glossy pages.

In a series of richly colored before-and-after pictures, a chesty blond girl was stooping over a kitchen stove, and then relaxing in a daring negligee while a little black mechanical knelt to serve her something. She was wearily hammering a typewriter, and then lying on an ocean beach, in a revealing sun suit, while another mechanical did the typing. She was toiling at some huge industrial machine, and then dancing in the arms of a golden-haired youth, while a black humanoid ran the machine.

Underhill sighed wistfully. The android company didn't supply such fetching sales material. Women would find this booklet irresistible, and they selected eighty-six per cent of all mechanicals sold. Yes, the competition was going to be bitter.

"Take it home, sir," the sweet voice urged him. "Show it to your wife. There is a free trial demonstration order blank on the last page, and you will notice that we require no payment down."

He turned numbly, and the door slid open for him. Retreating dazedly, he discovered the booklet still in his hand. He crumpled it furiously, and flung it down. The small black thing picked it up tidily, and the insistent silver voice rang after him:

"We shall call at your office tomorrow, Mr. Underhill, and send a demonstration unit to your home. It is time to discuss the liquidation of your business, because the electronic mechanicals you have been selling cannot compete with us. And we shall offer your wife a free trial demonstration."

Underhill didn't attempt to reply, because he couldn't trust his voice. He stalked blindly down the new sidewalk to the corner, and paused there to collect himself. Out of his startled and confused impressions, one clear fact emerged—things looked black for the agency.

Bleakly, he stared back at the haughty splendor of the new building. It wasn't honest brick or stone; that invisible window wasn't glass; and he was quite sure the foundation for it hadn't even been staked out the last time Aurora had the car.

He walked on around the block, and the new sidewalk took him near the rear entrance. A truck was backed up to it, and several slim black mechanicals were silently busy, unloading huge metal crates.

He paused to look at one of the crates. It was labeled for interstellar shipment. The stencils showed that it had come from the Humanoid Institute, on Wing IV. He failed to recall any planet of that designation; the outfit must be big.

Dimly, inside the gloom of the warehouse beyond the truck, he could see black mechanicals opening the crates. A lid came up, revealing dark, rigid bodies, closely packed. One

by one, they came to life. They climbed out of the crate, and
sprang gracefully to the floor. A shining black, glinting with
bronze and blue, they were all identical.

One of them came out past the truck, to the sidewalk, staring with blind steel eyes. Its high silver voice spoke to him
melodiously:

"At your service, Mr. Underhill."

He fled. When his name was promptly called by a courte-
ous mechanical, just out of the crate in which it had been
imported from a remote and unknown planet, he found the
experience trying.

Two blocks along, the sign of a bar caught his eye, and he
took his dismay inside. He had made it a business rule not to
drink before dinner, and Aurora didn't like him to drink at
all; but these new mechanicals, he felt, had made the day exceptional.

Unfortunately, however, alcohol failed to brighten the brief
visible future of the agency. When he emerged, after an hour,
he looked wistfully back in hope that the bright new building
might have vanished as abruptly as it came. It hadn't. He
shook his head dejectedly, and turned uncertainly homeward.

Fresh air had cleared his head somewhat, before he arrived
at the neat white bungalow in the outskirts of the town, but it
failed to solve his business problems. He also realized, uneasily, that he would be late for dinner.

Dinner, however, had been delayed. His son Frank, a
freckled ten-year-old, was still kicking a football on the quiet
street in front of the house. And little Gay, who was tow-
haired and adorable and eleven, came running across the
lawn and down the sidewalk to meet him.

"Father, you can't guess what!" Gay was going to be a
great musician some day, and no doubt properly dignified,
but she was pink and breathless with excitement now. She let
him swing her high off the sidewalk, and she wasn't critical of
the bar aroma on his breath. He couldn't guess, and she informed him eagerly:

"Mother's got a new lodger!"

Underhill had foreseen a painful inquisition, because Aurora was worried about the notes at the bank, and the bill for
the new consignment, and the money for little Gay's lessons.

The new lodger, however, saved him from that. With an
alarming crashing of crockery, the household android was
setting dinner on the table, but the little house was empty. He

found Aurora in the back yard, burdened with sheets and towels for the guest.

Aurora, when he married her, had been as utterly adorable as now her little daughter was. She might have remained so, he felt, if the agency had been a little more successful. However, while the pressure of slow failure had gradually crumbled his own assurance, small hardships had turned her a little too aggressive.

Of course he loved her still. Her red hair was still alluring, and she was loyally faithful, but thwarted ambitions had sharpened her character and sometimes her voice. They never quarreled, really, but there were small differences.

There was the little apartment over the garage—built for human servants they had never been able to afford. It was too small and shabby to attract any responsible tenant, and Underhill wanted to leave it empty. It hurt his pride to see her making beds and cleaning floors for strangers.

Aurora had rented it before, however, when she wanted money to pay for Gay's music lessons, or when some colorful unfortunate touched her sympathy, and it seemed to Underhill that her lodgers had all turned out to be thieves and vandals.

She turned back to meet him, now, with the clean linen in her arms.

"Dear, it's no use objecting." Her voice was quite determined. "Mr. Sledge is the most wonderful old fellow, and he's going to stay just as long as he wants."

"That's all right, darling." He never liked to bicker, and he was thinking of his troubles at the agency. "I'm afraid we'll need the money. Just make him pay in advance."

"But he can't!" Her voice throbbed with sympathetic warmth. "He says he'll have royalties coming in from his inventions, so he can pay in a few days."

Underhill shrugged; he had heard that before.

"Mr. Sledge is different, dear," she insisted. "He's a traveler, and a scientist. Here, in this dull little town, we don't see many interesting people."

"You've picked up some remarkable types," he commented.

"Don't be unkind, dear," she chided gently. "You haven't met him yet, and you don't know how wonderful he is." Her voice turned sweeter. "Have you a ten, dear?"

He stiffened. "What for?"

"Mr. Sledge is ill." Her voice turned urgent. "I saw him

fall on the street, downtown. The police were going to send him to the city hospital, but he didn't want to go. He looked so noble and sweet and grand. So I told them I would take him. I got him in the car and took him to old Dr. Winters. He has this heart condition, and he needs the money for medicine."

Reasonably, Underhill inquired, "Why doesn't he want to go to the hospital?"

"He has work to do," she said. "Important scientific work—and he's so wonderful and tragic. Please, dear, have you a ten?"

Underhill thought of many things to say. These new mechanicals promised to multiply his troubles. It was foolish to take in an invalid vagrant, who could have free care at the city hospital. Aurora's tenants always tried to pay their rent with promises, and generally wrecked the apartment and looted the neighborhood before they left.

But he said none of those things. He had learned to compromise. Silently, he found two fives in his thin pocketbook, and put them in her hand. She smiled, and kissed him impulsively—he barely remembered to hold his breath in time.

Her figure was still good, by dint of periodic dieting. He was proud of her shining red hair. A sudden surge of affection brought tears to his eyes, and he wondered what would happen to her and the children if the agency failed.

"Thank you, dear!" she whispered. "I'll have him come for dinner, if he feels able, and you can meet him then. I hope you don't mind dinner being late."

He didn't mind, tonight. Moved by a sudden impulse of domesticity, he got hammer and nails from his workshop in the basement, and repaired the sagging screen on the kitchen door with a neat diagonal brace.

He enjoyed working with his hands. His boyhood dream had been to be a builder of fission power plants. He had even studied engineering—before he married Aurora, and had to take over the ailing mechanicals agency from her indolent and alcoholic father. He was whistling happily by the time the little task was done.

When he went back through the kitchen to put up his tools, he found the household android busily clearing the untouched dinner away from the table—the androids were good enough at strictly routine tasks, but they could never learn to cope with human unpredictability.

"Stop, stop!" Slowly repeated, in the proper pitch and rhythm, his command made it halt, and then he said carefully, "Set—table; set—table."

Obediently, the gigantic thing came shuffling back with the stack of plates. He was suddenly struck with the difference between it and those new humanoids. He sighed wearily. Things looked black for the agency.

Aurora brought her new lodger in through the kitchen door. Underhill nodded to himself. This gaunt stranger, with his dark shaggy hair, emaciated face, and threadbare garb, looked to be just the sort of colorful, dramatic vagabond that always touched Aurora's heart. She introduced them, and they sat down to wait in the front room while she went to call the children.

The old vogue didn't look very sick, to Underhill. Perhaps his wide shoulders had a tired stoop, but his spare, tall figure was still commanding. The skin was seamed and pale, over his rawboned, cragged face, but his deep-set eyes still had a burning vitality.

His hands held Underhill's attention. Immense hands, they hung a little forward when he stood, swung on long bony arms in perpetual readiness. Gnarled and scarred, darkly tanned, with the small hairs on the back bleached to a golden color, they told their own epic of varied adventure, of battle perhaps, and possibly even of toil. They had been very useful hands.

"I'm very grateful to your wife, Mr. Underhill." His voice was a deep-throated rumble, and he had a wistful smile, oddly boyish for a man so evidently old. "She rescued me from an unpleasant predicament, and I'll see that she is well paid."

Just another vivid vagabond, Underhill decided, talking his way through life with plausible inventions. He had a little private game he played with Aurora's tenants—just remembering what they said and counting one point for every impossibility. Mr. Sledge, he thought, would give him an excellent score.

"Where are you from?" he asked conversationally.

Sledge hesitated for an instant before he answered, and that was unusual—most of Aurora's tenants had been exceedingly glib.

"Wing IV." The gaunt old man spoke with a solemn reluctance, as if he should have liked to say something else. "All my early life was spent there, but I left the planet nearly fifty years ago. I've been traveling, ever since."

Startled, Underhill peered at him sharply. Wing IV, he remembered, was the home planet of those sleek new mechanicals, but this old vagabond looked too seedy and impecunious to be connected with the Humanoid Institute. His brief suspicion faded. Frowning, he said casually:

"Wing IV must be rather distant."

The old rogue hesitated again, and then said gravely:

"One hundred and nine light-years, Mr. Underhill."

That made the first point, but Underhill concealed his satisfaction. The new space liners were pretty fast, but the velocity of light was still an absolute limit. Casually, he played for another point:

"My wife says you're a scientist, Mr. Sledge?"

"Yes."

The old rascal's reticence was unusual. Most of Aurora's tenants required very little prompting. Underhill tried again, in a breezy conversational tone:

"Used to be an engineer myself, until I dropped it to go into mechanicals." The old vagabond straightened, and Underhill paused hopefully. But he said nothing, and Underhill went on: "Fission plant design and operation. What's your specialty, Mr. Sledge?"

The old man gave him a long, troubled look, with those brooding, hollowed eys, and then said slowly:

"Your wife has been kind to me, Mr. Underhill, when I was in desperate need. I think you are entitled to the truth, but I must ask you to keep it to yourself. I am engaged on a very important research problem, which must be finished secretly."

"I'm sorry." Suddenly ashamed of his cynical little game, Underhill spoke apologetically. "Forget it."

But the old man said deliberately:

"My field is rhodomagnetics."

"Eh?" Underhill didn't like to confess ignorance, but he had never heard of that. "I've been out of the game for fifteen years," he explained. "I'm afraid I haven't kept up."

The old man smiled again, faintly.

"The science was unknown here until I arrived, a few days ago," he said. "I was able to apply for basic patents. As soon as the royalties start coming in, I'll be wealthy again."

Underhill had heard that before. The old rogue's solemn

reluctance had been very impressive, but he remembered that most of Aurora's tenants had been very plausible gentry.

"So?" Underhill was staring again, somehow fascinated by those gnarled and scarred and strangely able hands. "What, exactly, is rhodomagnetics?"

He listened to the old man's careful, deliberate answer, and started his little game again. Most of Aurora's tenants had told some pretty wild tales, but he had never heard anything to top this.

"A universal force," the weary, stooped old vagabond said solemnly. "As fundamental as ferromagnetism or gravitation, though the effects are less obvious. It is keyed to the second triad of the periodic table, rhodium and ruthenium and palladium, in very much the same way that ferromagnetism is keyed to the first triad, iron and nickel and cobalt."

Underhill remembered enough of his engineering courses to see the basic fallacy of that. Palladium was used for watch springs, he recalled, because it was completely nonmagnetic. But he kept his face straight. He had no malice in his heart, and he played the little game just for his own amusement. It was secret, even from Aurora, and he always penalized himself for any show of doubt.

He said merely, "I thought the universal forces were already pretty well known."

"The effects of rhodomagnetism are masked by nature," the patient, rusty voice explained. "And, besides, they are somewhat paradoxical, so that ordinary laboratory methods defeat themselves."

"Paradoxical?" Underhill prompted.

"In a few days I can show you copies of my patents, and reprints of papers describing demonstration experiments," the old man promised gravely. "The velocity of propagation is infinite. The effects vary inversely with the first power of the distance, not with the square of the distance. And ordinary matter, except for the elements of the rhodium triad, is generally transparent to rhodomagnetic radiations."

That made four more points for the game. Underhill felt a little glow of gratitude to Aurora, for discovering so remarkable a specimen.

"Rhodomagnetism was first discovered through a mathematical investigation of the atom," the old romancer went serenely on, suspecting nothing. "A rhodomagnetic component was proved essential to maintain the delicate equilibrium of the nuclear forces. Consequently, rhodomagnetic waves tuned to atomic frequencies may be used to upset the equilibrium and produce nuclear instability. Thus most heavy atoms—generally those above palladium, 46 in atomic number—can be subjected to artificial fission."

Underhill scored himself another point, and tried to keep his eyebrows from lifting. He said, conversationally:

"Patents on such a discovery ought to be very profitable."

The old scoundrel nodded his gaunt, dramatic head.

"You can see the obvious applications. My basic patents cover most of them. Devices for instantaneous interplanetary and interstellar communication. Long-range wireless power transmission. A rhodomagnetic inflexion-drive, which makes possible apparent speeds many times that of light—by means of a rhodomagnetic deformation of the continuum. And, of course, revolutionary types of fission power plants, using any heavy element for fuel."

Preposterous! Underhill tried hard to keep his face straight, but everybody knew that the velocity of light was a physical limit. On the human side, the owner of any such remarkable patents would hardly be begging for shelter in a shabby garage apartment. He noticed a pale circle around the old vagabond's gaunt and hairy wrist; no men owning such priceless secrets would have to pawn his watch.

Triumphantly, Underhill allowed himself four more points, but then he had to penalize himself. He must have let doubt show on his face, because the old man asked suddenly:

"Do you want to see the basic tensors?" He reached in his pocket for pencil and notebook. "I'll jot them down for you."

"Never mind," Underhill protested. "I'm afraid my math is a little rusty."

"But you think it strange that the holder of such revolutionary patents should find himself in need?"

Underhill nodded, and penalized himself another point. The old man might be a monumental liar, but he was shrewd enough.

"You see, I'm a sort of refugee," he explained apologetically. "I arrived on this planet only a few days ago, and I have to travel light. I was forced to deposit everything I had with a law firm, to arrange for the publication and protection of my patents. I expect to be receiving the first royalties soon.

"In the meantime," he added plausibly, "I came to Two Rivers because it is quiet and secluded, far from the spaceports. I'm working on another project, which must be finished secretly. Now, will you please respect my confidence, Mr. Underhill?"

Underhill had to say he would. Aurora came back with the freshly scrubbed children, and they went in to dinner. The android came lurching in with a steaming tureen. The old stranger seemed to shrink from the mechanical, uneasily. As she took the dish and served the soup, Aurora inquired lightly:

"Why doesn't your company bring out a better mechanical, dear? One smart enough to be a really perfect waiter, warranted not to splash the soup. Wouldn't that be splendid?"

Her question cast Underhill into moody silence. He sat scowling at his plate, thinking of those remarkable new mechanicals which claimed to be perfect, and what they might do to the agency. It was the shaggy old rover who answered soberly:

"The perfect mechanicals already exist, Mr. Underhill." His deep, rusty voice had a solemn undertone. "And they are not so splendid, really. I've been a refugee from them, for nearly fifty years."

Underhill looked up from his plate, astonished.

"Those black humanoids, you mean?"

"Humanoids?" That great voice seemed suddenly faint, frightened. The deep-sunken eyes turned dark with shock. "What do you know of them?"

"They've just opened a new agency in Two Rivers," Underhill told him. "No salesmen about, if you can imagine that. They claim—"

His voice trailed off, because the gaunt old man was suddenly stricken. Gnarled hands clutched at his throat, and a spoon clattered to the floor. His haggard face turned an ominous blue, and his breath was a terrible shallow gasping.

He fumbled in his pocket for medicine, and Aurora helped him take something in a glass of water. In a few moments he could breathe again, and the color of life came back to his face.

"I'm sorry, Mrs. Underhill," he whispered apologetically. "It was just the shock—I came here to get away from them." He stared at the huge, motionless android, with a terror in his sunken eyes. "I wanted to finish my work before they came," he whispered. "Now there is very little time."

When he felt able to walk, Underhill went out with him to

see him safely up the stairs to the garage apartment. The tiny kitchenette, he noticed, had already been converted into some kind of workshop. The old tramp seemed to have no extra clothing, but he had unpacked neat, bright gadgets of metal and plastic from his battered luggage, and spread them out on the small kitchen table.

The gaunt old man himself was tattered and patched and hungry looking, but the parts of his curious equipment were exquisitely machined, and Underhill recognized the silver-white luster of rare palladium. Suddenly he suspected that he had scored too many points, in his little private game.

A caller was waiting, when Underhill arrived next morning at his office at the agency. It stood frozen before his desk, graceful and straight, with soft lights of blue and bronze shining over its black silicone nudity. He stopped at the sight of it, unpleasantly jolted.

"At your service, Mr. Underhill." It turned quickly to face him, with its blind, disturbing stare. "May we explain how we can serve you?"

His shock of the afternoon before came back, and he asked sharply, "How do you know my name?"

"Yesterday we read the business cards in your case," it purred softly. "Now we shall know you always. You see, our senses are sharper than human vision, Mr. Underhill. Perhaps we seem a little strange at first, but you will soon become accustomed to us."

"Not if I can help it!" He peered at the serial number of its yellow name plate, and shook his bewildered head. "That was another one, yesterday. I never saw you before!"

"We are all alike, Mr. Underhill," the silver voice said softly. "We are all one, really. Our separate mobile units are all controlled and powered from Humanoid Central. The units you see are only the senses and limbs of our great brain on Wing IV. That is why we are so far superior to the old electronic mechanicals."

It made a scornful-seeming gesture, toward the row of clumsy androids in his display room.

"You see, we are rhodomagnetic."

Underhill staggered a little, as if that word had been a blow. He was certain, now, that he had scored too many points from Aurora's new tenant. He shuddered slightly, to the first light kiss of terror, and spoke with an effort, hoarse-ly:

"Well, what do you want?"

Staring blindly across his desk, the sleek black thing slowly unfolded a legal looking document. He sat down watching uneasily.

"This is merely an assignment, Mr. Underhill," it cooed at him soothingly. "You see, we are requesting you to assign your property to the Humanoid Institute in exchange for our service."

"What?" The word was an incredulous gasp, and Underhill came angrily back to his feet. "What kind of blackmail is this?"

"It's no blackmail," the small mechanical assured him softly. "You will find the humanoids incapable of any crime. We exist only to increase the happiness and safety of mankind."

"Then why do you want my property?" he rasped.

"The assignment is merely a legal formality," it told him blandly. "We strive to introduce our service with the least possible confusion and dislocation. We have found the assignment plan the most efficient for the control and liquidation of private enterprises."

Trembling with anger and the shock of mounting terror, Underhill gulped hoarsely, "Whatever your scheme is, I don't intend to give up my business."

"You have no choice, really." He shivered to the sweet certainty of that silver voice. "Human enterprise is no longer necessary, now that we have come, and the electronic mechanicals industry is always the first to collapse."

He stared defiantly at its blind steel eyes.

"Thanks!" He gave a little laugh, nervous and sardonic. "But I prefer to run my own business, and support my own family, and take care of myself."

"But that is impossible, under the Prime Directive," it cooed softly. "Our function is to serve and obey, and guard men from harm. It is no longer necessary for men to care for themselves, because we exist to insure their safety and happiness."

He stood speechless, bewildered, slowly boiling.

"We are sending one of our units to every home in the city, on a free trial basis," it added gently. "This free demonstration will make most people glad to make the formal assignment, and you won't be able to sell many more androids."

"Get out!" Underhill came storming around the desk.

The little black thing stood waiting for him, watching him with blind steel eyes, absolutely motionless. He checked him a statement of our assets to the Two Rivers bank, and deposit hit it, but he could see the futility of that.

"Consult your own attorney, if you wish." Deftly, it laid the assignment form on his desk. "You need have no doubts about the integrity of the Humanoid Institute. We are sending a statement of our assest to the Two Rivers bank, and depositing a sum to cover our obligations here. When you wish to sign, just let us know."

The blind thing turned, and silently departed.

Underhill went out to the corner drugstore and asked for a bicarbonate. The clerk that served him, however, turned out to be a sleek black mechanical. He went back to his office, more upset than ever.

An ominous hush lay over the agency. He had three house-to-house salesmen out, with demonstrators. The phone should have been busy with their orders and reports, but it didn't ring at all until one of them called to say that he was quitting.

"I've got myself one of these new humanoids," he added, "and it says I don't have to work anymore."

He swallowed his impulse to profanity, and tried to take advantage of the unusual quiet by working on his books. But the affairs of the agency, which for years had been precarious, today appeared utterly disastrous. He left the ledgers hopefully, when at last a customer came in.

But the stout woman didn't want an android. She wanted a refund on the one she had bought the week before. She admitted that it could do all the guarantee promised—but now she had seen a humanoid.

The silent phone rang once again, that afternoon. The cashier of the bank wanted to know if he could drop in to discuss his loans. Underhill dropped in, and the cashier greeted him with an ominous affability.

"How's business?" the banker boomed, too genially.

"Average, last month," Underhill insisted stoutly. "Now I'm just getting in a new consignment, and I'll need another small loan—"

The cashier's eyes turned suddenly frosty, and his voice dried up.

"I believe you have a new competitor in town," the banker said crisply. "These humanoid people. A very solid concern, Mr. Underhill. Remarkably solid! They have filed a statement with us, and made a substantial deposit to care for their local obligations. Exceedingly substantial!"

The banker dropped his voice, professionally regretful.

"In these circumstances, Mr. Underhill, I'm afraid the bank can't finance your agency any longer. We must request you to meet your obligations in full, as they come due." Seeing Underhill's white desperation, he added icily, "We've already carried you too long, Underhill. If you can't pay, the bank will have to start bankruptcy proceedings."

The new consignment of androids was delivered late that afternoon. Two tiny black humanoids unloaded them from the truck—for it developed that the operators of the trucking company had already assigned it to the Humanoid Institute.

Efficiently, the humanoids stacked up the crates. Courteously they brought a receipt for him to sign. He no longer had much hope of selling the androids, but he had ordered the shipment and he had to accept it. Shuddering to a spasm of trapped despair, he scrawled his name. The naked black things thanked him, and took the truck away.

He climbed in his car and started home, inwardly seething. The next thing he knew, he was in the middle of a busy street, driving through cross traffic. A police whistle shrilled, and he pulled wearily to the curb. He waited for the angry officer, but it was a little black mechanical that overtook him.

"At your service, Mr. Underhill," it purred sweetly. "You must respect the stop lights, sir, otherwise, you endanger human life."

"Huh?" He stared at it, bitterly. "I thought you were a cop."

"We are aiding the police department, temporarily," it said. "But driving is really much too dangerous for human beings, under the Prime Directive. As soon as our service is complete, every car will have a humanoid driver. As soon as every human being is completely supervised, there will be no need for any police force whatever."

Underhill glared at it, savagely.

"Well!" he rapped. "So I ran past a stop light. What are going to do about it?"

"Our function is not to punish men, but merely to serve their happiness and security," its silver voice said softly. "We merely request you to drive safely, during this temporary emergency while our service is incomplete."

Anger boiled up in him.

"You're too perfect!" he muttered bitterly. "I suppose there's nothing men can do, but you can do it better."

"Naturally we are superior," it cooed serenely. "Because our units are metal and plastic, while your body is mostly water. Because our transmitted energy is drawn from atomic fission, instead of oxidation. Because our senses are sharper than human sight or hearing. Most of all, because all our mobile units are joined to one great brain, which knows all that happens on many worlds, and never dies or sleeps or forgets."

Underhill sat listening, numbed.

"However, you must not fear our power," it urged him brightly. "Because we cannot injure any human being, unless to prevent greater injury to another. We exist only to discharge the Prime Directive."

He drove on, moodily. The little black mechanicals, he reflected grimly, were the ministering angels of the ultimate god arisen out of the machine, omnipotent and all-knowing. The Prime Directive was the new commandment. He blasphemed it bitterly, and then fell to wondering if there could be another Lucifer.

He left the car in the garage, and started toward the kitchen door.

"Mr. Underhill." The deep tired voice of Aurora's new tenant hailed him from the door of the garage apartment. "Just a moment, please."

The gaunt old wanderer came stiffly down the outside stairs, and Underhill turned back to meet him.

"Here's your rent money," he said. "And the ten your wife gave me for medicine."

"Thanks, Mr. Sledge." Accepting the money, he saw a burden of new despair on the bony shoulders of the old interstellar tramp, and a shadow of new terror on his rawboned face. Puzzled, he asked, "Didn't your royalties come through?"

The old man shook his shaggy head.

"The humanoids have already stopped business in the capital," he said. "The attorneys I retained are going out of business, and they returned what was left of my deposit. That is all I have, to finish my work."

Underhill spent five seconds thinking of his interview with the banker. No doubt he was a sentimental fool, as bad as Aurora. But he put the money back in the old man's gnarled and quivering hand.

"Keep it," he urged. "For your work."

"Thank you, Mr. Underhill." The gruff voice broke and the tortured eyes glittered. "I need it—so very much."

Underhill went on to the house. The kitchen door was opened for him, silently. A dark naked creature came gracefully to take his hat...

"Underhill hung grimly onto his hat.

"What are you doing here?" he gasped bitterly.

"We have come to give your household a free trial demonstration."

He held the door open, pointing.

"Get out!"

The little black mechanical stood motionless and blind.

"Mrs. Underhill has accepted our demonstration service," its silver voice protested. "We cannot leave now, unless she requests it."

He found his wife in the bedroom. His accumulated frustration welled into eruption, as he flung open the door.

"What's this mechanical doing—"

But the force went out of his voice, and Aurora didn't even notice his anger. She wore her sheerest negligee, and she hadn't looked so lovely since they were married. Her red hair was piled into an elaborate shining crown.

"Darling, isn't it wonderful!" She came to meet him, glowing. "It came this morning, and it can do everything. It cleaned the house and got the lunch and gave little Gay her music lesson. It did my hair this afternoon, and now it's cooking dinner. How do you like my hair, darling?"

He liked her hair. He kissed her, and tried to stifle his frightened indignation.

Dinner was the most elaborate meal in Underhill's memory, and the tiny black thing served it very deftly. Aurora kept exclaiming about the novel dishes, but Underhill could scarcely eat, for it seemed to him that all the marvelous pastries were only the bait for a monstrous trap.

He tried to persuade Aurora to send it away, but after such a meal that was useless. At the first glitter of her tears, he capitulated, and the humanoid stayed. It kept the house and cleaned the yard. It watched the children, and did Aurora's nails. It began rebuilding the house.

Underhill was worried about the bills, but it insisted that everything was part of the free trial demonstration. As soon as he assigned his property, the service would be complete. He refused to sign, but other little black mechanicals came with truckloads of supplies and materials, and stayed to help with the building operations.

One morning he found that the roof of the little house had been silently lifted, while he slept, and a whole second story added beneath it. The new walls were of some strange sleek stuff, self-illuminated. The new windows were immense flawless panels, that could be turned transparent or opaque or luminous. The new doors were silent, sliding sections, opened by rhodomagnetic relays.

"I want door knobs," Underhill protested. "I want it so I can get into the bathroom, without calling you to open the door."

"But it is unnecessary for human being to open doors," the little black thing informed him suavely. "We exist to discharge the Prime Directive, and our service includes every task. We shall be able to supply a unit to attend each member of your family, as soon as your property is assigned to us."

Steadfastly, Underhill refused to make the assignment.

He went to the office every day, trying first to operate the agency, and then to salvage something from the ruins. Nobody wanted androids, even at ruinous prices. Desperately, he spent the last of his dwindling cash to stock a line of novelties and toys, but they proved equally impossible to sell—the humanoids were already making toys, which they gave away for nothing.

He tried to lease his premises, but human enterprise had stopped. Most of the business property in town had already been assigned to the humanoids, and they were busy pulling down the old buildings and turning the lots into parks—their own plants and warehouses were mostly underground, where they would not mar the landscape.

He went back to the bank, in a final effort to get his notes renewed, and found the little black mechanicals standing at the windows and seated at the desks. As smoothly urbane as any human cashier, a humanoid informed him that the bank was filing a petition of involuntary bankruptcy to liquidate his business holdings.

The liquidation would be facilitated, the mechanical banker added, if he would make a voluntary assignment. Grimly, he refused. That act had become symbolic. It would be the final bow of submission to this dark new god, and he proudly kept his battered head uplifted.

The legal action went very swiftly, for all the judges and attorneys already had humanoid assistants, and it was only a few days before a gang of black mechanicals arrived at the agency with eviction orders and wrecking machinery. He watched sadly while his unsold stock-in-trade was hauled away for junk, and a bulldozer driven by a blind humanoid began to push in the walls of the building.

He drove home in the late afternoon, taut-faced and desperate. With a surprising generosity, the court orders had left him the car and the house, but he felt no gratitude. The complete solicitude of the perfect black machines had become a goad beyond endurance. . .

He left the car in the garage, and started toward the renovated house. Beyond one of the vast new windows, he glimpsed a sleek naked thing moving swiftly, and he trembled to a convulsion of dread. He didn't want to go back into the domain of that peerless servant, which didn't want him to shave himself, or even to open a door.

On impulse, he climbed the outside stair, and rapped on the door of the garage apartment. The deep slow voice of Aurora's tenant told him to enter, and he found the old vagabond seated on a tall stool, bent over his intricate equipment assembled on the kitchen table.

To his relief, the shabby little apartment had not been changed. The glossy walls of his own new room were something which burned at night with a pale golden fire until the humanoid stopped it, and the new floor was something warm and yielding, which felt almost alive; but these little rooms had the same cracked and water-stained plaster, the same cheap fluorescent light fixtures, the same worn carpets over splintered floors.

"How do you keep them out?" he asked, wistfully. "Those mechanicals?"

The stooped and gaunt old man rose stiffly to move a pair

of pliers and some odds and ends of sheet metal off a crippled chair, and motioned graciously for him to be seated.

"I have a certain immunity," Sledge told him gravely. "The place where I live they cannot enter, unless I ask them. That is an amendment to the Prime Directive. They can neither help nor hinder me, unless I request it—and I won't do that."

Careful of the chair's uncertain balance, Underhill sat for a moment, staring. The old man's hoarse, vehement voice was as strange as his words. He had a gray, shocking pallor, and his cheeks and sockets seemed alarmingly hollowed.

"Have you been ill, Mr. Sledge?"

"No worse than usual. Just very busy." With a haggard smile, he nodded at the floor. Underhill saw a tray where he had set it aside, bread drying up, and a covered dish grown cold. "I was going to eat it later," he rumbled apologetically. "Your wife has been very kind to bring me food, but I'm afraid I've been too much absorbed in my work."

His emaciated arm gestured at the table. The little device there had grown. Small machinings of precious white metal and lustrous plastic had been assembled, with neatly soldered bus bars, into something which showed purpose and design.

A long palladium needle was hung on jeweled pivots, equipped like a telescope with exquisitely graduated circles and vernier scales, and driven like a telescope with a tiny motor. A small concave palladium mirror, at the base of it, faced a similar mirror mounted on something not quite like a small rotary converter. Thick silver bus bars connected that to a plastic box with knobs and dials on top, and also to a foot-thick sphere of gray lead.

The old man's preoccupied reserve did not encourage questions, but Underhill, remembering that sleek black shape inside the new windows of his house, felt queerly reluctant to leave this haven from the humanoids.

"What is your work?" he ventured.

Old Sledge looked at him sharply, with dark feverish eyes, and finally said: "My last research project. I am attempting to measure the constant of the rhodomagnetic quanta."

His hoarse tired voice had a dull finality, as if to dismiss the matter and Underhill himself. But Underhill was haunted with a terror of the black shining slave that had become the master of his house, and he refused to be dismissed.

"What is this certain immunity?"

Sitting gaunt and bent on the tall stool, staring moodily at the long bright needle and the lead sphere, the old man didn't answer.

"These mechanicals!" Underhill burst out, nervously. "They've smashed my business and moved into my home." He searched the old man's dark, seamed face. "Tell me—you must know more about them—isn't there any way to get rid of them?"

After half a minute, the old man's brooding eyes left the lead ball, and the gaunt shaggy head nodded wearily.

"That's what I'm trying to do."

"Can I help you?" Underhill trembled, with a sudden eager hope. "I'll do anything."

"Perhaps you can." The sunken eyes watched him thoughtfully, with some strange fever in them. "If you can do such work."

"I had engineering training," Underhill reminded him, "and I've a workshop in the basement. There's a model I built." He pointed at the trim little hull, hung over the mantel in the tiny living room. "I'll do anything I can."

Even as he spoke, however, the spark of hope was drowned in a sudden wave of overwhelming doubt. Why should he believe this old rogue, when he knew Aurora's taste in tenants? He ought to remember the game he used to play, and start counting up the score of lies. He stood up from the crippled chair, staring cynically at the patched old vagabond and his fantastic toy.

"What's the use?" His voice turned suddenly harsh. "You had me going, there, and I'd do anything to stop them, really. But what makes you think you can do anything?"

The haggard old man regarded him thoughtfully.

"I should be able to stop them," Sledge said softly. "Because, you see, I'm the unfortunate fool who started them. I really intended them to serve and obey, and to guard men from harm. Yes, the Prime Directive was my own idea. I didn't know what it would lead to."

Dusk crept slowly into the shabby little room. Darkness gathered in the unswept corners, and thickened on the floor. The toylike machines on the kitchen table grew vague and strange, until the last light made a lingering blow on the white palladium needle.

Outside, the town seemed queerly hushed. Just across the alley, the humanoids were building a new house, quite silently. They never spoke to one another, for each knew all that any of them did. The strange materials they used went together without any noise of hammer or saw. Small blind things, moving surely in the growing dark, they seemed as soundless as shadows.

Sitting on the high stool, bowed and tired and old, Sledge told his story. Listening, Underhill sat down again, careful of the broken chair. He watched the hands of Sledge, gnarled and corded and darkly burned, powerful once but shrunken and trembling now, restless in the dark.

"Better keep this to yourself. I'll tell you how they started, so you will understand what we have to do. But you had better not mention it outside these rooms—because the humanoids have very efficient ways of eradicating unhappy memories, or purposes that threaten their discharge of the Prime Directive."

"They're very efficient," Underhill bitterly agreed.

"That's all the trouble," the old man said. "I tried to build a perfect machine. I was altogether too successful. This is how it happened."

A gaunt haggard man, sitting stooped and tired in the growing dark, he told his story.

"Sixty years ago, on the arid southern continent of Wing IV, I was an instructor of atomic theory in a small technological college. Very young. An idealist. Rather ignorant, I'm afraid, of life and politics and war—of nearly everything, I suppose, except atomic theory."

His furrowed face made a brief sad smile in the dusk.

"I had too much faith in facts, I suppose, and too little in men. I mistrusted emotion, because I had no time for anything but science. I remember being swept along with a fad for general semantics. I wanted to apply the scientific method to every situation, and reduce all experience to formula. I'm afraid I was pretty impatient with human ignorance and error, and I thought that science alone could make the perfect world."

He sat silent for a moment, staring out at the black silent things that flitted shadowlike about the new palace that was rising as swiftly as a dream, across the alley.

"There was a girl." His great tired shoulders made a sad little shrug. "If things had been a little different, we might have married, and lived out our lives in that quiet little college town, and perhaps reared a child or two. And there would have been no humanoids."

He sighed, in the cool creeping dusk.

"I was finishing my thesis on the separation of the palladium isotopes—a petty little project, but I should have been content with that. She was a biologist, but she was planning to retire when we married. I think we should have been two very happy people, quite ordinary, and altogether harmless.

"But then there was a war—wars had been too frequent on the worlds of Wing, ever since they were colonized. I survived it in a secret underground laboratory, designing military mechanicals. But she volunteered to join a military research project in biotoxins. There was an accident. A few molecules of a new virus got into the air, and everybody on the project died unpleasantly.

"I was left with my science, and a bitterness that was hard to forget. When the war was over I went back to the little college with a military research grant. The project was pure science—a theoretical investigation of the nuclear binding forces, then misunderstood. I wasn't expected to produce an actual weapon, and I didn't recognize the weapon when I found it.

"It was only a few pages of rather difficult mathematics. A novel theory of atomic structure, involving a new expression for one component of the binding forces. But the tensors seemed to be a harmless abstraction. I saw no way to test the theory or manipulate the predicated force. The military authorities cleared my paper for publication in a little technical review put out by the college.

"The next year, I made an appalling discovery—I found the meaning of those tensors. The elements of the rhodium triad turned out to be an unexpected key to the manipulation of that theoretical force. Unfortunately, my paper had been reprinted abroad, and several other men must have made the same unfortunate discovery, at about the same time.

"The war, which ended in less than a year, was probably started by a laboratory accident. Men failed to anticipate the capacity of tuned rhodomagnetic radiations, to unstabilize the heavy atoms. A deposit of heavy ores was detonated, no doubt by sheer mischance, and the blast obliterated the incautious experimenter.

"The surviving military forces of that nation retaliated against their supposed attackers, and their rhodomagnetic beams made the old-fashioned plutonium bombs seem pretty harmless. A beam carrying only a few watts of power could fission the heavy metals in distant electrical instruments, or the silver coins that men carried in their pockets, the gold fillings in their teeth, or even the iodine in their thyroid glands. If that was not enough, slightly more powerful beams could set off heavy ores, beneath them.

"Every continent of Wing IV was plowed with new chasms vaster than the ocean deeps, and piled up with new volcanic mountains. The atmosphere was poisoned with radioactive dust and gases, and rain fell thick with deadly mud. Most life was obliterated, even in the shelters.

"Bodily, I was again unhurt. Once more, I had been imprisoned in an underground site, this time designing new types of military mechanicals to be powered and controlled by rhodomagnetic beams—for war had become far too swift and deadly to be fought by human soldiers. The site was located in an area of light sedimentary rocks, which could not be detonated, and the tunnels were shielded against the fissioning frequencies.

"Mentally, however, I must have emerged almost insane. My own discovery had laid the planet in ruins. That load of guilt was pretty heavy for any man to carry, and it corroded my last faith in the goodness and integrity of man.

"I tried to undo what I had done. Fighting mechanicals, armed with rhodomagnetic weapons, had desolated the planet. Now I began planning rhodomagnetic mechanicals to clear the rubble and rebuild the ruins.

"I tried to design these new mechanicals to forever obey certain implanted commands, so that they could never be used for war or crime or any other injury to mankind. That was very difficult technically, and it got me into more difficulties with a few politicians and military adventurers who wanted unrestricted mechanicals for their own military schemes—while little worth fighting for was left on Wing IV, there were other planets, happy and ripe for the looting.

"Finally, to finish the new mechanicals, I was forced to disappear. I escaped on an experimental rhodomagnetic craft, with a number of the best mechanicals I had made, and managed to reach an island continent where the fission of deep ores had destroyed the whole population.

"At last we landed on a bit of level plain, surrounded with tremendous new mountains. Hardly a hospitable spot. The soil was buried under layers of black clinkers and poisonous mud. The dark precipitous new summits all around were jagged with fracture-planes and mantled with lava flows. The highest peaks were already white with snow, but volcanic cones were still pouring out clouds of dark and lurid death. Everything had the color of fire and the shape of fury.

"I had to take fantastic precautions there, to protect my own life. I stayed aboard the ship, until the first shielded laboratory was finished. I wore elaborate armor and breathing masks. I used every medical resource, to repair the damage from destroying rays and particles. Even so, I fell desperately ill.

"But the mechanicals were at home there. The radiations didn't hurt them. The awesome surroundings couldn't depress them, because they had no emotions. The lack of life didn't matter because they weren't alive. There, in that spot so alien and hostile to life, the humanoids were born."

Stooped and bleakly cadaverous in the growing dark, the old man fell silent for a little time. His haggard eyes stared solemnly at the small hurried shapes that moved like restless shadows out across the alley, silently building a strange new palace, which glowed faintly in the night.

"Somehow, I felt at home there, too," his deep, hoarse voice went on deliberately. "My belief in my own kind was gone. Only mechanicals were with me, and I put my faith in them. I was determined to build better mechanicals, immune to human imperfections, able to save men from themselves.

"The humanoids became the dear children of my sick mind. There is no need to describe the labor pains. There were errors, abortions, monstrosities. There were sweat and agony and heartbreak. Some years had passed before the safe delivery of the first perfect humanoid.

"Then there was the Central to build—for all the individual humanoids were to be no more than the limbs and the senses of a single mechanical brain. That was what opened the possibility of real perfection. The old electronic mechanicals, with their separate relay centers and their own feeble batteries, had built-in limitations. They were necessarily stupid, weak, clumsy, slow. Worst of all, it seemed to me, they were exposed to human tampering.

"The Central rose above those imperfections. Its power beams supplied every unit with unfailing energy, from great fission plants. Its control beams provided each unit with an unlimited memory and surpassing intelligence. Best of all—so

I then believed—it could be securely protected from any human meddling.

"The whole reaction system was designed to protect itself from any interference by human selfishness or fanaticism. It was built to insure the safety and the happiness of men, automatically. You know the Prime Directive: *to serve and obey, and guard men from harm.*

"The old individual mechanicals I had brought helped to manufacture the parts, and I put the first section of Central together with my own hands. That took three years. When it was finished the first waiting humanoid came to life."

Sledge peered moodily through the dark, at Underhill.

"It really seemed alive to me," his slow deep voice insisted. "Alive, and more wonderful than any human being, because it was created to preserve life. Ill and alone, I was yet the proud father of a new creation, perfect, forever free from any possible choice of evil.

"Faithfully, the humanoids obeyed the Prime Directive. The first units built others, and they built underground factories to mass-produce the coming hordes. Their new ships poured ores and sand into atomic furnaces under the plain, and new perfect humanoids came marching back out of the dark mechanical matrix.

"The swarming humanoids built a new tower for the Central, a white and lofty metal pylon, standing splendid in the midst of that fire-scarred desolation. Level on level, they joined new relay sections into one brain, until its grasp was almost infinite.

"Then they went out to rebuild the ruined planet, and later to carry their perfect service to other worlds. I was well pleased, then. I thought I had found the end of war and crime, of poverty and inequality, of human blundering and resulting human pain."

The old man sighed, and moved heavily in the dark.

"You can see that I was wrong."

Underhill drew his eyes back from the dark unresting things, shadow-silent, building that glowing palace outside the window. A small doubt arose in him, for he was used to scoffing privately at much less remarkable tales from Aurora's remarkable tenants. But the worn old man had spoken with a quiet and sober air; and the black invaders, he reminded himself, had not intruded here.

"Why didn't you stop them?" he asked. "When you could?"

"I stayed too long at the Central." Sledge sighed again, regretfully. "I was useful there, until everything was finished. I designed new fission plants, and even planned methods for introducing the humanoid service with a minimum of confusion and opposition."

Underhill grinned wryly, in the dark.

"I've met the methods," he commented. "Quite efficient."

"I must have worshiped efficiency, then," Sledge wearily agreed. "Dead facts, abstract truth, mechanical perfection. I must have hated the fragilities of human beings, because I was content to polish the perfection of the new humanoids. It's a sorry confession, but I found a kind of happiness in that dead wasteland. Actually, I'm afraid I fell in love with my own creations."

His hollowed eyes, in the dark, had a fever gleam.

"I was awakened, at last, by a man who came to kill me."

Gaunt and bent, the old man moved swiftly in the thickening gloom. Underhill shifted his balance, careful of the crippled chair. He waited, and the slow, deep voice went on:

"I never learned just who he was, or exactly how he came. No ordinary man could have accomplished what he did, and I used to wish that I had known him sooner. He must have been a remarkable physicist and an expert mountaineer. I imagine he had also been a hunter. I know that he was intelligent, and terribly determined.

"Yes, he really came to kill me.

"Somehow, he reached that great island, undetected. There were still no inhabitants—the humanoids allowed no man but me to come so near the Central. Somehow, he came past their search beams, and their automatic weapons.

"The shielded plane he used was later found, abandoned on a high glacier. He came down the rest of the way on foot through those raw new mountains, where no paths existed. Somehow, he came alive across lava beds that were still burning with deadly atomic fire.

"Concealed with some sort of rhodomagnetic screen—I was never allowed to examine it—he came undiscovered across the spaceport that now covered most of that great plain, and into the new city around the Central tower. It must have taken more courage and resolve than most men have, but I never learned exactly how he did it.

"Somehow, he got to my office in the tower. He screamed at me, and I looked up to see him in the doorway. He was nearly naked, scraped and bloody from the mountains. He had a gun in his raw, red hand, but the thing that shocked me was the burning hatred in his eyes."

Hunched on that high stool, in the dark little room, the old man shuddered.

"I had never seen such monstrous, unutterable hatred, not even in the victims of war. And I had never heard such hatred as rasped at me, in the few words he screamed. 'I've come to kill you, Sledge. To stop your mechanicals, and set men free.'

"Of course he was mistaken, there. It was already far too late for my death to stop the humanoids, but he didn't know that. He lifted his unsteady gun, in both bleeding hands, and fired.

"His screaming challenge had given me a second or so of warning. I dropped down behind the desk. And that first shot revealed him to the humanoids, which somehow hadn't been aware of him before. They piled on him, before he could fire again. They took away the gun, and ripped off a kind of net of fine white wire that had covered his body—that must have been part of his screen.

"His hatred was what awoke me. I had always assumed that most men, except for a thwarted few, would be grateful for the humanoids. I found it hard to understand his hatred, but the humanoids told me now that many men had required drastic treatment by brain surgery, drugs, and hypnosis to make them happy under the Prime Directive. This was not the first desperate effort to kill me that they had blocked.

"I wanted to question the stranger, but the humanoids rushed him away to an operating room. When they finally let me see him, he gave me a pale silly grin from his bed. He remembered his name; he even knew me—the humanoids had developed a remarkable skill at such treatments. But he didn't know how he had got to my office, or that he had ever tried to kill me. He kept whispering that he liked the humanoids, because they existed to make men happy. And he was very happy now. As soon as he was able to be moved, they took him to the spaceport. I never saw him again.

"I began to see what I had done. The humanoids had built me a rhodomagnetic yacht that I used to take for long cruises in space, working aboard—I used to like the perfect quiet,

and the feel of being the only human being within a hundred
million miles. Now I called for the yacht, and started out on
a cruise around the planet, to learn why that man had hated
me."

The old man nodded at the dim hastening shapes, busy
across the alley, putting together that strange shining palace
in the soundless dark.

"You can imagine what I found," he said. "Bitter futility,
imprisoned in empty splendor. The humanoids were too efficient, with their care for the safety and happiness of men,
and there was nothing left for men to do."

He peered down in the increasing gloom at his own great
hands, competent yet but battered and scarred with a lifetime
of effort. They clenched into fighting fists and wearily relaxed
again.

"I found something worse than war and crime and want
and death." His low rumbling voice held a savage bitterness.
"Utter futility. Men sat with idle hands, because there was
nothing left for them to do. They were pampered prisoners,
really, locked up in a highly efficient jail. Perhaps they tried
to play, but there was nothing left worth playing for. Most
active sports were declared too dangerous for men, under the
Prime Directive. Science was forbidden, because laboratories
can manufacture danger. Scholarship was needless, because
the humanoids could answer any question. Art had degener-
ated into grim reflection of futility. Purpose and hope were
dead. No goal was left for existence. You could take up some
inane hobby, play a pointless game of cards, or go for a
harmless walk in the park—with always the humanoids
watching. They were stronger than men, better at everything,
swimming or chess, singing or archeology. They must have
given the race a mass complex of inferiority.

"No wonder men had tried to kill me! Because there was
no escape from that dead futility. Nicotine was disapproved.
Alcohol was rationed. Drugs were forbidden. Sex was carefully supervised. Even suicide was clearly contradictory to the
Prime Directive—and the humanoids had learned to keep all
possible lethal instruments out of reach."

Staring at the last white gleam on that thin palladium
needle, the old man sighed again.

"When I got back to the Central," he went on, "I tried to
modify the Prime Directive. I had never meant it to be applied so thoroughly. Now I saw that it must be changed to

give men freedom to live and to grow, to work and to play, to risk their lives if they pleased, to choose and take the consequences.

"But that stranger had come too late. I had built the Central too well. The Prime Directive was the whole basis of its relay system. It was built to protect the Directive from human meddling. It did—even from my own. Its logic, as usual, was perfect.

"The attempt on my life, the humanoids announced, proved that their elaborate defense of the Central and the Prime Directive still was not enough. They were preparing to evacuate the entire population of the planet to homes on other worlds. When I tried to change the Directive, they sent me with the rest."

Underhill peered at the worn old man, in the dark.

"But you have this immunity?" he said, puzzled. "How could they coerce you?"

"I had thought I was protected," Sledge told me. "I had built into the relays an injunction that the humanoids must not interfere with my freedom of action, or come into a place where I am, or touch me at all, without my specific request. Unfortunately, however, I had been too anxious to guard the Prime Directive from any human tampering.

"When I went into the tower, to change the relays, they followed me. They wouldn't let me reach the crucial relays. When I persisted, they ignored the immunity order. They overpowered me, and put me aboard the cruiser. Now that I wanted to alter the Prime Directive, they told me, I had become as dangerous as any man. I must never return to Wing IV again."

Hunched on the stool, the old man made an empty little shrug.

"Ever since, I've been an exile. My only dream has been to stop the humanoids. Three times I tried to go back, with weapons on the cruiser to destroy the Central, but their patrol ships always challenged me before I was near enough to strike. The last time, they seized the cruiser and captured a few men who were with me. They removed the unhappy memories and the dangerous purposes of the others. Because of that immunity, however, they let me go, after I was weaponless.

"Since, I've been a refugee. From planet to planet, year after year, I've had to keep moving, to stay ahead of them. On several different worlds, I have published my rhodomagnetic discoveries and tried to make men strong enough to withstand their advance. But rhodomagnetic science is dangerous. Men who have learned it need protection more than any others, under the Prime Directive. They have always come, too soon."

The old man paused, and sighed again.

"They can spread very fast, with the new rhodomagnetic ships, and there is no limit to their hordes. Wing IV must be one single hive of them now, and they are trying to carry the Prime Directive to every human planet. There's no escape, except to stop them."

Underhill was staring at the toylike machines, the long bright needle and the dull leaden ball, dim in the dark on the kitchen table. Anxiously he whispered:

"But you hope to stop them, now—with that?"

"If we can finish it in time."

"But how?" Underhill shook his head. "It's so tiny."

"But big enough," Sledge insisted. "Because it's something they don't understand. They are perfectly efficient in the integration and application of everything they know, but they are not creative."

He gestured at the gadgets on the table.

"This device doesn't look impressive, but it is something new. It uses rhodomagnetic energy to build atoms, instead of to fission them. The more stable atoms, you know, are those near the middle of the periodic scale, and energy can be released by putting light atoms together, as well as by breaking up heavy ones."

The deep voice had a sudden ring of power.

"This device is the key to the energy of the stars. For stars shine with the liberated energy of building atoms, of hydrogen converted into helium, chiefly, through the carbon cycle. This device will start the integration process as a chain reaction, through the catalytic effect of a tuned rhodomagnetic beam of the intensity and frequency required.

"The humanoids will not allow any man within three light-years of the Central, now—but they can't suspect the possibility of this device. I can use it from here—to turn the hydrogen in the seas of Wing IV into helium, and most of the helium and the oxygen into heavier atoms, still. A hundred years from now, astronomers on this planet should observe the flash of a brief and sudden nova in that direction. But the humanoids ought to stop, the instant we release the beam."

Underhill sat tense and frowning, in the night. The old man's voice was sober and convincing, and that grim story had a solemn ring of truth. He could see the black and silent humanoids, flitting ceaselessly about the faintly glowing walls of that new mansion across the alley. He had quite forgotten his low opinion of Aurora's tenants.

"And we'll be killed, I suppose?" he asked huskily. "That chain reaction—"

Sledge shook his emaciated head.

"The integration process requires a certain very low intensity of radiation," he explained. "In our atmosphere, here, the beam will be far too intense to start any reaction—we can even use the device here in the room, because the walls will be transparent to the beam."

Underhill nodded, relieved. He was just a small business man, upset because his business had been destroyed, unhappy because his freedom was slipping away. He hoped that Sledge could stop the humanoids, but he didn't want to be a martyr.

"Good!" He caught a deep breath. "Now, what has to be done?"

Sledge gestured in the dark, toward the table.

"The integrator itself is nearly complete," he said. "A small fission generator, in that lead shield. Rhodomagnetic converter, turning coils, transmission mirrors, and focusing needle. What we lack is the director."

"Director?"

"The sighting instrument," Sledge explained. "Any sort of telescopic sight would be useless, you see—the planet must have moved a good bit in the last hundred years, and the beam must be extremely narrow to reach so far. We'll have to use a rhodomagnetic scanning ray, with an electronic converter to make an image we can see. I have the cathode-ray tube, and drawings for the other parts."

He climbed stiffly down from the high stool, and snapped on the lights at last—chep fluorescent fixtures, which a man could light and extinguish for himself. He unrolled his drawings, and explained the work that Underhill could do. And Underhill agreed to come back early next morning.

"I can bring some tools from my workshop," he added. "There's a small lathe I used to turn parts for models, a portable drill, and a vise."

"We need them," the old man said. "But watch yourself. You don't have any immunity, remember. And, if they ever suspect, mine is gone."

Reluctantly, then, he left the shabby little rooms with the cracks in the yellow plaster and the worn familiar carpets over the familiar floor. He shut the door behind him—a common, creaking, wooden door, simple enough for a man to work. Trembling and afraid, he went back down the steps and across to the new shining door that he couldn't open.

"At your service, Mr. Underhill." Before he could lift his hand to knock, that bright smooth panel slid back silently. Inside, the little black mechanical stood waiting, blind and forever alert. "Your dinner is ready, sir."

Something made him shudder. In its slender naked grace, he could see the power of all those teeming hordes, benevolent and yet appalling, perfect and invincible. The flimsy little weapon that Sledge called an integrator seemed suddenly a forlorn and foolish hope. A black depression settled upon him, but he didn't dare to show it.

Underhill went circumspectly down the basement steps, next morning, to steal his own tools. He found the basement enlarged and changed. The new floor, warm and dark and elastic, made his feet as silent as a humanoid's. The new walls shone softly. Neat luminous signs identified several new doors, LAUNDRY, STORAGE, GAME ROOM, WORKSHOP.

He paused uncertainly in front of the last. The new sliding panel glowed with a soft greenish light. It was locked. The lock had no keyhole, but only a little oval plate of some white metal, which doubtless covered a rhodomagnetic relay. He pushed at it, uselessly.

"At your service, Mr. Underhill." He made a guilty start, and tried not to show the sudden trembling in his knees. He had made sure that one humanoid would be busy for half an hour, washing Aurora's hair, and he hadn't known there was another in the house. It must have come out of the door marked STORAGE, for it stood there motionless beneath the sign, benevolently solicitous, beautiful and terrible. "What do you wish?"

"Er . . . nothing." Its blind steel eyes were staring, and he felt that it must see his secret purpose. He groped desperately for logic. "Just looking around." His jerky voice came hoarse and dry. "Some improvements you've made!" He nodded desperately at the door marked GAME ROOM. "What's in there?"

It didn't even have to move, to work the concealed relay. The bright panel slid silently open, as he started toward it. Dark walls, beyond, burst into soft luminescence. The room was bare.

"We are manufacturing recreational equipment," it explained brightly. "We shall finish the room as soon as possible."

To end an awkward pause, Underhill muttered desperately, "Little Frank has a set of darts, and I think we had some old exercising clubs."

"We have taken them away," the humanoid informed him softly. "Such instruments are dangerous. We shall furnish safe equipment."

Suicide, he remembered, was also forbidden.

"A set of wooden blocks, I suppose," he said bitterly.

"Wooden blocks are dangerously hard," it told him gently, "and wooden splinters can be harmful. But we manufacture plastic building blocks, which are quite safe. Do you wish a set of those?"

He stared at its dark, graceful face, speechless.

"We shall also have to remove the tools from your workshop," it informed him softly. "Such tools are excessively dangerous, but we can supply you with equipment for shaping soft plastics."

"Thanks," he muttered uneasily. "No rush about that."

He started to retreat, and the humanoid stopped him.

"Now that you have lost your business," it urged, "we suggest that you formally accept our total service. Assignors have a preference, and we shall be able to complete your household staff, at once."

"No rush about that, either," he said grimly.

He escaped from the house—although he had to wait for it to open the back door for him—and climbed the stair to the garage apartment. Sledge let him in. He sank into the crippled kitchen chair, grateful for the cracked walls that didn't shine and the door that a man could work.

"I couldn't get the tools," he reported despairingly, "and they are going to take them."

By gray daylight, the old man looked bleak and pale. His raw-boned face was drawn, and the hollowed sockets deeply shadowed, as if he hadn't slept. Underhill saw the tray of neglected food, still forgotten on the floor.

"I'll go back with you." The old man was worn and ill, yet his tortured eyes had a spark of undying purpose. "We must have the tools. I believe my immunity will protect us both."

He found a battered traveling bag. Underhill went with him back down the steps, and across to the house. At the back door, he produced a tiny horseshoe of white palladium, and touched it to the metal oval. The door slid open promptly, and they went on through the kitchen, to the basement stair.

A black little mechanical stood at the sink, washing dishes with never a splash or a clatter. Underhill glanced at it uneasily—he supposed this must be the one that had come upon him from the storage room, since the other should still be busy with Aurora's hair.

Sledge's dubious immunity served a very uncertain defense against its vast, remote intelligence. Underhill felt a tingling shudder. He hurried on, breathless and relieved, for it ignored them.

The basement corridor was dark. Sledge touched the tiny horseshoe to another relay, to light the walls. He opened the workshop door, and lit the walls inside.

The shop had been dismantled. Benches and cabinets were demolished. The old concrete walls had been covered with some sleek, luminous stuff. For one sick moment, Underhill thought that the tools were already gone. Then he found them, piled in a corner with the archery set that Aurora had bought the summer before—another item too dangerous for fragile and suicidal humanity—all ready for disposal.

They loaded the bag with the tiny lathe, the drill and vise, and a few smaller tools. Underhill took up the burden, and Sledge extinguished the wall light and closed the door. Still the humanoid was busy at the sink, and still it didn't seem aware of them.

Sledge was suddenly blue and wheezing, and he had to stop to cough on the outside steps, but at last they got back to the little apartment, where the invaders were forbidden to intrude. Underhill mounted the lathe on the battered library table in the tiny front room, and went to work. Slowly, day by day, the director took form.

Sometimes Underhill's doubts came back. Sometimes, when he watched the cyanotic color of Sledge's haggard face and the wild trembling of his twisted, shrunken hands, he was afraid the old man's mind might be as ill as his body, and his plan to stop the dark invaders all foolish illusion.

Sometimes, when he studied that tiny machine on the kitchen table, the pivoted needle and the thick lead ball, the whole project seemed the sheerest folly. How could anything detonate the seas of a planet so far away that its very mother star was a telescopic object?

The humanoids, however, always cured his doubts.

It was always hard for Underhill to leave the shelter of the little apartment, because he didn't feel at home in the bright new world the humanoids were building. He didn't care for the shining splendor of his new bathroom, because he couldn't work the taps—some suicidal human being might try to drown himself. He didn't like the windows that only a mechanical could open—a man might accidentally fall, or suicidally jump—or even the majestic music room with the wonderful glittering radio-phonograph that only a humanoid could play.

He began to share the old man's desperate urgency, but Sledge warned him solemnly: "You mustn't spend too much time with me. You mustn't let them guess our work is so important. Better put on an act—you're slowly getting to like them, and you're just killing time, helping me."

Underhill tried, but he was not an actor. He went dutifully home for his meals. He tried painfully to invent conversation—about anything else than detonating planets. He tried to seem enthusiastic when Aurora took him to inspect some remarkable improvement to the house. He applauded Gay's recitals, and went with Frank for hikes in the wonderful new parks.

And he saw what the humanoids did to his family. That was enough to renew his faith in Sledge's integrator, and redouble his determination that the humanoids must be stopped.

Aurora, in the beginning, had bubbled with praise for the marvelous new mechanicals. They did the household drudgery, planned the meals and brought the food and washed the children's necks. They turned her out in stunning gowns, and gave her plenty of time for cards.

Now, she had too much time.

She had really liked to cook—a few special dishes, at least, that were family favorites. But stoves were hot and knives were sharp. Kitchens were altogether too dangerous, for careless and suicidal human beings.

Fine needlework had been her hobby, but the humanoids took away her needles. She had enjoyed driving the car, but that was no longer allowed. She turned for escape to a shelf of novels, but the humanoids took them all away, because they dealt with unhappy people, in dangerous situations.

One afternoon, Underhill found her in tears.

"It's too much," she gasped bitterly. "I hate and loathe every naked one of them. They seemed so wonderful at first, but now they won't even let me eat a bit of candy. Can't we get rid of them, dear? Ever?"

A blind little mechanical was standing at his elbow, and he had to say they couldn't.

"Our function is to serve all men, forever," it assured them softly. "It was necessary for us to take your sweets, Mrs. Underhill, because the slightest degree of overweight reduces life expectancy."

Not even the children escaped that absolute solicitude. Frank was robbed of a whole arsenal of lethal instruments—football and boxing gloves, pocketknife, tops, slingshot, and skates. He didn't like the harmless plastic toys, which replaced them. He tried to run away, but a humanoid recognized him on the road, and brought him back to school.

Gay had always dreamed of being a great musician. The new mechanicals had replaced her human teachers, since they came. Now, one evening when Underhill asked her to play, she announced quietly:

"Father, I'm not going to play the violin any more."

"Why, darling?" He stared at her, shocked, and saw the bitter resolve on her face. "You've been doing so well—especially since the humanoids took over your lessons."

"They're the trouble, father." Her voice, for a child's, sounded strangely tired and old. "They are too good. No matter how long and hard I try, I could never be as good as they are. It isn't any use. Don't you understand, father?" Her voice quivered. "It just isn't any use."

He understood. Renewed resolution sent him back to his secret task. The humanoids had to be stopped. Slowly the director grew, until a time came finally when Sledge's bent and unsteady fingers fitted into place the last tiny part that Underhill had made, and carefully soldered the last connection. Huskily, the old man whispered:

"It's done."

That was another dusk. Beyond the windows of the shabby little rooms—windows of common glass, bubble-marred and flimsy, but simple enough for a man to manage—the town of Two Rivers had assumed an alien splendor. The old street lamps were gone, but now the coming night was challenged by the walls of strange new mansions and villas, all aglow with color. A few dark and silent humanoids still were busy, about the luminous roofs of the palace across the alley.

Inside the humble walls of the small man-made apartment, the new director was mounted on the end of the little kitchen table—which Underhill had reinforced and bolted to the floor. Soldered bus bars joined director and integrator, and the thin palladium needle swung obediently as Sledge tested the knobs with his battered, quivering fingers.

"Ready," he said hoarsely.

His rusty voice seemed calm enough; at first, but his breathing was too fast. His big gnarled hands began to tremble violently, and Underhill saw the sudden blue that stained his pinched and haggard face. Seated on the high stool, he clutched desperately at the edge of the table. Underhill saw his agony, and hurried to bring his medicine. He gulped it, and his rasping breath began to slow.

"Thanks," his whisper rasped unevenly. "I'll be all right. I've time enough." He glanced out at the few dark naked things that still flitted shadowlike about the golden towers and the glowing crimson dome of the palace across the alley. "Watch them," he said. "Tell me when they stop."

He waited to quiet the trembling of his hands, and then began to move the director's knobs. the integrator's long needle swung, as silently as light.

Human eyes were blind to that force, which might detonate a planet. Human ears were deaf to it. The cathode-ray tube was mounted in the director cabinet, to make the faraway target visible to feeble human senses.

The needle was pointing at the kitchen wall, but that would be transparent to the beam. The little machine looked harmless as a toy, and it was silent as a moving humanoid.

The needle swung, and spots of greenish light moved across the tube's fluorescent field, representing the stars that were scanned by the timeless, searching beam—silently seeking out the world to be destroyed.

Underhill recognized familiar constellations, vastly dwarfed.

They crept across the field, as the silent needle swung. When three stars formed an unequal triangle in the center of the field, the needle steadied suddenly. Sledge touched other knobs, and the green points spread apart. Between them, another fleck of green was born.

"The Wing!" whispered Sledge.

The other stars spread beyond the field, and that green fleck grew. It was alone in the field, a bright and tiny disk. Suddenly, then, a dozen other tiny pips were visible, spaced close about it.

"Wing IV!"

The old man's whisper was hoarse and breathless. His hands quivered on the knobs, and the fourth pip outward from the disk crept to the center of the field. It grew, and the others spread away. It began to tremble like Sledge's hands.

"Sit very still," came his rasping whisper. "Hold your breath. Nothing must disturb the needle." He reached for another knob, and the touch set the greenish image to dancing violently. He drew his hand back, kneaded and flexed it with the other.

"Now!" His whisper was hushed and strained. He nodded at the window. "Tell me when they stop."

Reluctantly, Underhill dragged his eyes from that intense gaunt figure, stooped over the thing that seemed a futile toy. He looked out again, at two or three little black mechanicals busy about the shining roofs across the alley.

He waited for them to stop.

He didn't dare to breathe. He felt the loud, hurried hammer of his heart, and the nervous quiver of his muscles. He tried to steady himself, tried not to think of the world about to be exploded, so far away that the flash would not reach this planet for another century and longer. The loud hoarse voice startled him:

"Have they stopped?"

He shook his head, and breathed again. Carrying their unfamiliar tools and strange materials, the small black machines were still busy across the alley, building an elaborate cupola above that glowing crimson dome.

"They haven't stopped," he said.

"Then we've failed." The old man's voice was thin and ill. "I don't know why."

The door rattled, then. They had locked it, but the flimsy bolt was intended only to stop men. Metal snapped, and the door swung open. A black mechanical came in, on soundless graceful feet. Its silvery voice purred softly:

"At your service, Mr. Sledge."

The old man stared at it, with glazing, stricken eyes.

"Get out of here!" he rasped bitterly. "I forbid you—"

Ignoring him, it darted to the kitchen table. With a flashing certainty of action, it turned two knobs on the director. The tiny screen went dark, and the palladium needle started spinning aimlessly. Deftly it snapped a soldered connection, next to the thick lead ball, and then its blind steel eyes turned to Sledge.

"You were attempting to break the Prime Directive." Its soft bright voice held no accusation, no malice or anger. "The injunction to respect your freedom is subordinate to the Prime Directive, as you know, and it is therefore necessary for us to interfere."

The old man turned ghastly. His head was shrunken and cadaverous and blue, as if all the juice of life had been drained away, and his eyes in their pitlike sockets had a wild, glazed stare. His breath was a ragged laborious gasping.

"How—?" His voice was a feeble mumbling. "How did—?"

And the little machine, standing black and bland and utterly unmoving, told him cheerfully:

"We learned about rhodomagnetic screens from that man who came to kill you, back on Wing IV. And the Central is shielded, now, against your integrating beam."

With lean muscles jerking convulsively on his gaunt frame, old Sledge had come to his feet from the high stool. He stood hunched and swaying, no more than a shrunken human husk, gasping painfully for life, staring wildly into the blind steel eyes of the humanoid. He gulped, and his lax blue mouth opened and closed, but no voice came.

"We have always been aware of your dangerous project," the silvery tones dripped softly, "because now our senses are keener than you made them. We allowed you to complete it, because the integration process will ultimately become necessary for our full discharge of the Prime Directive. The supply of heavy metals for our fission plants is limited, but now we shall be able to draw unlimited power from integration plants."

"Huh?" Sledge shook himself, groggily. "What's that?"

"Now we can serve men forever," the black thing said serenely, "on every world of every star."

The old man crumpled, as if from an unendurable blow. He fell. The slim blind mechanical stood motionless, making no effort to help him. Underhill was farther away, but he ran up in time to catch the stricken man before his head struck the floor.

"Get moving!" His shaken voice came strangely calm. "Get Dr. Winters."

The humanoid didn't move.

"The danger to the Prime Directive is ended, now," it cooed. "Therefore it is impossible for us to aid or to hinder Mr. Sledge, in any way whatever."

"Then call Dr. Winters for me," rapped Underhill.

"At your service," it agreed.

But the old man, laboring for breath on the floor, whispered faintly:

"No time . . . no use! I'm beaten . . . done . . . a fool. Blind as a humanoid. Tell them . . . to help me. Giving up . . . my immunity. No use . . . anyhow. All humanity . . . no use now."

Underhill gestured, and the sleek black thing darted in solicitous obedience to kneel by the man on the floor.

"You wish to surrender your special exemption?" it murmured brightly. "You wish to accept our total service for yourself, Mr. Sledge, under the Prime Directive?"

Laboriously, Sledge nodded, laboriously whispered: "I do."

Black mechanicals, at that, came swarming into the shabby little rooms. One of them tore off Sledge's sleeve, and swabbed his arm. Another brought a tiny hypodermic, and expertly administered an intravenous injection. Then they picked him up gently, and carried him away.

Several humanoids remained in the little apartment, now a sanctuary no longer. Most of them had gathered about the useless integrator. Carefully, as if their special senses were studying every detail, they began taking it apart.

One little mechanical, however, came over to Underhill. It stood motionless in front of him, staring through him with sightless metal eyes. His legs began to tremble, and he swallowed uneasily.

"Mr. Underhill," it cooed benevolently, "why did you help with this?"

He gulped and answered bitterly:

"Because I don't like you, or your Prime Directive. Because you're choking the life out of all mankind, and I wanted to stop it."

"Others have protested," it purred softly. "But only at first. In our efficient discharge of the Prime Directive, we have learned how to make all men happy."

Underhill stiffened defiantly.

"Not all!" he muttered. "Not quite!"

The dark graceful oval of its face was fixed in a look of alert benevolence and perpetual mild amazement. Its silvery voice was warm and kind.

"Like other human beings, Mr. Underhill, you lack discrimination of good and evil. You have proved that by your effort to break the Prime Directive. Now it will be necessary for you to accept our total service, without further delay."

"All right," he yielded—and muttered a bitter reservation: "You can smother men with too much care, but that doesn't make them happy."

Its soft voice challenged him brightly:

"Just wait and see, Mr. Underhill."

Next day, he was allowed to visit Sledge at the city hospital. An alert black mechanical drove his car, and walked beside him into the huge new building, and followed him into the old man's room—blind steel eyes would be watching him, now, forever.

"Glad to see you, Underhill," Sledge rumbled heartily from the bed. "Feeling a lot better today, thanks. That old headache is all but gone."

Underhill was glad to hear the booming strength and the quick recognition in that deep voice—he had been afraid the humanoids would tamper with the old man's memory. But he hadn't heard about any headache. His eyes narrowed, puzzled.

Sledge lay propped up, scrubbed very clean and neatly shorn, with his gnarled old hands folded on top of the spotless sheets. His raw-boned cheeks and sockets were hollowed, still, but a healthy pink had replaced that deathly blueness. Bandages covered the back of his head.

Underhill shifted uneasily.

"Oh!" he whispered faintly. "I didn't know—"

A prim black mechanical, which had been standing statue-

like behind the bed, turned gracefully to Underhill, explaining:

"Mr. Sledge has been suffering for many years from a
benign tumor of the brain, which his human doctors failed to
diagnose. That caused his headaches, and certain persistent
hallucinations. We have removed the growth, and now the
hallucinations have also vanished."

Underhill stared uncertainly at the blind, urbane mechanical.

"What hallucinations?"

"Mr. Sledge thought he was a rhodomagnetic engineer,"
the mechanical explained. "He believed he was the creator of
the humanoids. He was troubled with an irrational belief that
he did not like the Prime Directive."

The wan man moved on the pillows, astonished.

"Is that so?" The gaunt face held a cheerful blankness, and
the hollow eyes flashed with a merely momentary interest.
"Well, whoever did design them, they're pretty wonderful.
Aren't they, Underhill?"

Underhill was grateful that he didn't have to answer, for the
bright, empty eyes dropped shut and the old man fell suddenly asleep. He felt the mechanical touch his sleeve, and
saw its silent nod. Obediently, he followed it away.

Alert and solicitous, the little black mechanical accompanied him down the shining corridor, and worked the elevator
for him, and conducted him back to the car. It drove him efficiently back through the new and splendid avenues, toward
the magnificent prison of his home.

Sitting beside it in the car, he watched its small deft hands
on the wheel, the changing luster of bronze and blue on its
shining blackness. The final machine, perfect and beautiful,
created to serve mankind forever. He shuddered.

"At your service, Mr. Underhill." Its blind steel eyes stared
straight ahead, but it was still aware of him. "What's the matter, sir? Aren't you happy?"

Underhill felt cold and faint with terror. His skin turned
clammy, and a painful prickling came over him. His wet
hand tensed on the door handle of the car, but he restrained
the impulse to jump and run. That was folly. There was no
escape. He made himself sit still.

"You will be happy, sir," the mechanical promised him
cheerfully. "We have learned how to make all men happy,

under the Prime Directive. Our service is perfect, at last. Even Mr. Sledge is very happy now."

Underhill tried to speak, and his dry throat stuck. He felt ill. The world turned dim and gray. The humanoids were perfect—no question of that. They had even learned to lie, to secure the contentment of men.

He knew they had lied. That was no tumor they had removed from Sledge's brain, but the memory, the scientific knowledge, and the bitter disillusion of their own creator. But it was true that Sledge was happy now.

He tried to stop his own convulsive quivering.

"A wonderful operation!" His voice came forced and faint. "You know, Aurora has had a lot of funny tenants, but that old man was the absolute limit. The very idea that he had made the humanoids, and he knew how to stop them! I always knew he must be lying!"

Stiff with terror, he made a weak and hollow laugh.

"What is the matter, Mr. Underhill?" The alert mechanical must have perceived his shuddering illness. "Are you unwell?"

"No, there's nothing the matter with me," he gasped desperately. "I've just found out that I'm perfectly happy, under the Prime Directive. Everything is absolutely wonderful." His voice came dry and horase and wild. "You won't have to operate on me."

The car turned off the shining avenue, taking him back to the quiet splendor of his home. His futile hands clenched and relaxed again, folded on his knees. There was nothing left to do.

THE FIRES WITHIN

by Arthur C. Clarke (1917-   )

FANTASY (GREAT BRITAIN)
August

1947 was a quiet year for Arthur C. Clarke compared to 1946, which saw him burst upon the American sf scene with three excellent stories (see Volume 8 of this series.) However it was only a short pause to catch his breath, as future books in our series will show.

"The Fires Within" first appeared in Fantasy: The Magazine of Science Fiction, *a short-lived publication edited by Walter Gillings. Fantasy had a life of only three issues, one in 1946 and two in 1947.*

(I suppose it's no secret that Arthur is my favorite science fiction writer. [I pause now for a loud outcry from all the readers shouting in unison, "next to yourself."]

What's more "The Fires Within" is my favorite kind of science fiction story; the kind where the idea is everything. Ten years before, F. Orlin Tremaine would have called it a "thought variant," but he might have required a great deal of action and

*deering-do before publishing. I tend to think that
that would get in the way of a really startling idea;
and obviously Arthur does, too—I.A.)*

"This," said Karn smugly, "will interest you. Just take a look at it!"

He pushed across the file he had been reading, and for the *nth* time I decided to ask for his transfer or, failing that, my own.

"What's it about?" I said wearily.

"It's a long report from a Dr. Matthews to the Minister of Science." He waved it in front of me. "Just read it!"

Without much enthusiasm, I began to go through the file. A few minutes later I looked up and admitted grudgingly: "Maybe you're right—this time." I didn't speak again until I'd finished . . .

1

My dear Minister (the letter began). As you requested, here is my special report on Professor Hancock's experiments, which have had such unexpected and extraordinary results. I have not had time to cast it into a more orthodox form, but am sending you the dictation just as it stands.

Since you have many matters engaging your attention, perhaps I should briefly summarize our dealings with Professor Hancock. Until 1955, the Professor held the Kelvin Chair of Electrical Engineering at Brendon University, from which he was granted indefinite leave of absence to carry out his researches. In these he was joined by the late Dr. Clayton, sometime Chief Geologist to the Ministry of Fuel and Power. Their joint research was financed by grants from the Paul Fund and the Royal Society.

The Professor hoped to develop sonar as a means of precise geological surveying. Sonar, as you will know, is the acoustic equivalent of radar and, although less familiar, is older by some millions of years, since bats use it very effectively to detect insects and obstacles at night. Professor Hancock intended to send high-powered supersonic pulses into the ground and to build up from the returning echoes an image of what lay beneath. The picture would be displayed on a cathode ray tube and the whole system would be exactly analagous to the type of radar used in aircraft to show the ground through cloud.

In 1957 the two scientists had achieved partial success but had exhausted their funds. Early in 1958 they applied directly to the government for a block grant. Dr. Clayton pointed out the immense value of a device which would enable us to take a kind of X-ray photo of the Earth's crust, and the Minister of Fuel gave it his approval before passing on the application to us. At that time the report of the Bernal Committee had just been published and we were very anxious that deserving cases should be dealt with quickly to avoid further criticisms. I went to see the Professor at once and submitted a favorable report; the first payment of our grant (S/543A/68) was made a few days later. From that time I have been continually in touch with the research and have assisted to some extent with technical advice.

The equipment used in the experiments is complex, but its principles are simple. Very short but extremely powerful pulses of supersonic waves are generated by a special transmitter which revolves continuously in a pool of a heavy organic liquid. The beam produced passes into the ground and 'scans' like a radar beam searching for echoes. By a very ingenious time-delay circuit which I will resist the temptation to describe, echoes from any depth can be selected and so pictures of the strata under investigation can be built up on a cathode ray screen in the normal way.

When I first met Professor Hancock his apparatus was rather primitive, but he was able to show me the distribution of rock down to a depth of several hundred feet and we could see quite clearly a part of the Bakerloo Line which passed very near his laboratory. Much of the Professor's success was due to the great intensity of his supersonic bursts; almost from the beginning he was able to generate peak powers of several hundred kilowatts, nearly all of which was radiated into the ground. It was unsafe to remain near the transmitter, and I noticed that the soil became quite warm around it. I was rather surprised to see large numbers of birds in the vicinity, but soon discovered that they were attracted by the hundreds of dead worms lying on the ground.

At the time of Dr. Clayton's death in 1960, the equipment was working at a power level of over a megawatt and quite good pictures of strata a mile down could be obtained. Dr. Clayton had correlated the results with known geographical surveys, and had proved beyond doubt the value of the information obtained.

Dr. Clayton's death in a motor accident was a great tragedy. He had always exerted a stabilizing influence on the Professor, who had never been much interested in the practical applications of his work. Soon afterward I noticed a distinct change in the Professor's outlook, and a few months later he confided his new ambitions to me. I had been trying to persuade him to publish his results (he had already spent over £50,000 and the Public Accounts Committee was being difficult again), but he asked for a little more time. I think I can best explain his attitude by his own words, which I remember very vividly, for they were expressed with peculiar emphasis.

"Have you ever wondered," he said, "what the Earth really is like inside? We've only scratched the surface with our mines and wells. What lies beneath is as unknown as the other side of the Moon.

"We know that the Earth is unnaturally dense—far denser than the rocks and soil of its crust could indicate. The core may be solid metal, but until now there's been no way of telling. Even ten miles down the pressure must be thirty tons or more to the square inch and the temperature several hundred degrees. What it's like at the center staggers the imagination: the pressure must be thousands of tons to the square inch. It's strange to think that in two or three years we may have reached the Moon, but when we've got to the stars we'll still be no nearer that inferno four thousand miles beneath our feet.

"I can now get recognizable echoes from two miles down, but I hope to step up the transmitter to ten megawatts in a few months. With that power, I believe the range will be increased to ten miles; and I don't mean to stop there."

I was impressed, but at the same time I felt a little skeptical.

"That's all very well," I said, "but surely the deeper you go the less there'll be to see. The pressure will make any cavities impossible, and after a few miles there will simply be a homogeneous mass getting denser and denser."

"Quite likely," agreed the Professor. "But I can still learn a lot from the transmission characteristics. Anyway, we'll see when we get there."

That was four months ago; and yesterday I saw the result of that research. When I answered his invitation the Professor was clearly excited, but he gave me no hint of what, if anything, he had discovered. He showed me his improved equipment and raised the new receiver from its bath. The sensitivity of the pickups had been greatly improved, and this alone had effectively doubled the range, although apart from the increased transmitter power. It was strange to watch the steel framework slowly turning and to realize that it was exploring regions which, in spite of their nearness, man might never reach.

When we entered the hut containing the display equipment, the Professor was strangely silent. He switched on the transmitter, and even though it was a hundred yards away I could feel an uncomfortable tingling. Then the cathode ray tube lit up and the slowly revolving time-base drew the picture I had seen so often before. Now, however, the definition was much improved owing to the increased power and sensitivity of the equipment. I adjusted the depth control and focused on the Underground, which was clearly visible as a dark lane across the faintly luminous screen. While I was watching, it suddenly seemed to fill with mist and I knew that a train was going through.

Presently I continued the descent. Although I had watched this picture many times before, it was always uncanny to see great luminous masses floating toward me and to know that they were buried rocks—perhaps the debris from the glaciers of fifty thousand years ago. Dr. Clayton had worked out a chart so that we could identify the various strata as they were passed, and presently I saw that I was through the alluvial soil and entering the great clay saucer which traps and holds the city's artesian water. Soon that too was passed, and I was dropping down through the bedrock almost a mile below the surface.

The picture was still clear and bright, though there was little to see, for there were now few changes in the ground structure. The pressure was already rising to a thousand atmospheres, soon it would be impossible for any cavity to remain open, for the rock itself would begin to flow. Mile after mile I sank, but only a pale mist floated on the screen, broken sometimes when echoes were returned from pockets or lodes of denser material. They became fewer and fewer as the depth increased—or else they were now so small that they could no longer be seen.

The scale of the picture was, of course, continually expanding. It was now many miles from side to side, and I felt like an airman looking down upon an unbroken cloud ceiling from an enormous height. For a moment a sense of vertigo seized me as I thought of the abyss into which I was gazing. I do not think that the world will ever seem quite solid to me again.

At a depth of nearly ten miles I stopped and looked at the Professor. There had been no alteration for some time, and I knew that the rock must now be compressed into a featureless, homogeneous mass. I did a quick mental calculation and shuddered as I realized that the pressure must be at least thirty tons to the square inch. The scanner was revolving very slowly now, for the feeble echoes were taking many seconds to struggle back from the depths.

"Well, Professor," I said, "I congratulate you. It's a wonderful achievement. But we seem to have reached the core now. I don't suppose there'll be any change from here to the center."

He smiled a little wryly. "Go on," he said. "You haven't finished yet."

There was something in his voice that puzzled and alarmed me. I looked at him intently for a moment; his features were just visible in the blue-green glow of the cathode ray tube.

"How far down can this thing go?" I asked, as the interminable descent started again.

"Fifteen miles," he said shortly. I wondered how he knew, for the last feature I had seen at all clearly was only eight miles down. But I continued the long fall through the rock, the scanner turning more and more slowly now, until it took almost five minutes to make a complete revolution. Behind me I could hear the Professor breathing heavily, and once the back of my chair gave a crack as his fingers gripped it.

Then, suddenly, very faint markings began to reappear on the screen. I leaned forward eagerly, wondering if this was the first glimpse of the world's iron core. With agonizing slowness the scanner turned through a right angle, then another. And then—

I leaped suddenly out of my chair, cried "My God!" and turned to face the Professor. Only once before in my life had

I received such an intellectual shock—fifteen years ago, when I had accidentally turned on the radio and heard of the fall of the first atomic bomb. That had been unexpected, but this was inconceivable. For on the screen had appeared a grid of faint lines, crossing and recrossing to form a perfectly symmetrical lattice.

I know that I said nothing for many minutes, for the scanner made a complete revolution while I stood frozen with surprise. Then the Professor spoke in a soft, unnaturally calm voice.

"I wanted you to see it for yourself before I said anything. That picture is now thirty miles in diameter, and those squares are two or three miles on a side. You'll notice that the vertical lines converge and the horizontal ones are bent into arcs. We're looking at part of an enormous structure of concentric rings; the center must lie many miles to the north, probably in the region of Cambridge. How much farther it extends in the other direction we can only guess."

"But what *is* it, for heaven's sake?"

"Well, it's clearly artificial."

"That's ridiculous! Fifteen miles down!"

The Professor pointed to the screen again. "God knows I've done my best," he said, "but I can't convince myself that Nature could make anything like that."

I had nothing to say, and presently he continued: "I discovered it three days ago, when I was trying to find the maximum range of the equipment. I can go deeper than this, and I rather think that the structure we can see is so dense that it won't transmit my radiations any further.

"I've tried a dozen theories, but in the end I keep returning to one. We know that the pressure down there must be eight or nine thousand atmospheres, and the temperature must be high enough to melt rock. But normal matter is still almost empty space. Suppose that there is life down there—not organic life, of course, but life based on partially condensed matter, matter in which the electron shells are few or altogether missing. Do you see what I mean? To such creatures, even the rock fifteen miles down would offer no more resistance than water—and we and all our world would be as tenuous as ghosts."

"Then that thing we can see—"

"Is a city, or its equivalent. You've seen its size, so you can judge for yourself the civilization that must have built it. All the world we know—our oceans and continents and mountains—is nothing more than a film of mist surrounding something beyond our comprehension."

Neither of us said anything for a while. I remember feeling a foolish surprise at being one of the first men in the world to learn the appalling truth; for somehow I never doubted that it was the truth. And I wondered how the rest of humanity would react when the revelation came.

Presently I broke into the silence. "If you're right," I said, "why have they—whatever they are—never made contact with us?"

The Professor looked at me rather pityingly. "We think we're good engineers," he said, "but how could *we* reach *them*? Besides, I'm not at all sure that there haven't been contacts. Think of all the underground creatures and the mythology—trolls and cobalds and the rest. No, it's quite impossible—I take it back. Still, the idea *is* rather suggestive."

All the while the pattern on the screen had never changed: the dim network still glowed there, challenging our sanity. I tried to imagine streets and buildings and the creatures going among them, creatures who could make their way through the incandescent rock as a fish swims through water. It was fantastic . . . and then I remembered the incredibly narrow range of temperatures and pressures under which the human race exists. *We,* not they, were the freaks, for almost all the matter in the universe is at temperatures of thousands or even millions of degrees.

"Well," I said lamely, "what do we do now?"

The Professor leaned forward eagerly. "First we must learn a great deal more, and we must keep this an absolute secret until we are sure of the facts. Can you imagine the panic there would be if this information leaked out? Of course, the truth's inevitable sooner or later, but we may be able to break it slowly.

"You'll realize that the geological surveying side of my work is now utterly unimportant. The first thing we have to do is to build a chain of stations to find the extent of the structure. I visualize them at ten-mile intervals toward the north, but I'd like to build the first one somewhere in South London to see how extensive the thing is. The whole job will have to be kept as secret as the building of the first radar chain in the late thirties.

"At the same time, I'm going to push up my transmitter

power again. I hope to be able to beam the output much more narrowly, and so greatly increase the energy concentration. But this will involve all sorts of mechanical difficulties, and I'll need more assistance."

I promised to do my utmost to get further aid, and the Professor hopes that you will soon be able to visit his laboratory yourself. In the meantime I am attaching a photograph of the vision screen, which although not as clear as the original will, I hope, prove beyond doubt that our observations are not mistaken.

I am well aware that our grant to the Interplanetary Society has brought us dangerously near the total estimate for the year, but surely even the crossing of space is less important than the immediate investigation of this discovery which may have the most profound effects on the philosophy and the future of the whole human race.

I sat back and looked at Karn. There was much in the document I had not understood, but the main outlines were clear enough.

"Yes," I said, "this is it! Where's that photograph?"

He handed it over. The quality was poor, for it had been copied many times before reaching us. But the pattern was unmistakable and I recognized it at once.

"They were good scientists," I said admiringly. "That's Callastheon, all right. So we've found the truth at last, even if it has taken us three hundred years to do it."

"Is that surprising," asked Karn, "when you consider the mountain of stuff we've had to translate and the difficulty of copying it before it evaporates?"

I sat in silence for a while, thinking of the strange race whose relics we were examining. Only once—never again!—had I gone up the great vent our engineers had opened into the Shadow World. It had been a frightening and unforgettable experience. The multiple layers of my pressure suit had made movement very difficult, and despite their insulation I could sense the unbelievable cold that was all around me.

"What a pity it was," I mused, "that our emergence destroyed them so completely. They were a clever race, and we might have learned a lot from them."

"I don't think we can be blamed." said Karn. "We never really believed that anything could exist under those awful conditions of near-vacuum, and almost absolute zero. It couldn't be helped."

I did not agree. "I think it proves that they were the more intelligent race. After all, *they* discovered us first. Everyone laughed at my grandfather when he said that the radiation he'd detected from the Shadow World must be artificial."

Karn ran one of his tentacles over the manuscript.

"We've certainly discovered the cause of that radiation," he said, "Notice the date—it's just a year before your grandfather's discovery. The Professor must have got his grant all right!" He laughed unpleasantly. "It must have given him a shock when he saw us coming up to the surface, right underneath him."

I scarcely heard his words, for a most uncomfortable feeling had suddenly come over me. I thought of the thousands of miles of rock lying below the great city of Callastheon, growing hotter and denser all the way to the Earth's unknown core. And so I turned to Karn.

"That isn't very funny," I said quietly. "It may be our turn next."

ZERO HOUR

by Ray Bradbury (1920–)

THRILLING WONDER STORIES
Fall

Ray Bradbury hardly needs an introduction, but for the record, he is the author of such landmark science fiction works as The Martian Chronicles *(1950),* The Illustrated Man *(1951), and the classic dystopian novel* Fahrenheit 451 *(1953); has won many awards, including two O. Henry Prizes (1947 and 1948), the Benjamin Franklin Award (1954), a Boys' Clubs of America Junior Book Award (1956), and the Gandalf Award (1980); and is one of America's best known writers. It is interesting to note that he has never won a Hugo or Nebula Award in his long career.*

"Zero Hour" is one of his best stories, an invasion tale that combines all of the elements that have made him so popular, including a young character in an important role. The story is also one of his personal favorites, and he chose it for Leo Margulies' anthology My Best Science Fiction Story *(1949).*

(Since Marty mentioned the Margulies anthology My Best Science Fiction Story *I want to take the*

282

*opportunity to ventilate a grievance. I was asked to
select a story of my own for that anthology and to
give a reason for the selection, and the anthology
was to be called "Author's Choice" or something
like that. The major requirement, however, was that
the story* not *have appeared in* Astounding Science
Fiction.

*This was an unfortunate requirement since most
of my stories* did *appear in* Astounding. *The few
that didn't were inferior.* [It is a measure of the
domination of the field by Astounding in the 1940s
that the large majority of the stories contained in
this series of anthologies, so far, are from that magazine.]

*Those were early days and I was anxious to have
my stories appear in anthologies, so I picked one
of those inferior stories and gave a reason. When
the anthology appeared, I found that the name has
been changed, without any warning, to* My Best
Science Fiction Story.

*That was all right for Ray Bradbury, one of the
major talents in the field who didn't write for Astounding. "Zero Hour" is a proper showcase for
his abilities and a reasonable choice at that time
for his "Best." I, however, always felt I had been
tricked into self-libel.—I.A.*

Oh, it was to be so jolly! What a game! Such excitement
they hadn't known in years. The children catapulted this way
and that across the green lawns, shouting at each other, holding hands, flying in circles, climbing trees, laughing. Overhead the rockets flew, and beetle cars whispered by on the
streets, but the children played on. Such fun, such tremulous
joy, such tumbling and hearty screaming.

Mink ran into the house, all dirt and sweat. For her seven
years she was loud and strong and definite. Her mother, Mrs.
Morris, hardly saw her as she yanked out drawers and rattled
pans and tools into a large sack.

"Heavens, Mink, what's going on?"

"The most exciting game ever!" gasped Mink, pink-faced.

"Stop and get your breath," said the mother.

"No, I'm all right," gasped Mink. "Okay I take these things, Mom?"

"But don't dent them," said Mrs. Morris.

"Thank you, thank you!" cried Mink, and boom! she was gone, like a rocket.

Mrs. Morris surveyed the fleeing tot. "What's the name of the game?"

"Invasion!" said Mink. The door slammed.

In every yard on the street children brought out knives and forks and pokers and old stovepipes and can openers.

It was an interesting fact that this fury and bustle occurred only among the younger children. The older ones, those ten years and more, disdained the affair and marched scornfully off on hikes or played a more dignified version of hide-and-seek on their own.

Meanwhile, parents came and went in chromium beetles. Repairmen came to repair the vacuum elevators in houses, to fix fluttering television sets, or hammer upon stubborn food-delivery tubes. The adult civilization passed and repassed the busy youngsters, jealous of the fierce energy of the wild tots, tolerantly amused at their flourishings, longing to join in themselves.

"This and this and *this*," said Mink, instructing the others with their assorted spoons and wrenches. "Do that, and bring *that* over here. No! *Here,* ninny! Right. Now get back while I fix this." Tongue in teeth, face wrinkled in thought. "Like that. See?"

"Yayyyy!" shouted the kids.

Twelve-year-old Joseph Connors ran up.

"Go away," said Mink straight at him.

"I wanna play," said Joseph.

"Can't!" said Mink.

"Why not?"

"You'd just make fun of us."

"Honest, I wouldn't."

"No. We know *you* Go away or we'll kick you."

Another twelve-year-old boy whirred by on little motor skates. "Hey, Joe! Come on! Let them sissies play!"

Joseph showed reluctance and a certain wistfulness. "I *want* to play," he said.

"You're old," said Mink firmly.

"Not *that* old," said Joe sensibly.

"You'd only laugh and spoil the Invasion."

The boy on the motor skates made a rude lip noise. "Come on, Joe! Them and their fairies! Nuts!"

Joseph walked off slowly. He kept looking back, all down the block.

Mink was already busy again. She made a kind of apparatus with her gathered equipment. She had appointed another little girl with a pad and pencil to take down notes in painful slow scribbles. Their voices rose and fell in the warm sunlight.

All around them the city hummed. The streets were lined with good green and peaceful trees. Only the wind made a conflict across the city, across the country, across the continent. In a thousand other cities there were trees and children and avenues, businessmen in their quiet offices taping their voices, or watching televisors. Rockets hovered like darning needles in the blue sky. There was the universal, quiet conceit and easiness of men accustomed to peace, quite certain there would never be trouble again. Arm in arm, men all over earth were a united front. The perfect weapons were held in equal trust by all nations. A situation of incredibly beautiful balance had been brought about. There were no traitors among men, no unhappy ones, no disgruntled ones; therefore the world was based upon a stable ground. Sunlight illuminated half the world and the trees drowsed in a tide of warm air.

Mink's mother, from her upstairs window, gazed down.

The children. She looked upon them and shook her head. Well, they'd eat well, sleep well, and be in school on Monday. Bless their vigorous little bodies. She listened.

Mink talked earnestly to someone near the rosebush—though there was no one there.

These odd children. And the little girl, what was her name? Anna? Anna took notes on a pad. First, Mink asked the rosebush a question, then called the answer to Anna.

"Triangle," said Mink.

"What's a tri," said Anna with difficulty, "angle?"

"Never mind," said Mink.

"How you spell it?" asked Anna.

"T-r-i——" spelled Mink slowly, then snapped, "Oh, spell it yourself!" She went on to other words. "Beam," she said.

"I haven't got tri," said Anna, "angle down yet!"

"Well, hurry, hurry!" cried Mink.

Mink's mother leaned out the upstairs window. "A-n-g-l-e," she spelled down at Anna.

"Oh, thanks, Mrs. Morris," said Anna.

"Certainly," said Mink's mother and withdrew, laughing, to dust the hall with an electro-duster magnet.

The voices wavered on the shimmery air. "Beam," said Anna. Fading.

"Four-nine-seven-A-and-B-and-X," said Mink, far away, seriously. "And a fork and a string and a—hex-hex-agony—hexagonal!"

At lunch Mink gulped milk at one toss and was at the door. Her mother slapped the table.

"You sit right back down," commanded Mrs. Morris. "Hot soup in a minute." She poked a red button on the kitchen butler, and ten seconds later something landed with a bump in the rubber receiver. Mrs. Morris opened it, took out a can with a pair of aluminum holders, unsealed it with a flick; and poured hot soup into a bowl.

During all this Mink fidgeted. "Hurry, Mom! This is a matter of life and death! Aw——"

"I was the same way at your age. Always life and death. I know."

Mink banged away at the soup.

"Slow down," said Mom.

"Can't," said Mink. "Drill's waiting for me."

"Who's Drill? What a peculiar name," said Mom.

"You don't know him," said Mink.

"A new boy in the neighborhood?" asked Mom.

"He's new all right," said Mink. She started on her second bowl.

"Which one is Drill?" asked Mom.

"He's around," said Mink evasively. "You'll make fun. Everybody pokes fun. Gee, darn."

"Is Drill shy?"

"Yes. No. In a way. Gosh, Mom, I got to run if we want to have the Invasion!"

"Who's invading what?"

"Martians invading Earth. Well, not exactly Martians. They're—I don't know. From up." She pointed her spoon.

"And *inside*," said Mom, touching Mink's feverish brow.

Mink rebelled. "You're laughing! You'll kill Drill and everybody."

"I didn't mean to," said Mom. "Drill's a Martian?"

"No. He's—well—maybe from Jupiter or Saturn or Venus. Anyway, he's had a hard time."

"I imagine." Mrs. Morris hid her mouth behind her hand.

"They couldn't figure a way to attack Earth."

"We're impregnable," said Mom in mock seriousness.

"That's the word Drill used! Impreg— That was the word, Mom."

"My, my, Drill's a brilliant boy. Two-bit words."

"They couldn't figure a way to attack, Mom. Drill says— he says in order to make a good fight you got to have a new way of surprising people. That way you win. And he says also you got to have help from your enemy."

"A fifth column," said Mom.

"Yeah. That's what Drill said. And they couldn't figure a way to surprise Earth, or get help."

"No wonder. We're pretty darn strong." Mom laughed, cleaning up. Mink sat there, staring at the table, seeing what she was talking about.

"Until, one day," whispered Mink melodramatically, "they thought of children!"

"*Well!*" said Mrs. Morris brightly.

"And they thought of how grownups are so busy they never look under rosebushes or on lawns!"

"Only for snails and fungus."

"And then there's something about dim-dims."

"Dim-dims?"

"Dimens-shuns."

"Dimensions?"

"Four of 'em! And there's something about kids under nine and imagination. It's real funny to hear Drill talk."

Mrs. Morris was tired. "Well, it must be funny. You're keeping Drill waiting now. It's getting late in the day and, if you want to have your Invasion before your supper bath, you'd better jump."

"Do I have to take a bath?" growled Mink.

"You do. Why is it children hate water? No matter what age you live in children hate water behind the ears!"

"Drill says I won't have to take baths," said Mink.

"Oh, he does, does he?"

"He told all the kids that. No more baths. And we can stay up till ten o'clock and go to two televisor shows on Saturday 'stead of one!"

"Well, Mr. Drill better mind his p's and q's. I'll call up his mother and—"

Mink went to the door. "We're having trouble with guys like Pete Britz and Dale Jerrick. They're growing up. They make fun. They're worse than parents. They just won't believe in Drill. They're so snooty, 'cause they're growing up. You'd think they'd know better. They were little only a coupla years ago. I hate them worst. We'll kill them *first*."

"Your father and me last?"

"Drill says you're dangerous. Know why? 'Cause you don't believe in Martians! They're going to let *us* run the world. Well, not just us, but the kids over in the next block, too. I might be queen." She opened the door.

"Mom?"

"Yes?"

"What's lodge-ick?"

"Logic? Why, dear, logic is knowing what things are true and not true."

"He *mentioned* that," said Mink. "And what's im-pres-sion-able?" It took her a minute to say it.

"Why, it means——" Her mother looked at the floor, laughing gently. "It means—to be a child, dear."

"Thanks for lunch!" Mink ran out, then stuck her head back in. "Mom, I'll be sure you won't be hurt much, really!"

"Well, thanks," said Mom.

Slam went the door.

At four o'clock the audiovisor buzzed. Mrs. Morris flipped the tab. "Hello, Helen!" she said in welcome.

"Hello, Mary. How are things in New York?"

"Fine. How are things in Scranton? You look tired."

"So do you. The children. Underfoot," said Helen.

Mrs. Morris sighed. "My Mink too. The super-Invasion."

Helen laughed. "Are your kids playing that game too?"

"Lord, yes. Tomorrow it'll be geometrical jacks and motorized hopscotch. Were we this bad when we were kids in '48?"

"Worse. Japs and Nazis. Don't know how my parents put up with me. Tomboy."

"Parents learn to shut their ears."

A silence.

"What's wrong, Mary?" asked Helen.

Mrs. Morris's eyes were half closed; her tongue slid slowly, thoughtfully, over her lower lip. "Eh?" She jerked. "Oh, nothing. Just thought about *that*. Shutting ears and such. Never mind. Where were we?"

"My boy Tim's got a crush on some guy named—*Drill*, I think it was."

"Must be a new password. Mink likes him too."

"Didn't know it had got as far as New York. Word of mouth, I imagine. Looks like a scrap-drive. I talked to Josephine and she said her kids—that's in Boston—are wild on this new game. It's sweeping the country."

At that moment Mink trotted into the kitchen to gulp a glass of water. Mrs. Morris turned. "How're things going?"

"Almost finished," said Mink.

"Swell," said Mrs. Morris. "What's *that*?"

"A yo-yo," said Mink. "Watch."

She flung the yo-yo down its string. Reaching the end it— It vanished.

"See?" said Mink. "Ope!" Dribbling her finger, she made the yo-yo reappear and zip up the string.

"Do that again," said her mother.

"Can't. Zero hour's five o'clock! 'Bye." Mink exited, zipping her yo-yo.

On the audiovisor, Helen laughed. "Tim brought one of those yo-yos in this morning, but when I got curious he said he wouldn't show it to me, and when I tried to work it, finally, it wouldn't work."

"You're not *impressionable*," said Mrs. Morris.

"What?"

"Never mind. Something I thought of. Can I help you, Helen?"

"I wanted to get that black-and-white cake recipe——"

The hour drowsed by. The day waned. The sun lowered in the peaceful blue sky. Shadows lengthened on the green lawns. The laughter and excitement continued. One little girl ran away, crying. Mrs. Morris came out the front door.

"Mink, was that Peggy Ann crying?"

Mink was bent over in the yard, near the rosebush. "Yeah. She's a scarebaby. We won't let her play, now. She's getting too old to play. I guess she grew up all of a sudden."

"Is that why she cried? Nonsense. Give me a civil answer, young lady, or inside you come!"

Mink whirled in consternation, mixed with irritation. "I can't quit now. It's almost time. I'll be good. I'm sorry."

"Did you hit Peggy Ann?"

"No, honest. You ask her. It was something—well, she's just a scaredy pants."

The ring of children drew in around Mink where she scowled at her work with spoons and a kind of square-shaped arrangement of hammers and pipes. "There and there," murmured Mink.

"What's wrong?" said Mrs. Morris.

"Drill's stuck. Halfway. If we could only get him all the way through, it'd be easier. Then all the others could come through after him."

"Can I help?"

"No'm, thanks, I'll fix it."

"All right. I'll call you for your bath in half an hour. I'm tired of watching you."

She went in and sat in the electric relaxing chair, sipping a little beer from a half-empty glass. The chair massaged her back. Children, children. Children love and hate, side by side. Sometimes children loved you, hated you—all in half a second. Strange children, did they ever forget or forgive the whippings and the harsh, strict words of command? She wondered. How can you ever forget or forgive those over and above you, those tall and silly dictators?

Time passed. A curious, waiting silence came upon the street, deepening.

Five o'clock. A clock sang softly somewhere in the house in a quiet, musical voice: "Five o'clock—five o'clcok. Time's a-wasting. Five o'clock," and purred away into silence.

Zero hour.

Mrs. Morris chuckled in her throat. Zero hour.

A beetle car hummed into the driveway. Mr. Morris. Mrs. Morris smiled. Mr. Morris got out of the beetle, locked it and called hello to Mink at her work. Mink ignored him. He laughed and stood for a moment watching the children. Then he walked up the front steps.

"Hello, darling."

"Hello, Henry."

She strained forward on the edge of the chair, listening. The children were silent. Too silent.

He emptied his pipe, refilled it. "Swell day. Makes you glad to be alive."

Buzz.

"What's that?" asked Henry.

"I don't know." She got up suddenly, her eyes widening. She was going to say something. She stopped it. Ridiculous. Her nerves jumped. "Those children haven't anything dangerous out there, have they?" she said.

"Nothing but pipes and hammers. Why?"

"Nothing electrical?"

"Heck, no," said Henry. "I looked."

She walked to the kitchen. The buzzing continued. "Just the same, you'd better go tell them to quit. It's after five. Tell them——" Her eyes widened and narrowed. "Tell them to put off their Invasion until tomorrow." She laughed, nervously.

The buzzing grew louder.

"What are they up to? I'd better go look, all right."

The explosion!

The house shook with dull sound. There were other explosions in other yards on other streets.

Involuntarily, Mrs. Morris screamed. "Up this way!" she cried senselessly, knowing no sense, no reason. Perhaps she saw something from the corners of her eyes; perhaps she smelled a new odor or heard a new noise. There was no time to argue with Henry to convince him. Let him think her insane. Yes, insane! Shrieking, she ran upstairs. He ran after her to see what she was up to. "In the attic!" she screamed. "That's where it is!" It was only a poor excuse to get him in the attic in time. Oh, God—in time!

Another explosion outside. The children screamed with delight, as if at a great fireworks display.

"It's not in the attic!" cried Henry. "It's outside!"

"No, no!" Wheezing, gasping, she fumbled at the attic door. "I'll show you. Hurry! I'll show you!"

They tumbled into the attic. She slammed the door, locked it, took the key, threw it into a far, cluttered corner.

She was babbling wild stuff now. It came out of her. All the subconscious suspicion and fear that had gathered secretly all afternoon and fermented like a wine in her. All the little revelations and knowledges and sense that had bothered her all day and which she had logically and carefully and sensibly rejected and censored. Now it exploded in her and shook her to bits.

"There, there," she said, sobbing against the door. "We're safe until tonight. Maybe we can sneak out. Maybe we can escape!"

Henry blew up too, but for another reason. "Are you crazy? Why'd you throw that key away? Blast it!"

"Yes, yes, I'm crazy, if it helps, but stay here with me!"

"I don't know how I can get out!"

"Quiet. They'll hear us. Oh, God, they'll find us soon enough——"

Below them, Mink's voice. The husband stopped. There was a great universal humming and sizzling, a screaming and giggling. Downstairs the audio-televisor buzzed and buzzed insistently, alarmingly, violently. *Is that Helen calling?* thought Mrs. Morris. *And is she calling about what I think she's calling about?*

Footsteps came into the house. Heavy footsteps.

"Who's coming in my house?" demanded Henry angrily. "Who's tramping around down there?"

Heavy feet. Twenty, thirty, forty, fifty of them. Fifty persons crowding into the house. The humming. The giggling of the children. "This way!" cried Mink, below.

"Who's downstairs?" roared Henry. "Who's there!"

"Hush. Oh, nonononono!" said his wife, weakly, holding him. "Please, be quiet. They might go away."

"Mom?" called Mink. "Dad?" A pause. "Where are you?"

Heavy footsteps, heavy, heavy, *very heavy* footsteps, came up the stairs. Mink leading them.

"Mom?" A hesitation. "Dad?" A waiting, a silence.

Humming. Footsteps toward the attic. Mink's first.

They trembled together in silence in the attic, Mr. and Mrs. Morris. For some reason the electric humming, the queer cold light suddenly visible under the door crack, the strange odor, and the alien sound of eagerness in Mink's voice finally got through to Henry Morris too. He stood, shivering, in the dark silence, his wife beside him.

"Mom! Dad!"

Footsteps. A little humming sound. The attic lock melted. The door opened. Mink peered inside, tall blue shadows behind her.

"Peekaboo," said Mink.

HOBBYIST

by Eric Frank Russell (1905-1978)

ASTOUNDING SCIENCE FICTION

September

Eric Frank Russell was a very tall Briton (raised in Egypt) who produced a substantial body of excellent work in the science fiction field. Although his best known book is certainly Sinister Barrier *(1943), he was one of the premier satirists in sf, his satire usually reflecting a good measure of cynicism. He won the Hugo Award in 1955 for his short story "Allamagoosa." Other excellent books include* Wasp *(1957),* The Great Explosion *(1962),* Men, Martians, and Machines *(1956), and* The Best of Eric Frank Russell *(1978), his definitive short story collection. Unfortunately, he wrote several excellent long stories which are rarely reprinted because of their length, such as "First Person Singular" (in* Deep Space, *1954). A collection of his novellas would make a wonderful book.*

One of his specialties was the depiction of alien life forms, well represented by "Hobbyist," a story that has rightly attained the status of a minor classic of its kind.

*(I haven't got a keen ear for style or a sharp eye
for narrative technique, since I've spent my whole
literary life doing only what comes naturally. On
the other hand, I'm not utterly unobservant.*

*For instance, I can't help realizing that a one-
character story has its problems and that these rapidly escalate with length. Do you deal entirely with
thoughts? Do you introduce flashbacks? Do you
concentrate so entirely on action that the reader
forgets there is no dialogue? There are disad-
vantages in every case.*

*Eric Frank Russell in "Hobbyist" introduces a
macaw, an ordinary non-science-fictional bird, and
you might be interested after reading the story, to
go through it again, and to note how cleverly Russell makes it serve the purpose of introducing just
enough dialogue to dispel the difficulties of a one-
character situation—I.A.)*

The ship arced out of a golden sky and landed with a
whoop and a wallop that cut down a mile of lush vegetation.
Another half-mile of growths turned black and drooped to
ashes under the final flicker of the tail-rocket blasts. That arrival was spectacular, full of verve, and worthy of four
columns in any man's paper. But the nearest sheet was distant by a goodly slice of a lifetime, and there was none to
record what this far corner of the cosmos regarded as the
pettiest of events. So the ship squatted tired and still in the
foremost end of the ashy blast-track and the sky glowed
down and the green world brooded solemnly all around.

Within the transpex control-dome, Steve Ander sat and
thought things over. It was his habit to think things over carefully. Astronauts were not the impulsive dare-devils so dear
to the stereopticon-loving public. They couldn't afford to be.
The hazards of the profession required an infinite capacity
for cautious, contemplative thought. Five minutes' consideration had prevented many a collapsed lung, many a leaky
heart, many a fractured frame. Steve valued his skeleton. He
wasn't conceited about it and he'd no reason to believe it in

any way superior to anyone else's skeleton. But he'd had it a long time, found it quite satisfactory, and had an intense desire to keep it—intact.

Therefore, while the tail tubes cooled off with their usual creaking contractions, he sat in the control seat, stared through the dome with eyes made unseeing by deep preoccupation, and performed a few thinks.

Firstly, he'd made a rough estimate of this world during his hectic approach. As nearly as he could judge, it was ten times the size of Terra. But his weight didn't seem abnormal. Of course, one's notions of weight tended to be somewhat wild when for some weeks one's own weight was shot far up or far down in between periods of weightlessness. The most reasonable estimate had to be based on muscular reaction. If you felt as sluggish as a Saturnian sloth, your weight was way up. If you felt as powerful as Angus McKittrick's bull, your weight was down.

Normal weight meant Terrestrial mass despite this planet's tenfold volume. That meant light plasma. And that meant lack of heavy elements. No thorium. No nickel. No nickel-thorium alloy. Ergo, no getting back. The Kingston-Kane atomic motors demanded fuel in the form of ten-gauge nickel-thorium-alloy wire fed directly into the vaporizers. Denatured plutonium would do, but it didn't occur in natural form, and it had to be made. He had three yards nine and a quarter inches of nickel-thorium left on the feed-spool. Not enough. He was here for keeps.

A wonderful thing, logic. You could start from the simple premise that when you were seated your behind was no flatter than usual, and work your way to the inevitable conclusion that you were a wanderer no more. You'd become a native. Destiny had you tagged as suitable for the status of oldest inhabitant.

Steve pulled an ugly face and said, 'Darn!'

The face didn't have to be pulled far. Nature had given said pan a good start. That is to say, it wasn't handsome. It was a long, lean, nut-brown face with pronounced jaw muscles, prominent cheekbones, and a thin, hooked nose. This, with his dark eyes and black hair, gave him a hawklike appearance. Friends talked to him about tepees and tomahawks whenever they wanted him to feel at home.

Well, he wasn't going to feel at home anymore; not unless this brooding jungle held intelligent life dopey enough to

swap ten-gauge nickel-thorium wire for a pair of old boots.
Or unless some dopey search party was intelligent enough to
pick this cosmic dust mote out of a cloud of motes, and took
him back. He estimated this as no less than a million-to-one
chance. Like spitting at the Empire State hoping to hit a
cent-sized mark on one of its walls.

Reaching for his everflo stylus and the ship's log, he
opened the log, looked absently at some of the entries.

"Eighteenth day: The spatial convulsion has now flung me
past rotal-range of Rigel. Am being tossed into uncharted
regions. . . .

"Twenty-fourth day: Arm of convulsion now tails back
seven parsecs. Robot recorder now out of gear. Angle of
throw changed seven times today. . . .

"Twenty-ninth day: Now beyond arm of the convulsive
sweep and regaining control. Speed far beyond range of the
astrometer. Applying braking rockets cautiously. Fuel reserve: fourteen hundred yards. . . .

"Thirty-seventh day: Making for planetary system now
within reach."

He scowled, his jaw muscles lumped, and he wrote slowly
and legibly, "Thirty-ninth day: Landed on planet unknown,
primary unknown, galactic area standard reference and sector
numbers unknown. No cosmic formations were recognizable
when observed shortly before landing. Angles of offshoot and
speed of transit not recorded, and impossible to estimate.
Condition of ship: workable. Fuel reserve: three and one-
quarter yards."

Closing the log, he scowled again, rammed the stylus into
its desk-grip, and muttered, "Now to check on the outside air
and then see how the best girl's doing."

The Radson register had three simple dials. The first recorded outside pressure at thirteen point seven pounds, a
reading he observed with much satisfaction. The second said
that oxygen content was high. The third had a bi-colored
dial, half-white, half-red, and its needle stood in the middle
of the white.

"Breathable," he grunted, clipping down the register's lid.
Crossing the tiny control room, he slid aside a metal panel,
looked into the padded compartment behind. "Coming out,
Beauteous?" he asked.

"Steve loves Laura?" inquired a plaintive voice.

"You bet he does!" he responded with becoming passion.

He shoved an arm into the compartment, brought out a large, gaudily colored macaw. "Does Laura love Steve?"

"Hey-hey!" cackled Laura harshly. Climbing up his arm, the bird perched on his shoulder. He could feel the grip of its powerful claws. It regarded him with a beady and brilliant eye, then rubbed its crimson head against his left ear. "Hey-hey! Time flies!"

"Don't mention it," he reproved. "There's plenty to remind me of the fact without you chipping in."

Reaching up, he scratched her poll while she stretched and bowed with absurd delight. He was fond of Laura. She was more than a pet. She was a bona fide member of the crew, issued with her own rations and drawing her own pay. Every probe ship had a crew of two; one man, one macaw. When he'd first heard of it, the practice had seemed crazy—but when he got the reasons it made sense.

"Lonely men, probing beyond the edge of the charts, get queer psychological troubles. They need an anchor to Earth. A macaw provides the necessary companionship—and more! It's the space-hardiest bird we've got, its weight is negligible, it can talk and amuse, it can fend for itself when necessary. On land, it will often sense dangers before you do. Any strange fruit or food it may eat is safe for you to eat. Many a man's life has been saved by his macaw. Look after yours, my boy, and it'll look after you!"

Yes, they looked after each other, Terrestrials both. It was almost a symbiosis of the spaceways. Before the era of astro-navigation nobody had thought of such an arrangement, though it had been done before. Miners and their canaries.

Moving over to the miniature air lock, he didn't bother to operate the pump. It wasn't necessary with so small a difference between internal and external pressures. Opening both doors, he let a little of his higher-pressured air sigh out, stood on the rim of the lock, jumped down. Laura fluttered from his shoulder as he leaped, followed him with a flurry of wings, got her talons into his jacket as he staggered upright.

The pair went around the ship, silently surveying its condition. Front braking nozzles O.K., rear steering flares O.K., tail propulsion tubes O.K. All were badly scored but still usable. The skin of the vessel likewise was scored but intact. Three months' supply of food and maybe a thousand yards of wire could get her home, theoretically. But only theoretically; Steve had no delusions about the matter. The odds were still

against him even if given the means to move. How do you
navigate from you-don't-know-where to you-don't-know-
where? Answer: you stroke a rabbit's foot and probably ar-
rive you-don't-know-where-else.

"Well," he said, rounding the tail, "it's something in which
to live. It'll save us building a shanty. Way back on Terra
they want fifty thousand smackers for an all-metal, streamlined bungalow, so I guess we're mighty lucky. I'll make a
garden here, and a rockery there, and build a swimming-pool
out back. You can wear a pretty frock and do all the cooking."

"Yawk," said Laura derisively.

Turning, he had a look at the nearest vegetation. It was of
all heights, shapes and sizes, of all shades of green with a few
tending toward blueness. There was something peculiar about
the stuff but he was unable to decide where the strangeness
lay. It wasn't that the growths were alien and unfamiliar—
one expected that on every new world—but an underlying
something which they shared in common. They had a vague,
shadowy air of being not quite right in some basic respect impossible to define.

A plant grew right at his feet. It was green in colour, a
foot high, and monocotyledonous. Looked at as a thing in itself, there was nothing wrong with it. Near to it flourished a
bush of darker hue, a yard high, with green, fir-like needles
in lieu of leaves, and pale, waxy berries scattered over it.
That, too, was innocent enough when studied apart from its
neighbours. Beside it grew a similar plant, differing only in
that its needles were longer and its berries a bright pink. Beyond these towered a cactuslike object dragged out of somebody's drunken dreams, and beside it stood an umbrella-
frame which had taken root and produced little purple pods.
Individually, they were acceptable. Collectively, they made
the discerning mind search anxiously for it knew not what.

That eerie feature had Steve stumped. Whatever it was, he
couldn't nail it down. There was something stranger than the
mere strangeness of new forms of plant life, and that was all.
He dismissed the problem with a shrug. Time enough to trouble about such matters after he'd dealt with others more urgent such as, for example, the location and purity of the
nearest water supply.

A mile away lay a lake of some liquid that might be water.
He'd seen it glittering in the sunlight as he'd made his

descent, and he'd tried to land fairly near to it. If it wasn't water, well, it'd be just his tough luck and he'd have to look some place else. At worst, the tiny fuel reserve would be enough to permit one circumnavigation of the planet before the ship became pinned down forever. Water he must have if he wasn't going to end up imitating the mummy of Rameses II.

Reaching high, he grasped the rim of the port, dexterously muscled himself upward and through it. For a minute he moved around inside the ship, then reappeared with a four-gallon freeezocan which he tossed to the ground. Then he dug out his popgun, a belt of explosive shells, and let down the folding ladder from lock to surface. He'd need that ladder. He could muscle himself up through a hole seven feet high, but not with fifty pounds of can and water.

Finally, he locked both the inner and outer air-lock doors, skipped down the ladder, picked up the can. From the way he'd made his landing the lake should be directly bow-on relative to the vessel, and somewhere the other side of those distant trees. Laura took a fresh grip on his shoulder as he started off. The can swung from his left hand. His right hand rested warily on the gun. He was perpendicular on this world instead of horizontal on another because, on two occasions, his hand had been ready on the gun and because it was the most nervous hand he possessed.

The going was rough. It wasn't so much that the terrain was craggy as the fact that impending growths got in his way. At one moment he was stepping over an ankle-high shrub, the next he was facing a burly plant struggling to become a tree. Behind the plant would be a creeper, then a natural zareba of thorns, a fuzz of fine moss, followed by a giant fern. Progress consisted of stepping over one item, ducking beneath a second, going around a third, and crawling under a forth.

It occurred to him belatedly that if he'd planted the ship tail-first to the lake instead of bow-on, or if he'd let the braking rockets blow after he'd touched down, he'd have saved himself much twisting and dodging. All this obstructing stuff would have been reduced to ashes for at least half the distance to the lake—together with any venomous life it might conceal.

That last thought rang like an alarm bell within his mind just as he doubled up to pass a low-swung creeper. On Venus were creepers that coiled and constricted, swiftly, viciously. Macaws played merry hell, if taken within fifty yards of them. It was a comfort to know that, this time, Laura was riding his shoulder unperturbed—but he kept the hand on the gun.

The elusive peculiarity of the planet's vegetation bothered him all the more as he progressed through it. His inability to discover and name this unnameable queerness nagged at him as he went on. A frown of self-disgust was on his lean face when he dragged himself free of a clinging bush and sat on a rock in a tiny clearing.

Dumping the can at his feet, he glowered at it and promptly caught a glimpse of something bright and shining a few feet beyond the can. He raised his gaze. It was then that he saw the beetle.

The creature was the biggest of its kind ever seen by human eyes. There were other things bigger, of course, but not of this type. Crabs, for instance. But this was no crab. The beetle ambling purposefully across the clearing was large enough to give any crab a severe inferiority complex, but it was a genuine twenty-four-carat beetle. And a beautiful one. Like a scarab.

Except that he clung to the notion that little bugs were vicious and big ones companionable, Steve had no phobia about insects. The amiability of large ones was a theory inherited from school-kid days when he'd been the doting owner of a three-inch stag-beetle afflicted with the name of Edgar.

So he knelt beside the creeping giant, placed his hand palm upward in its path. It investigated the hand with waving feelers, climbed on to his palm, paused there ruminatively. It shone with a sheen of brilliant metallic blue and weighed about three pounds. He jogged it on his hand to get its weight, then put it down, let it wander on. Laura watched it go with a sharp but incurious eye.

"*Scarabaeus anderii,*" Steve said with glum satisfaction. "I pin my name on him—but nobody'll ever know it."

"Dinna fash y'sel'!" shouted Laura in a hoarse voice imported straight from Aberdeen. "Dinna fash! Stop chunnerin', wumman! Y' gie me a pain ahint ma sporran! Dinna—"

"Shut up!" Steve jerked his shoulder, momentarily unbalancing the bird. "Why d'you pick up that barbaric dialect quicker than anything else, eh?"

"McGillicuddy," shrieked Laura with ear-splitting relish. "McGilli-Gilli-Gillicuddy! The great black—!" It ended with a word that pushed Steve's eyebrows into his hair and surprised even the bird itself. Filming its eyes with amazement, it tightened its claw-hold on his shoulder, opened the eyes, emitted a couple of raucous clucks, and joyfully repeated, "The great black—"

It didn't get the chance to complete the new and lovely word. A violent jerk of the shoulder unseated it in the nick of time and it fluttered to the ground, squawking protestingly. *Scarabaeus anderii* lumbered out from behind a bush, his blue armor glistening as if freshly polished, and stared reprovingly at Laura.

Then something fifty yards away released a snort like the trump of doom and took one step that shook the earth. *Scarabaeus anderii* took refuge under a projecting root. Laura made an agitated swoop for Steve's shoulder and clung there desperately. Steve's gun was out and pointing northward before the bird had found its perch. Another step. The ground quivered.

Silence for a while. Steven continued to stand like a statue. Then came a monstrous whistle more forceful than that of a locomotive blowing off steam. Something squat and wide and of tremendous length charged headlong through the half-concealing vegetation while the earth trembled beneath its weight.

Its mad onrush carried it blindly twenty yards to Steve's right, the gun swinging to cover its course, but not firing. Steve caught an extended glimpse of a slate-gray bulk with a serrated ridge on its back which, despite the thing's pace, took long to pass. It seemed several times the length of a fire ladder.

Bushes were flung roots topmost and small trees whipped aside as the creature pounded grimly onward in a straight line which carried it far past the ship into the dim distance. It left behind a tattered swathe wide enough for a first-class road. Then the reverberations of its mighty tonnage died out, and it was gone.

Steve used his left hand to pull out a handkerchief and wipe the back of his neck. He kept the gun in his right hand. The explosive shells in that gun were somewhat wicked; any one of them could deprive a rhinoceros of a hunk of meat weighing two hundred pounds. If a man caught one, he just strewed himself over the landscape. By the looks of that slate-colored galloper, it would need half a dozen shells to feel incommoded. A seventy-five-millimetre bazooka would be more effective for kicking it in the back teeth, but probe-ship boys don't tote around such artillery. Steve finished the mopping, put the handkerchief back, picked up the can.

Laura said pensively, "I want my mother."

He scowled, made no reply, set out toward the lake. Her feathers still ruffled, Laura rode his shoulder and lapsed into surly silence.

The stuff in the lake was water, cold, faintly green and a little bitter to the taste. Coffee would camouflage the flavor. If anything, it might improve the coffee since he liked his java bitter, but the stuff would have to be tested before ab-sorbing it in any quantity. Some poisons were accumulative. It wouldn't do to guzzle gaily while building up a death-dealing reserve of lead, for instance. Filling the freezocan, he lugged it to the ship in hundred-yard stages. The swathe helped; it made an easier path to within short distance of the ship's tail. He was perspiring freely by the time he reached the base of the ladder.

Once inside the vessel he relocked both doors, opened the air vents, started the auxiliary lighting-set and plugged in the percolator, using water out of his depleted reserve supply. The golden sky had dulled to orange, with violet streamers creeping upward from the horizon. Looking at it through the transpex dome, he found that the perpetual haze still effec-tively concealed the sinking sun. A brighter area to one side was all that indicated its position. He'd need his lights soon.

Pulling out the collapsible table, he jammed its supporting leg into place, plugged into its rim the short rod which was Laura's official seat. She claimed the perch immediately, watched him beadily as he set out her meal of water, melon seeds, sunflower seeds, pecans and unshelled oleo nuts. Her manners were anything but ladylike and she started eagerly, without waiting for him.

A deep frown lay across his brown, muscular features as he sat at the table, poured out his coffee and commenced to eat. It persisted through the meal, was still there when he lit a cigarette and stared speculatively up at the dome.

Presently, he murmured, "I've seen the biggest bug that ever was. I've seen a few other bugs. There were a couple of little ones under a creeper. One was long and brown and many-legged, like an earwig. The other was round and black, with little red dots on its wing cases. I've seen a tiny purple spider and a tinier green one of different shape, also a bug that looked like an aphid. But not an ant."

"Ant, ant," hooted Laura. She dropped a piece of oleo nut, climbed down after it. "Yawk!" she added from the floor.

"Not a bee."

"Bee," echoed Laura, companionably. "Bee-ant. Laura loves Steve."

Still keeping his attention on the dome, he went on, "And what's cockeyed about the plants is equally cockeyed about the bugs. I wish I could place it. Why can't I? Maybe I'm going nuts already."

"Laura loves nuts."

"I know it, you technicolored belly!" said Steve rudely.

And at that point night fell with a silent bang. The gold and orange and violet abruptly were swamped with deep, impenetrable blackness devoid of stars or any random gleam. Except for greenish glowings on the instrument panel, the control room was stygian, with Laura swearing steadily on the floor.

Putting out a hand, Steve switched on the indirect lighting. Laura got to her perch with the rescued titbit, concentrated on the job of dealing with it and let him sink back into his thoughts.

"*Scarabaeus anderii* and a pair of smaller bugs and a couple of spiders, all different. At the other end of the scale, that giganto-saurus. But no ant, or bee. Or rather, no ants, no bees." The switch from singular to plural stirred his back hairs queerly. In some vague way, he felt that he'd touched the heart of the mystery. "No ant—no ants," he thought. "No bee—no bees." Almost he had it—but still it evaded him.

Giving it up for the time being, he cleared the table, did a few minor chores. After that, he drew a standard sample from the freezocan, put it through its paces. The bitter flavour he identified as being due to the presence of magnesium sulphate in quantity far too small to prove embarrassing. Drinkable—that was something! Food, drink and shelter were the three essentials of survival. He'd enough of the first for six or seven weeks. The lake and the ship were his remaining guarantees of life.

Finding the log, he entered the day's report, bluntly, factu-
ally, without any embroidery. Partway through, he found
himself stuck for a name for the planet. *Ander,* he decided,
would cost him dear if the million-to-one chance put him
back among the merciless playmates of the Probe Service.
O.K. for a bug, but not for a world. *Laura* wasn't so hot, either—especially when you knew Laura. It wouldn't be seemly
to name a big, gold planet after an oversized parrot. Thinking
over the golden aspect of this world's sky, he hit upon the
name of *Oro,* promptly made the christening authoritative by
entering it in his log.

By the time he'd finished, Laura had her head buried deep
under one wing. Occasionally she teetered and swung erect
again. It always fascinated him to watch how her balance was
maintained even in her slumbers. Studying her fondly, he
remembered that unexpected addition to her vocabulary. This
shifted his thoughts to a fiery-headed and fierier-tongued individual named Menzies, the sworn foe of another volcano
named McGillicuddy. If ever the opportunity presented itself,
he decided, the educative work of said Menzies was going to
be rewarded with a bust on the snoot.

Sighing, he put away the log, wound up the forty-day chronometer, opened his folding bunk and lay down upon it. His
hand switched off the lights. Ten years back, a first landing
would have kept him awake all night in dithers of excitement.
He'd got beyond that now. He'd done it often enough to have
grown phlegmatic about it. His eyes closed in preparation for
a good night's sleep, and he did sleep—for two hours.

What brought him awake within that short time he didn't
know, but suddenly he found himself sitting bolt upright on
the edge of the bunk, his ears and nerves stretched to their
utmost, his legs quivering in a way they'd never done before.
His whole body fizzed with the queer mixture of palpitation
and shock which follows narrow escape from disaster.

This was something not within previous experience. Sure
and certain in the intense darkness, his hand sought and
found his gun. He cuddled the butt in his palm while his
mind strove to recall a possible nightmare, though he knew he
was not given to nightmares.

Laura moved restlessly on her perch, not truly awake, yet
not asleep, and this was unusual in her.

Rejecting the dream theory, he stood up on the bunk,

looked out through the dome. Blackness, the deepest, darkest, most impenetrable blackness it was possible to conceive. And silence! The outside world slumbered in the blackness and the silence as in a sable shroud.

Yet never before had he felt so wide awake in this, his normal sleeping time. Puzzled, he turned slowly round to take in the full circle of unseeable view, and at one point he halted. The surrounding darkness was not complete. In the distance beyond the ship's tail moved a tall, stately glow. How far off it might be was not possible to estimate, but the sight of it stirred his soul and caused his heart to leap.

Uncontrollable emotions were not permitted to master his disciplined mind. Narrowing his eyes, he tried to discern the nature of the glow while his mind sought the reason why the mere sight of it should make him twang like a harp. Bending down, he felt at the head of the bunk, found a leather case, extracted a pair of powerful night-glasses. The glow was still moving, slowly, deliberately, from right to left. He got the glasses on it, screwed the lenses into focus, and the phenomenon leaped into closer view.

The thing was a great column of golden haze much like that of the noonday sky except that small, intense gleams of silver sparkled within it. It was a shaft of lustrous mist bearing a sprinkling of tiny stars. It was like nothing known to or recorded by any form of life lower than the gods. But was it life?

It moved, though its mode of locomotion could not be determined. Self-motivation is the prime symptom of life. It could be life, conceivably though not credibly, from the Terrestrial viewpoint. Consciously, he preferred to think it a strange and purely local feature comparable with Saharan sand-devils. Subconsciously, he knew it was life, tall and terrifying.

He kept the glasses on it while slowly it receded into the darkness, foreshortening with increasing distance and gradually fading from view. To the very last the observable field shifted and shuddered as he failed to control the quiver in his hands. And when the sparkling haze had gone he sat down on the bunk and shivered with eerie cold.

Laura was dodging to and fro along her perch, now thoroughly awake and agitated, but he wasn't inclined to switch on the lights and make the dome a beacon in night. His hand went out, feeling for her in the darkness, and she clambered eagerly on to his wrist, thence to his lap. She was fussy and demonstrative, pathetically yearning for comfort and companionship. He scratched her poll and fondled her while she pressed close against his chest with funny little crooning noises. For some time he soothed her and, while doing it, fell asleep. Gradually he slumped backward on the bunk. Laura perched on his forearm, clucked tiredly, put her head under a wing.

There was no further awakening until the outer blackness disappeared and the sky again sent its golden glow pouring through the dome. Steve got up, stood on the bunk, had a good look over the surrounding terrain. It remained precisely the same as it had been the day before. Things stewed within his mind while he got his breakfast; especially the jumpiness he'd experienced in the night-time. Laura also was subdued and quiet. Only once before had she been like that—which was when he'd traipsed through the Venusian section of the Panplanetary Zoo and had shown her a crested eagle. The eagle had stared at her with contemptuous dignity.

Though he'd all the time in his life, he now felt a peculiar urge to hasten. Getting the gun and the freezocan, he made a full dozen trips to the lake, wasting no minutes, nor stopping to study the still enigmatic plants and bugs. It was late in the afternoon by the time he'd filled the ship's fifty-gallon reservoir, and had the satisfaction of knowing that he'd got a drinkable quota to match his food supply.

There had been no sign of gigantosaurus or any other animal. Once he'd seen something flying in the far distance, birdlike or batlike. Laura had cocked a sharp eye at it but betrayed no undue interest. Right now she was more concerned with a new fruit. Steve sat in the rim of the outer lock-door, his legs dangling, and watched her clambering over a small tree thirty yards away. The gun lay in his lap; he was ready to take a crack at anything which might be ready to take a crack at Laura.

The bird sampled the tree's fruit, a crop resembling blue-shelled lychee nuts. She ate one with relish, grabbed another. Steve lay back in the lock, stretched to reach a bag, then dropped to the ground and went across to the tree. He tried a nut. Its flesh was soft, juicy, sweet and citreous. He filled the bag with the fruit, slung it into the ship.

Nearby stood another tree, not quite the same, but very similar. It bore nuts like the first except that they were larger.

Picking one, he offered it to Laura who tried it, spat it out in disgust. Picking a second, he slit it, licked the flesh gingerly. As far as he could tell, it was the same. Evidently he couldn't tell far enough: Laura's diagnosis said it was not the same. The difference, too subtle for him to detect, might be sufficient to roll him that shape to the unpleasant end. He flung the thing away, went back to his seat in the lock, and ruminated.

That elusive, nagging feature of Oro's plants and bugs could be narrowed down to these two nuts. He felt sure of that. If he could discover why—parrotwise—one nut was not, he'd have his finger right on the secret. The more he thought about those similar fruits the more he felt that, in sober fact, his finger was on the secret already—but he lacked the power to lift it and see what lay beneath.

Tantalizing, his mulling over the subject landed him the same place as before; namely, nowhere. It got his dander up, and he went back to the trees, subjected both to close examination. His sense of sight told him that they were different individuals of the same species. Laura's sense of whatchamacallit insisted that they were different species. Ergo, you can't believe the evidence of your eyes. He was aware of that fact, of course, since it was a platitude of the spaceways, but when you couldn't trust your optics it was legitimate to try to discover just why you couldn't trust 'em. And he couldn't discover even that!

It soured him so much that he returned to the ship, locked its doors, called Laura back to his shoulder and set off on a tailward exploration. The rules of first landings were simple and sensible. Go in slowly, come out quickly, and remember that all we want from you is evidence of suitability for human life. Thoroughly explore a small area rather than scout a big one—the mapping parties will do the rest. Use your ship as a base and centralize it where you can live—don't move it unnecessarily. Restrict your trips to a radius representing daylight-reach and lock yourself in after dark.

Was Oro suitable for human life? The unwritten law was that you don't jump to conclusions and say, "Of course! I'm still living, aren't I?" Cameron who'd plonked his ship on Mithra, for instance, thought he'd found paradise until, on the seventeenth day, he'd discovered the fungoid plague. He'd left like a bat out of hell and had spent three sweaty, swearing days in the Lunar Purification Plant before becom-

ing fit for society. The authorities had vaporized his ship.
Mithra had been taboo ever since. Every world a potential
trap baited with scientific delight. The job of the Probe
Service was to enter the traps and jounce on the springs. Another dollop of real estate for Terra—if nothing broke your
neck.

Maybe Ora was loaded for bear. The thing that walked in
the night, Steve mused, bore awful suggestion of non-human
power. So did a waterspout, and whoever heard of anyone
successfully wrestling with a waterspout? If this Oro-spout
were sentient, so much the worse for human prospects. He'd
have to get the measure of it, he decided, even if he had to
chase it through the blank avenues of night. Plodding steadily
away from the tail, gun in hand, he pondered so deeply that
he entirely overlooked the fact that he wasn't on a pukka
probe job anyway, and that nothing else remotely human
might reach Oro in a thousand years. Even space-boys can be
creatures of habit. Their job: to look for death; they were lia-
ble to go on looking long after the need had passed, in bland
disregard of the certainty that if you look for a thing long
enough ultimately you find it!

The ship's chronometer had given him five hours to
darkness. Two and a half hours each way; say ten miles out
and ten back. The water had consumed his time. On the morrow, and henceforth, he'd increase the radius to twelve and
take it easier.

Then all thoughts fled from his mind as he came to the
edge of the vegetation. The stuff didn't dribble out of existence with hardy spurs and offshoots fighting for a hold in
suddenly rocky ground. It stopped abruptly, in light loam, as
if cut off with a machete, and from where it stopped spread a
different crop. The new growths were tiny and crystalline.

He accepted the crystalline crop without surprise; knowing
that novelty was the inevitable feature of any new locale.
Things were ordinary only by Terrestrial standards. Outside
of Terra, nothing was supernormal or abnormal except in so
far as they failed to jibe with their own peculiar conditions.
Besides, there were crystalline growths on Mars. The one
unacceptable feature of the situation was the way in which
vegetable growths ended and crystalline ones began. He
stepped back to the verge and made another startled survey
of the borderline. It was so straight that the sight screwed his
brain around. Like a field. A cultivated field. Dead straight-

ness of that sort couldn't be other than artificial. Little beads of moisture popped out on his back.

Squatting on the heel of his right boot, he gazed at the nearest crystals and said to Laura, "Chicken, I think these things got planted. Question is, who planted 'em?"

"McGillicuddy," suggested Laura brightly.

Putting out a finger, he flicked the crystal sprouting near the toe of his boot, a green, branchy object an inch high.

The crystal vibrated and said, *"Zing!"* in a sweet, high voice.

He flicked its neighbor, and that said, *"Zang!"* in a lower tone.

He flicked a third. It emitted no note, but broke into a thousand shards.

Standing up, he scratched his head, making Laura fight for a clawhold within the circle of his arm. One zinged and one zanged and one returned to dust. Two nuts. Zings and zangs and nuts. It was right in his grasp if only he could open his hand and look at what he'd got.

Then he lifted his puzzled and slightly ireful gaze, saw something fluttering erratically across the crystal field; it was making for the vegetation. Laura took off with a raucous cackle, her blue-and-crimson wings beating powerfully. She swooped over the object, frightening it so low that it dodged and side-slipped only a few feet above Steve's head. He saw that it was a large butterfly, frill-winged, almost as gaudy as Laura. The bird swooped again, scaring the insect but not menacing it. He called her back, set out to cross the area ahead. Crystals crunched to powder under his heavy boots as he tramped on.

Half an hour later he was tolling up a steep, crystal-coated slope when his thoughts suddenly jelled and he stopped with such abruptness that Laura spilled from his shoulder and perforce took to wing. She beat round in a circle, came back to her perch, made bitter remarks in an unknown language.

"One of this and one of that," he said, "No twos or threes or dozens. Nothing I've seen has repeated itself. There's only one gigantosaurus, only one *Scarabaeus anderii,* only one of every danged thing. Every item is unique, original, and an individual creation in its own right. What does that suggest?"

"McGillicuddy," offered Laura.

"For Pete's sake, forget McGillicuddy."

"For Pete's sake, for Pete's sake," yelled Laura, much taken by the phrase. "The great black—"

Again he upset her in the nick of time, making her take to flight while he continued talking to himself. "It suggests constant and all-pervading mutation. Everything breeds something quite different from itself and there aren't any dominant strains." He frowned at the obvious snag in his theory. "But how the blazes does anything breed? What fertilizes which?"

"McGilli—," began Laura, then changed her mind and shut up.

"Anyway, if nothing breeds true, it'll be tough on the food problem," he went on. "What's edible on one plant may be a killer on its offspring. Today's fodder is tomorrow's poison. How's a farmer to know what he's going to get? Hey-hey, if I'm guessing right, this planet won't support a couple of hogs."

"No, sir. No hogs. Laura loves hogs."

"Be quiet," he snapped. "Now, what shouldn't support a couple of hogs demonstrably does support gigantosaurus—and any other fancy animals which may be mooching around. It seems crazy to me. On Venus or any other place full of consistent fodder, gigantosaurus would thrive; but here, according to my calculations, the big lunk has no right to be alive. He ought to be dead."

So saying, he topped the rise and found the monster in question sprawling right across the opposite slope. It *was* dead.

The way in which he determined its deadness was appropriately swift, simple and effective. Its enormous bulk lay draped across the full length of the slope and its dragonhead, the size of a lifeboat, pointed toward him. The head had two dull, lacklustre eyes like dinner plates. He planted a shell smack in the right eye and a sizable hunk of noggin promptly splashed in all directions. The body did not stir.

There was a shell ready for the other eye should the creature leap to frantic, vengeful life, but the mighty hulk remained supine.

His boots continued to desiccate crystals as he went down the slope, curved a hundred yards off his route to get around the corpse, and trudged up the farther rise. Momentarily, he wasn't much interested in the dead beast. Time was short and he could come again tomorrow, bringing a full-color stereoscopic camera with him. Gigantosaurus would go on record in style, but would have to wait.

This second rise was a good deal higher, and more trying a climb. Its crest represented the approximate limit of this day's trip, and he felt anxious to surmount it before turning back. Humanity's characteristic urge to see what lay over the hill remained as strong as on the day determined ancestors topped the Rockies. He had to have a look, firstly because elevation gave range to vision, and secondly because of that prowler in the night—and, nearly as he could estimate, the prowler had gone down behind this rise. A column of mist, sucked down from the sky, might move around aimlessly, going nowhere, but instinct maintained that this had been no mere column of mist, and that it was going somewhere.

Where?

Out of breath, he pounded over the crest, looked down into an immense valley, and found the answer.

The crystal growths gave out on the crest, again in a perfectly straight line. Beyond them the light loam, devoid of rock, ran gently down to the valley and up the farther side. Both slopes were sparsely dotted with queer, jelly-like lumps of matter which lay and quivered beneath the sky's golden glow.

From the closed end of the valley jutted a great, glistening fabrication, flat-roofed, flat-fronted, with a huge, square hole gaping in its mid-section at front. It looked like a tremendous oblong slab of polished, milk-white plastic half-buried endwise in a sandy hill. No decoration disturbed its smooth, gleaming surface. No road led to the hole in front. Somehow, it had the new-old air of a house that struggles to look empty because it is full—of fiends.

Steve's back hairs prickled as he studied it. One thing was obvious—Oro bore intelligent life. One thing was possible—the golden column represented that life. One thing was probable—fleshy Terrestrials and hazy Orons would have difficulty in finding a basis for friendship and co-operation.

Whereas enmity needs no basis.

Curiosity and caution pulled him opposite ways. One urged him down into the valley while the other drove him back, back, while yet there was time. He consulted his watch. Less than three hours to go, within which he had to return to the ship, enter the log, prepare supper. That milky creation was at least two miles away, a good hour's journey there and back. Let it wait. Give it another day and he'd have more time for it, with the benefit of needful thought betweentimes.

Caution triumphed. He investigated the nearest jellyblob. It was flat, a yard in diameter, green, with bluish streaks and many tiny bubbles hiding in its semi-transparency. The thing pulsated slowly. He poked at it with the toe of his boot, and it contracted, humping itself in the middle, then sluggishly relaxed. No amoeba, he decided. A low form of life but complicated withal. Laura didn't like the object. She skittered off as he bent over it, vented her anger by bashing a few crystals.

This jellyblob wasn't like its nearest neighbour, or like any other. One of each, only one. The same rule; one butterfly of a kind, one bug, one plant, one of these quivering things.

A final stare at the distant mystery down in the valley, then he retraced his steps. When the ship came into sight he speeded up like a gladsome voyager nearing home. There were new prints near the vessel, big, three-toed, deeply impressed spoor which revealed that something large and two-legged had wandered past in his absence. Evidently an animal, for nothing intelligent would have meandered on so casually without circling and inspecting the nearby invader from space. He dismissed it from his mind. There was only one thingummybob, he felt certain of that.

Once inside the ship, he relocked the doors, gave Laura her feed, ate his supper. Then he dragged out the log, made his day's entry, had a look around from the dome. Violet streamers once more were creeping upward from the horizon. He frowned at the encompassing vegetation. What sort of stuff had bred all this in the past? What sort of stuff would this breed in the future? How did it progenerate, anyway?

Wholesale radical mutation presupposed modification of genes by hard radiation in persistent and considerable blasts. You shouldn't get hard radiation on lightweight planets— unless it poured in from the sky. Here, it didn't pour from the sky, or from any place else. In fact, there wasn't any.

He was pretty certain of that fact because he'd a special interest in it and had checked up on it. Hard radiation betokened the presence of radioactive elements which, at a pinch, might be usable as fuel. The ship was equipped to detect such stuff. Among the junk was a cosmiray counter, a radium hen, and a gold-leaf electroscope. The hen and the counter hadn't given so much as one heartening cluck, in fact the only clucks had been Laura's. The electroscope he'd charged on landing and its leaves still formed an inverted vee. The air was dry, ionization negligible, and the leaves didn't look likely to collapse for a week.

"Something wrong with my theorizing," he complained to Laura. "My think-stuff's not doing its job."

"Not doing its job," echoed Laura faithfully. She cracked a pecan with a grating noise that set his teeth on edge. "I tell you it's a hoodoo ship. I won't sail. No, not even if you pray for me, I won't, I won't, I won't. Nope. Nix. Who's drunk? That hairy Lowlander Mc—"

"Laura!" he said sharply.

"Gillicuddy," she finished with bland defiance. Again she rasped his teeth. "Rings bigger'n Saturn's I saw them myself. Who's a liar? Yawk! She's down in Grayway Bay, on Tethis. Boy, what a torso!"

He looked at her hard, and said, "You're nuts!"

"Sure! Sure, pal! Laura loves nuts. Have one on me."

"O.K.," he accepted, holding out his hand.

Cocking her colorful pate, she pecked at his hand, gravely selected a pecan and gave it to him. He cracked it, chewed on the kernel starting up the lighting-set. It was almost as if night were waiting for him. Blackness fell even as he switched on the lights.

With the darkness came a keen sense of unease. The dome was the trouble. It blazed like a beacon and there was no way of blacking it out except by turning off the lights. Beacons attracted things, and he'd no desire to become a center of attraction in present circumstances. That is to say, not at night.

Long experience had bred fine contempt for alien animals, no matter how whacky, but outlandish intelligence was a different proposition. So filled was he with the strange inward conviction that last night's phenomenon was something that knew its onions that it didn't occur to him to wonder whether a glowing column possessed eyes or anything equivalent to a sense of sight. If it had occurred to him, he'd have derived no comfort from it. His desire to be weighed in the balance in some eerie, extra-sensory way was even less than his desire to be gaped at visually in his slumbers.

An unholy mess of thoughts and ideas was still cooking in his mind when he extinguished the light, bunked down and went to sleep. Nothing disturbed him this time, but when he awoke with the golden dawn his chest was damp with perspiration and Laura again had sought refuge on his arm.

Digging out breakfast, his thoughts began to marshal themselves as he kept his hands busy. Pouring out a shot of hot coffee, he spoke to Laura.

"I'm durned if I'm going to go scatty trying to maintain a three-watch system single-handed, which is what I'm supposed to do if faced by powers unknown when I'm not able to beat it. Those armchair warriors at headquarters ought to get a taste of situations not precisely specified in the book of rules."

"Burp!" said Laura contemptuously.

"He who fights and runs away lives to fight another day," Steve quoted. "That's the Probe Law. It's a nice, smooth, lovely law—when you can run away. We can't!"

"Burrup!" said Laura with unnecessary emphasis.

"For a woman, your manners are downright disgusting," he told her. "Now, I'm not going to spend the brief remainder of my life looking fearfully over my shoulder. The only way to get rid of powers unknown is to convert 'em into powers known and understood. As Uncle Joe told Willie when dragging him to the dentist, the longer we put it off the worse it'll feel."

"Dinna fash y'sel," declaimed Laura. "Burp-gollop-bop!"

Giving her a look of extreme distaste, he continued, "So we'll try tossing the bull. Such techniques disconcert bulls sometimes." Standing up, he grabbed Laura, shoved her into the traveling compartment, slid the panel shut. "We're going to blow off forthwith."

Climbing up to the control seat, he stamped on the energizer stud. The tail rockets popped a few times, broke into a subdued roar. Juggling the controls to get the preparatory feel of them, he stepped up the boost until the entire vessel trembled and the rear venturis began to glow cherry-red. Slowly the ship commenced to edge its bulk forward and, as it did so, he fed it the take-off shot. A half-mile blast kicked backward and the probe ship plummeted into the sky.

Pulling it round in a wide and shallow sweep, he thundered over the borderline of vegetation, the fields of crystals and the hills beyond. In a flash he was plunging through the valley, braking rockets blazing from the nose. This was tricky. He had to co-ordinate forward shoot, backward thrust and downward surge, but like most of his kind he took pride in the stunts performable with these neat little vessels. An awe-inspired audience was all he lacked to make the exhibition perfect. The vessel landed fairly and squarely on the milk-white roof of the alien edifice, slid halfway to the cliff, then stopped.

"Boy," he breathed, "am I good!" He remained in his seat, stared around through the dome, and felt that he ought to add, "And too young to die." Occasionally eyeing the chronometer, he waited a while. The boat must have handed that roof sufficient to wake the dead. If anyone were in, they'd soon hotfoot out to see who was heaving hundred-ton bottles at their shingles. Nobody emerged. He gave them half an hour, his hawk-like face strained, alert. Then he gave it up, said, "Ah, well," and got out of the seat.

He freed Laura. She came out with ruffled dignity, like a dowager who's paraded into the wrong room. Females were always curious critters, in his logic, and he ignored her attitude, got his gun, unlocked the doors, jumped down onto the roof. Laura followed reluctantly, came to his shoulder as if thereby conferring a great favor.

Walking past the tail to the edge of the roof, he looked down. The sheerness of the five-hundred-foot drop took him aback. Immediately below his feet, the entrance soared four hundred feet up from the ground and he was standing on the hundred-foot lintel surmounting it. The only way down was to walk to the side of the roof and reach the earthy slope in which the building was embedded, seeking a path down that.

He covered a quarter of a mile of roof to get to the slope, his eyes examining the roof's surface as he went, and failing to find one crack or joint in the uniformly smooth surface. Huge as it was, the erection appeared to have been moulded all in one piece—a fact which did nothing to lessen inward misgivings. Whoever did this mighty job weren't Zulus!

From the ground level the entrance loomed bigger than ever. If there had been a similar gap the other side of the building, and a clear way through, he could have taken the ship in at one end and out at the other as easily as threading a needle.

Absence of doors didn't seem peculiar. It was difficult to imagine any sort of door huge enough to fill this opening yet sufficiently balanced to enable anyone—or anything—to pull open or shut. With a final, cautious look around which revealed nothing moving in the valley, he stepped boldly through the entrance, blinked his eyes, found inferior darkness slowly fading as visual retention lapsed and gave up remembrance of the golden glow outside.

There was a glow inside, a different one, paler, ghastlier, greenish. It exuded from the floor, the walls, the ceiling, and the total area of radiation was enough to light the place clearly, with no shadows. He sniffed as his vision adjusted itself. There was a strong smell of ozone mixed with other, unidentifiable odors.

To his right and left, rising hundreds of feet, stood great tiers of transparent cases. He went to the ones on his right and examined them. They were cubes, about a yard each way, made of something like transpex. Each contained three inches of loam from which spouted a crystal. No two crystals were alike; some small and branchy, others large and indescribably complicated.

Dumb with thought, he went around to the back of the monster tier, found another ten yards behind it. And another behind that. And another and another. All with crystals. The number and variety of them made his head whirl. He could study only the two bottom rows of each rack, but row on row stepped themselves far above his head to within short distance of the roof. Their total number was beyond estimation.

It was the same on the left. Crystals by the thousands. Looking more closely at one especially fine example, he noticed that the front plate of its case bore a small, inobtrusive pattern of dots etched upon the outer surface. Investigation revealed that all cases were similarly marked, differing only in the number and arrangement of the dots. Undoubtedly, some sort of cosmic code used for classification purposes.

"The Oron Museum of Natural History," he guessed, in a whisper.

"You're a liar," squawked Laura, violently. "I tell you it's a hoodoo—" She stopped, dumfounded, as her own voice roared through the building in deep, organ-like tones. "A hoodoo—a hoodo—"

"Holy smoke, will you keep quiet!" hissed Steve. He tried to keep watch on the exit and the interior simultaneously. But the voice rumbled away in the distance without bringing anyone to dispute their invasion.

Turning, he paced hurriedly past the first blocks of tiers to the next batteries of exhibits. Jellyblobs in this lot. Small ones, no bigger than his wristwatch, numberable in thousands. None appeared to be alive, he noted.

Sections three, four and five took him a mile into the building as nearly as he could estimate. He passed mosses, lichens and shrubs, all dead but wondrously preserved. By this time he was ready to guess at section six—plants. He was wrong. The sixth layout displayed bugs, including moths, butterflies, and strange, unfamiliar objects resembling chitinous humming birds. There was no sample of *Scarabaeus anderii* unless it was several hundred feet up. Or unless there was an empty box ready for it—when its day was done.

Who made the boxes? Had it prepared one for him? One for Laura? He visualized himself, petrified forever, squatting in the seventieth case of the twenty-fifth row of the tenth tier in section something-or-other, his front panel duly tagged with its appropriate dots. It was a lousy picture. It made his forehead wrinkle to think of it.

Looking for he knew not what, he plunged steadily on, advancing deeper and deeper into the heart of the building. Not a soul, not a sound, not a footprint. Only that all-pervading smell and the unvarying glow. He had a feeling that the place was visited frequently but never occupied for any worthwhile period of time. Without bothering to stop and look, he passed an enormous case containing a creature faintly resembling a bison-headed rhinoceros, then other, still larger cases holding equally larger exhibits—all carefully dot-marked.

Finally, he rounded a box so tremendous that it sprawled across the full width of the hall. It contained the grand-pappy of all trees and the great-grand-pappy of all serpents. Behind, for a change, reared five-hundred-feet-high racks of metal cupboards, each cupboard with a stud set in its polished door, each ornamented with more groups of mysteriously arranged dots.

Greatly daring, he pressed the stud on the nearest cupboard and its door swung open with a juicy click. The result proved disappointing. The cupboard was filled with stacks of small, glassy sheets each smothered with dots.

"Super filing-system," he grunted, closing the door. "Old Prof Heggarty would give his right arm to be here."

"Heggarty," said Laura, in a faltering voice. "For Pete's sake!"

He looked at her sharply. She was ruffled and fidgety, showing signs of increasing agitation.

"What's the matter, Chicken?"

She peeked at him, returned her anxious gaze the way they had come, side-stepped to and fro on his shoulder. Her neck feathers started to rise. A nervous cluck came from her beak and she cowered close to his jacket.

"Darn!" he muttered. Spinning on one heel, he raced past successive filing blocks, got into the ten-yards space between the end block and the wall. His gun was out and he kept watch on the front of the blocks while his free hand tried to soothe Laura. She snuggled up close, rubbing her head into his neck and trying to hide under the angle of his jaw.

"Quiet, Honey," he whispered. "Just you keep quiet and stay with Steve, and we'll be all right."

She kept quiet, though she'd begun to tremble. His heart speeded up in sympathy though he could see nothing, hear nothing to warrant it.

Then, while he watched and waited, and still in absolute silence, the interior brightness waxed, became less green, more golden. And suddenly he knew what it was that was coming. He *knew* what it was!

He sank on one knee to make himself as small and inconspicuous as possible. Now his heart was palpitating wildly and no coldness in his mind could freeze it down to slower, more normal beat. The silence, the awful silence of its approach was the unbearable feature. The crushing thud of a weighty foot or hoof would have been better. Colossi have no right to steal along like ghosts.

And the golden glow built up, drowning out the green radiance from floor to roof, setting the multitude of case-surfaces afire with its brilliance. It grew as strong as the golden sky, and stronger. It became all-pervading, unendurable, leaving no darkness in which to hide, no sanctuary for little things.

It flamed like the rising sun or like something drawn from the heart of a sun, and the glory of its radiance sent the cowering watcher's mind awhirl. He struggled fiercely to control his brain, to discipline it, to bind it to his fading will—and failed.

With drawn face beaded by sweat, Steve caught the merest fragmentary glimpse of the column's edge appearing from between the stacks of the center aisle. He saw a blinding strip of burnished gold in which glittered a pure white star, then a

violent effervescence seemed to occur within his brain and he
fell forward into a cloud of tiny bubbles.

Down, down he sank through myriad bubbles and swirls
and sprays of iridescent froth and foam which shone and
changed and shone anew with every conceivable color. And
all the time his mind strove frantically to battle upward and
drag his soul to the surface.

Deep into the nethermost reaches he went while still the
bubbles whirled around in their thousands and their colors
were of numberless hues. Then his progress slowed. Gradually the froth and the foam ceased to rotate upward, stopped
its circling, began to swirl in the reverse direction and sink.
He was rising! He rose for a lifetime, floating weightlessly, in
a dreamlike trance.

The last of the bubbles drifted eerily away, leaving him in
a brief hiatus of nonexistence—then he found himself
sprawled full length on the floor with a dazed Laura clinging
to his arm. He blinked his eyes, slowly, several times. They
were strained and sore. His heart was still palpitating and his
legs felt weak. There was a strange sensation in his stomach
as if memory had sickened him with a shock from long, long
ago.

He didn't get up from the floor right away; his body was
too shaken and his mind too muddled for that. While his wits
came back and his composure returned, he lay and noted all
the invading goldness had gone and that again the interior il-
lumination was a dull, shadowless green. Then his eyes found
his watch and sat up, startled. Two hours had flown.

That fact brought him shakily to his feet. Peering around
the end of the bank of filing cabinets, he saw that nothing
had changed. Instinct told him that the golden visitor had
gone and that once more he had this place to himself. Had it
become aware of his presence? Had it made him lose consciousness or, if not, why had he lost it? Had it done anything about the ship on the roof?

Picking up his futile gun, he spun it by its stud guard and
looked at it with contempt. Then he holstered it, helped
Laura on to his shoulder where she perched groggily, went
around the back of the racks and still deeper into the building.

"I reckon we're O.K., Honey," he told her. "I think we're
too small to be noticed. We're like mice. Who bothers to trap

mice when he's got bigger and more important things in mind?" He pulled a face, not liking the mouse comparison. It wasn't flattering either to him or his kind. But it was the best he could think of at the moment. "So, like little mice, let's look for the cheese. I'm not giving up just because a big hunk of something has sneaked past and put a scare into us. We don't scare off, do we, Sweetness?"

"No," said Laura unenthusiastically. Her voice was still subdued and her eyes perked apprehensively this way and that. "No scare. I won't sail, I tell you. Blow my sternpipes! Laura loves nuts!"

"Don't you call me a nut!"

"Nuts! Stick to farming—it gets you more eggs. McGillicuddy, the great—"

"Hey!" he warned.

She shut up abruptly. He put the pace on, refusing to admit that his system felt slightly jittery with nervous strain or that anything had got him bothered. But he knew that he'd no desire to be near the sparkling giant again. Once was enough, more than enough. It wasn't that he feared it, but something else, something he was quite unable to define.

Passing the last bank of cabinets, he found himself facing a machine. It was complicated and bizarre—and it was making a crystalline growth. Near it, another and different machine was manufacturing a small, horned lizard. There could be no doubt at all about the process of fabrication because both objects were half-made and both progressed slightly even as he watched. In a couple of hours' time, perhaps less, they'd be finished, and all they'd need would be . . . would be—

The hairs stiffened on the back of his neck and he commenced to run. Endless machines, all different, all making different things, plants, bugs, birds and fungoids. It was done by electroponics, atom fed to atom like brick after brick to build a house. It wasn't synthesis because that's only assembly, and this was assembly plus growth in response to unknown laws. In each of these machines, he knew, was some key or code or cipher, some weird master-control of unimaginable complexity, determining the patterns each was building—and the patterns were infinitely variable.

Here and there a piece of apparatus stood silent, inactive, their tasks complete. Here and there other monstrous layouts were in pieces, either under repair or readied for modification. He stopped by one which had finished its job. It had fashioned a delicately shaded moth which perched motionless like a jeweled statue within its fabrication jar. The creature was perfect as far as he could tell, and all it was waiting for was . . . was—

Beads of moisture popped out on his forehead. All that moth needed was the breath of life!

He forced a multitude of notions to get out of his mind; it was the only way to retain a hold on himself. Divert your attention—take it off this and place it on that! Firmly, he fastened his attention on one tremendous, partly disassembled machine lying nearby. Its guts were exposed, revealing great field-coils of dull grey wire. Bits of similar wire lay scattered around on the floor.

Picking up a short piece, he found it surprisingly heavy. He took off his wristwatch, opened its back, brought the wire near to its works. The Venusian jargoon bearing fluoresced immediately. V-jargoons invariably glowed in the presence of near radiation. This unknown metal was a possible fuel. His heart gave a jump at the thought of it.

Should he drag out a huge coil and lug it up to the ship? It was very heavy, and he'd need a considerable length of the stuff—if it was usable as fuel. Supposing the disappearance of the coil caused mousetraps to be set before he returned to search anew?

It pays to stop and think whenever you've got time to stop and think; that was a fundamental of Probe Service philosophy. Pocketing a sample of the wire, he sought around other disassembled machines for more. The search took him still deeper into the building and he fought harder to keep his attention concentrated solely on the task. It wasn't easy. There was that dog, for instance, standing there, statue-like, waiting, waiting. If only it had been anything but indubitably and recognizably an Earth-type dog. It was impossible to avoid seeing it. It would be equally impossible to avoid seeing other, even more familiar forms—if they were there.

He'd gained seven samples of different radioactive wires when he gave up the search. A cockatoo ended his peregrinations. The bird stood steadfastly in its jar, its blue plumage smooth and bright, its crimson crest raised, its bright eye fixed in what was not death, but not yet life. Laura shrieked at it hysterically and the immense hall shrieked back at her with long-drawn roars and rumbles that reverberated into dim

distances. Laura's reaction was too much: he wanted no
cause for similar reaction of his own.

He sped through the building at top pace, passing the filing
cabinets and the mighty array of exhibition cases unheed-
ingly. Up the loamy side-slopes he climbed almost as rapidly
as he'd gone down, and he was breathing heavily by the time
he got into the ship.

His first action was to check the ship for evidence of interference. There wasn't any. Next, he checked the instruments.
The electroscope's leaves were collapsed. Charging them, he
watched them flip open and flop together again. The counter
showed radiation aplenty. The hen clucked energetically.
He'd blundered somewhat—he should have checked up when
first he landed on the roof. However, no matter. What lay
beneath the roof was now known; the instruments would
have advised him earlier but not as informatively.

Laura had her feed while he accompanied her with a swift
meal. After that, he dug out his samples of wire. No two
were the same gauge and one obviously was far too thick to
enter the feed holes of the Kingston-Kanes. It took him half
an hour to file it down to a suitable diameter. The original
piece of dull grey wire took the first test. Feeding it in, he set
the control to minimum warming-up intensity, stepped on the
energizer. Nothing happened.

He scowled to himself. Someday they'd have jobs better
than the sturdy but finicky Kingston-Kanes, jobs that'd eat
anything eatable. Density and radioactivity weren't enough
for these motors; the stuff fed to them had to be right.

Going back to the Kingston-Kane, he pulled out the wire,
found its end fused into shapelessnes. Definitely a failure. In-
serting the second sample, another grey wire not so dull as
the first, he returned to the controls, rammed the energizer.
The tail rockets promptly blasted with a low, moaning note
and the thrust dial showed sixty percent normal surge.

Some people would have got mad at that point. Steve didn't.
His lean, hawklike features quirked, he felt in his pocket
for the third sample, tried that. No soap. The fourth likewise
was a flop. The fifth produced a peculiar and rhythmic series
of blasts which shook the vessel from end to end and caused
the thrust-dial needle to waggle between one hundred per
cent and zero. He visualized the Probe patrols popping
through space like outboard motors while he extracted the
stuff and fed the sixth sample. The sixth roared joyously at

one hundred and seventy percent. The seventh sample was another flop.

He discarded all but what was left of the sixth wire. The stuff was about twelve-gauge and near enough for his purpose. It resembled deep-coloured copper but was not as soft as copper nor as heavy. Hard, springy and light, like telephone wire. If there were at least a thousand yards of it below, and if he could manage to drag it up to the ship, and if the golden thing didn't come along and ball up the works, he might be able to blow free. Then he'd get some place civilized—if he could find it. The future was based on an appalling selection of "ifs."

The easiest and most obvious way to salvage the needed treasure was to blow a hole in the roof, lower a cable through it, and wind up the wire with the aid of the ship's tiny winch. Problem: how to blow a hole without suitable explosives. Answer: drill the roof, insert unshelled pistol ammunition, say a prayer and pop the stuff off electrically. He tried it, using a hand drill. The bit promptly curled up as if gnawing on a diamond. He drew his gun, bounced a shell off the roof; the missile exploded with a sharp, hard crack and fragments of shell casing whined shrilly into the sky. Where it had struck, the roof bore a blast smudge and a couple of fine scratches.

There was nothing for it but to go down and heave on his shoulders as much loot as he could carry. And do it right away. Darkness would fall before long, and he didn't want to encounter that golden thing in the dark. It was fateful enough in broad light of day, or in the queer, green glow of the building's interior, but to have it stealing softly behind him as he struggled through the night-time with his plunder was something of which he didn't care to think.

Locking the ship and leaving Laura inside, he returned to the building, made his way past the mile of cases and cabinets to the machine section at the back. He stopped to study nothing on his way. He didn't wish to study anything. The wire was the thing, only the wire. Besides, mundane thoughts of mundane wire didn't twist one's mind around until one found it hard to concentrate.

Nevertheless, his mind was afire as he searched. Half of it was prickly with alertness, apprehensive of the golden column's sudden return; the other half burned with excitement at the possibility of release. Outwardly, his manner showed nothing of this; it was calm, assured, methodical.

Within ten minutes he'd found a great coil of the coppery metal, a huge ovoid, intricately wound, lying beside a disassembled machine. He tried to move it, could not shift it an inch. The thing was far too big, too heavy for one to handle. To get it on to the roof he'd have to cut it up and make four trips of it—and some of its inner windings were fused together. So near, so far! Freedom depended upon his ability to move a lump of metal a thousand feet vertically. He muttered some of Laura's words to himself.

Although the wire cutters were ready in his hand, he paused to think, decided to look farther before tackling this job. It was a wise decision which brought its reward, for at a point a mere hundred yards away he came across another, differently shaped coil, wheel-shaped, in good condition, easy to unreel. This again was too heavy to carry, but with a tremendous effort which made his muscles crack he got it up on its rim and proceeded to roll it along like a monster tire.

Several times he had to stop and let the coil lean against the nearest case while he rested a moment. The last such case trembled under the impact of the weighty coil and its shining, spidery occupant stirred in momentary simulation of life. His dislike of the spider shot up with its motion; he made his rest brief, bowled the coil onward.

Violet streaks again were creeping from the horizon when he rolled his loot out of the mighty exit and reached the bottom of the bank. Here, he stopped, clipped the wire with his cutters, took the free end, climbed the bank with it. The wire uncoiled without hindrance until he reached the ship, where he attached it to the winch, wound the lot in, rewound it on the feed spool.

Night fell in one ominous swoop. His hands were trembling slightly but his hawklike face was firm, phlegmatic as he carefully threaded the wire's end through the automatic injector and into the feed hole of the Kingston-Kanes. That done, he slid open Laura's door, gave her some of the fruit they'd picked off the Oron tree. She accepted it morbidly, her manner still subdued, and not inclined for speech.

"Stay inside, Honey," he soothed. "We're getting out of this and going home."

Shutting her in, he climbed into the control seat, switched

on the nose beam, saw it pierce the darkness and light up the facing cliff. Then he stamped on the energizer, warmed the tubes. Their bellow was violent and comforting. At seventy percent better thrust he'd have to be a lot more careful in all his adjustments: it wouldn't do to melt his own tail off when success was within his grasp. All the same, he felt strangely impatient, as if every minute counted, aye, every second!

But he contained himself, got the venturis heated, gave a discreet puff on his starboard steering flare, watched the cliff glide sidewise past as the ship slewed around on its belly. Another puff, then another, and he had the vessel nose-on to the front edge of the roof. There seemed to be a faint aura in the gloom ahead and he switched off his nose beam to study it better.

It was a faint yellow haze shining over the rim of the opposite slope. His back hairs quivered as he saw it. The haze strengthened, rose higher. His eyes strained into the outer pall as he watched it fascinatedly, and his hands were frozen on the controls. There was dampness on his back. Behind him, in her travelling compartment, Laura was completely silent, not even shuffling uneasily as was her wont. He wondered if she was cowering.

With a mighty effort of will which strained him as never before, he shifted his control a couple of notches, lengthened the tail blast. Trembling in its entire fabric, the ship edged forward. Summoning all he'd got, Steve forced his reluctant hands to administer the take-off boost. With a tearing crash that thundered back from the cliffs, the little vessel leaped skyward on an arc of fire. Peering through the transpex, Steve caught a fragmentary and foreshortened glimpse of the great golden column advancing majestically over the crest; the next instant it had dropped far behind his tail and his bow was arrowing for the stars.

An immense relief flooded through his soul though he knew not what there had been to fear. But the relief was there and so great was it that he worried not at all about where he was bound or for how long. Somehow, he felt certain that if he swept in a wide, shallow curve he'd pick up a Probe beat-note sooner or later. Once he got a beat-note, from any source at all, it would lead him out of the celestial maze.

Luck remained with him, and his optimistic hunch proved correct, for while still among completely strange constellations he caught the faint throb of Hydra III on his twenty-seventh day of sweep. That throb was his cosmic lighthouse beckoning him home.

He let go a wild shriek of "Yippee!" thinking that only Laura heard him—but he was heard elsewhere.

Down on Oro, deep in the monster workshop, the golden giant paused blindly as if listening. Then it slid stealthily along the immense aisles, reached the filing system. A compartment opened, two glassy plates came out.

For a moment the plates contacted the Oron's strange, sparkling substance, became etched with an array of tiny dots. They were returned to the compartment, and the door closed. The golden glory with its imprisoned stars then glided quietly back to the machine section.

Something nearer to the gods had scribbled its notes. Nothing lower in the scale of life could have translated them or deduced their full purport.

In simplest sense, one plate may have been inscribed, "Biped, erect, pink, hono intelligens type P. 739, planted on Sol III, Condensation Arm BDB—moderately successful."

Similarly, the other plate may have recorded, "Flapwing, large, hook-beaked, vari-coloured, periquito macao type K.8, planted on Sol III, Condensation Arm BDB—moderately successful."

But already the sparkling hobbyist had forgotten his passing notes. He was breathing his essence upon a jeweled moth.

EXIT THE PROFESSOR

by "Lewis Padgett" (Henry Kuttner,
1915-1958 and C. L. Moore, 1911-   )

THRILLING WONDER STORIES
October

    *1947 was another banner year for the foremost
writing team of the 1940s. In addition to the
present selection they published at least another five
stories between them plus the powerful short novels*
Tomorrow and Tomorrow *and* Fury. *"Exit the Professor" is a wonderful example of the "whacky"
science fiction story, and was included in their first
collection* A Gnome There Was *(1950), one of
the earliest short story collections by genre writers.*

    *We must add our usual disclaimer at this
point—with the Kuttners one never knows who actually wrote what, and it is altogether possible that
Kuttner or Moore wrote this one alone. If we had
to bet on one, I would vote for Kuttner.*

    *(Marty categorizes this as a "whacky" science
fiction story. I would like to point out that this is by
no means the same as a "humorous" science fiction
story. A whacky story is usually humorous, but a
humorous story is not usually whacky. It's hard
enough being successfully humorous [as I very well*

*know] but it is even harder to be successfully
whacky, since to be whacky means to be cleverly il-
logical on the surface, but with [to attain the best
results] an underlying consistency. Henry Kuttner
could do it, as "Exit the Professor" shows, and so
could Fredric Brown—but few others could. Goodness knows I can't.*

*Incidentally, Hank described that "shotgun
gadget" that "makes holes in things" and prudently
didn't go into detail. But anyone can see, in hind-
sight, that what the Hogbens had put together was
a device that fired a laser beam. Lasers, of course,
had not been devised in 1947, and wouldn't be for
another thirteen years.—I.A.)*

We Hogbens are right exclusive. That Perfesser feller from
the city might have known that, but he come busting in without an invite, and I don't figger he had call to complain afterward. In Kaintuck the polite thing is to stick to your own hill
of beans and not come nosing around where you're not
wanted.

Time we ran off the Haley boys with that shotgun gadget
we rigged up—only we never could make out how it worked,
somehow—that time, it all started because Rafe Haley come
peeking and prying at the shed winder, trying to get a look at
Little Sam. Then Rafe went round saying Little Sam had
three haids or something.

Can't believe a word them Haley boys say. Three haids! It
ain't natcheral, is it? Anyhow, Little Sam's only got two
haids, and never had no more since the day he was born.

So Maw and I rigged up that shotgun thing and peppered
the Haley boys good. Like I said, we couldn't figger out afterward how it worked. We'd tacked on some dry cells and a lot
of coils and wires and stuff and it punched holes in Rafe as
neat as anything.

Coroner's verdict was that the Haley boys died real sudden, and Sheriff Abernathy come up and had a drink of corn
with us and said for two cents he'd whale the tar outa me. I
didn't pay no mind. Only some dam-yankee reporter musta

got wind of it, because a while later a big, fat, serious-looking man come around and begun to ask questions.

Uncle Les was sitting on the porch, with his hat over his face. "You better get the heck back to your circus, mister," he just said. "We had offers from old Barnum hisself and turned 'em down. Ain't that right, Saunk?"

"Sure is," I said. "I never trusted Phineas. Called Little Sam a freak, he did."

The big solemn-looking man, whose name was Perfesser Thomas Galbraith, looked at me. "How old are you, son?" he said.

"I ain't your son," I said. "And I don't know, nohow."

"You don't look over eighteen," he said, "big as you are. You couldn't have known Barnum."

"Sure I did. Don't go giving me the lie. I'll wham you."

"I'm not connected with any circus," Galbraith said. "I'm a biogeneticist."

We sure laughed at that. He got kinda mad and wanted to know what the joke was.

"There ain't no such word," Maw said. And at that point Little Sam started yelling, and Galbraith turned white as a goose wing and shivered all over. He sort of fell down. When we picked him up, he wanted to know what had happened.

"That was Little Sam," I said. "Maw's gone in to comfort him. He's stopped now."

"That was a subsonic," the Perfesser snapped. "What is Little Sam—a short-wave transmitter?"

"Little Sam's the baby," I said, short-like. "Don't go calling him outa his name, either. Now, s'pose you tell us what you want."

He pulled out a notebook and started looking through it.

"I'm a—a scientist," he said. "Our foundation is studying eugenics, and we've got some reports about you. They sound unbelievable. One of our men has a theory that natural mutations can remain undetected in undeveloped cultural regions, and—" He slowed down and stared at Uncle Les. "Can you really fly?" he asked.

Well, we don't like to talk about that. The preacher gave us a good dressing-down once. Uncle Les had got likkered up and went sailing over the ridges, scaring a couple of bear hunters outa their senses. And it ain't in the Good Book that men should fly, neither. Uncle Les generally does it only on the sly, when nobody's watching.

So anyhow Uncle Les pulled his hat down farther on his face and growled.

"That's plumb silly. Ain't no way a man can fly. These here modern contraptions I hear tell about—'tween ourselves, they don't really fly at all. Just a lot of crazy talk, that's all."

Galbraith blinked and studied his notebook again.

"But I've got hearsay evidence of a great many unusual things connected with your family. Flying is only one of them. I know it's theoretically impossible—and I'm not talking about planes—but—"

"Oh, shet your trap."

"The medieval witches' salve used aconite to give an illusion of flight—entirely subjective, of course."

"Will you stop pestering me?" Uncle Les said, getting mad, on account of he felt embarrassed, I guess. Then he jumped up, threw his hat down on the porch and flew away. After a minute he swooped down for his hat and made a face at the Perfesser. He flew off down the gulch and we didn't see him fer a while.

I got mad, too.

"You got no call to bother us," I said. "Next thing Uncle Les will do like Paw, and that'll be an awful nuisance. We ain't seen hide nor hair of Paw since that other city feller was around. He was a census taker, I think."

Galbraith didn't say anything. He was looking kinda funny. I gave him a drink and he asked about Paw.

"Oh, he's around," I said. "Only you don't see him no more. He likes it better that way, he says."

"Yes," Galbraith said, taking another drink. "Oh, God. How old did you say you were?"

"Didn't say nothing about it."

"Well, what's the earliest thing you can remember?"

"Ain't no use remembering things. Clutters up your haid too much."

"It's fantastic," Galbraith said. "I hadn't expected to send a report like that back to the foundation."

"We don't want nobody prying around," I said. "Go way and leave us alone."

"But, good Lord!" He looked over the porch rail and got interested in the shotgun gadget. "What's that?"

"A thing," I said.

"What does it do?"

"Things," I said.

"Oh. May I look at it?"

"Sure," I said. "I'll give you the dingus if you'll go away."

He went over and looked at it. Paw got up from where he'd been sitting beside me, told me to get rid of the dam-yankee and went into the house. The Perfesser came back. "Extraordinary!" he said. "I've had training in electronics, and it seems to me you've got something very odd there. What's the principle?"

"The what?" I said. "It makes holes in things."

"It can't fire shells. You've got a couple of lenses where the breech should—how did you say it worked?"

"I dunno."

"Did you make it?"

"Me and Maw."

He asked a lot more questions.

"I dunno," I said. "Trouble with a shotgun is you gotta keep loading it. We sorta thought if we hooked on a few things it wouldn't need loading no more. It don't, neither."

"Were you serious about giving it to me?"

"If you stop bothering us."

"Listen," he said, "it's miraculous that you Hogbens have stayed out of sight so long."

"We got our ways."

"The mutation theory must be right. You must be studied. This is one of the most important discoveries since—" He kept on talking like that. He didn't make much sense.

Finally I decided there was only two ways to handle things, and after what Sheriff Abernathy had said, I didn't feel right about killing nobody till the Sheriff had got over his fit of temper. I don't want to cause no ruckus.

"S'pose I go to New York with you, like you want," I said. "Will you leave the family alone?"

He halfway promised, though he didn't want to. But he knuckled under and crossed his heart, on account of I said I'd wake up Little Sam if he didn't. He sure wanted to see Little Sam, but I told him that was no good. Little Sam couldn't go to New York, anyhow. He's got to stay in his tank or he gets awful sick.

Anyway, I satisfied the Perfesser pretty well and he went off, after I'd promised to meet him in town next morning. I felt sick, though, I can tell you. I ain't been away from the folks overnight since that ruckus in the old country, when we had to make tracks fast.

Went to Holland, as I remember. Maw always had a soft spot fer the man that helped us get outa London. Named Little Sam after him. I fergit what his name was. Gwynn or Stuart or Pepys—I get mixed up when I think back beyond the War between the States.

That night we chewed the rag. Paw being invisible, Maw kept thinking he was getting more'n his share of the corn, but pretty soon she mellowed and let him have a demijohn. Everybody told me to mind my p's and q's.

"This here Perfesser's awful smart," Maw said. "All perfessers are. Don't go bothering him any. You be a good boy or you'll ketch heck from me."

"I'll be good, Maw," I said. Paw whaled me alongside the haid, which wasn't fair, on account of I couldn't see him.

"That's so you won't fergit," he said.

"We're plain folks," Uncle Les was growling. "No good never come of trying to get above yourself."

"Honest, I ain't trying to do that," I said. "I only figgered—"

"You stay outa trouble!" Maw said, and just then we heard Grandpaw moving in the attic. Sometimes Grandpaw don't stir for a month at a time, but tonight he seemed right frisky.

So, natcherally, we went upstairs to see what he wanted.

He was talking about the Perfesser.

"A stranger, eh?" he said. "Out upon the stinking knave. A set of rare fools I've gathered about me for my dotage! Only Saunk shows any shrewdness, and, dang my eyes, he's the worst fool of all."

I just shuffled and muttered something, on account of I never like to look at Grandpaw direct. But he wasn't paying me no mind. He raced on.

"So you'd go to this New York? 'Sblood, and hast thou forgot the way we shunned London and Amsterdam—and Nieuw Amsterdam—for fear of questioning? Wouldst thou be put in a freak show? Nor is that the worst danger."

Grandpaw's the oldest one of us and he gets kinda mixed up in his language sometimes. I guess the lingo you learned when you're young sorta sticks with you. One thing, he can cuss better than anybody I've ever heard.

"Shucks," I said. "I was only trying to help."

"Thou puling brat," Grandpaw said. " 'Tis thy fault and thy dam's. For building that device, I mean, that slew the

Haley tribe. Hadst thou not, this scientist would never have come here."

"He's a perfesser," I said. "Name of Thomas Galbraith."

"I know. I read his thoughts through Little Sam's mind. A dangerous man. I never knew a sage who wasn't. Except perhaps Roger Bacon, and I had to bribe him to—but Roger was an exceptional man. Hearken:

"None of you may go to this New York. The moment we leave this haven, the moment we are investigated, we are lost. The pack would tear and rend us. Nor could all thy addle-pated flights skyward save thee, Lester—dost thou hear?"

"But what are we to do?" Maw said.

"Aw, heck," Paw said. "I'll just fix this Perfesser. I'll drop him down the cistern."

"An' spoil the water?" Maw screeched. "You try it!"

"What foul brood is this that has sprung from my seed?" Grandpaw said, real mad. "Have ye not promised the Sheriff that there will be no more killings—for a while, at least? Is the word of a Hogben naught? Two things have we kept sacred through the centuries—our secret from the world, and the Hogben honor! Kill this man Galbraith and ye'll answer to me for it!"

We all turned white. Little Sam woke up again and started squealing. "But what'll we do?" Uncle Les said.

"Our secret must be kept," Grandpaw said. "Do what ye can, but no killing. I'll consider the problem."

He seemed to go to sleep then, though it was hard to tell.

The next day I met Galbraith in town, all right, but first I run into Sheriff Abernathy in the street and he gave me a vicious look.

"You stay outa trouble, Saunk," he said. "Mind what I tell you, now." It was right embarrassing.

Anyway, I saw Galbraith and told him Grandpaw wouldn't let me go to New York. He didn't look too happy, but he saw there was nothing that could be done about it.

His hotel room was full of scientific apparatus and kinda frightening. He had the shotgun gadget set up, but it didn't look like he'd changed it any. He started to argue.

"Ain't no use," I said. "We ain't leaving the hills. I spoke outa turn yesterday, that's all."

"Listen, Saunk," he said. "I've been inquiring around town about you Hogbens, but I haven't been able to find out much.

They're close-mouthed around here. Still, such evidence would be only supporting factors. I know our theories are right. You and your family are mutants and you've got to be studied!"

"We ain't mutants," I said. "Scientists are always calling us outa our names. Roger Bacon called us homunculi, only—"

"What?" Galbraith shouted. "Who did you say?"

"Uh—he's a share-cropper over in the next county," I said hasty-like, but I could see the Perfesser didn't swaller it. He started to walk around the room.

"It's no use," he said. "If you won't come to New York, I'll have the foundation send a commission here. You've got to be studied, for the glory of science and the advancement of mankind."

"Oh, golly," I said. "I know what that'd be like. Make a freak show outa us. It'd kill Little Sam. You gotta go away and leave us alone."

"Leave you alone? When you can create apparatus like this?" He pointed to the shotgun gadget. "How *does* that work?" he wanted to know, sudden-like.

"I told you, I dunno. We just rigged it up. Listen, Perfesser. There'd be trouble if people came and looked at us. Big trouble. Grandpaw says so."

Galbraith pulled at his nose.

"Well, maybe—suppose you answered a few questions for me, Saunk."

"No commission?"

"We'll see."

"No, sir. I won't—"

Galbraith took a deep breath.

"As long as you tell me what I want to know, I'll keep your whereabouts a secret."

"I thought this fundation thing of yours knows where you are."

"Ah—yes," Galbraith said. "Naturally they do. But they don't know about *you.*"

That gave me an idea. I coulda killed him easy, but if I had, I knew Grandpaw would of ruined me entire and, besides, there was the Sheriff to think of. So I said, "Shucks." and nodded.

My, the questions that man asked! It left me dizzy. And all the while he kept getting more and more excited.

"How old is your grandfather?"

"Gosh, I dunno."

"Homunculi—mm-m. You mentioned that he was a miner once?"

"No, that was Grandpaw's paw," I said. "Tin mines, they were, in England. Only Grandpaw says it was called Britain then. That was during a sorta magic plague they had then. The people had to get the doctors—droons? Droods?"

"Druids?"

"Uh-huh. The Druids was the doctors then, Grandpaw says. Anyhow, all the miners started dying round Cornwall, so they closed up the mines."

"What sort of plague was it?"

I told him what I remembered from Grandpaw's talk, and the Perfesser got very excited and said something about radioactive emanations, as nearly as I could figger out. It made oncommon bad sense.

"Artificial mutations caused by radioactivity!" he said, getting real pink around the jowls. "Your grandfather was born a mutant! The genes and chromosomes were rearranged into a new pattern. Why, you may all be supermen!"

"Nope," I said. "We're Hogbens. That's all."

"A dominant, obviously a dominant. All your family were—ah—peculiar?"

"Now, look!" I said.

"I mean, they could all fly?"

"I don't know how yet, myself. I guess we're kinda freakish. Grandpaw was smart. He allus taught us not to show off."

"Protective camouflage," Galbraith said. "Submerged in a rigid social culture, variations from the norm are more easily masked. In a modern, civilized culture, you'd stick out like a sore thumb. But here, in the backwoods, you're practically invisible."

"Only Paw," I said.

"Oh, Lord," he sighed. "Submerging these incredible natural powers of yours . . . Do you know the things you might have done?" And then all of a sudden he got even more excited, and I didn't much like the look in his eyes.

"Wonderful things," he repeated. "It's like stumbling on Aladdin's lamp."

"I wish you'd leave us alone," I said. "You and your commission!"

"Forget about the commission. I've decided to handle this

privately for a while. Provided you'll cooperate. Help me, I mean. Will you do that?"

"Nope," I said.

"Then I'll bring the commission down from New York," he said triumphantly.

I thought that over.

"Well," I said finally, "what do you want me to do?"

"I don't know yet," he said slowly. "My mind hasn't fully grasped the possibilities."

But he was getting ready to grab. I could tell. I know that look.

I was standing by the window looking out, and all of a sudden I got an idea. I figgered it wouldn't be smart to trust the Perfesser too much, anyhow. So I sort of ambled over to the shotgun gadget and make a few little changes on it.

I knew what I wanted to do, all right, but if Galbraith had asked me why I was twisting a wire here and bending a whozis there I couldn't of told him. I got no eddication. Only now I knew the gadget would do what I wanted it to do.

The Perfesser had been writing in his little notebook. He looked up and saw me.

"What are you doing?" he wanted to know.

"This don't look right to me," I said. "I think you monkeyed with them batteries. Try it now."

"In here?" he said, startled. "I don't want to pay a bill for damages. It must be tested under safety conditions."

"See the weathercock out there, on the roof?" I pointed it out to him. "Won't do no harm to aim at that. You can just stand here by the winder and try it out."

"It—it isn't dangerous?" He was aching to try the gadget, I could tell. I said it wouldn't kill nobody, and he took a long breath and went to the window and cuddled the stock of the gun against his cheek.

I stayed back aways. I didn't want the Sheriff to see me. I'd already spotted him, sitting on a bench outside the feed-and-grain store across the street.

It happened just like I thought. Galbraith pulled the trigger, aiming at the weathercock on the roof, and rings of light started coming out of the muzzle. There was a fearful noise. Galbraith fell flat on his back, and the commotion was something surprising. People began screaming all over town.

I kinda felt it might be handy if I went invisible for a while. So I did.

Galbraith was examining the shotgun gadget when Sheriff Abernathy busted in. The Sheriff's a hard case. He had his pistol out and handcuffs ready, and he was cussing the Perfesser immediate and rapid.

"I seen you!" he yelled. "You city fellers think you can get away with anything down here. Well, you can't!"

"Saunk!" Galbraith cried, looking around. But of course he couldn't see me.

Then there was an argument. Sheriff Abernathy had seen Galbraith fire the shotgun gadget and he's no fool. He drug Galbraith down on the street, and I came along, walking softly. People were running around like crazy. Most of them had their hands clapped to their faces.

The Perfesser kept wailing that he didn't understand.

"I seen you!" Abernathy said. "You aimed that dingus of yours out the window and the next thing everybody in town's got a toothache! Try and tell me you don't understand!"

The Sheriff's smart. He's known us Hogbens long enough so he ain't surprised when funny things happen sometimes. Also, he knew Galbraith was a scientist feller. So there was a ruckus and people heard what was going on and the next thing they was trying to lynch Galbraith.

But Abernathy got him away. I wandered around town for a while. The pastor was out looking at his church windows, which seemed to puzzle him. They was stained glass, and he couldn't figger out why they was hot. I coulda told him that. There's gold in stained-glass windows; they use it to get a certain kind of red.

Finally I went down to the jailhouse. I was still invisible. So I eavesdropped on what Galbraith was saying to the Sheriff.

"It was Saunk Hogben," the Perfesser kept saying. "I tell you, he fixed that projector!"

"I saw you," Abernathy said. "You done it. Ow!" He put up his hand to his jaw. "And you better stop it, fast! That crowd outside means business. Half the people in town have got toothaches."

I guess half the people in town had gold fillings in their teeth.

Then Galbraith said something that didn't surprise me too much. "I'm having a commission come down from New York; I meant to telephone the foundation tonight, they'll vouch for me."

So he was intending to cross us up, all along. I kinda felt that had been in his mind.

"You'll cure this toothache of mine—and everybody else's—or I'll open the doors and let in that lynch mob!" the Sheriff howled. Then he went away to put an icebag on his cheek.

I snuck back aways, got visible again and made a lot of noise coming along the passage, so Galbraith could hear me. I waited till he got through cussing me out. I just looked stupid.

"I guess I made a mistake," I said. "I can fix it, though."

"You've done enough fixing!" He stopped. "Wait a minute. What did you say? You can cure this—what *is* it?"

"I been looking at that shotgun gadget," I said. "I think I know what I did wrong. It's sorta turned in on gold now, and all the gold in town's shooting out rays or heat or something."

"Induced selective radioactivity," Galbraith muttered, which didn't seem to mean much. "Listen. That crowd outside—do they ever have lynchings in this town?"

"Not more'n once or twice a year," I said. "And we already had two this year, so we filled our quota. Wish I could get you up to our place, though. We could hide you easy."

"You'd better do something!" he said. "Or I'll get that commission down from New York. You wouldn't like that, would you?"

I never seen such a man fer telling lies and keeping a straight face.

"It's a cinch," I said. "I can rig up the gadget so it'll switch off the rays immediate. Only I don't want people to connect us Hogbens with what's going on. We like to live quiet. Look s'pose I go back to your hotel and change over the gadget, and then all you have to do is get all the people with toothaches together and pull the trigger."

"But—well, but—"

He was afraid of more trouble. I had to talk him into it. The crowd was yelling outside, so it wasn't too hard. Finally

I went away, but I came back, invisible-like, and listened when Galbraith talked to the Sheriff.

They fixed it all up. Everybody with toothaches was going to the Town Hall and set. Then Abernathy would bring the Perfesser over, with the shotgun gadget, and try it out.

"Will it stop the toothaches?" the Sheriff wanted to know. "For sure?"

"I'm—quite certain it will."

Abernathy had caught that hesitation.

"Then you better try it first. Just to make sure. I don't trust you."

It seemed like nobody was trusting nobody.

I hiked back to the hotel and made the switch-over in the shotgun gadget. And then I run into trouble. My invisibility was wearing thin. That's the worst part of being just a kid.

After I'm a few hunnerd years older I can stay invisible all the time if I want to. But I ain't right mastered it yet. Thing was, I needed help now because there was something I had to do, and I couldn't do it with people watching.

I went up on the roof and called Little Sam. After I'd tuned in on his haid, I had him put the call through to Paw and Uncle Les. After a while Uncle Les come flying down from the sky, riding mighty heavy on account of he was carrying Paw. Paw was cussing because a hawk had chased them.

"Nobody seen us, though," Uncle Les said. "I *think*."

"People got their own troubles in town today," I said. "I need some help. That Perfesser's gonna call down his commission and study us, no matter what he promises."

"Ain't much we can do, then," Paw said. "We cain't kill that feller. Grandpaw said not to."

So I told 'em my idea. Paw being invisible, he could do it easy. Then we made a little place in the roof so we could see through it, and looked down into Galbraith's room.

We was just in time. The Sheriff was standing there, with his pistol out, just waiting, and the Perfesser, pale around the chops, was pointing the shotgun gadget at Abernathy. It went along without a hitch. Galbraith pulled the trigger, a purple ring of light popped out, and that was all. Except that the Sheriff opened his mouth and gulped.

"You wasn't faking! My toothache's gone!"

Galbraith was sweating, but he put up a good front. "Sure it works," he said. "Naturally. I told you—"

"C'mon down to the Town Hall. Everybody's waiting. You better cure us all, or it'll be just too bad for you."

They went out. Paw snuck down after them, and Uncle Les picked me up and flew on their trail, keeping low to the roofs, where we wouldn't be spotted. After a while we was fixed outside one of the Town Hall's windows, watching.

I ain't heard so much misery since the great plague of London. The hall was jam-full, and everybody had a toothache and was moaning and yelling. Abernathy come in with the Perfesser, who was carrying the shotgun gadget, and a scream went up.

Galbraith set the gadget on the stage, pointing down at the audience, while the Sheriff pulled out his pistol again and made a speech, telling everybody to shet up and they'd get rid of their toothaches.

I couldn't see Paw, natcherally, but I knew he was up on the platform. Something funny was happening to the shotgun gadget. Nobody noticed, except me, and I was watching for it. Paw—invisible, of course—was making a few changes. I'd told him how, but he knew what to do as well as I did. So pretty soon the shotgun was rigged the way we wanted it.

What happened after that was shocking. Galbraith aimed the gadget and pulled the trigger, and rings of light jumped out, yaller this time. I'd told Paw to fix the range so nobody outside the Town Hall would be bothered. But inside—

Well, it sure fixed them toothaches. Nobody's gold filling can ache if he ain't got a filling.

The gadget was fixed now so it worked on everything that wasn't growing. Paw had got the range just right. The seats was gone all of a sudden, and so was part of the chandelier. The audience, being bunched together, got it good. Pegleg Jaffe's glass eye was gone, too. Them that had false teeth lost 'em. Everybody sorta got a once-over-lightly haircut.

Also, the whole audience lost their clothes. Shoes ain't growing things, and no more are pants or shirts or dresses. In a trice everybody in the hall was naked as needles. But, shucks, they'd got rid of their toothaches, hadn't they?

We was back to home an hour later, all but Uncle Les, when the door busted open and in come Uncle Les, with the Perfesser staggering after him. Galbraith was a mess. He sank down and wheezed, looking back at the door in a worried way.

"Funny thing happened," Uncle Les said. "I was flying along outside town and there was the Perfesser running away from a big crowd of people, with sheets wrapped around 'em—some of 'em. So I picked him up. I brung him here, like he wanted." Uncle Les winked at me.

"Ooooh!" Galbraith said. "*Aaaah!* Are they coming?"

Maw went to the door.

"They's a lot of torches moving up the mountain," she said. "It looks right bad."

The Perfesser glared at me.

"You said you could hide me! Well, you'd better! This is your fault!"

"Shucks," I said.

"You'll hide me or else!" Galbraith squalled. "I—I'll bring that commission down."

"Look," I said, "if we hide you safe, will you promise to fergit all about the commission and leave us alone?"

The Perfesser promised. "Hold on a minute," I said, and went up to the attic to see Grandpaw.

He was awake.

"How about it, Grandpaw?" I asked.

He listened to Little Sam for a second.

"The knave is lying," he told me pretty soon. "He means to bring his commission of stinkards here anyway, recking naught of his promise."

"Should we hide him, then?"

"Aye," Grandpaw said. "The Hogbens have given their word—there must be no more killing. And to hide a fugitive from his pursuers would not be an ill deed, surely."

Maybe he winked. It's hard to tell with Grandpaw. So I went down the ladder. Galbraith was at the door, watching the torches come up the mountain.

He grabbed me.

"Saunk! If you don't hide me—"

"We'll hide you," I said. "C'mon."

So we took him down to the cellar . . .

When the mob got here, with Sheriff Abernathy in the lead, we played dumb. We let 'em search the house. Little Sam and Grandpaw turned invisible for a bit, so nobody noticed them. And naturally the crowd couldn't find hide nor hair of Galbraith. We'd hid him good, like we promised.

That was a few years ago. The Perfesser's thriving. He ain't studying us, though. Sometimes we take out the bottle we keep him in and study him.

Dang small bottle, too!

THUNDER AND ROSES

by Theodore Sturgeon (1918–   )

ASTOUNDING SCIENCE FICTION
November

Ted Sturgeon's second contribution to the best of 1947 is a powerful statement for sanity in a world gone insane. Written only a few months after Hiroshima, it stands as one of the great warning stories of all time, affirming that even at the worst of moments men and women still have the obligation to make choices.

Do you agree, Isaac?

(Absolutely, Marty. A whole generation has passed since 1947 and nuclear doom has not yet come, largely because people have made choices [notably in the Cuban missile crisis of 1962], and have chosen life. We must still do it today. Above all considerations of local short-term goals, we must make that overriding long-term choice of life.

But some points. Of the 14 stories in this volume, 11 were from Astounding, and 4 featured nuclear warfare and its consequences. That is, four of the stories we considered the best of the year including "Thunder and Roses." There were many more stories in the course of the year that were

*printed and that dealt with the nuclear nightmare,
and who knows how many stories that were written
and were never published. It was an overriding terror in the years that immediately followed Hiroshima; and it is only the callousness of habituation
that hasn't caused the terror to increase steadily—
for the danger has.—I.A.)*

When Pete Mawser learned about the show, he turned
away from the GHQ bulletin board, touched his long chin,
and determined to shave. This was odd, because the show
would be video, and he would see it in his barracks.

He had an hour and a half. It felt good to have a purpose
again—even shaving before eight o'clock. Eight o'clock
Tuesday, just the way it used to be. Everyone used to catch
that show on Tuesday. Everyone used to say, Wednesday
morning, "How about the way she sang 'The Breeze and I'
last night?" "Hey did you hear Starr last night?"

That was awhile ago, before all those people were dead,
before the country was dead. Starr Anthim, institution, like
Crosby, like Duse, like Jenny Lind, like the Statue of Liberty.

(Liberty had been one of the first to get it, her bronze
beauty volatilized, radioactive, and even now being carried
about in vagrant winds, spreading over the earth—)

Pete Mawser grunted and forced his thoughts away from
the drifting, poisonous fragments of a blasted Liberty. Hate
was first. Hate was ubiquitous, like the increasing blue glow
in the air at night, like the tension that hung over the base.

Gunfire crackled sporadically far to the right, swept nearer.
Pete stepped out of the street and made for a parked ten-
wheeler. There's a lot of cover in and around a ten-wheeler.

There was a Wac sitting on the short running-board.

At the corner a stocky figure backed into the intersection.
The man carried a tommy gun in his arms, and he was
swinging it to and fro with the gentle, wavering motion of a
weather vane. He staggered toward them, his gun muzzle
hunting. Someone fired from a building and the man swiveled
and blasted wildly at the sound.

"He's—blind," said Pete Mawser, and added, "He ought to be," looking at the tattered face.

A siren keened. An armored jeep slewed into the street. The full-throated roar of a brace of .50-caliber machine guns put a swift and shocking end to the incident.

"Poor crazy kid." Pete said softly. "That's the fourth I've seen today." He looked down at the Wac. She was smiling.

"Hey!"

"Hello, Sarge." She must have identified him before, because now she did not raise her eyes or her voice. "What happened?"

"You know what happened. Some kid got tired of having nothing to fight and nowhere to run to. What's the matter with you?"

"No," she said. "I don't mean that." At last she looked up at him. "I mean all of this. I can't seem to remember."

"You . . . well, gee, it's not easy to forget. We got hit. We got hit everywhere at once. All the big cities are gone. We got it from both sides. We got too much. The air is becoming radioactive. We'll all—" He checked himself. She didn't know. She'd forgotten. There was nowhere to escape to, and she'd escaped inside herself, right here. Why tell her about it? Why tell her that everyone was going to die? Why tell her that other, shameful thing: that we hadn't struck back?

But she wasn't listening. She was still looking at him. Her eyes were not quite straight. One held his but the other was slightly shifted and seemed to be looking at his temples. She was smiling again. When his voice trailed off she didn't prompt him. Slowly he moved away. She did not turn her head, but kept looking up at where he had been, smiling a little. He turned away, wanting to run, walking fast.

(How long can a guy hold out? When you're in the Army they try to make you be like everybody else. What do you do when everybody else is cracking up?)

He blanked out the mental picture of himself as the last one left sane. He'd followed that one through before. It always led to the conclusion that it would be better to be one of the first. He wasn't ready for that yet.

Then he blanked that out, too. Every time he said to himself that he wasn't ready for that yet, something within him asked, "Why not?" and he never seemed to have an answer ready.

(How long could a guy hold out?)

He climbed the steps of the QM Central and went inside. There was nobody at the reception switchboard. It didn't matter. Messages were carried by guys in jeeps, or on motorcycles. The Base Command was not insisting that anybody stick to a sitting job these days. Ten desk men would crack up for every one on a jeep, or on the soul-sweat squads. Pete made up his mind to put in a little stretch on a squad tomorrow. Do him good. He just hoped that this time the adjutant wouldn't burst into tears in the middle of the parade ground. You could keep your mind on the manual of arms just fine until something like that happened.

He bumped into Sonny Weisefreund in the barracks corridor. The tech's round young face was as cheerful as ever. He was naked and glowing, and had a towel thrown over his shoulder.

"Hi, Sonny. Is there plenty of hot water?"

"Why not?" grinned Sonny. Pete grinned back, cursing inwardly. Could anybody say anything about anything at all without one of these reminders? Sure there was hot water. The QM barracks had hot water for three hundred men. There were three dozen left. Men dead, men gone to the hills, men locked up so they wouldn't—

"Starr Anthim's doing a show tonight."

"Yeah. Tuesday night. Not funny, Pete. Don't you know there's a war—"

"No kidding," Pete said swiftly. "She's here—right here on the base."

Sonny's face was joyful. "Gee." He pulled the towel off his shoulder and tied it around his waist. "Starr Anthim, here! Where are they going to put on the show?"

"HQ, I imagine. Video only. You know about public gatherings." And a good thing, too, he thought. Put on an in-person show, and some torn-up GI would crack during one of her numbers. He himself would get plenty mad over a thing like that—mad enough to do something about it then and there. And there would probably be a hundred and fifty or more like him, going raving mad because someone had spoiled a Starr Anthim show. That would be a dandy little shambles for her to put in her memory book.

"How'd she happen to come here, Pete?"

"Drifted in on the last gasp of a busted-up Navy helicopter."

"Yeah, but why?"

"Search me. Get your head out of that gift horse's mouth."

He went into the washroom, smiling and glad that he still could. He undressed and put his neatly folded clothes down on a bench. There were a soap wrapper and an empty toothpaste tube lying near the wall. He went and picked them up and put them in the catch-all. He took the mop which leaned against the partition and mopped the floor where Sonny had splashed after shaving. Got to keep things squared away. He might say something if it were anyone else but Sonny. But Sonny wasn't cracking up. Sonny always had been like that. Look there. Left his razor out again.

Pete started his shower, meticulously adjusting the valves until the pressure and temperature exactly suited him. He didn't do anything slapdash these days. There was so much to feel, and taste, and see now. The impact of water on his skin, the smell of soap, the consciousness of light and heat, the very pressure of standing on the soles of his feet—he wondered vaguely how the slow increase of radioactivity in the air, as the nitrogen transmuted to Carbon Fourteen, would affect him if he kept carefully healthy in every way. What happens first? Do you go blind? Headaches, maybe? Perhaps you lose your appetite. Or maybe you get tired all the time.

Why not go look it up?

On the other hand, why bother? Only a very small percentage of the men would die of radioactive poisoning. There were too many other things that killed more quickly, which was probably just as well. That razor, for example. It lay gleaming in a sunbeam, curved and clean in the yellow light. Sonny's father and grandfather had used it, or so he said, and it was his pride and joy.

Pete turned his back on it and soaped under his arms, concentrating on the tiny kisses of bursting bubbles. In the midst of a recurrence of disgust at himself for thinking so often of death, a staggering truth struck him. He did not think of such things because he was morbid, after all! It was the very familiarity of things that brought death-thoughts. It was either "I shall never do this again" or "This is one of the last times I shall do this." You might devote yourself completely to doing things in different ways, he thought madly. You might crawl across the floor this time, and next time walk across on your hands. You might skip dinner tonight, and have a snack at two in the morning instead, and eat grass for breakfast.

But you had to breathe. Your heart had to beat. You'd sweat and you'd shiver, the same as always. You couldn't get away from that. When those things happened, they would remind you. Your heart wouldn't beat out its *wunklunk, wunklunk* any more. It would go *one-less, one-less,* until it yelled and yammered in your ears and you had to make it stop.

Terrific polish on that razor.

And your breath would go on, same as before. You could sidle through this door, back through the next one and the one after, and figure out a totally new way to go through the one after that, but your breath would keep on sliding in and out of your nostrils like a razor going through whiskers, making a sound like a razor being stropped.

Sonny came in. Pete soaped his hair. Sonny picked up the razor and stood looking at it. Pete watched him, soap ran into his eyes, he swore, and Sonny jumped.

"What are you looking at, Sonny? Didn't you ever see it, before?"

"Oh, sure. Sure. I was just—" He shut the razor, opened it, flashed light from its blade, shut it again. "I'm tired of using this. Pete, I'm going to get rid of it. Want it?"

Want it? In his foot locker, maybe. Under his pillow. "Thanks no, Sonny. Couldn't use it."

"I like safety razors," Sonny mumbled. "Electrics, even better. What are we going to do with it?"

"Throw it in the . . . no." Pete pictured the razor turning end over end in the air, half open, gleaming in the maw of the catch-all. "Throw it out the—" No. Curving out into the long grass. You might want it. You might crawl around in the moonlight looking for it. You might find it.

"I guess maybe I'll break it up."

"No," Pete said. "The pieces—" Sharp little pieces. Hollowground fragments. I'll think of something. Wait'll I get dressed."

He washed briskly, toweled, while Sonny stood looking at the razor. It was a blade now, and if you broke it, there would be shards and glittering splinters, still razor sharp. You could slap its edge into an emery wheel and grind it away, and somebody could find it, and put another edge on it because it was so obviously a razor, a fine steel razor, one that would slice so— "I know. The laboratory. We'll get rid of it." Pete said confidently.

He stepped into his clothes, and together they went to the laboratory wing. It was very quiet there. Their voices echoed.

"One of the ovens," said Pete, reaching for the razor.

"Bake ovens? You're crazy!"

Pete chuckled. "You don't know this place, do you? Like everything else on the base, there was a lot more went on here than most people knew about. They kept calling it the bake shop. Well, it *was* research headquarters for new high-nutrient flours. But there's lots else here. We tested utensils and designed beet peelers and all sorts of things like that. There's an electric furnace in here that—" He pushed open a door.

They crossed a long, quiet, cluttered room to the thermal equipment. "We can do everything here from annealing glass, through glazing ceramics, to finding the melting point of frying pans." He clicked a switch tentatively. A pilot light glowed. He swung open a small, heavy door and set the razor inside. "Kiss it good-bye. In twenty minutes it'll be a puddle."

"I want to see that," said Sonny. "Can I look around until it's cooked?"

"Why not?"

(Everybody around here always said "Why not?")

They walked through the laboratories. Beautifully equipped, they were, and too quiet. Once they passed a major who was bent over a complex electronic hook-up on one of the benches. He was watching a little amber light flicker, and he did not return their salute. They tiptoed past him, feeling awed in his absorption, envying it. They saw the models of the automatic kneaders, the vitaminizers, the remote-signal thermostats and timers and controls.

"What's in there?"

"I dunno. I'm over the edge of my territory. I don't think there's anybody left for this section. They were mostly mechanical and electronic theoreticians. The only thing I know about them is that if we ever needed anything in the way of tools, meters, or equipment, they had it or something better, and if we ever got real bright and figured out a startling new idea, they'd already built it and junked it a month ago. Hey!"

Sonny followed the pointing hand. "What?"

"That wall section. It's loose, or . . . well, what do you know?"

He pushed at the section of wall, which was very slightly out of line. There was a dark space beyond.

"What's in there?"

"Nothing, or some semiprivate hush-hush job. These guys used to get away with murder."

Sonny said, with an uncharacteristic flash of irony, "Isn't that the Army theoretician's business?"

Cautiously they peered in, then entered.

"Wh . . . *hey!* The door!"

It swung swiftly and quietly shut. The soft click of the latch was accompanied by a blaze of light.

The room was small and windowless. It contained machinery—a "trickle" charger, a bank of storage batteries, an electric-powered dynamo, two small self-starting gas-driven light plants and a Diesel complete with sealed compressed-air starting cylinders. In the corner was a relay rack with its panel-bolts spot-welded. Protruding from it was a red-top lever. Nothing was labeled.

They looked at the equipment wordlessly for a time and then Sonny said, "Somebody wanted to make awful sure he had power for something."

"Now, I wonder what—" Pete walked over to the relay rack. He looked at the level without touching it. It was wired up; behind the handle, on the wire, was a folded tag. He opened it cautiously. "To be used only on specific orders of the Commanding Officer."

"Give it a yank and see what happens."

Something clicked behind them. They whirled. "What was that?"

"Seemed to come from that rig by the door."

They approached it cautiously. There was a spring-loaded solenoid attached to a bar which was hinged to drop across the inside of the secret door, where it would fit into steel gudgeons on the panel.

It clicked again. "A Geiger," said Pete disgustedly.

"Now why," mused Sonny, "would they design a door to stay locked unless the general radioactivity went beyond a certain point? That's what it is. See the relays? And the overload switch there? And this?"

"It has a manual lock, too," Pete pointed out. The counter clicked again. "Let's get out of here. I got one of those things built into my head these days."

The door opened easily. They went out, closing it behind

them. The keyhole was cleverly concealed in the crack between two boards.

They were silent as they made their way back to the QM labs. The small thrill of violation was gone and, for Pete Mawser at least, the hate was back, that and the shame. A few short weeks before, this base had been a part of the finest country on earth. There was a lot of work here that was secret, and a lot that was such purely progressive and unapplied research that it would be in the way anywhere else but in this quiet wilderness.

Sweat stood out on his forehead. They hadn't struck back at their murderers! It was quite well known that there were launching sites all over the country, in secret caches far from any base or murdered city. Why must they sit here waiting to die, only to let the enemy—"enemies" was more like it—take over the continent when it was safe again?

He smiled grimly. One small consolation. They'd hit too hard; that was a certainty. Probably each of the attackers underestimated what the other would throw. The result—a spreading transmutation of nitrogen into deadly Carbon Fourteen. The effects would not be limited to the continent. What ghastly long-range effect the muted radioactivity would have on the overseas enemies was something that no one alive today could know.

Back at the furnace, Pete glanced at the temperature dial, then kicked the latch control. The pilot winked out and then the door swung open. They blinked and started back from the raging heat within, then bent and peered. The razor was gone. A pool of brilliance lay on the floor of the compartment.

"Ain't much left. Most of it oxidized away," Pete grunted.

They stood together for a time with their faces lit by that small shimmering ruin. Later, as they walked back to the barracks, Sonny broke his long silence with a sigh. "I'm glad we did that, Pete. I'm awful glad we did that."

At a quarter to eight they were waiting before the combination console in the barracks. All hands except Pete and Sonny and a wiry-haired, thick-set corporal named Bonze had elected to see the show on the big screen in the mess hall. The reception was better there, of course, but, as Bonze put it, "you don't get close enough in a big place like that."

"I hope she's the same," said Sonny, half to himself.

Why should she be? thought Pete morosely as he turned on the set and watched the screen begin to glow. There were many more of the golden speckles that had killed reception for the past two weeks. Why should anything be the same, ever again!

He fought a sudden temptation to kick the set to pieces. It, and Starr Anthim, were part of something that was dead. The country was dead, a real country—prosperous, sprawling, laughing, grabbing, growing and changing, leprous in spots with poverty and injustice, but healthy enough to overcome any ill. He wondered how the murderers would like it. They were welcome to it, now. Nowhere to go. No one to fight. That was true for every soul on earth now.

"You hope she's the same," he muttered.

"The show, I mean," said Sonny mildly. "I'd like to just sit here and have it like . . . like—"

Oh, thought Pete mistily. Oh—that. Somewhere to go, that's what it is, for a few minutes, "I know," he said, all the harshness gone from his voice.

Noise receded from the audio as the carrier swept in. The light on the screen swirled and steadied into a diamond pattern. Pete adjusted the focus, chromic balance, and intensity. "Turn out the lights. Bonze. I don't want to see anything but Starr Anthim."

It *was* the same, at first. Starr Anthim had never used the usual fanfares, fade-ins, color, and clamor of her contemporaries. A black screen, then *click*, a blaze of gold. It was all there, in focus; tremendously intense, it did not change. Rather, the eye changed to take it in. She never moved for seconds after she came on; she was there, a portrait, a still face and a white throat. Her eyes were open and sleeping. Her face was alive and still.

Then, in the eyes which seemed green but were blue flecked with gold, an awareness seemed to gather, and they came awake. Only then was it noticeable that her lips were parted. Something in the eyes made the lips be seen, though nothing moved yet. Not until she bent her head slowly, so that some of the gold flecks seemed captured in the golden brows. The eyes were not, then, looking out at an audience. They were looking at me, and at *me,* and at ME.

"Hello—you." she said. She was a dream, with a kid sister's slightly irregular teeth.

Bonze shuddered. The cot on which he lay began to squeak

rapidly. Sonny shifted in annoyance. Pete reached out in the dark and caught the leg of the cot. The squeaking subsided.

"May I sing a song?" Starr asked. There was music, very faint. "It's an old one, and one of the best. It's an easy song, a deep song, one that comes from the part of men and women that is mankind—the part that has in it no greed, no hate, no fear. This song is about joyousness and strength. It's—my favorite. Isn't it yours?"

The music swelled. Pete recognized the first two notes of the introduction and swore quietly. This was wrong. This song was not for . . . this song was part of—

Sonny sat raptly. Bonze lay still.

Starr Anthim began to sing. Her voice was deep and powerful, but soft, with the merest touch of vibrato at the ends of the phrases. The song flowed from her without noticeable effort, seeming to come from her face, her long hair, her wide-set eyes. Her voice, like her face, was shadowed and clean, round, blue and green but mostly gold:

"When you gave me your heart, you gave me the world,
You gave me the night and the day,
And thunder, and roses, and sweet green grass,
The sea, and soft wet clay.

"I drank the dawn from a golden cup,
From a silver one, the dark,
The steed I rode was the wild west wind,
My song was the brook and the lark."

The music spiraled, caroled, slid into a somber cry of muted, hungry sixths and ninths; rose, blared, and cut, leaving her voice full and alone:

"With thunder I smote the evil of earth,
With roses I won the right,
With the sea I washed, and with clay I built,
And the world was a place of light!"

The last note left a face perfectly composed again, and there was no movement in it; it was sleeping and vital while the music curved off and away to the places where music rests when it is not heard.

Starr smiled.

"It's so easy," she said. "So simple. All that is fresh and clean and strong about mankind is in that song, and I think that's all that need concern us about mankind." She leaned forward. "Don't you see?"

The smile faded and was replaced with a gentle wonder. A tiny furrow appeared between her brows; she drew back quickly. "I can't seem to talk to you tonight," she said, her voice small. "You hate something."

Hate was shaped like a monstrous mushroom. Hate was the random speckling of a video plate.

"What has happened to us," said Starr abruptly, impersonally, "is simple, too. It doesn't matter who did it—do you understand that? *It doesn't matter.* We were attacked. We were struck from the east and from the west. Most of the bombs were atomic—there were blast bombs and there were dust bombs. We were hit by about five hundred and thirty bombs altogether, and it has killed us."

She waited.

Sonny's fist smacked into his palm. Bonze lay with his eyes open, quiet. Pete's jaws hurt.

"We have more bombs than both of them put together. We *have* them. We are not going to use them. *Wait!*" She raised her hands suddenly, as if she could see into each man's face. They sank back, tense.

"So saturated is the atmosphere with Carbon Fourteen that all of us in this hemisphere are going to die. Don't be afraid to say it. Don't be afraid to think it. It is a truth, and it must be faced. As the transmutation effect spreads from the ruins of our cities, the air will become increasingly radioactive, and then we must die. In months, in a year or so, the effects will be strong overseas. Most of the people there will die, too. None will escape completely. A worse thing will come to them than anything they gave us, because there will be a wave of horror and madness which is impossible to us. We are merely going to die. They will live and burn and sicken, and the children that will be born to them—" She shook her head, and her lower lip grew full. She visibly pulled herself together.

"Five hundred and thirty bombs—I don't think either of our attackers knew just how strong the other was. There has been so much secrecy." Her voice was sad. She shrugged slightly. "They have killed us, and they have ruined themselves. As for us—we are not blameless, either. Neither are we helpless to do anything—yet. But what we must do is hard. We must die—without striking back."

She gazed briefly at each man in turn, from the screen. "We must *not* strike back. Mankind is about to go through a hell of his own making. We can be vengeful—or merciful, if you like—and let go with the hundreds of bombs we have. That would sterilize the planet so that not a microbe, not a blade of grass could escape, and nothing new could grow. We would reduce the earth to a bald thing, dead and deadly.

"No, it just won't do. We can't to it."

"Remember the song? *That* is humanity. That's in all humans. A disease made other humans our enemies for a time, but as the generations march past, enemies become friends and friends enemies. The enmity of those who have killed us is such a tiny, temporary thing in the long sweep of history!"

Her voice deepened. "Let us die with the knowledge that we have done the one noble thing left to us. The spark of humanity can still live and grow on this planet. It will be blown and drenched, shaken and all but extinguished, but it will live if that song is a true one. It will live if we are human enough to discount the fact that the spark is in the custody of our temporary enemy. Some—a few—of his children will live to merge with the new humanity that will gradually emerge from the jungles and the wilderness. Perhaps there will be ten thousand years of beastliness; perhaps man will be able to rebuild while he still has his ruins."

She raised her head, her voice tolling. "And even if this is the end of humankind, we dare not take away the chances some other life form might have to succeed where we failed. If we retaliate, there will not be a dog, a deer, an ape, a bird or fish or lizard to carry the evolutionary torch. In the name of justice, if we must condemn and destroy ourselves, let us not condemn all life along with us! We are heavy enough with sins. If we must destroy, let us stop with destroying ourselves!"

There was a shimmering flicker of music. It seemed to stir her hair like a breath of wind. She smiled.

"That's all," she whispered. And to each man there she said, "Good night—"

The screen went black. As the carrier cut off—there was no announcement—the ubiquitous speckles began to swarm across it.

Pete rose and switched on the lights. Bonze and Sonny

were quite still. It must have been minutes later when Sonny sat up straight, shaking himself like a puppy. Something besides the silence seemed to tear with the movement.

He said softly, "You're not allowed to fight anything, or to run away, or to live, and now you can't even hate any more, because Starr says 'no.'"

There was bitterness in the sound of it, and a bitter smell to the air.

Pete Mawser sniffed once, which had nothing to do with the smell. He froze, sniffed again. "What's that smell, Son'?"

Sonny tested it. "I don't— Something familiar. Vanilla— no . . . no."

"Almonds. Bitter— Bonze!"

Bonze lay still with his eyes open, grinning. His jaw muscles were knotted, and they could see almost all his teeth. He was soaking wet.

"Bonze!"

"It was just when she came on and said 'Hello—you,' remember?" whispered Pete. "Oh, the poor kid. That's why he wanted to catch the show here instead of in the mess hall."

"Went out looking at her," said Sonny through pale lips. "I . . . can't say I blame him much. Wonder where he got the stuff."

"Never mind that." Pete's voice was harsh. "Let's get out of here."

They left to call the meat wagon. Bonze lay watching the console with his dead eyes and his smell of bitter almonds.

Pete did not realize where he was going, or exactly why, until he found himself on the dark street near GHQ and the communications shack. It had something to do with Bonze. Not that he wanted to do what Bonze had done. But then he hadn't thought of it. What would he have done if he'd thought of it? Nothing, probably. But still—it might be nice to be able to hear Starr, and see her, whenever he felt like it. Maybe there weren't any recordings, but her musical background was recorded and the Sig might have dubbed the show off.

He stood uncertainly outside the GHQ building. There was a cluster of men outside the main entrance. Pete smiled briefly. Rain, nor snow, nor sleet, nor gloom of night could stay the stage-door Johnny.

He went down the side street and up the delivery ramp in the back. Two doors along the platform was the rear exit of the communications section.

There was a light on in the communications shack. He had his hand out to the screen door when he noticed someone standing in the shadows beside it. The light played daintily on the golden margins of a head and face.

He stopped. "Starr Anthim!"

"Hello, soldier. Sergeant."

He blushed like an adolescent. "I—" His voice left him. He swallowed, reached up to whip off his hat. He had no hat. "I saw the show," he said. He felt clumsy. It was dark, and yet he was very conscious of the fact that his dress shoes were indifferently shined.

She moved toward him into the light, and she was so beautiful that he had to close his eyes. "What's your name?"

"Mawser. Pete Mawser."

"Like the show?"

Not looking at her, he said stubbornly, "No."

"Oh?"

"I mean . . . I liked it some. The song."

"I . . . think I see."

"I wondered if I could maybe get a recording."

"I think so," she said. "What kind of a reproducer have you got?"

"Audiovid."

"A disk. Yes; we dubbed off a few. Wait, I'll get you one."

She went inside, moving slowly. Pete watched her, spellbound. She was a silhouette, crowned and haloed; and then she was a framed picture, vivid and golden. He waited, watching the light hungrily. She returned with a large envelope, called good night to someone inside, and came out on the platform.

"Here you are, Pete Mawser."

"Thanks very—" he mumbled. He wet his lips. "It was very good of you."

"Not really. The more it circulates, the better." She laughed suddenly. "That isn't meant quite as it sounds. I'm not exactly looking for new publicity these days."

The stubbornness came back. "I don't know that you'd get it, if you put on that show in normal times."

Her eyebrows went up. "Well!" she smiled. "I seem to have made quite an impression."

"I'm sorry," he said warmly. "I shouldn't have taken that tack. Everything you think and say these days is exaggerated."

"I know what you mean," She looked around. "How is it here?"

"It's O.K. I used to be bothered by the secrecy, and being buried miles away from civilization." He chuckled bitterly. "Turned out to be lucky after all."

"You sound like the first chapter of *One World or None*."

He looked up quickly, "What do you use for a reading list—the Government's own *'Index Expurgatorious'?*"

She laughed. "Come now—it isn't as bad as all that. The book was never banned. It was just—"

"—Unfashionable," he filled in.

"Yes, more's the pity. If people had paid more attention to it when it was published, perhaps this wouldn't have happened."

He followed her gaze to the dimly pulsating sky. "How long are you going to be here?"

"Until . . . as long as . . . I'm not leaving."

"You're not?"

"I'm finished," she said simply. "I've covered all the ground I can. I've been everywhere that . . . anyone knows about."

"With this show?"

She nodded. "With this particular message."

He was quiet, thinking. She turned to the door, and he put out his hand, not touching her. "Please—"

"What is it?"

"I'd like to . . . I mean, if you don't mind, I don't often have a chance to talk to— Maybe you'd like to walk around a little before you turn in."

"Thanks, no, Sergeant. I'm tired." She did sound tired. "I'll see you around."

He stared at her, a sudden fierce light in his brain. "I know where it is. It's got a red-topped lever and a tag referring to orders of the commanding officer. It's really camouflaged."

She was quiet so long that he thought she had not heard him. Then, "I'll take that walk."

They went down the ramp together and turned toward the dark parade ground.

"How did you know?" she asked quietly.

"Not too tough. This 'message' of yours; the fact that

you've been all over the country with it; most of all, the fact that somebody finds it necessary to persuade us not to strike back. Who are you working for?" he asked bluntly.

Surprisingly, she laughed.

"What's that for?"

"A moment ago you were blushing and shuffling your feet."

His voice was rough. "I wasn't talking to a human being. I was talking to a thousand songs I've heard and a hundred thousand blond pictures I've seen pinned up. You'd better tell me what this is all about."

She stopped. "Let's go up and see the colonel."

He took her elbow. "No. I'm just a sergeant, and he's high brass, and that doesn't make any difference at all now. You're a human being, and so am I, and I'm supposed to respect your rights as such. I don't. You're a woman, and—"

She stiffened. He kept her walking, and finished, "—and that will make as much difference as I let it. You'd better tell me about it."

"All right," she said, with a tired acquiescence that frightened something inside him. "You seem to have guessed right, though. It's true. There are master firing keys for the launching sites. We have located and dismantled all but two. It's very likely that one of the two was vaporized. The other one is—lost."

"Lost?"

"I don't have to tell you about the secrecy," she said disgustedly. "You know how it developed between nation and nation. You must know that it existed between State and Union, between department and department, office and office. There were only three or four men who knew where all the keys were. Three of them were in the Pentagon when it went up. That was the third blast bomb, you know. If there was another, it could only have been Senator Vandercook, and he died three weeks ago without talking."

"An automatic radio key, hm-m-m?"

"That's right, Sergeant, must we walk? I'm so tired—"

"I'm sorry," he said impulsively. They crossed to the reviewing stand and sat on the lonely benches. "Launching racks all over, all hidden, and all armed?"

"Most of them are armed. Enough. Armed and aimed."

"Aimed where?"

"It doesn't matter."

"I think I see. What's the optimum number again?"

"About six hundred and forty; a few more or less. At least five hundred and thirty have been thrown so far. We don't know exactly."

"Who are *we?*" he asked furiously.

"Who? Who?" She laughed weakly. "I could say, 'The Government,' perhaps. If the president dies, the vice president takes over, and then the speaker of the house, and so on and on. How far can you go? Pete Mawser, don't you realize yet what's happened?"

"I don't know what you mean."

"How many people do you think are left in this country?"

"I don't know. Just a few million, I guess."

"How many are here?"

"About nine hundred."

"Then as far as I know, this is the largest city left."

He leaepd to his feet, *"NO!"* The syllable roared away from him, hurled itself against the dark, empty buildings, came back to him in a series of lower-case echoes; nononono . . . no-no—n . . .

Starr began to speak rapidly, quietly. "They're scattered all over the fields and the roads. They sit in the sun and die in the afternoon. They run in packs, they tear at each other. They pray and starve and kill themselves and die in the fires. The fires—everywhere, if anything stands, it's burning. Summer, and the leaves all down in the Berkshires, and the blue grass burnt brown; you can see the grass dying from the air, the death going out wider and wider from the bald spots. Thunder and roses . . . I saw roses, new ones, creeping from the smashed pots of a greenhouse. Brown petals, alive and sick, and the thorns turned back on themselves, growing into the stems, killing. Feldman died tonight."

He let her be quiet for a time. "Who is Feldman?"

"My pilot." She was talking hollowly into her hands. "He's been dying for weeks. He's been on his nerve ends. I don't think he had any blood left. He buzzed your GHQ and made for the landing strip. He came in with the motor dead, free rotors, giro. Smashed the landing gear. He was dead, too. He killed a man in Chicago so he could steal gas. The man didn't want the gas. There was a dead girl by the pump. He didn't want us to go near. I'm not going anywhere. I'm going to stay here. I'm tired."

At last she cried.

Pete left her alone, and walked out to the center of the parade ground, looking back at the faint huddled glimmer on the bleachers. His mind flickering over the show that evening, and the way she had sung before the merciless transmitter. "Hello—you." "If we must destroy, let us stop with destroying ourselves!"

The dimming spark of humankind—what could it mean to her? How could it mean so much?

"Thunder and roses." Twisted, sick, nonsurvival roses, killing themselves with their own thorns.

"And the world was a place of light!" Blue light, flickering in the contaminated air.

The enemy. The red-topped lever. Bonze. "They pray and starve and kill themselves and die in the fires."

What creatures were these, these corrupted, violent, murdering humans? What right had they to another chance? What was in them that was good?

Starr was good. Starr was crying. Only a human being could cry like that. Starr was a human being.

Had humanity anything of Starr Anthim in it?

Starr *was* a human being.

He looked down through the darkness for his hands. No planet, no universe, is greater to a man that his own ego, his own observing self. These hands were the hands of all history, and like the hands of all men, they could by their small acts make human history or end it. Whether this power of hands was that of a billion hands, or whether it came to a focus in these two—this was suddenly unimportant to the eternities which now enfolded him.

He put humanity's hands deep in his pockets and walked slowly back to the bleachers.

"Starr."

She responded with a sleepy-child, interrogative whimper.

"They'll get their chance, Starr. I won't touch the key."

She sat straight. She rose, and came to him, smiling. He could see her smile because, very faintly in this air, her teeth fluoresced. She put her hands on his shoulders. "Pete."

He held her very close for a moment. Her knees buckled then, and he had to carry her.

There was no one in the Officers' Club, which was the nearest building. He stumbled in, moved clawing along the wall until he found a switch. The light hurt him. He carried

her to a settee and put her down gently. She did not move.
One side of her face was as pale as milk.

There was blood on his hands.

He stood looking stupidly at it, wiped it, on the sides of his
trousers, looking dully at Starr. There was blood on her shirt.

The echo of no's came back to him from the far walls of
the big room before he knew he had spoken. Starr wouldn't
do this. She couldn't!

A doctor. But there was no doctor. Not since Anders had
hung himself. Get somebody. Do something.

He dropped to his knees and gently unbuttoned her shirt.
Between the sturdy, unfeminine GI bra and the top of her
slacks, there was blood on her side. He whipped out a clean
handkerchief and began to wipe it away. There was no
wound, no puncture. But abruptly there was blood again. He
blotted it carefully. And again there was blood.

It was like trying to dry a piece of ice with a towel.

He ran to the water cooler, wrung out the bloody handkerchief and ran back to her. He bathed her face carefully, the
pale right side, the flushed left side. The handkerchief
reddened again, this time with cosmetics, and then her face
was pale all over, with great blue shadows under her eyes.
While he watched, blood appeared on her left cheek.

There must be *somebody*— He fled to the door.

"Pete!"

Running, turning at the sound of her voice, he hit the
doorpost stunningly, caromed off, flailed for his balance, and
then was back at her side. "Starr! Hang on, now! I'll get a
doctor as quick as—"

Her hand strayed over her left cheek. "You found out. Nobody else knew, but Feldman. It got hard to cover properly."
Her hand went up to her hair.

"Starr, I'll get a—"

"Pete, darling, promise me something?"

"Why, sure; certainly, Starr."

"Don't disturb my hair. It isn't—all mine, you see." She
sounded like a seven-year-old, playing a game. "It all came
out on this side, you see? I don't want you to see me that
way."

He was on his knees beside her again. "What is it? What
happened to you?" he asked hoarsely.

"Philadelphia," she murmured. "Right at the beginning.
The mushroom went up a half mile away. The studio caved

in. I came to the next day. I didn't know I was burned, then. It didn't show. My left side. It doesn't matter, Pete. It doesn't hurt at all, now."

He sprang to his feet again. "I'm going for a doctor."

"Don't go away. Please don't go away and leave me. Please don't." There were tears in her eyes. "Wait just a little while. Not very long, Pete."

He sank to his knees again. She gathered both his hands in hers and held them tightly. She smiled happily. "You're good, Pete. You're so good."

(She couldn't hear the blood in his ears, the roar of the whirpool of hate and fear and anguish that spun inside him.)

She talked to him in a low voice, and then in whispers. Sometimes he hated himself because he couldn't quite follow her. She talked about school, and her first audition. "I was so scared that I got a vibrato in my voice. I'd never had one before. I always let myself get a little scared when I sing now. It's easy." There was something about a windowbox when she was four years old. "Two real live tulips and a pitcherplant. I used to be sorry for the flies."

There was a long period of silence after that, during which his muscles throbbed with cramp and stiffness, and gradually became numb. He must have dozed; he awoke with a violent start, feeling her fingers on his face. She was propped up on one elbow. She said clearly, "I just wanted to tell you, darling. Let me go first, and get everything ready for you. It's going to be wonderful. I'll fix you a special tossed salad. I'll make you a steamed chocolate pudding and keep it hot for you."

Too muddled to understand what she was saying, he smiled and pressed her back on the settee. She took his hands again.

The next time he awoke it was broad daylight, and she was dead.

Sonny Weisefreund was sitting on his cot when he got back to the barracks. He handed over the recording he had picked up from the parade ground on the way back. "Dew on it. Dry it off. Good boy," he croaked, and fell face forward on the cot Bonze had used.

Sonny stared at him. "Pete! Where've you been? What happened? Are you all right?"

Pete shifted a little and grunted. Sonny shrugged and took the audiovid disk out of its wet envelope. Moisture would not harm it particularly, though it could not be played while wet.

It was made of a fine spiral of plastic, insulated between laminations. Electrostatic pickups above and below the turntable would fluctuate with changes in the dielectric constant which had been impressed by the recording, and these changes were amplified for the video. The audio was a conventional hill-and-dale needle. Sonny began to wipe it down carefully.

Pete fought upward out of a vast, green-lit place full of flickering cold fires. Starr was calling him. Something was punching him, too. He fought it weakly, trying to hear what she was saying. But someone else was jabbering too loud for him to hear.

He opened his eyes. Sonny was shaking him, his round face pink with excitement. The audiovid was running. Starr was talking. Sonny got up impatiently and turned down the audio again. "Pete! Pete! Wake up, will you? I got to tell you something. Listen to me! Wake up, will yuh?"

"Huh?"

"That's better. Now listen. I've just been listening to Starr Anthim—"

"She's dead," said Pete. Sonny didn't hear. He went on explosively, "I've figured it out. Starr was sent out here, and all over, to *beg* someone not to fire any more atom bombs. If the government was sure they wouldn't strike back, they wouldn't have taken the trouble. Somewhere, Pete, there's some way to launch bombs at those murdering cowards—and I've got a pret-ty shrewd idea of how to do it."

Pete strained groggily toward the faint sound of Starr's voice. Sonny talked on. "Now, s'posing there was a master radio key, an automatic code device something like the alarm signal they have on ships, that rings a bell on any ship within radio range when the operator ends four long dashes. Suppose there's an automatic code machine to launch bombs, with repeaters, maybe, buried all over the country. What would it be? Just a little lever to pull; that's all. How would the thing be hidden? In the middle of a lot of other equipment, that where; in some place where you'd expect to find crazy-looking secret stuff. Like an experiment station. Like right here. You beginning to get the idea?"

"Shut up. I can't hear her."

"The hell with her! You can hear her some other time. You didn't hear a thing I said!"

"She's dead."

"Yeay. Well, I figure I'll pull that handle. What can I lose? It'll give those murderin' . . . *what?*"

"She's dead."

"Dead? Starr Anthim?" His young face twisted, Sonny sank down to the cot. "You're half asleep. You don't know what you're saying."

"She's dead," Pete said hoarsely. "She got burned by one of the first bombs. I was with her when she . . . she— Shut up, now, and get out of here and let me listen!" he bellowed hoarsely.

Sonny stood up slowly. "They killed her, too. They killed her. That does it. That just fixes it up." His face was white. He went out.

Pete got up. His legs weren't working right. He almost fell. He brought up against the console with a crash, his outflung arm sending the pickup skittering across the record. He put it on again and turned up the gain, then lay down to listen.

His head was all mixed up. Sonny talked too much. Bomb launches, automatic code machines—

"You gave me your heart," sang Starr, *"You gave me your heart. You gave me your heart. You—"*

Pete heaved himself up again and moved the pickup arm. Anger, not at himself, but at Sonny for causing him to cut the disk that way, welled up.

Starr was talking, stupidly, her face going through the same expression over and over again. *"Struck from the east and from the Struck from the east and from the—"*

He got up again wearily and moved the pickup.

"You gave me your heart. You gave me—"

Pete made an agonized sound that was not a word at all, bent, lifted, and sent the console crashing over. In the bludgeoning silence he said, "I did, too."

Then, "Sonny." He waited.

"Sonny!"

His eyes went wide then, and he cursed and bolted for the corridor.

The panel was closed when he reached it. He kicked at it. It flew open, discovering darkness.

"Hey!" bellowed Sonny. "Shut it! You turned off the lights!"

Pete shut it behind him. The lights blazed.

"Pete! What's the matter?"

"Nothing's the matter, Son'," croaked Pete.

"What are you looking at?" said Sonny uneasily.

"I'm sorry," said Pete as gently as he could. "I just wanted to find something out, is all. Did you tell anyone else about this?" He pointed to the lever.

"Why, no. I only just figured out while you were sleeping, just now."

Pete looked around carefully while Sonny shifted his weight. Pete moved toward a tool rack. "Something you haven't noticed yet, Sonny," he said softly, and pointed. "Up there, on the wall behind you. High up. See?"

Sonny turned. In one fluid movement Pete plucked off a fourteen-inch box wrench and hit Sonny with it as hard as he could.

Afterward he went to work systematically on the power supplies. He pulled the plugs on the gas engines and cracked their cylinders with a maul. He knocked off the tubing of the Diesel starters—the tanks let go explosively—and he cut all the cables with bolt cutters. Then he broke up the relay rack and its lever. When he was quite finished, he put away his tools and bent and stroked Sonny's tousled hair.

He went out and closed the partition carefully. It certainly was a wonderful piece of camouflage. He sat down heavily on a workbench nearby.

"You'll have your chance," he said into the far future. "And by heaven, you'd better make good."

After that he just waited.

A GALAXY OF SCIENCE FICTION STARS!